PHOENIX OF SCARLET

NecroSeam Chronicles Book IV

NECROSEAM CHRONICLES

Available in eBook, Paperback, Hardcover, and Audiobook (for select titles)

Prequel 1: Princess of Shadow and Dream
Prequel 2: Princess of Grim

Book I: Willow of Ashes
Book II: Orbs of Azure
Book III: Pearl of Emerald
Book IV: Phoenix of Scarlet
Book V: Blossom of Gold

OTHER WORKS BY ELLIE RAINE
Adult
Nightingale: A Paranormal Noir

Children's Illustration
Ballad of the Ice Fairy

Phoenix of Scarlet

NecroSeam Chronicles Book IV

Ellie Raine

Phoenix of Scarlet
NecroSeam Chronicles | Book Four

Copyright © 2019 by Ellie Raine

Cover Design by Ellie Raine
Interior Formatting by Tamara Cribley
Author Photograph by Melissa Giles Photography
Map © 2021 Chris Seckinger

Printed in the United States of America

ISBNs: 978-1-7323238-4-1 (Hardcover), 978-1-7323238-3-4 (Paperback), 978-1-7323238-2-7 (Ebook)

Library of Congress Control Number: 2019905703
First Printing, Edition I: 2019

Published by
ScyntheFy Press, LLC
Peachtree Corners, GA
www.ScyntheFy.com

For information about special discounts available for bulk purchases, sales promotions, fund-raising and educational needs, contact ScyntheFy Press at: www.ScyntheFy.com/contact

For special bonus features and up-to-date news, visit the official NecroSeam web site: www.NecroSeam.com

For my wonderful husband Josh, my sweet daughter the dragon princess Felicity, and all my loving friends and family. Thank you for your continued support and encouragement. Also, special thanks to my amazing beta readers for your valuable feedback.

AUTHOR'S NOTE

Dear Adventurer,

Congratulation on reaching the next save-point in the NecroSeam Chronicles. If you've made it this far in the Reapers' adventures, you are my favorite reader! By now, I'm sure you realize that as the series has advanced, so have the characters along with the world itself. To help you keep track, I've included an updated Nirussian Travel Guide at the end of this book. As you continue your quest, be warned: this new adventure is not for the faint of heart. Pack your bags and don't look down as you depart on your next journey toward the floating islands of the Sky realm.

Happy Reading!
~Ellie Raine

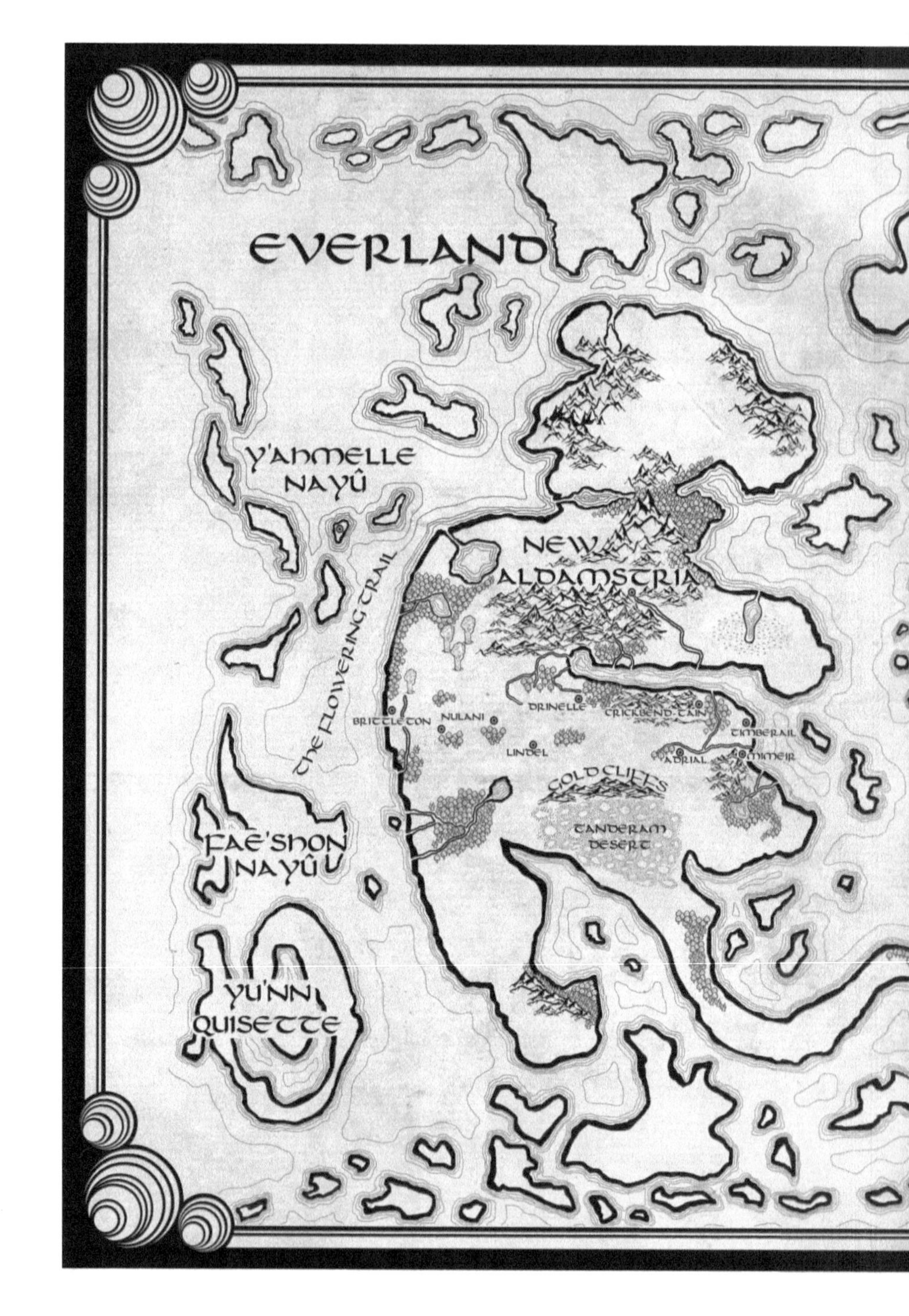

EVERLAND
Y'AHMELLE NAYÛ
NEW ALDAMSTRIA
THE FLOWERING TRAIL
DRINELLE
CRICKBEND-CAIN
BRITTLETON
NULANI
TIMBERAIL
LINDEL
ADRIAL
MIMEIR
GOLD CLIFFS
FAE'SHON NAYÛ
TANDERAM DESERT
YU'NNI QUISETTE

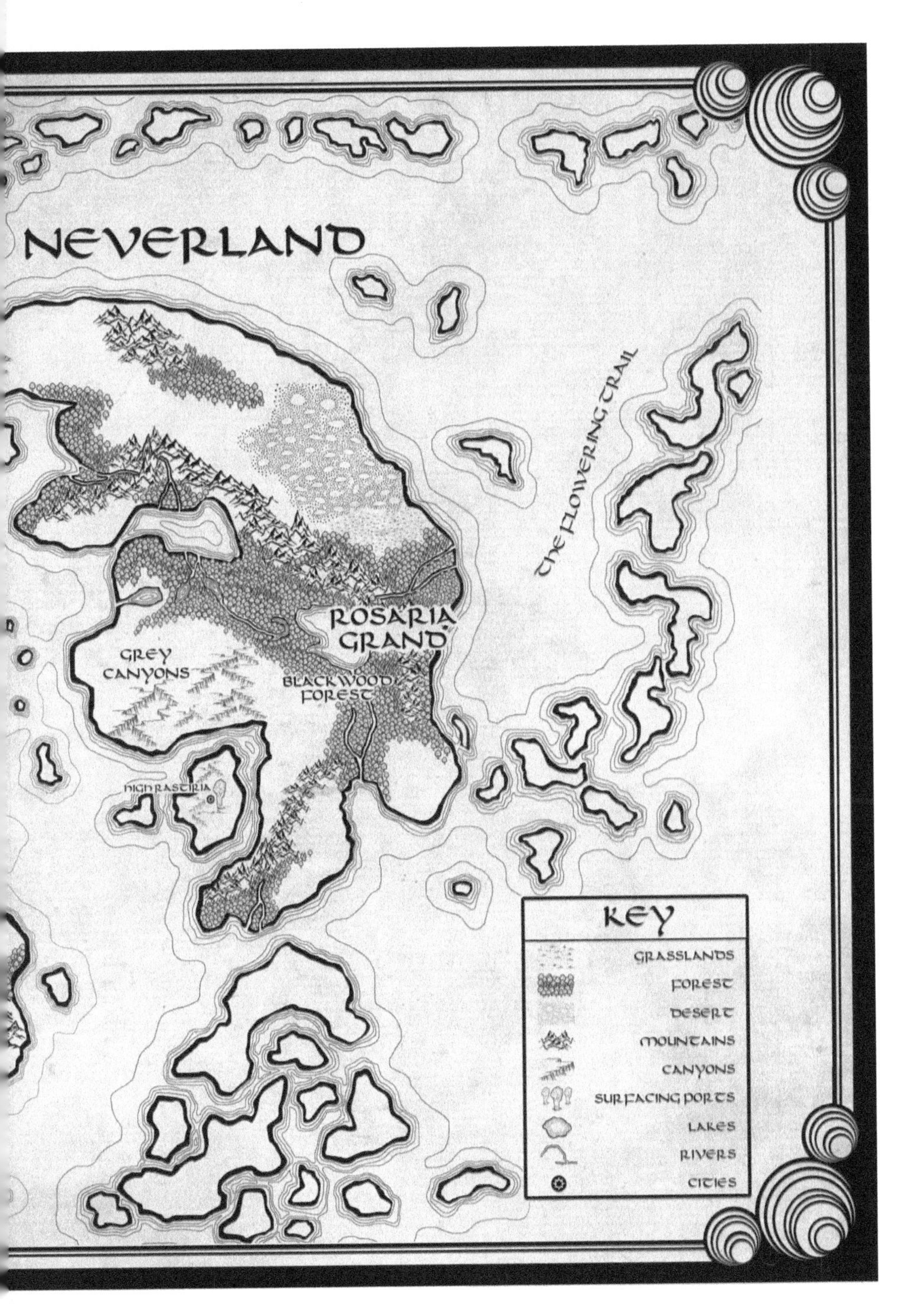

NEVERLAND
THE FLOWERING TRAIL
ROSARIA GRAND
GREY CANYONS
BLACKWOOD FOREST
HIGH RASTIRIA
KEY
GRASSLANDS
FOREST
DESERT
MOUNTAINS
CANYONS
SURFACING PORTS
LAKES
RIVERS
CITIES

TABLE OF CONTENTS

"Then, in truth, was it I who brought this upon us, Father? This was, after all, my doing. In my selfishness, have I killed us all...?"

—The King of Dreams, 2092 A.B.

PROLOGUE
SAVIOR

MACARIUS

506 YEARS PRIOR

Snow wept over the beautiful city of Aldamstria. I stood on a balcony in Everland's palace, allowing the crisp breeze to wash over my scales as I breathed in its icy scent and relished the flakes that drifted onto my halfmoon spectacles. This truly was a night to remember. The beauty, the majesty... the serenity of this moment that teetered on the cusp of our survival.

Behind me flapped the velvet curtain that hid the ballroom. Not moments ago, it had been alive with music and dancing guests, their pleasant laughter still echoing in my memory.

But better than their laughter was their screams.

Clang!

The muffled ring of steel split through the curtain from inside the hidden ballroom. The sounds of clashing swords were muffled out here, the insulating snow muting the sharpness of the duel.

Inside, King Adam fought for his life against Kael. The surgeon had slaughtered the visiting royals long ago, along with anyone who'd foolishly stepped in his path toward the king. Guests, guards, lords, ladies... the ballroom had been painted with their blood as Kael used his infection Hallows to burn away their souls and melt their blackening skin off their bones...

It was magnificent.

Had I known killing Cilia—the one shifter who controlled the fate of his fragile sanity—would create such a masterpiece, I would have done it sooner. The brilliant part was that I'd so perfectly, *seamlessly* framed the king for it all. It had been a stroke of *genius*.

My fingers were still stained with her blood. My clothes were splotched as well. Though I'd washed it all, there was just too much to rub clean without more time. I'd been rushed to leave before Kael returned home to find his wife's pieces. And there were a *lot* of pieces. Thanks to my sore arm, I now had a new admiration for butchers. It was incredibly laborious work.

But Shel, was it satisfying.

A chill split down my fingers, remembering the *crunch* of her wrist bones, the thirsty *gush* of the cleaver sinking into her throat and splitting her vocal cords. Most thrilling, though, had been the *crack* of her ribs as I hollowed out her chest, and the *rip* of her arteries when I yanked out her heart. The most ingenious part had been the artful placement of the detached muscle between her thighs. It had been a comical statement, really, giving literal meaning to the phrase "A whore's heart is between her legs". It was something her former employer at the brothel had said, and I knew Kael would remember it. Even if he didn't, I thought it still hilarious.

Kael's enraged cries were muffled from behind the curtain. As he and King Adam continued their duel, I leaned my hands on the balcony's snow-covered railing, admiring the cityscape in the distance. The white blanket of powder coating the stone buildings was so serene. It dressed the evergreens in entrancing gowns and fluttered from the sky in lovely flurries.

Do not worry, people of Aldamstria, I thought in a long sigh as I pushed up my spectacles, *All people of Nirus… I will deliver you from the End. I will be your shepherd.*

"—Macar."

The rasping voice came from the curtain behind me.

I twisted back. My brother, Accursius, stood under the arched opening. He wore his gilded armor, save for his helmet, which I noticed had fallen to the snow at his plated feet. Without it, his brown-and-blond streaked hair waved freely at his cheeks, and the identical, spectacle-less face of myself stared back at me like a mirror. His tanned scales were pale with disgust. His brown eyes were rimmed red as his furious glare welled with betrayal.

I leaned back against the railing, the wet snow soaking my silken doublet as I crossed my arms and grinned. "You seem distraught, Accur. Is something on your mind?"

His voice was a rumbling whisper. "How could you…?"

"How could I… what?" I hummed. "Last I saw, Kael is the one poisoning the others—"

"Do not *dare* take me for a fool, Macar!" He hissed, his long fangs unfolding as venom leaked threateningly. "I Saw the vision…! I Saw what you've done…!

But I…! I don't understand…" His glare wrenched into desperation. "Why…? What purpose does it serve…?"

I scoffed. "You *are* a fool if you cannot see its purpose. I'm ensuring our safety—*everyone's* safety. If you haven't been listening for the last month, the End of Existence is coming. It is just at our door, hanging by a thread."

"Of course, I've been listening!" He tossed a gauntleted hand back toward the curtain. "But how in Land will *this* save us all?! You heard Dream's plan just as well as I! Not once was *murder* ever part of his design—!"

"His design is *weak!*" I roared, my own fangs unfolding, venom stinging sweetly over my tongue. "It will not protect a single shifter! Hear me now, Accur, I will see that our demise is averted at all costs. These miniscule souls would be honored to know the *billions* of lives their sacrifice will save. I will guide them to Aspirre. In the Dream realm, time will not expire—the crises will *never* come to pass."

Accur gritted his teeth, fangs hanging in front. "And who will protect them from the Noctis Golems? I can do nothing in Aspirre—I'm only a Seer, Macar! You were blessed with illusions *and* dream walking, but how do you expect me to help you protect them in a realm I cannot walk within?"

I cocked my head with a flat expression. "Well. If you cannot contribute due to your… 'lack of ability'," I drawled, "I suppose you'll have to appreciate what you have and… what was it you told me those years ago? 'Find a new career'?"

His face wrenched resentfully. Those had been his words to me when I wished to join the royal guard, as he had. He denied me the chance to even apply, claiming that I had too soft of a soul, and that I was better off with my 'dusty old books'. While he was promoted to Everland's chief military general, he suggested I apply as the royal Dreamcatcher instead. But despite having won the role, despite the fact that I had excelled at my duty to keep the royal family and the servants and the guards—even Accur *himself!*—alive for five Gods damned years while they slept in blissful ignorance of the dangers their dreams were guarded from… He still looked at me as a feral wolf would a domesticated hound. Pitying. Pompous. Patronizing…

But no longer.

"I think it's time you lived in *my* shadow, don't you think?" I sneered. "In the shadow of *all* Dreamcatchers? You foolish land-walkers are a fragile *bubble* away from an eaten soul every… Gods… Damned… *Night.*" The last word crunched ruefully. "We are the ones who always save your pathetic spirits—more than you've ever saved with that rusty sword of yours." I nodded curtly at the blade strapped to his hip. "And for what? For the rest of the world to dust their hands of us? To spit on us? To wish us dead because we make them *uncomfortable?*"

I shook my head. "No more. This time, you will be at *our* mercy as we save you from the End of Existence… as *I* save you."

Accur was silent for a very long, strained moment. Then he hushed, "Dream said we *both* were needed…"

"Dream was wrong," I hissed. "I have found another path to salvation. To Sanctuary… a *better* path."

Accur's face fell sickly. "Macar… what's happened to you…?"

"An epiphany, dear brother. And do you want to know what I've concluded?" I folded my arms behind my back. Then evoked my dream Hallows. I created a phantom copy of myself, coloring the air with a false man that mimicked my figure perfectly. Then I discreetly used my illusion Hallows to paint myself invisible, and stepped back from behind the phantom copy I'd created.

Accur's gaze was distracted on the phantom as I strolled behind him without notice.

My phantom spoke to keep his attention away from my snowy footprints, my own voice projecting from the copy as it said, "I have deduced that splitting abilities between us weakens potential. If we continue the path Dream wishes of us, we will fail due to the simple fact that *you*, Accur, would weigh me down."

My true self quietly slid my brother's sword from its scabbard.

Accur stiffened when the weight at his hip vanished, and he whirled just as I dropped my invisible guise—and *thrust* his blade straight through his throat.

"What I have found, Accur," I said as a thrilled grin split my lips hungrily, "is a path that doesn't need you."

NEVERLAND

1

EXILED EMPEROR

KURN

TRANSLATED FROM FERRET

PRESENT DAY

I watched as the scarlet-winged Sky prince and princess—the siblings Roji and Zyl—accepted their platter of sandwiches that a servant had brought them in their guest chambers within Neverland's palace.

My mouth watered.

"Steady…" I said to myself in my huffing language, crouching down and flattening my round ears as I stealthily hid within the open vent. My sights were locked onto the sandwich platter. "Nearly there…"

When the two turned away, I slinked my way toward them. "Almost…" I stretched my long neck and cautiously peeled open my maw. "And…"

Crunch!

I clamped my teeth into one of the sandwiches and scampered back into the vent. The winged siblings shouted after me in their Culatian language.

"Ec-fell-fior!" I huffed in triumph with my mouth full of the bounty I'd won, retreating deeper into the palace vents to be sure those giant bi-pedals couldn't follow after me

I passed several slitted openings throughout the building, hearing the familiar voices of Ringëd's company in the different rooms.

"… not sure I like the idea of this 'parade'," the burly, scar-faced man grunted in one room. I believe they often called the warrior Kurrick. He was in some sort of armory, by the looks of it, throwing on heavy plate beside the goat-horned Seer they called Linus.

The goat was eyeing a sword mounted on the wall as he hummed, "Our long-lost queen has finally returned to us after centuries of our people struggling under the oppressive thumb of her usurper. It's only reasonable that we should hold a parade in her honor."

Kurrick snorted his disapproval, and I hobbled onward through the vents.

The next vent held a more chaotic scene with two children running about and driving the adults with them to insanity. One child was a winged, brown-skinned boy, and the other was a scaled, web-eared lad with long emerald hair.

"Oliver!" the bat-winged woman called angrily, waving two small suits in the air by their hangers. "Fuérr! Cease your tomfoolery and come get dressed! We've only an hour's time before this parade, and I want you to look your best!"

"But we ain't gonna be *in* the parade, Mama!" the winged boy whined.

The bat gritted her teeth, leathery wings lowering testily. "I'm sorry, dear. *What* was that?"

Oliver blushed and grumbled in a more proper speech, "We *aren't* going to be in the parade, *Mother...*"

The bat smiled. "That's better. And it doesn't matter if you won't be in the parade, you're the son of a noblewoman now, and you will dress as one."

The boy whined again. "But Mother—"

The other adult with them, the fanged one with blond hair and rectangular spectacles, clasped a scaled hand on the boy's shoulder. "Come on, kiddo, just do what your Ma wants, yeah?" He crossed his arms expectantly. "It'll be a Void-of-a-lot more hassle if you don't, trust me."

I carried on my way.

I reached a cross-road in the metal tunnels and found the passageway I needed. Unfortunately, it was several feet above me. It was too high to reach, and the walls were too slippery to climb.

I sighed and drew in a long breath, mentally accessing the nano-tech in my blood. The tiny bots had been injected at birth, like all young ferrets from my home planet. Except, being born as royalty, I had additional upgrades that the average citizen lacked.

I felt my body hum and vibrate as the nanites activated, and my paws lifted off the metal vent. I levitated in the air, rising upward and upward until my claws reached the tunnel I sought. I felt the humming tech dwindle in my blood, their power draining quickly, and I dropped onto the vent once more, skittering forward on my paws like before.

Along the way, I heard a robotic female's voice announce in my thoughts, *"KURN'S DEFENSIVE ENERGY LEVELS LOW... NANITE POWER AT 4%."*

"4%?" I groaned. "Just from that?"

The woman's voice replied, *"JUST FROM THAT."*

This was why I hated to use the nanites for levitation too often. Truthfully, that feature was for defensive purposes, for catching oneself from a fall and such. The nanites had a terrible lifespan, though. They constantly needed to be recharged. I'd used an awful lot of power just doing that much. Waiting for my body to recharge them would take days… Nothing for it. I would have to find Ringëd's communicator and drain some of its battery again when he wasn't looking.

I turned corners in the spacious vents and hurried on my way. Luckily for me, Ringëd had stayed at this fine castle with his pack long enough for me to learn the ventilation tunnels by heart, so I easily navigated my way through it.

I passed a third vent—

"I DON'T KNOW WHAT THAT MEANS!" a woman's voice roared through the slits, making me stumble to my side in a startled yelp.

Who was THAT? Dazed, I rolled back on my paws and scuttled to the vent, peeking through warily.

It was the pregnant, ashen-haired Death Princess, Her Highness Willow. She was in her guest chambers with her husband, one of the odd-eyed twins whom I knew was named Xavier. Willow's fox ears were grown and curled tight to her white locks as she gave the most blood-curdling glare at the bearded man—who was backing away and raising pacifying hands.

Xavier swallowed. "N… now, darling—"

"DON'T YOU 'DARLING' ME!" She barked. "You can't keep spouting about 'FEELING' this and 'PUSH HARDER' that to normal Evocators! I need *actual* instruction! I need *real* terminology that I can understand! I'm sorry I'm not a Bloody genius Necrovoker who can randomly create a NecroSeam for a living soul with a mere wave of his *hand!*" Her fists burst into flames at the last word, and she was panting heavily by the end of her rant. Then her expression wrenched into sadness and she sniffled—and broke into a sob.

"Death," Xavier winced and came to console her. "No, no, no—Willow, it's all right! I'm sorry! You'll get it, you just need to… er…"

Poor fellow. I grimaced in sympathy from my view behind the vent. Now that the princess's growing baby was twenty weeks along, it seemed her mood swings were at full-force. I was glad *I* didn't have to be on the receiving end of it.

I scurried onward, finally reaching the east tower where the aviary was located. I poked my head out through the vent's just-large-enough slit to be sure no bi-pedals were about. I was in luck, it seemed. Only a flock of aimless pigeons and trained falcons were here in their designated coop, along with many of the Reapers' black-feathered companions who croaked and cawed to their hearts content as they fluttered about the aviary at their leisure. There was Shade, whom I was most familiar with, his brother Ace, the small crow called Clover, Bridge, Dusk, Paschal, Lady Lilac, the tiny royal crow named Jewel, and the twins: Mal and Chai.

I was pleased to see that all my feathered soldiers were in attendance. They fought bravely in the Battle of Blackwood Forest two months prior—with their wise emperor leading them to victory, of course—and as any ruler knows, it was of the most importance to allow my subjects time to rest and recuperate.

I squeezed the rest of my long body through the vent's wide slit, ruffling my fur in the process, and kept a wary eye on the falcons and owls whose beady gazes were now focused solely on me. Predatory bastards. My first visit to this aviary nearly ended with me being swallowed by those savages. Thankfully, my loyal entourage of black birds vastly outnumbered those uncivilized fowl, and they have proven to be most effective guards for their emperor.

Sighing contentedly, I set down my sandwich bounty to begin my feast with elated, though dignified, nibbles.

My feathered comrades glanced my way when I entered, and they greeted me kindly.

One of them, Ace, craned his head to look at my meal. "What's that you got there, Kurn?"

I huffed between nibbles and stuck up my nose. "It is a meal that I acquired all on my own, and is *mine*, young Ace," I said. I knew he couldn't understand me since the nanite-translation implants only translated languages for *me*. But I wagered my guarded body language was enough to tip the raven off. "Go scavenge someone else's scraps—*Hey!*"

Ace ignored my warning and grabbed the entire sandwich in his beak.

His brother, Shade, flapped over next and grabbed a bit of the meal for himself before Ace swallowed the thing whole, crumbs left on his black talons.

"No…!" I lamented and slapped furious paws on Ace's wings, crying the loss of my hard-earned treat. "How dare you…! You… you lazy ingrate…!" I sniffled and mourned over the fallen crumbs. "You'd starve your emperor so carelessly…?"

Blast it, now I'll have to find food some other way. *Well,* I thought in a dreary sigh, *I suppose the kitchens are a good start.* I searched the crowd of feathered messengers and found one who didn't seem preoccupied with anything. It was the youngest of the murder, Clover.

"You there," I said, clearing my throat as I hobbled over to the crow. "Could you perhaps assist me?"

The youngling cocked his head at me curiously, not understanding my words, but acknowledging my gestures. "Oh, it's the little furry thing," he said. "Do ya want something?"

"I've tired myself whilst venturing up here, I'm afraid," I bemoaned, sure to give him the most piteous look I could manage and folded my round ears downward. "Could you provide your emperor with a means of transportation down to the palace kitchens?"

"Uh… do ya want another ride somewhere?" Clover guessed. He lowered a wing to allow me aboard his back. "I can do that. I wanted to find Oliver soon, anyway. I can feel him pouting from up here, and I think he wants to see me."

"Ah, brilliant!" I climbed onto my willing mount. Then I mentally activated the nanites to make myself pseudo-levitate again. This time, it was only a fraction of what I'd done earlier, just enough to make myself lighter to allow the crow to carry me without weighing him down, and without draining too much power. "Thank you, young one."

The crow gave a winded caw when I settled on his back. "Bloods, you're heavier than usual…" the crow replied in a grumble. He flew us out of the aviary regardless, heading downward as I steered him toward the kitchens by gently pulling on his neck-feathers.

"KURN'S DEFENSIVE ENERGY LEVELS LOW," the robotic voice in my thoughts announced again, *"NANITE POWER AT 3%… RECHARGE SUGGESTED."*

"Oh, all right," I muttered. "I'll find Ringëd's com and recharge with its batteries soon… It's a good thing Ringëd's wife is probably in the kitchens anyway."

"A LUCKY BREAK," agreed the nanites' representative. *"BECAUSE KURN'S HUNGER LEVELS ARE ALSO AT 3%… RECHARGE SUGGESTED."*

"And heeded!" I huffed and patted Clover's neck. "Best we hurried, young one!"

HERRIN

It has been two months since Neverland's queen fell at the hands of Land's lost Relicblood, I wrote on the sheet of parchment on my desk, *and Queen Anabelle has swiftly assumed her role as Neverland's monarch.*

There has been no sign of the former queen, nor of the Sentient Necrofera who had fled from the Shadowblood after the rebellion's takeover. It's still thought that the queen has been Changed… I think it likely we will see her again. Though as to when, I don't know. My hope is that it won't be soon.

I put down my quill and leaned back, my wooden chair creaking under my weight. My wings spread to either side of the chair and draped to the floor.

Then a light, ceramic clatter sounded to my left and snagged my attention. *Oh.* It was Marian. The cardinal-shifter carried a tray of tea with a single cup next to the kettle. It looked like some cakes were there, too.

She wore a cream, long sleeved smock today, buttoned all the way to her neck, and her hands were veiled with tight-fitting gloves. Her auburn, feathered hair was braided over one shoulder, and as she made her way to me, her wings flexed and contracted to avoid desks and bookcases that were scattered around the room.

"I thought you might be in need of a break, Archchancellor," she said shyly, hovering beside me with the tray.

"Oh," I said. "Sure. Just put it on the desk, I guess."

She did, pouring the tea into the single cup in silence.

I rubbed my neck. "Thanks... but you know you don't have to do this every day. Do your parents even know you come here?"

"I'm an orphan, Archchancellor." Her tone was light, but respectful. "The Chapel Mother houses me and the others at the school. She encouraged me to help you anyway I could, as you are the Chief of Knowledge of my guild."

"Oh." *Huh*, I thought, *Crysalette never mentioned she was an orphan.* I only thought Marian worked at the chapel as an apprentice or something. "My siblings and I came from an orphanage, too," I said. "Well, just us younger three. We weren't there for long though, our oldest brother Dalen busted us out so we wouldn't be separated and—"

"Thus, began your thieving days as arms-traders," she finished, clasping her hands behind her back. "As is told in volume IV of the Chronicles you've written."

I blinked at her. "But I haven't finished volume IV."

Her bronze face flushed pink. "I... *may* have been reading over your shoulder when I bring your tea... And you have a spelling error on page 34, paragraph three, line five. You left out the *t* in *next*."

"Uh... oh," I said, kind of embarrassed. "Is that why you've been coming here every day? To read the Chronicles?"

She was bright red now. "Well, that and perhaps to... i-if you would allow, of course, Archchancellor, I had hoped to..." She swallowed, taking a deep breath, then said, "I wish to come with you when you leave for Culatia today."

My eyes went wide. "What? Why?"

"With Mrs. Elliot leading the Neverlandish Enlighteners, I'm of little use here," she explained sheepishly. "And I've always wanted to see the other realms—and with the Shadowblood no less. I've spent my entire life having visions of their future without ever meeting them. It's as if I was raised with them here beside me."

"Wait, wait, wait." I shifted my weight to turn to her fully. "You've had visions of them, too? Like Oliver and Linus and Ringëd?"

She nodded, her wings drooping. "I typically See their future, just as the owl boy does."

"Bloods, does *every* oracle See them?" I rubbed my eyes. "Maybe I should look at some writings of past oracles. This keeps happening, it wouldn't surprise me if you Seers have been having visions of them for centuries."

She hummed. "I imagine only His Majesty Dream has Seen those visions for so long."

"What makes you say that?"

"To start, Oliver and I—who are younger than the Shadowblood—have Seen them since we were born. But both Linolius and Ringëd claim their visions did not start until they were six years of age. Both have even named the same date: the first of Spiridel, 2082 A.B."

I ruffled my feathered hair. "The day the twins were born…" Bloods, how did I miss that in my interviews with them? I should have asked that. Stupid, stupid, *stupid!* My lids narrowed at her. "You asked the other oracles about that already?"

"Of course," she said, "When I read of the other Seers in your Chronicles, I wished to know if their visions coincided with any of mine."

"And did they?"

"Quite of a lot of them, yes." She sounded excited, smiling now. "Of course, Oliver and I synchronize the most, with the future. Though, since he's still young, his visions are chaotic and he has trouble sifting through them to determine which timeline is the present."

"Doesn't he have a 'crystal' ball for that?" I asked. "The rubber one?"

"Yes. But he is still learning to utilize it to its fullest potential. It took me some years to master it myself."

"Oh!" I snapped my fingers, opening a drawer on the desk. "That reminds me. Some of the servants found this a few days ago."

I pulled out the crystal ball from the drawer. It was newly washed of the blood flecks that were splattered there before. I offered it out to her. "This was found in the dungeons," I said. "I know you said you were freed by our rebel soldiers from there, so I figured this was probably yours—"

"Get that away from me."

I paused, surprised by her suddenly callous tone. She stared at the orb with a haunted look, her face wrenched tight.

"But… Isn't it yours?" I asked, retracting. "I mean, it looked like the one you dropped when you first ran into me in town—"

"It's because of that orb that the previous queen found your camp," she said, pulling off one glove and rolling up a sleeve, revealing the crisscrossed lacerations trailing all over her arm like painful, puckered wires. "It's because of that orb that I'll wear these scars for the rest of my life. I will never touch that orb, nor another like it, again. If… if you will only take me on your journey for my foresight…" She draped her sleeve back over her arm, her eyes glazing while replacing her glove. "Then I suppose I'm of no use to you… It was truly a pleasure meeting you, Archchancellor."

She spun on her heels and started out, hugging herself as if to keep her arms from shaking.

"Wait!" I said, rising as my chair made a small screech over the floor. "If you don't want to use your foresight anymore, I-I get it. Really. Sorry for bringing it up…" I rubbed my knuckles. "And I mean, we have enough Seers with us anyway to take care of that. But I guess… I could use an assistant Enlightener?"

She glanced back at me, her wings dipping. "Assistant?"

"Yeah," I said. "You actually thought to ask Linus and Ringëd questions I never considered. And you're apparently good at finding spelling errors. Interviewing everyone about the same events, especially as they're happening, is getting really hard with only me here. I could really use the extra set of hands." I scratched my neck. "If you want to, I mean."

Her eyes brightened, but they were still wet. "I… I would be honored, Archchancellor."

"Great." I smiled. "And call me Herrin."

2

ROYAL GUARD

ALEXANDER

"They've repaired it?" I asked Ana, ducking under another archway that had been tangled in browning vines.

The autumn season hadn't been kind to the potted plants in her palace halls, though she didn't seem to mind. Ana strolled at my side with her arms folded behind her back, one finger radiating with a golden light as she used her Arborvoking Hallows to part the draping vines away from her head. *Bloody show-off queen and her theatrics.*

"I've heard from Prince Roji," the golden-haired queen said in that soft, gentle voice of hers. "The Skyport is fully restored and ten of its Airships are fully operational."

"Finally," I grunted. It only took two Gods damned months of waiting. While the break from all the fighting was a relief, sitting on my rear all day for months was growing unnerving.

"And I suppose it's grand timing," she added, smiling. "I expect things have settled in the kingdom enough to enjoy Death's Festival today. Everyone was so busy rebuilding their homes and grieving their losses, there seemed to be no appropriate time to celebrate the Night of Dreams last month."

I muttered, "After everything that's happened, I'd say 'celebrating' falls any-where between ludicrous and outright trivial."

"Trivial to you, perhaps." The lion-eared woman lifted a finger as if chiding me. "But one mustn't forget, Alexander: It is *because* we have all been through so much strife and sorrow that clearing our minds of it for a small time, how-ever trivial, can help us focus on our tasks in the coming months. It can serve as a rebirth for our determination, one could say."

"I think you mean boredom." I grimaced. Then the flap of small wings sounded behind me, and I turned to see my messenger raven, Mal, was soaring toward me through the corridor. He alighted on my shoulder and settled there as his throat rumbled in annoyance, in tune with my own irritation, and the raven began biting an itch over his flight feathers.

I peered at Ana questioningly. "If the Skyport is rebuilt, what of the Surfacing Ports? Is there a way to reestablish commerce with Grim?"

"Commerce, yes," she said. "The trading of goods and produce has been active again, barely. But transportation for shifters has perhaps another month or two left before it will be operational again."

I exchanged another disdainful glance with Mal. "Then no way home, still."

"… sure you're up for this trip, darling?" My brother's voice echoed ahead of us within the west wing's atrium. "I know how you are with heights, and you're under so much stress already…"

Ana and I entered the atrium and found Xavier at the foot of the marble steps. He was offering a hand to his ashen-haired wife as she stepped down to meet him. Willow's belly had only just begun to show the growing baby within, and her bump showed through her gown.

The royal couple wore splendid, alabaster garbs today, silver skull-crowns adorning both their heads. Xavier's doublet was lined with polished buttons, his long hair tied back with a white ribbon while his shadow-grey bangs fell freely at his bearded cheeks. The scar running down his right eye was currently hidden under an intricate white mask. Willow wore a mask herself, though hers was far more elegant and shaped like a butterfly over her azure eyes. Her flowing maternity gown was wrapped in delicate chiffon that shimmered with silver beadwork, patterned in the same butterfly motif that mimicked her festive mask. She wore her ashen hair down today, the curling strands wafting behind her as she leisurely made her way down the steps, the ends dragging over the floor and nearly blending with her white skirts. Clipped to either side of her head were her silver marriage-vines that connected at her forehead by the diamond center-piece, the silken chains and imbedded gemstones glittering from the outside sunlight that filtered in through the arching windows in brilliant, golden rays.

Behind the Death Princess floated a young ghost. The translucent boy seemed meek yet eager as he glided around Willow to stay dutifully at Xavier's side.

Ah, I thought curiously while I watched the ghost boy, *so that's where Hugh had been this past month? Hanging at his master Reaper's ear, at his beck and call?* That explained the ghost's lack of hurrying to me to resurrect his vessel every fortnight. Xavier must have been giving his apprentice verbal lessons for a time. Then, I supposed Hugh was partly to blame for Xavier's cluttered schedule.

"Xavier," Willow sighed as she stepped down to meet him at the foot of the steps. She gripped his gloved hand in assurance. "I'll be fine. *We'll* be fine. I'm not due for another two months, and it takes but *one* to reach Culatia's capital. Little Lucas won't surprise us on the ship."

My brother released a breath through his nose and brought her fingers to his lips. "If you're sure... I'd rather avoid any complications if we can help it, and..." He trailed off when he noticed Ana and me approach. "Ah, Alex!" He brightened, striding over. "Bloods be good, it feels like weeks since I last saw you."

"Try *six* weeks," I muttered and crossed my arms. "A whole month. But I suppose I'll have to grow accustomed to it. A Death Prince scarcely has an open schedule, I imagine. Even for his only brother."

His mismatched eyes fell solemnly from behind his mask. He ran a hand through his bangs and managed to neither untangle the tail that was tied over his shoulder nor disturb the silver crown atop his head. "I suppose there's so much happening at once, I..."

I forced a grin, unwinding my arms to look a little less... hurt. "Relax. I know you're busy. I'm only envious. You have so many things to do and I've nothing to distract myself with but Dream and Fuérr's relentless training."

He winced at that. An apologetic look creased his face, as if he were sorry for having missed so much training over the month.

Xavier almost formed a reply at last, but Willow interrupted. "Is that your wardrobe for today, Alexander?" she asked and inspected my casual dress-shirt and trousers with a frown. My clothes were still quite noble, to be fair, but compared to *their* festive attire, I may as well have worn my sleepwear around Ana's palace. Willow cocked her head curiously and hummed, "It seems a bit informal for the parade."

I scowled. "What parade?"

Xavier's gloom was replaced with a wide smile. "For Death's Festival. Ana, you'll be there as well, yes?"

Ana chuckled beside me. "Of course. Appearances in such festive times are part of a queen's duties to her country."

"Her, I understand," I said. "And obviously, the Prince and Princess of Death ought to be present for Death's Festival... but I've no place in a blasted parade."

Ana protested, "Oh, but you do. The people wish to see more of the Shadowblood. You are as much the champion as Xavier, it is most appropriate for you to join."

"As if I whimsically *decided* to be the Gods damned Shadowblood," I snorted. "I think I shall pass."

Xavier scratched at his recently groomed beard. "Are you sure?"

Why the disappointed tone? He'd spent the last month acting as if I didn't exist, shouldn't he be used to my absence by now?

I strode through the towering, opened doors that led outside. "I'd rather not subject the public to my lowly self so unnecessarily. Parades are for royalty. But do let me know how it goes."

Now in the orchards, I snapped an apple straight from its stem and crunched into it.

"Wait." Xavier came to linger under the doorway behind me. "If not as the Shadowblood..." He glanced away for a moment as if struggling to find the words. Death's Head, he was already turning into Father. And with the full beard, I had to admit he was beginning to *look* like Father as well, though drastically thinner. When he seemed sure of himself again, he took a breath and said, "Would you join as captain of our guard?"

I staggered, not having expected that. "I thought Lilli was to be captain?" I asked.

"Lilli is in line to be Willow's first Hand, when she becomes queen," he said, hopeful. "And she's denied the role as captain, with Oliver taking up half her schedule. Willow hadn't any candidates of her own to choose from, so she's left the decision to me. I thought you could, perhaps..." He rubbed his neck. "Well, I thought it would be a good chance to see more of you, this way. And it's not as if you aren't qualified. Death, but you're the best candidate we have."

He was serious? I stared at him, dumbfounded. "You've thought about this, then? You aren't offering on an impulse just to get me in that Bloody parade?"

"Of course not." He allowed himself a small smile. "I need to trust my guard with not only my life, but with Willow's. There's no one I trust more, Alex. I want my brother with me. I promised we would die together, and I don't intend to change that plan." His smile faltered, uncertain. "Say you will?"

I turned the apple in hand. *Bloods, captain of a royal guard... as Mother had been...*

I gripped the apple. Took a popping bite and chewed thoughtfully. Then said, "I want Jaq as my lieutenant."

His shoulders slacked with relief. "I expected as much. You can recruit whomever you wish for your squadron."

I tossed the apple over a shoulder and walked back inside, passing him. "Then I suppose I ought to snatch Octavius from whatever leisure he's confined himself to." I paused and twisted back. "I'm not expected to follow your royal posterior on foot at this thing, am I?"

"You'll get a horse," he assured, "all of your team will."

"Good." I grinned and went inside, throwing a fist to my chest in a lazy salute as I crossed paths with Willow, humming cheerfully, "Afternoon, dear sister. Do take care of my nephew."

She offered me a puzzled gaze, but yielded to a chuckle and went to meet her husband, rubbing her extended belly tenderly along the way.

Now, to find my team. I knew Octavius would be with his hybrid lady-friend. But where was Jaq—?

I slammed into someone's shoulder when I turned a corner. It was Matthiel Inion. *Ah.* This one would do.

"Matthiel." I patted the befuddled Howllord's shoulder, his sienna eyes blinking at me as he brushed his raven-black hair into place. "How would you like to…"

"Not now, Alexander," Matthiel interrupted, glancing over his shoulder as if afraid of his own shadow. Then he spotted something and blanched, ducking behind me instead. "Blast it, they're too Bloody fast…!"

My brow knitted at the frightened man, then I craned my gaze around the corner. "Who is too Bloody fast?"

A gaggle of women staggered when they saw me, stopping in their tracks and whispering in hushed tones. One, I recognized as Lëtta, Sirra-Lynn's teen-aged Necrovoking Mistress. The giggling Grimish girl led the pack as their demeanor suddenly changed to a poorly feigned nonchalance while they strolled past Matthiel and me.

I felt him cringe against my back, pointedly darting his gaze away and shielding his eyes with a bashful hand.

Only when they disappeared down the steps did Matthiel relax. "Death, you're a savior!" he said, slicking back his hair again. "They've been tailing me all damned month! I scarcely have a moment to myself anymore!"

I sent him a sidelong glance. "Accrued ourselves some admirers, have we?"

"More like scavengers." He calmed in an exhale. "What was it you wanted?"

"I've just been appointed captain of our fair prince and princess's royal guard," I said, opening a hand in his direction. "I thought to offer you a posi-tion, if you'll accept?" *As if he wouldn't,* came the afterthought.

"Oh?" He stood taller, his face brightening, as expected. "Why, I'd be honored!"

"I thought you might be." I thumped his back, strolling onward. "Be dressed within the hour. I'll gather the rest of our team and meet you by the stables."

I was gone before he could reply.

One down, three to go. Now, where would Jaq be at this hour?

My steps slowed when I spied a branch-like tail swaying from an opened doorway, the creature's brown scales coated like bark. *Ah. That would be Bianca's Barkdragon. Bazil, wasn't it?*

My lips wrenched into a smile, and I tucked my arms behind me and strolled toward the doorway. The lanky dragon noticed me first, its head creaking to the side. I patted the woody beast's hindquarters and peered inside. My smile widened when I spotted Bianca with her new guild members, all of them tinkering with tonics and adjusting burners. She, however, was currently giving attention to her right-hand assistant, Red.

The young man, whom I could have sworn was in his twenties despite his suddenly shy demeanor, was hunched over a desk and sweating like a feral hog. A fountain pen was gripped in his fingers so tightly, I half expected the thing to break in two, drawing each letter as if afraid they would jump off the page and sting him.

Oddly, my brother's messenger raven, Chai, was perched beside him on the same desk, balancing his own fountain pen with his beak and talons and scratching out each scripted letter *better* than Red.

Red noticed the mortifying skill difference, shooting the raven a rueful glare before returning his focus on his own writing.

Bianca hovered over him in examination, her large goggles drawn over her head and her overalls stained in soot along with her oversized gloves. Her orange rabbit ears were draped down as her mouth twisted in a grumble. "How did you teach yourself to read, but not write?" she asked him.

Red muttered, "I never got to that part, all right? Bloody woman, stickin' her nose where it don't belong…"

Bianca's chocolate eyes flicked in my direction then. She smiled, stretching my own lips as a wash of bliss fell over me. Death, it was good to see that smile again. How long had it been since she looked at me that way?

She left Red to his studies, striding to me with a cheerful wave. "Hey, Alex. You're in a good mood today."

Bloods, her voice was like candied honey. "I've just been appointed captain of the royal guard for Xavier and Willow," I announced, more than a little proud.

She gave a toothy grin and punched my shoulder. "It's about time. Xavier dragged his feet with it, didn't he?"

"You're not surprised?"

"He's your twin." She shifted weight to one foot and set a fist at her hip. "And he spent a good six years trapped in your body. He knows better than anyone that you're the most qualified candidate."

"He knows better than anyone but you, you mean?" I asked. "She-who-knows-everything-before-everyone-else?"

"I can't help being smarter than you all." She winked, her button nose scrunching with another radiant smile.

"So I see," I said, slipping into a euphoric daze as I gazed into those brilliant eyes.

Eyes which flicked away.

"Alex," she said, her tone now stern, taking a breath as if to collect herself. "Stop."

I hummed, my mind still miles away. "Stop what?"

"Stop looking like you still…" Her expression saddened. "Like *we* still…"

Sobriety was a bitter mistress.

"A-Ah…" My throat dried, and I cleared it swiftly. "Yes. Right. Lilli…" *My fiancée.*

Bianca sighed. "You're still set on all that, then? You're going to marry her?"

My voice hollowed. "I…"

"—*Please,*" a haunting voice whispered in my memory, Mother Maria's crimson face flickering to mind. Her blood covered my arms as I tried to carry her, but she was too heavy for my young muscles to go any farther than the corridor. *"Please,"* she begged, tears streaking her cheeks and mixing with the red. *"Take care of my Lilli…"*

"—Alex?" a new voice called behind me, snapping me out of my daze.

It was Jaq, coming to stop beside me. He was with Lilli, and little Oliver and Fuérr were at their heels, all dressed formally for the festival.

"Mate?" Jaq asked cautiously. "You all right?"

Lilli looked concerned as well, reaching a hand toward me. But she retracted it after glancing at Bianca behind me… who silently withdrew, returning to Red and his studies. She did not look back.

"Fine." I cleared my throat, regaining focus. "Jaq, fetch your best armor. You're now the lieutenant of the royal guard." I nodded to Lilli, my gaze set on the floor instead. "And Lilli, you're qualified for a position as well, if you wish… report at the palace stables within the hour. I need to fetch Octavius."

I stormed past them, trying with all my might to keep my wolf ears from sprouting. I found no success.

Three hours after lining up along the streets with my new squadron in formation, the damned parade began later than expected. But large events like this were wont to being delayed, I supposed. Xavier and I had grown accustomed to such annoyances in our youth, having been forced to attend public hearings and festival speeches Father would hold in Low Drinelle's square back in Grim's caverns.

I sighed harshly while riding my grey-spotted horse behind Xavier's and Willow's open carriage, flooded with a twisting wave of homesickness. My raven, Mal, croaked from the sky and fluttered onto my armored shoulder, nudging his beak against my scruffy cheek. My dismal mood must have transferred to him through our Bond.

"Sorry, Mal," I grumbled and scratched his feathered neck. "I'm just… looking forward to descending back to Grim. I'm long past sick of the surface."

"Si-*ck!*" Mal croaked in agreement, our Bond surging with a rueful vibration. "Si-*ck!* Ho-*me!*"

I exhaled. "I'm glad I'm not the only one missing the caves."

He cocked his head at me one last time, then flew off to patrol the skies again, joining the other messengers soaring overhead. I could feel his sense of vigilance burning even from down here on my horse. With as many demon hordes as we've encountered, it was a small wonder why everyone's black birds were habitually on alert. Not to mention the fact we had several demons *with* us now. Reapers befriending Necrofera was a new concept to all of us. It seemed our messengers were having trouble acquainting themselves with the notion as well.

The setting sun left a golden halo that kissed the flat-roofed cityscape's horizon. Neverlandish citizens, Reapers, and Stormchasers alike packed the streets to watch the parade. Trumpets blared behind me and drums beat in front.

Queen Anabelle sat poised and smiling in the front carriage, drawn by three Landragons and guarded on either side by her two boringly faithful guards: Kurrick and Linus.

The two were hardly ever away from her flanks, and I swore they had arranged their own 'designated side' beforehand because the bulky lion always took her left while the goat took her right. They never deviated from the formation when around her. Yet they rarely seemed to communicate. How they figured it out was beyond me.

Following the queen's carriage at the rear was her newest guard, Sil Genevieve. The woman wasn't much of a conversationalist either. A few grunted answers here and there, the occasional flat stare at Willow, the usual deadly glare at Xavier and me… I didn't know what to make of her. But Ana seemed to trust her enough. That was all I need be concerned with, I wagered.

The people cheered and waved their flags that were crested with Shel's golden emblem as their lion-eared queen passed. My attention drifted idly over the crowd—

Jaq punched my shoulder.

I kept my horse steady and turned to the viper, who was on horseback himself beside me, his silver plate glimmering in the setting sun.

"D'ya do it yet?" he asked me.

I lifted a brow, confused. "Do what?"

He pointed his scaled chin toward Lilli to my left. The bat rode beside Matthiel and Neal—Octavius's older brother—who were adorned in the same matching armor.

I glowered at Jaq, now understanding what he'd meant. "You're still on about that, are you?"

"Time's up," he said. "Deal was, if you didn't get somethin' and give it to her in two months, ya gotta use what *I* got for ya."

I brushed a stray, purple leaf from my shoulder-guard. "Why are you so set on this?" I asked. "It doesn't concern you."

"Like Death it doesn't." He shoved a long, velvet box in my gauntleted hand, his plate clattering with the motion. "I'm callin' best man. Xavier ain't gettin' it, 'cos I did way more for ya."

I glared at the box, annoyance simmering as my fingers gripped around it, knowing what was inside the infernal thing.

Jaq punched my shoulder again. "Go on. Deal's a deal. Your lazy ass wasn't gonna get nothin' in the first place 'n ya know it. I saved ya the time."

I scowled one last time, then growled, "Fine… Bloody nosy, you are."

I sucked in a breath, let it out harshly, and pulled the reins to slow my horse while I veered the feral creature to the left. Once beside Lilli, who was busy smiling at the crowd and keeping her leathery wings curled to her back, I cleared my throat, startling her.

"Here," I grunted and offered the long box to her. "These were overdue, I suppose."

Her orange-brown eyes went wide at me. She stared at the box, gently taking it from my fingers, and opened it.

Hm. This was the first time I'd actually seen the contents. The engagement-vines were made of silver chains that glittered with rose-pink gemstones, the separate centerpiece the same rosy color.

"They're beautiful." She sounded mesmerized, fanning a hand to her collarbone in wonder. She turned her entranced gaze at me. "These are mine?"

"No," I drawled nasally, "I thought Willow could use a second pair."

She chuckled and pulled the vines from the case—leaving the centerpiece inside—and clipped them to either side of her hair. The pink gems glinted in the sunlight, the chains looking sleek and glossy between them.

She wore a warm smile now. This was, perhaps, the happiest I'd seen her. *Odd.*

"Thank you," she said. Bloods, she looked on the verge of tears, but she wiped a discreet finger over her lid and sighed, as if relieved. "I was beginning to think you'd forgotten entirely."

If only, I brooded in silence. Jaq had been relentless these last months, it was impossible to even pretend to forget.

"I take it you approve?" I asked, gritting my teeth. *Try.* Try to be delighted.

"I love them," she said, laying a hand over mine. "And the gems are my favorite color."

My brow knitted. Her favorite color? I twisted back to Jaq quizzically. The viper gave a fang-filled smirk and lifted his thumb approvingly.

"Yes, well." I cleared my throat behind a fist. "I'm glad you like them."

Before she could reply, I unceremoniously steered my horse back into position beside Jaq.

"Did she like 'em?" he asked, a little too eager for my liking.

I hummed. "Incredibly, yes. I'm guessing you asked for her favorite color?"

He snorted. "She's always wearin' pink, it ain't brain surgery."

"Hrm. I never noticed."

"Yeah, I figured…" He glanced at me sidelong. "So?"

"So what?"

"I get best man. No arguin'. Come on, you're impressed, ain't ya?"

I sighed hard, rubbing my eyes. "You're set on this, are you? Fine. You'll have it."

He punched my shoulder in triumph. "Thanks, mate! Won't let ya down."

I exhaled dismally. Off in the crowd, I saw a certain rabbit eared woman offer a satchel full of tonics to a local vendor, exchanging Mel beads for quite a few glasses of her brews.

Two children ran around her in a playful chase, Fuérr and Oliver: the youngling Prince of Ocean and the owlet Seer whom Lilli had all but adopted by now.

I let out a solemn breath, watching Oliver's wings give a flutter, waving a flag some of the parade's organizers were handing out. The boy's little crow, Clover, soared with a spritely flap alongside him.

Lilli clearly wasn't going to abandon the child. She was set on his adoption. And, if I was to wed her… Well, Xavier wouldn't be the only father among us.

Oliver and Fuérr rushed here and there, laughing and grabbing at the rabbit's overalls until she groaned and bought them a candied sweet from the vendor next door.

Bianca... I slouched over the saddle, watching her drearily. My wolf ears grew from under my helm.

Then I snorted and turned forward, glaring ahead to where Xavier sat beside his wife in their personal carriage.

3

PAINFUL PARADE

XAVIER

I watched Alex ride alongside Jaq behind our open carriage. He looked oddly morose. What was that face about? He'd seemed so ecstatic to have the job earlier, what had happened?

Octavius followed behind them, taking riding lessons on the go from El as she stifled several laughs at his awkward attempts. This was Octavius's first time on a saddle, apparently. He looked terrified, but I think El's company helped ease his nerves.

El was here under Sky Princess Zylveia's request. Zylveia rode beside her brother's family, scowling and muttering under her breath in her homeland's tongue, her wings jerking open every so often when her horse would dip.

Next to me in the carriage sat Willow, poised and waving at the enthusiastic crowd of shifters celebrating Death's Festival. Her tiny crow, Jewel, hopped excitedly and twittered from her shoulder while my own messenger raven, Chai, was perched on the seat's back beside my head. Chai's gaze swiveled all round, our Bond thrumming with his curious thrill at the festivities.

Willow glanced over her shoulder, tucking a long strand of ashen hair behind her ear. "Lilli has her vines now?"

I peered round to see for myself. "Why, that she does. And here I thought Alex had forgotten entirely."

"As had I." She hid a laugh behind her fingers. "I've never seen her so happy. What a lovely gift."

"Indeed. And speaking of gifts…" I reached under our bench and pulled out a box with sleek, black wrappings and silver butterfly designs. "I believe today is someone's *Rae'u Shelic*." I tossed the box up and down. "Now I wonder, whose could it be?"

She grinned, taking the offered box. "Haven't you given me enough gifts over the years?"

"For *Mal Aschay*, there is never enough to give." I paused and added, "I also wanted to make up for earlier this morning… I'm sorry I'm not the best Hallows instructor…"

She sighed. "No, *I'm* sorry for snapping at you… I suppose I'm still a bit… *testy* when it comes to my dismal Hallows' strength…" She gave me a half-grin. "It's just not fair. I've lived my entire life struggling to control the most basic Evocations between my six elements. Now you and Alexander have seven, and you're already masters at all of them."

I rubbed my neck. "Well, ours are still halved…"

"Still." She shook her head in a huff. "It's not fair… but I'll get over it. Now, what did you get me?"

As she slipped off the silken ribbon from the box, I chuckled. "Something I think you'll enjoy. I admit it isn't quite as exciting as past gifts. But it *did* take me all morning to find, you should know."

She peeled off the wrappings and lifted the lid. Her head cocked. "An apple?" She scooped the fruit up and turned it over curiously. Then she smirked. "Half green and half red… you remembered my favorite." She took a cheerful bite.

"I did." I smiled. "I hope you don't mind something so mundane."

"Oh, I was worried you'd gotten me another trinket to add to the plethora of jewelry I already have. Thank you, love. I was craving one anyway." She bit a second time, chewing happily—then she jolted, laying a hand on her swollen belly.

My breath caught, and I pressed a hand beside hers on her belly. "Is he kicking?"

"It's faint," she said. "But he's certainly active today. I suspect those drums are exciting him."

The tiniest of knocks bounced under my hand from in there, and I flinched.

Willow snorted. "I can't tell if you're terrified or exhilarated."

"Is it possible to be both?" I laughed nervously, lifting my hand and stared at it in awe. It had been such a feeble kick, so small, so fragile… There was a little *person* in there, inside my wife. Alive. *Moving.*

"Do you think…" I began, curling my gloved fingers anxiously. "Do you think he'll like me?"

Her next look was inquisitive. "Xavier, he'll love you. Why would you ask such a silly thing?"

"It's easy for you to say," I muttered. "He can't possibly hate his mother. But what if the moment he meets me, he wants nothing to do with me? What if I don't hold him correctly, what if I make a mistake, what if I…"

"Darling." She shoved her apple over my lips to hush me. "I love you. And he will love you. You've nothing to fuss about."

I sighed, taking a bite of the apple and chewed thoughtfully. Perhaps she was right. I shouldn't work myself up over such things so soon. There was time yet before I would meet him.

Time yet for me to be… to be *ready*—

"Get down!" Alex hollered suddenly from behind. I whipped round in time to see him kick his horse forward and stop at the side of the carriage in front of me, then he leapt off his horse and tackled Willow and me to the carriage's floor, our messengers fluttering away in alarmed croaks and twitters.

"A-Alex!" I hollered under him, flabbergasted. "What are you—?!"

—An arrow shot at his horse's side. The arrow's glass tip shattered on impact, flecks of the jagged shards digging into its skin as black, tendril-like veins slithered out of the broken arrowhead. The horse whinnied in pain and swerved out of control, its knobby knees buckling before it collapsed to the ground.

"Death!" I shoved Alexander off and fumbled to my feet, ripping off my gloves. I sucked in a breath and exhaled, evoking my ice Hallows. My internal coldness poured out of my soul and crystalized into frost at my palms, fog licking between my fingers. I had the ice shape into a wide, rough shield, then planted it into the carriage's floor in front of the three of us.

Shnk!

Shnk!

Two arrows knocked against my ice, their glass tips shattering just like the first as tiny, dangerous shards puffed in a glittering shower. The force shoved me backward against Alexander, who shielded Willow with his body. As before, the broken arrowheads festered with black veins, the sticky worms crawling up and over my ice-shield—heading for my hands.

I hurriedly ripped the shield off before the veins could reach me, the ice cracking over the stones beneath the hovering carriage. The veins uselessly slithered over the ground, then evaporated.

"What in Death…?" I panted, perplexed.

Then I heard a faint grunt, followed by a crash within the crowd, then shouting.

I whipped my gaze up and found our teenaged vassal, Vendy, was hopping up and down in the crowd. Her brown rabbit ears were perked straight up in alarm, her glowing sword flailing above her head as if attempting to swat at something.

And indeed, there *was* something above her. Our second vassal, Dalen, was flying over her head above the crowd. He had a woman with a crossbow in his grasp and he dangled her by her ankle. Vendy was hurtling curses at the woman, her Crystal sword trying in vain to swat at her wriggling head.

"We got 'er, *Da'torr!*" Dalen shouted over at us. He shook his catch, who gave a shriek and dropped her crossbow—nearly hitting Vendy beneath her.

Thank Death we thought to resurrect them before this, I thought in relief. Still, I didn't lower my guard and produced a new ice-shield, hopping off the carriage alongside Alexander. I then helped Willow down and turned to my brother, asking, "Are there more?"

He was still for a moment, his eyes glazing over.

Then five other men—no, five other *Alexanders*—swept *through* the crowd, *through* Willow and me, *through* Octavius and Jaq, and were sucked into the original Alexander who stood before me. Those must have been Alexander's phantom 'copies': doubles of himself that couldn't touch anything physically but could gather information and deliver it to the original caster. I'd seen him produce those intangible scouts before with his half of our Somniovoking. It seemed he'd found a great use for them over the month.

After a moment, Alex blinked back to reality, having gathered the information his copies had collected. "Two more." He pointed into the crowd. "There, and there."

Behind us, Jaq kicked his steed forward. "On it!"

He dashed into the crowd after one assailant, and Octavius did the same for the second. Lilli spread her wings and took flight overhead to scout.

I nodded to Alex in thanks. "Your Somniovoker copies have improved since last I saw."

His stern brow didn't soften, mismatched eyes still sweeping over the mass. "I did say Dream's training was relentless."

My stomach churned. *I've missed so much training. He must be so far ahead… But now is not the time for self-pity.* Focusing on the matter at hand, I checked over Willow.

"Are you all right?" I hesitantly pressed a hand to her belly. I felt another drum of faint kicks and sighed in relief, cupping her face. "Were you hurt?"

"No," she assured, though still sounded alarmed. "Either their aim is terrible, or I wasn't the target."

"Where are your vassals?"

"It's Death's Festival, Xavier," she reminded. "I gave them leave to do as they pleased today."

I grunted. "Blast, but we could use Rossette's lightning…"

Master, a young voice fuzzed in my thoughts. Then the ghost of a boy appeared behind me, floating through El's horse. It was my apprentice and vassal, the teenaged Hugh. "What's happened?" he asked warily.

"Assassins," I growled to Hugh's ghost, sweeping an arm in front of him to keep him back. I doubted enemy demons were nearby, given that our ravens weren't sounding any alarms, but after losing the boy once, I wasn't about to take any chances with my apprentice's afterlife now.

Hugh hesitated. "Can I help, Master?"

"It's being handled, Hugh," I assured. "Though, this will be added to your lessons. Observe what Alexander and his team are doing in this situation."

Hugh nodded, now turning his gaze to Alexander with impressive intent.

From her mount, Princess Zylveia called down in broken Landish. "What be wrong, wolf prince?"

"Everyone, dismount," I urged. "There are more bowmen in the area—"

A sharp crack came from the ground, and I whirled in time to see Anabelle was stepping down from her carriage and ripping apart the stones at her feet with her glittering-gold rock Hallows. She shaped them into two thickened spearheads, which she *thrust* into the crowd, steering them around the cluster of civilians until they found their marks—

Two women were sent flying from the mass, both their heads impaled by the spearheads with an eerie silence. Neither had a chance to cry out. To gasp. To so much as blink.

"*Hu'choft Necros*," I cursed in Grimish. I thought I'd be ill.

Anabelle stepped beside me, her soft voice haunting as she gazed upon her kills, then at us. "Are either of you harmed?"

I swallowed. "No."

"I am glad," she whispered. "Please, tell your vassal to bring forth his catch. I wish to question her."

"Dalen," I called, tapping into our mental, vassal-Necrovoker connection so I wouldn't have to shout over the crowing crowd. "Bring her here."

Roger that, Da'torr, came his reply from my thoughts, and he flapped toward us.

Jaq came galloping to my side with his horse, shaking his head. "No more on this end."

Octavius approached after him. "None over here either."

I let myself relax, but only slightly. My ice-shield was melting in the autumn warmth, forming a puddle at my feet. Those black veins from before were gone. But I knew I hadn't imagined them…

From the skies, Chai returned and alighted on my shoulder. He croaked and flared his neck feathers, still on the alert.

I glanced at Anabelle. "Do you think they're from the rebellion?"

Bloods, that felt odd to say. Not months ago, *we* were the rebellion. But I supposed those who win the wars become the 'just' side. Those who lose become the new rebels.

Anabelle's gaze was affixed on the dangling assassin heading our way. "We shall see."

Dalen flew down with the woman in tow, keeping her arms twisted behind her, and shoved her before us. She was a tigress, round ears curled tight to her head in vehemence. She stumbled into the puddle and splashed the hem of Anabelle's shimmering, white gown. The golden-haired queen made no air of offence.

Anabelle snatched the woman's chin, turning her face in examination. "State your purpose," Ana commanded in a whisper, "Or I will begin your afterlife early."

The tigress woman snarled, "The End draws ever nearer. And you harbor our *deaths*." She gave Alexander and me a viciously odious sneer so severe it sent my spine in a shudder. "Sanctuary will be our salvation. We must follow the Lightcaster... or we all die."

Her teeth sharpened. Then she jerked out of Ana's hold and ripped her teeth into her own shoulder, tearing open a sewn pocket and bit into a hidden lozenge—

From the lozenge burst forth a flurry of black, jagged veins. They crawled out of her mouth and rooted into her flesh, burning the skin like acid as her bones gleaned through at the cheeks and now-exposed, rotting gums.

Then, from her pores, a blackened mist rose and evaporated, the woman sighing a final breath before collapsing and growing still.

Silence fell among us.

"Mu necros neschali yettek..." I hushed, raising fist to my chest and bowed my head in prayer.

I heard Octavius breathe meekly behind me, "Those veins... That looked like..."

"Like your Infeciovoking," I finished for him. "She mentioned the Lightcaster."

Alex growled, "Then she was with Macarius."

I glanced back at Octavius, my wolf ears grown and curled. "It seems we must speak with your father posthaste."

4

ADJUSTING

CILIA

The cool breeze wafted past my windowsill perch, a trail of red and purple leaves riding the wind as my grey hair swept forward.

I reached out and caught a beautiful crimson leaf. Its black veins stretched across the thin membrane like a charred tree caught aflame.

I sighed and laid back against the windowsill, tossing the leaf aside and watching it flutter to the palace gardens below.

There were people down there, some servants and some… more. That ice-spewing fish man—Janson's formal vassal who was currently resurrected—was down there painting a portrait of his green-feathered model: his Astravoking associate. Another one of Janson's previous vassals.

Khol, our third Ancient Necrofera 'king', if you could call the coward that, was admiring the artist's painting while he himself trimmed away at a hedge, as if the sorry excuse for a demon had appointed himself the royal gardener.

Two ghosts floated among them and gestured praises or perhaps critiques. One was that large bear shifter, Nathaniel? The other was a winged adolescent, from the look of him. Aiden? I still was unsure who these souls were. They didn't seem to be any of this group's vassals, of that I was confident.

I glowered at them all. They looked so peaceful down there, laughing and chittering as if the world around them wasn't crumbling; as if I wasn't lurking in their shadow.

"—Any change?"

I turned to the sudden voice. A shark man had appeared on the stone awning above me, his white pupils piercing. Hecrûshou looked particularly modern today. He wore a new brown jacket, the hood folded to his shoulders to allow his translucent, indigo hair to flow freely in the autumn wind. His demon-slaying trident was wrapped in a cloth and strapped to his back as always. His little pet Bindragon, Aahn, was coiled around the top of his trident's staff and snoozing with his serpentine head between the three prongs of the fork.

I stretched my arms behind my head in a yawn. "It's been pleasantly boring, I'm happy to report. Have you and Miranda found traces of La'lunaî?"

"None, as of yet," he said in that watery accent of his. He crouched over his long knees, which were hidden under a pair of slim, black trousers. Where was he finding all these nice clothes? All the shops I stole mine from never had anything *hip*. "But we cannot be too careful. We know she is out there, and it's likely the old queen of this palace has become her toy. She may well be building an army to come for us."

Wonderful. I closed my eyes in a sigh. Yet another danger to worry over. At this rate, I may sprout wrinkles with all this stress, un-aging body or not.

I peeked open an eye at Hecrûshou. "Where is Miranda?"

"Returning on foot with the Queen of Land," he informed. "Something had happened during the festival. She wishes to stay close to the queen, to protect her."

I frowned, sitting up. "What happened?"

"An assassination attempt."

"On the queen?"

He sat and crossed his legs, arms folding. "On the twins. At least, that is our speculation."

"Any reason for such speculating?"

Land, but the man's gaze was dark. "They caught one of the assassins," he said. "She swallowed a Metaglass lozenge full of Infection Hallows that destroyed her flesh and her soul at once... but not before she gave praise to the Lightcaster."

My cat ears sprouted with fury, my inner fire flaring. "Macarius."

My manipulator. My puppeteer.

My murderer.

"So it seems," Hecrûshou rumbled. "From what we've learned between you and Claude, there is no one else it could be."

My claws scratched the windowsill. "Does this mean he knows what I've learned? He knows I've cut my strings?"

"I'm not sure," he admitted, seeming troubled. "But they are on their way to speak with Claude on the matter. To perhaps shed some light on those soul-erasing lozenges and arrows."

"Which room?" I asked. "Is there a window to listen from?"

He lifted a brow at me. "Would you not benefit from being included directly?"

My laugh was cynical. "As if they would humor the thought of including me."

"But you may have information they need."

"I've told them everything I know. I was kept in the dark about most of his plans in the first place. And after what I've done under his demands, they… well, it's not unjust that they hate the Bloody slippers on my feet."

He nodded ponderously. "But they understand it is because of Macarius that you've caused them such troubles."

I swung my legs over the sill. "And I suppose this makes us grand friends, does it?"

"It makes you allies," he considered. "You share at least one common goal. For now, I expect that should be enough."

"For now." My expression dampened.

Of course, he was right. Once I could rip off Macarius's head, eat his soul, and find Kael, I didn't intend to shuffle my feet around these Reapers and wait for them to kill me.

I pushed up, arms stretching over my head. "Well, if you'll excuse me, Hecrûshou, I have a conversation to listen in on. If you say they're looking for my descendant, then I believe I know where he'll be."

Claude was a baker, that much I'd learned over the months spent in their shadows. He would surely be in the kitchens.

I didn't bother waiting for Hecrûshou to reply and hopped down to the next sill, then the next. Then the next. It would have been easier to simply jump the whole length of the palace, but lately I've been taking pains to be more discreet. Making a show of myself was now the last thing I wished to—

"Oh, Cilia!"

I jolted, glaring at whomever had called. It had come from the gardens.

There, seated at a table and waving at me like a prim lunatic with an azure-haired baby suckling at her breast, was the Queen of Dreams. Her flaming orange hair was difficult to miss even from this distance.

"Cilia!" She called again brightly. "Cilia! Oh, do come down for a moment, won't you?"

My brow furrowed. *What does she want?*

She kept waving, calling, not about to cease her attention-drawing acts. I growled, cat ears growing, and leapt down to the soft grass.

Upon my landing, Janson's former vassals turned to glare at me. Then they promptly packed up their supplies of paint and canvas and strode to a different area of the grounds. Away from me.

Khol merely looked frightened when he saw me. His webbed ears flicked before he hefted his hedge clippers and trotted after the two vassals, those other two ghosts following him.

"Cilia!" The fiery haired queen cried yet again, waving more vigorously while balancing the baby in her other arm. "Over here!"

One of my cat ears flicked back in suspicion. I approached slowly, reaching the table which, I discovered, was set with two cups of purple tea, the floral-painted pot still steaming from its spout.

The queen lifted a pair of large sunshades away from her eyes and tucked the things into her curly hair.

"Come, sit with me," she all but pleaded, motioning to the second chair across from her. "Everyone left for the parade and these servants are such dull conversation."

I watched her cautiously while lowering myself in the wooden chair. "Where is your husband?" I asked.

She wavered a hand dismissively. "Oh, Dream's gone to fetch me something sweet before his nap." She tilted her head toward the suckling baby in her arm. "It was his turn to tend to Eryn last night, so I'd gotten more rest."

"I see." I stared at the second cup of tea that was placed before me. Did she expect me to pick it up? To leave it be? I gave her a narrow look and questioned, "Are you not frightened of me?"

She laughed. Hysterically. "Don't be silly, dear! Oh, sure, you can rip my skull open with your bare hands and feast on my innards and whatnot, but you've no reason to at the moment, now have you?"

I stared deadpanned at her. What in Land was wrong with this woman?

She was still chuckling, wiping at an entertained tear. "Silly girl. You're still very funny, even after death." She sighed and leaned back in her chair, relaxed. "Oh, how I did miss our chats, Cilia. I'm glad our paths have crossed again."

Again? "Your husband… Dream…" I tapped a nail over the ceramic teacup, the following ring giving faint *tink, tink, tinks* and making the purple liquid quiver. "He mentioned his… your… daughters would play with my son? With Caleb?"

Her smile was ever pleasant. "Those were my favorite years, you know. Isn't it strange? We've lived five hundred of them, and only five are truly the most memorable."

"Memorable for you," I muttered.

She hummed, fiddling with her baby's azure locks. "Ah, right… I suppose you don't remember me, do you?"

"Not even a little." I paused, adding, "sorry."

"Nothing to be sorry over, dear. It was Macar who did this to you, and it is still Macar who holds your memories hostage, as it were."

"Why can't I remember more, yet?" I asked. If anyone would have answers, it would be her or Dream. "I only barely remember your husband's face, and despite having spent two months with you all, I remember nothing of you, Cr... Crys..."

"Crysalette," she sighed, dismayed. "But you used to call me Crysa. You and I were friends once, you know. Perhaps the only friend I could truly claim, anyway."

"Once..." I gazed down at my untouched tea, steam licking from the gilded rim. "And now? After what I've done, do you still think of me as a friend?"

She flicked her eyes up for a moment, silent. Thinking.

My claws threatened to sharpen. *Fool, Cilia.* My crimes were unforgivable. I may have destroyed every chance I had at having 'friends' again.

"Oddly," she began, her smile making me blink. "Yes."

I gawked. "*Yes?*"

"Strange, isn't it?" the madwoman giggled.

My claws did grow, and my cat ears curled. I slammed a fist on the table, knocking over my tea.

"How?" I demanded. "*Why?* I've killed thousands—hundreds of thousands! — over the last five centuries! I've let my own murderer manipulate me into bringing war across the globe, I have caused so much grief...!" My ears draped to my neck, fists loosening. My sinking stomach forced my legs to cave, and I lowered back into my chair, my voice soft. "I've cause you all *so much* grief. So much pain..."

She took up her tea and sipped in another hum. "I know. And it's the oddest thing. I'm aware of the horrors you've inflicted upon the world, yet..." She set down her cup. "Here and now, it doesn't feel like anything has changed. I'm not sure why."

My gaze was pained. Confused. "Crysa," I said. "You are perhaps the most perplexing woman I've ever met."

She chuckled. "And this isn't the first time you've told me so."

She cooed to her baby and wagged a finger at his face. The child gripped her finger playfully.

Then a scuffle of footfalls echoed from the breezeway behind me. I inched my gaze back—and froze.

A black-haired woman approached us. Her lime green eyes found mine, and her step paused. It was my descendant. The one who shared my face.

She was holding a tray of cakes and other pastries. A pet ferret was stretched over her neck from shoulder to shoulder, nibbling on a piece of muffin.

The woman and I stared at one another for but a moment, then she let out a snort and stalked over to our table.

"Dream said you wanted sweets?" She asked the queen and placed the tray on the table.

Crysa ogled the pastries, setting the baby on her knee and closed her blouse. "Ah! They smell delicious, Mikani. Thank you."

Mikani. So that was her name. Finally, I at least knew one of my descendants' names, aside from Claude.

Mikani grinned. "No problem." Her eyes flicked to me next, and I grew cold. "Cilia, right?" she asked.

She was… talking to me? "Yes," I answered, cautious.

Her gaze drifted to the spilt tea in front of me, and she grunted, righting the cup on its saucer and filled it again from the pot.

"So," she muttered, setting the pot down and folding her arms. "Everyone won't shut up about how I look like you."

"Likewise." Praise Shel, one of my descendants was actually *talking* to me? On purpose? By choice…! I dared to add with a smirk, "You're welcome, by the way. Not everyone is blessed with such beautiful ancestors from which to gain their genes."

She grinned! It was only for a brief moment, but Shel damn it, it was the most positive response any of my family had given me.

That ferret on her shoulder crawled onto the table and sniffed at the array of pastries. It prepared to swipe a corner—

"Nuh-uh," my descendant chided, snapping her fingers in front of the weasel's nose and caused a burst of fire to puff there.

The ferret huffed in both fright and anger, scuttling into my lap and curled into a ball. My tone turned flighty as I asked, "You're a Pyrovoker as well?"

She cocked an eyebrow at me. "What, should I thank you for that, too?"

I couldn't help my smile. "Well, I'm hardly one to gloat."

"Clearly."

The queen flapped her hand excitedly and reached out a cake to me. "Oh, Cilia, you must try some of her pastries! They are very nearly your own recipes from when you were alive, it's uncanny."

The lovely Mikani frowned at me. "You were a baker?"

"I was." I took the pastry, hesitating, then took a small bite.

—I took a small bite of the apricot cake, the crisp, flaky dough crinkling under my teeth.

I swallowed and chuckled, wiping a crumb from Caleb's cheek after he'd taken his own bite, the boy giggling.

"And that's how you make mama's special apricot cakes."

The memory vanished.

I was still chewing the small piece of cake. But now, my vision was blurred, eyes having welled without warning.

"Caleb," I whispered, joy blossoming so sweet, my lungs felt like cotton. "I… I showed Caleb how to make this same cake. It was his favorite. And Kael's…"

The Dream Queen put a hand to her chest, saddened.

Mikani picked up the ferret from my lap, her tone softening. "I guess you miss him, huh?"

I let my tears do as they willed, each bead boiling black and slithering into the swirling lines on my fingers in quiet hisses. I was so *happy*, then. We were all so happy…

"Well," Mikani sighed and slipped her hands in her pockets. "If it helps, he seemed to miss you, too."

My attention jolted. "Who?"

"Kael," she said, shrugging half-heartedly. "He found me in that prison. Talked about you a little."

"You've seen Kael?" How could I have missed this? "What did he say?"

"He said I reminded him of his wife." Her head wavered. "So, guess he meant you. He still thinks you're dead, though. Well… The *real* kind of dead."

"Did he seem angry with me?" The last memory I had of Kael, he had just walked out on me, cursing me. Wanting nothing to do with me.

Her face twisted in bewilderment. "Angry? Bloods, he looked downright crushed. He's still wearing his wedding ring and stud, even."

"He is?" I gripped my chair's arm, hope swelling.

She looked across the yard toward the breezeway. "You know… everyone keeps talking about the horrible stuff he did. They call him a stone-cold killer and a lunatic." She shook her head. "But I didn't see that in Tanderam. All I saw was a sad man who missed his wife so much, it broke him. And looking at your scars…" She pointed to the ugly line running across my neck, and then the ones looping my wrists. "You look like you were chopped up. Like Bloody livestock. If I came home and found Ringëd like that…" Her black cat ears grew, curling tight. "Well, I can't say I wouldn't snap either. I'd find the son of a bitch who took him from me and burn him to a crisp. Along with anyone who got in my way." She rubbed her neck. "I can't really ignore what everyone's saying you both did, but… I get it. Thought I should tell you that, at least."

The tears resurfaced. "Thank you."

She sniffed, wiping a finger under her nose. Then she said, "And, um, if you're the one we get our recipes from…" She blushed only a little. "I guess I wouldn't mind if you came around the kitchens and showed us some things you didn't get to write down or whatever. Dad probably wouldn't mind either."

She walked off. I stifled a choking sob of joy, chuckling as I stared after that wonderful, wonderful woman.

Crysa giggled across from me. "She reminds me of you."

I shot her a flat look.

But laughed.

5

NEW DANGERS

XAVIER

Claude's honey-yellow eyes glared at the Metaglass tipped arrow. He rolled the shaft between his fingers, his cat ears sprouting.

From across the counter, cluttered with various pots and pans, I watched the infectious veins quiver and lick about inside the glass as if it were a living creature all its own. A simmering hiss sounded from the other chefs who were fiddling with the stoves, spices and peppers perfuming the kitchens in thick clouds of steam. Claude's daughter, Mikani, had abandoned her ovens to stand beside him and inspect the strange arrow with one cat ear flicked forward. Octavius watched his father as well, shifting uncomfortably beside Alexander while his platemail clattered.

After a long, grueling silence from him, Claude let out a gnarled breath at last. "I don't like it."

"What does it mean?" I asked.

"It means two things," said Claude as he turned the arrow upside down in examination, his lips wrenched in a foreboding frown. "One, that Macar figured out how to utilize our era's Metaglass with Kael's infection Hallows. And two, we're screwed up the ass."

"How terribly?" Alex asked from behind me.

Beside him, Willow placed a hand at her hip and inquired, "how much of a threat will this be if only one man is able to produce the poisons?"

Claude handed me back the arrow and rubbed his neck. "Hard to tell, Princess. It depends how much time Kael has on his hands right now. But then, this is the first we've seen of these things. Safe to say it's pretty fresh, so there can't be too many of them right now. My bet is, these were prototypes they fired at you. Shel knows they didn't have this idea when I was with them."

"—Let me see that arrow," a sudden voice croaked to my right, startling me. Dream had appeared out of thin air. No doubt, the blue-haired king must have come from Aspirre with the Orbs of Azure again, abandoning any sense of decorum by electing *not* to use the Bloody door like everyone else. I should be accustomed to his sudden appearances by now, yet I still found myself jumping even now.

But good *Gods*, he looked terrible. His bloodshot eyes had developed heavy, dark bags that dragged down the lids, his curling azure hair a greasy mess, his hopefully *sweat* stained jacket wrinkled and stiff.

Lords, is that what I have to look forward to as a father? I wondered as fright shook my blood. Aside from what Alexander had told me of his training with Dream, Aspirre's king hadn't been seen much by the rest of us, he and Crysalette being busy with their newborn son. And my own son was to be born in two months' time. That gave us less than twenty weeks. *Gods help me through those first weeks of exhaustion.* I swallowed the lump in my throat, seeing Dream's crusted, swollen eyes could barely stay open. *How am I to survive THAT?*

I'd been so busy staring, I'd forgotten Dream's request. The teenaged king plucked the arrow from my fingers and inspected it with those heavy, red-rimmed eyes. He made no sound. His exhausted expression didn't change.

Then he yawned and said, "These aren't prototypes. Kael must have begun production of these weapons nearly the moment Claude left them. See for yourself."

He offered me the arrow again. *He means with my prophetic Hallows,* I realized. Of course. I should have thought of that first. Have I fallen so out of habit?

My fingers hesitated, but I took the shaft once more, this time evoking my prophetic Hallows as my fingers gleamed blue around the arrow. Then, my point of view changed, Seeing through someone else's eyes.

—That lying bastard...!

He shoved the lizard woman blocking his path to the Sky Port's entrance, keeping his hood firmly cinched over his black hair.

He'd looked at every possible angle, hadn't he? Could that fool of a prince have been lying himself?

His teeth sharpened, and he slammed his Mel beads onto the ticket master's counter, demanding a ticket to Culatia's capital city.

He was getting to the bottom of this. If she was here... if his angel was still among them...

He wanted it to be true. Damn him, but he wanted that prince to be right. If by some merciful will of Nira he could see her again, demon or not, he would damn well find her if it meant upturning every blade of grass and cracked stone on this Godsforsaken planet.

Though oddly, despite the thrashing waves of absolute fury boiling within him and the tears stinging his eyes, he found himself smiling.

The present time dripped back into view. I found my eyes wet with Kael's tears, and quickly dabbed them dry. Upon receiving these visions with my new prophetic Hallows, I found that the narrator's emotions had a habit of leaking into my own as though *I* were experiencing them myself. It was damned annoying at times. It often took a few seconds for their emotions to fully fade.

"He knows," I said, the surprise thick on my tongue. "Cayden's told him Cilia is here. He's heading to Culatia's palace to confront Macar."

Dream blinked at me, then snatched the arrow back. "What?" His eyes went stale, his fingers brightened blue, but he frowned skeptically. "I don't See any of that."

"It was months ago, I think," I said.

Alex came beside me and took the arrow from Dream, evoking his own prophetic Hallows.

"Gods, he's right," Alex announced. "Kael's just arrived in Culatia's capital."

"Culatia?" A new voice asked.

My head snapped to Cilia, who had perched herself on the sill of an open window in the kitchens. Her cat ears were grown and perked forward; her glowing white pupils dedicated to us.

Willow's fox ears grew, and she sneered, "I don't recall asking *you* to join this meeting, witch."

Cilia glared for only a moment, then turned her nose to the sky and pierced a claw into a bowl of purple grapes on a nearby table. "Then forgive me for being the *subject* of this meeting, Princess. I should think it my business if my husband is looking for me."

Willow's lips curled back in a snarl, but she raised no further protest.

Cilia popped a grape in her mouth. When she finished chewing and sank her claw into another, she hummed. "Why is Kael in Culatia?"

I folded my arms. "Macarius is there, it seems. One of our allies in Everland told Kael you were the demon queen Macarius had been using. Now your murdering husband is about to demand answers."

"Do you think he'll kill Macar?" She asked excitedly, swinging her legs inside and kicking them in the air like a gleeful child. "Oh, I hope he waits for me to see him shrivel that snake into a poisoned, charred lizard...!"

"As simple as it would make our jobs," Dream muttered, yielding to another yawn and rubbing his eyes with his too-long sleeve, "if Kael has gone to merely question Macar, it sounds as though he isn't fully convinced. He's only hopeful you're still here, Cilia. I'm afraid it will be too easy for Macar to dismiss it."

Cilia grimaced, but quickly composed herself and popped another grape in her mouth, swallowing. She glanced at Dream sidelong. "But we are going to Culatia ourselves, aren't we?"

I tapped a finger over my arm. "We are… though knowing Macar is there already worries me."

"It worries me as well," grunted Dream. "I'm certain he seeks Sky's Relic. Though I imagine Rojired is in no condition to give Macar a coherent answer for where to find it. Currently, we have the advantage, with Sky being here with us."

Alexander's platemail rattled when he shifted his weight. "I'll tell Prince Roji to be on guard before we leave."

"Very good," Dream yawned, nodding as he slipped onto an empty stool and rested his head over the flour-covered countertop. "I had hoped…" Another yawn, his eyes closing. "We'd have more time… before seeing him again…"

Dream sighed softly and drifted into slumber—then vanished into Aspirre in a white flash, the Orbs of Azure he'd had on his person transporting him there physically as they usually did when the man fell asleep with them.

Willow shook her head and turned to Alexander, who still held the infection arrow. "Perhaps you should hand that off to someone who's better equipped with immunity?" She suggested.

Alex grimaced, then passed the arrow to Octavius beside him.

Octavius looked from the arrow to Willow, then to me questioningly. "Um, what do I do with it?"

I smoothed the beard at my chin thoughtfully. "Why don't you bring it to our Alchemists? See if they can't come up with a defense against these things?"

"—Sure, we can do that," the voice of Bianca affirmed from the kitchen door suddenly.

We all turned to her, and her rabbit ears stiffened straight up, as if regretting speaking up. She was halfway in the kitchens as if she'd been listening to us in secret, not wanting to be seen. But now that she'd made herself known, she sighed and entered officially. Her Barkdragon, Basil, followed at her heels timidly. Bianca was sure to give Alex a sharp glare before stepping beside Octavius to examine the poison-arrow he held. The Metaglass tip clinked softly as the cluster of black veins slithered inside it, writhing like a living creature trying to escape.

Bianca tapped a finger over the glass tip, thoughtful. "There might just be a way to counter it…" she murmured, her nose scrunching. "But I'm going to need Octavius's poison Hallows to find it." She lifted her gaze to Octavius. "Think you can spare a couple hours a day in the next month while I run some tests?"

He didn't look all that thrilled about it, but he hummed. "I guess… What all would I need to do?"

"I'll need you to infect a ghost—lightly, obviously. Not enough to destroy the soul, but enough so I can test out some tonics to fight against it. But let me find some old Healing books first." She delicately plucked the arrow from his fingers and walked toward the door, handling the dangerous weapon with care as she murmured, "I need to do some research before we do any testing. I'll come find you when I'm ready." She lifted the arrow to the light, humming as she left. "Very interesting…"

When Bianca was gone, Willow grumbled a curse and spun on her heels to leave the kitchens as well, scowling in deep thought. "I must speak with my father about this," she said, rubbing her temples. "If these soul-poisoning arrows are shipped to High Everland as well, he must be warned of the possible threat."

I followed at her side. I saw from over my shoulder that Alexander had used his Somniovoking to split himself into several copies, all of which fanned out to scout the hallways while the original stayed close behind us as a personal guard.

"I'll contact my mother and father as well," I said. "Perhaps they can come up with a counter against such an attack."

Willow nodded her agreement and pulled out a communicator from the Storagesphere chained round her waist. I did the same for my own com, plucking it from my doublet's pocket and dialed the proper number for my mother's personal com. From the embedded Vision-gem, a projected screen of light brightened to life before my nose and swirled in a stirring motion as I awaited an answer. After a moment, Mother's narrow face fuzzed into view, her grey wolf ears perking in my direction on the screen.

"Ah, Xavier," Mother greeted bluntly. Her hair was braided over one of her plated shoulders, sharp clatters sounding from the com's small speakers as though her armor were clinking noisily during her walk. I could swear I spied a fleck of blood on her breastplate as she gave a nasally hum. *"You've grand timing. We've just seized the city of High Adrial successfully. We project to march on High Timberail within the month."*

"Grand progress," I commended. Beside me, Willow had begun her report to the Death King. She spoke with him through her own com's screen of light and exchanged hard tones. I returned my attention to Mother. "I'm afraid I have less… positive news to report, Mistress. There was an incident here at Neverland's capital during the parade. Assassins shot at us with peculiar, Metaglass-tipped arrows—"

"SEAMSTRESS CLEANSE ME!" Mother cried so shrilly I had to cringe away from the com to keep my eardrums from bursting. Her hardened expression contorted to frightened shock, wolf ears draping to her neck as her shrieks tumbled over themselves. *"Was Willow harmed?! Has she seen the Healers?! Is the baby all right—for the love of Nira, IS THE BABY ALL RIGHT?!"*

"Y-yes, they're both safe!" I assured, twisting back to Alexander to exchange a grimace. He hid a chuckling snort behind a hand. "But there's something about these—"

"Keep her in bed and do your Bloody duty as a husband to bring her the meals she needs! What was she doing out there in the first place?! She should be resting and staying out of harms' way! Stress is not good for the baby! I did NOT raise you to put your expecting wife in danger—!"

"Mother, she's *fine*," I growled, my wolf ears growing. I rubbed a finger in one to stop the blasted ringing from that abuse. "As am *I*, thank you for asking… Anabelle did away with the assassins swiftly. There's no need for alarm. Though, the weapons we found on the women were alarming."

Mother's panic quelled some, but her drastic frown showed she still hadn't calmed. *"What do you mean?"*

"They had poisoned-tipped arrows." I paused, then amended, "*Infection*-tipped arrows. Metaglass arrowheads filled with Infection Hallows. They melted the flesh from a horse and destroyed the soul of one assassin who took her own life before we could question her."

"Infection Hallows…?" Her brows creased in deliberation, tapping a gauntleted finger to her chin. *"Then, is Kael behind this weapon?"*

"We've no doubt that he is. Though, since he is the only manufacturer, we don't think there are very many in production just yet. Regardless, it seemed prudent to inform you of this new danger, in case you see any in High Everland as well."

She nodded, brooding. *"Yes… I'll inform your father. If we see such arrows, we'll need a counter measure prepared."*

"My thoughts exactly," I said. "I'll keep you posted if anything else should arise upon our departure tomorrow—"

"Oh, wait now!" she interrupted desperately. *"Is Willow there with you? Could I speak with her? It's been far too long since I had a pleasant chat with my daughter-in-law!"*

I glanced at Willow beside me. She was still on call with her father.

"… and sure you're drinking enough water?" the Death King questioned her intently from her screen. *"And don't forget to take your vitamins! And get some rest

should you tire! Your mother and I think you should postpone your flight to Culatia, especially after such a stressful event—!"

"Father, for the last time, I am *fine*," she muttered and curled back her grown fox ears. "And you know well we can't postpone the flight. If we're to stop the war with Culatia and Marincia, Prince Roji must take the throne from his father immediately."

"But you shouldn't have to concern yourself with such things in your condition!"

"My condition is not preventing me from being any less of a shifter-being! And for another thing, how is any of this at all relevant to…!"

They continued bickering, and I swallowed, glancing back at Mother from *my* screen. "Erm," I began meekly and cleared my throat. "She's a tad… busy, Mother. Perhaps another time?"

Mother deflated. *"Oh, very well… Do see that she's taken care of, then?"*

I chuckled. "Of course. Why would I do any less? It's my son just as well as hers, Mother."

Mother snorted. *"You wouldn't understand. You aren't the one growing him."*

I grimaced. "Yes, well… until next time, Mother…"

I ended the call in a long, irked breath. Most of my calls with Mother and Father had ended this way, lately. And each time, I was left feeling overwhelmingly irritated. While I acknowledged that yes, Willow was bearing the brunt of the load with our son, *why* did it feel like I hadn't any claim to him whatsoever?

"FATHER!" Willow blurted at her com screen. "Will you *please* calm yourself! I. Am. *Fine*. All will be well. We have *numerous* Seers and Healers joining us on our flight, and even Grandfather and Grandmother will be there. You've nothing to worry over, now if you don't mind, I have other important matters to see to!" She ended the call in a huff.

Then a passing servant strolled by and Willow snagged the woman's arm tersely. "Excuse me, miss," she said through clenched teeth, trying like Death to sound less furious than she looked. "Could you please send for someone to bring up three lemon cakes, a quart of spiced cider, and an entire bottle of pickled beets to our guest chambers? *Immediately*."

The servant woman hesitated, still caught in Willow's tight grip. "O-oh, yes, Your Grace… I'll send for someone right away."

"Thank you." Willow released her, and we watched the woman scurry away toward the kitchens we'd left behind, bumping into Alexander in her hurry.

With that, Willow huffed again and strutted up a curling flight of stairs. "Why does *every* conversation with my parents have to turn into 'baby this' and 'baby that' and 'you oughtn't be doing this'? Bah!" She threw up her hands. "I am not some delicate flower! I've fought demons, I've fought dragons, I've fought *countless* soldiers for Death's sake! There are expecting mothers who have done far more and survived it all with no complications!"

Alex gave her a dead-panned look as he strode behind us. "Are there, now? I wasn't aware that 'running into battle during a war' was the new hobby for pregnant women. Who needs knitting these days?"

She gave a twisted look, blinked, then grunted. "Well… all right, perhaps I was a *tad* reckless at the beginning… But it's not as if I'm charging the front-lines now."

"They're only worried," I reminded her and wrapped an arm around her waist as we walked through the second floor's halls toward our chambers. I chuckled in a small grimace. "Though, I must admit, even my own parents are being exceedingly overbearing… at least you're getting all the attention. I may as well not exist anymore."

"Which is just as ridiculous," she said. "I am not the only expecting parent here. Why can't they dote on you for a change and give me a Bloody break?"

"According to my mother," I muttered. "It's because *I'm not the one grow-ing him*, and *I wouldn't understand.* Is that true, darling? Do you think I don't understand what you're going through?"

She cocked an eyebrow at me. "Perhaps not in a literal sense, but I know I'm not the only one affected. I don't think you've left my side often in the past month, in fact. You've even been holding Hugh's lessons wherever *I* am. When have you had time to see your friends? Or even Alexander here?" She waved a hand to Alexander behind us.

My brother scoffed and folded his arms. "I've hardly seen him all month."

I rubbed my neck in a mumble, "I *did* apologize for that…"

"Perhaps it would do you some good to get out more?" She said. We reached our chamber doors and strode inside. Alexander didn't join us, saying he would remain posted *outside* to guard the door. Willow turned the latch behind us and sighed. "It may do us both some good to… to gain a bit of *space?*"

I blinked at her. "Are you kicking me out?"

"No, no!" She flushed slightly. "I merely meant that, if you'd prefer, you haven't an obligation to stay with me. Not that I don't appreciate the company," she assured. "It's just that you seemed rather… distraught today while speaking with Alexander. If you would rather spend time with him and the others—"

"Willow, that's why I offered him the position as captain of our guard." I lowered into a leather chaise by the open balcony entry, the curtains ruffling gently in the outside breeze. "Aside from the obvious fact he's the best damned candidate in existence for it, this way I wouldn't have to give up time with either of you."

"But you really ought to find time with him *alone,*" she insisted. "And with the others. I admit, even I haven't spent much time with Lilli, and I know I should do better for her sake—especially before our child is born, when we'll have even *less* time to do so."

I leaned back in the chaise and sighed, rubbing my eyes. "Oh, very well… I suppose you're right. Our lives are about to change in the next twenty weeks, I suppose we don't have to start that change any earlier, eh?"

"Precisely." She lowered beside me and stole my lips, steam simmering from her Pyrovoker's heat and my Glaciavoker's chill. Then she chuckled and began kissing up my neck, the trail warming over my iced veins up to my ear. She then crawled over my lap and played with my beard with a suddenly hungry leer. "But such can wait for tomorrow," she purred. "Alexander can have you when I'm done with you today…"

My skin trembled with pleasure as her breath heated my throat, and I ran my fingers through her ashen hair. "As you demand, darling," I rasped and tasted along her smooth jaw.

A servant knocked on the doors and called about the meals Willow had ordered, but they were unheeded as we lost ourselves in each other's arms.

6

A FATEFUL MEETING

DREAM

510 YEARS PRIOR

"*Crysa…*" *I murmured, letting the name play over my tongue. It sounded so familiar now, after saying it aloud for so long. "Crysa… Crysa… Crysa…"*

Blast it, if only I'd had more time with my unborn granddaughter that last round! I was sure she'd said I'd meet this mythical 'Crysa' around this century.

I lowered back over my floating shepherd's crook, folding my arms behind my head as the crook glided through the empty depths of Aspirre. This part of Aspirre seemed free of any Noctis Golems thus far, but one couldn't be too careful, so I'd woven myself a clear barrier to ward them off, should any decide to hunt me on my lazy trek.

What if this 'Crysa' hadn't been born yet? Even worse, what if I find her as a child and won't recognize her until Gods know how long? Confound it all!

I pulled my hood over my face and deflated, letting my arms drape as my back stretched over the crook, feeling like a wet towel hung up to dry.

How many more hundred years did I have to wait to experience this… this 'romance' everyone speaks of? Why did everyone dream of it so frequently? Why did their dreams of sex look so thrilling? Why did holding hands and sharing the touch of one's lips appear in almost everyone's subconscious? What was it about this love business that made everyone's dreams look so…

So happy?

I groaned and tugged my hood to my chin. "Crysa, where are you?" I lamented. "I'm so Bloody BORED—"

My crook slammed into something at the front, and I nearly fell off.

I scrambled to balance myself on the crook again, looking up to see an opaque, azure sphere was blocking my way. It was the average size of a shifter's subconscious, so it must have been a Somniovoker's barrier.

Hmm. I cupped my chin, looking right, then left. Twisting round to peer behind me.

There were barriers such as this in the area, above and below. But they were a plain, solid azure and purple, looking drab compared to this pristine, glittering barrier in front of me.

Curious, I pushed a hand over it. Its walls felt smooth and clean, as pure as crystal… Admirable work. Let's see whose handy work this was.

I pushed on the wall further to pass through as I usually did—

It didn't budge.

I blinked, pushing again, shoving my shoulder against it. My fox ears grew, irritated. In all my fifteen-hundred years, I've never once been kept out of someone's subconscious. And I wasn't about to start now, pretty barrier or not.

I grabbed my shepherd's crook and began thwacking the damned thing, now eager as ever to see who in Void dared to keep me out of their dreams.

"Stop that blasted knocking, will you?" A young man's voice snapped from the other side of the barrier. "Mind your own dreams."

I paused, crook hesitating over my head. "Oh. Sorry." I cleared my throat and lowered the staff, asking awkwardly, "Whose dream is this, then?"

"Bloody fool, you are." The boy gave a haughty laugh. "As if I'm one to give my name so freely to every trespassing Somniovoker that waltzes into my barrier."

"I don't suppose you could make an exception?"

Another laugh. "Think we're entitled to everyone's dreams, eh? Think we're the little blue king himself?"

I grimaced. "I quite think I've outgrown that name, thank you."

He was silent behind his barrier. Then a tiny piece of it disappeared, revealing a single, brown eye that peered through suspiciously.

His hostility dissolved. "Oh. Your Majesty. A thousand pardons."

A larger piece of the barrier vanished, wide enough to be an enormous door as the young man—a snake shifter—could now be seen in full splendor, pushing up his half-moon eyeglasses.

I stiffened. Suddenly, the inexistent air grew very, very cold.

"Please, come in," the boy encouraged, gesturing welcomingly. "I apologize for the suspicion. I'm sure you understand, you can't trust every dream walker that wanders through."

The boy looked to be fifteen, his scales an Everlandish bronze, brown hair streaked with blond strands. His subconscious had him wearing a clean pressed, long-sleeved tunic the color of luscious cream, the tie strings at the collar hanging loose. This marked him as a relaxed, yet refined mind.

I, on the other hand, was anything but relaxed while staring at that scaled, smiling face. It was a face that has haunted me for near two-thousand years.

It was the Lightcaster.

The boy floated into his subconscious—floated, without the aid of a woven pair of wings or a cloud to sit on or anything Somniovokers usually used to move about Aspirre.

He traveled this realm as I did. Someone so young…

The Lightcaster turned back and smiled warmly. "I wondered if I'd have a chance to meet you. They say most of us do, if you find us worthy or notable."

What was I to say to the Lightcaster? The one who may well bring the End of Existence? He was so young. So unexpectedly… pleasant.

Should I do something? Should I try and kill him now, just in case? I've never killed anyone before… And what if I was wrong about the vision?

No, I should run. Only the Shadowblood is said to be his match, right or wrong. Damn me, I should run now while I could and search for the Shadowblood. If the Lightcaster has come, then surely his rival has followed? Bloods, I'm not prepared for this, I need more time, I…!

I looked into the barrier.

"Iri," I breathed, awed into silence.

It was a library. An enormous, incredible library filled with shelves that seemed miles high and encircled the entirety of the globed subconscious. Suspended in the center of these maze-like shelves were various chairs, tables, desks, papers, notebooks, quills and ink bottles, all floating there in the air without a care.

The boy floated to one notebook in particular and grabbed a quill that hovered beside it.

"Now," he said and made his way back to me while dipping his quill nib in the accompanying ink well. "Being the only individual who has personally lived during it, can you give a more detailed recollection of what befell the sunken city of Corros in the year 512 A.B?"

I stared at the Caster. "What?"

"The sunken city," he reiterated, circling the quill urgently. "According to the texts, there once was a city named Corros in the Marincian isles that supposedly sank to the bottom of the sea in ancient times. Did it ever exist, and if so, did it actually sink? How so? There is little detail offered of the event, save for a few infuriatingly vague mentions in passing."

My brow furrowed. "You've waited to see me to ask that specific question?"

"Well, no," he admitted. "I've compiled a few books of other questions I wished to ask you, if you ever came around. Both physically and subconsciously."

My expression flattened. "You wished to meet the King of Dreams to ask him history questions?"

"Of course." He pushed up his eyeglasses, readying his quill. "You are the only shifter alive who can actually answer them as a primary source. The ghosts I've interviewed only know up to three hundred years in the past, since their afterlives tend to end after that. None of them know even a smidgen of the knowledge you alone hold."

I stared at the lad a moment longer. Then took a breath. "Corros was built in the sea to begin with. Only the fish shifters could travel there without drowning."

His eyes lightened with pure delight, then he let out a joyous laugh and quickly scribbled down his notes. "Of course…! But then, how do you know of it if you yourself aren't a fish shifter?"

"Well, being the King of Dreams has its perks," I explained. "The Ocean King at the time was proud of the new city and invited me to see it. He made me a personal air bubble to travel with him there."

"But according to the Marincians of this era," he protested, "Even they think it's only a legend."

I shrugged. "The city only lasted a few decades before feral Seadragons overran the place and chased the shifters out. They've made it their nest, to my understanding, so everyone forgot about it after a few hundred years. Myself included, until you asked."

He scribbled down more notes, nodding. "Fascinating… Well, that's one question out of the way. Next—Was Fangs Gabbum VIII really ten feet tall?"

PRESENT DAY

Clunk!

My chin cracked against the flour-dusted counter the moment I awoke and I tumbled onto the kitchen's tiled floor in a pained yelp.

I shook my bleary head, sobering while I took in my suddenly physical surroundings. *Hmm.* Someone had moved the stool I'd fallen asleep on. How long had it been since I dozed off? The others were nowhere in sight now.

"You all right down there, Dream?" Claude asked above me from the other side of the counter. The baker was rolling dough over a wooden board, his daughter and her demon-doppelganger pausing their own work to glance down at me from the far corner.

I waved a hand, signaling that I was fine, and pushed to my bare feet. Peering out the window, I saw it was dark now. Apparently, I'd been asleep for some hours.

Well, I thought in a shudder. *Best I found my wife, else she has my balls for shirking my fatherly duties with baby Eryn.*

I yawned and shuffled out of the kitchen.

—Cilia gasped in surprise suddenly as she was pushed aside by the invisible force that came from the Orbs I had tied in their sack on my belt. *Ah, that's right.* I'd forgotten Sentients couldn't near the Relics. I waved to the demon queen in apology, yawning once more, and made my way through the palace halls.

Once reaching my designated guest room, I closed the doors behind me, finding Crysa sitting in the rocking chair, baby Eryn sleeping on her bosom.

She turned when I entered, smiling.

My returning smile was brief.

Concerned, she rose and gently set Eryn in his crib before padding toward me.

"Dream?" she murmured, cupping my bristled chin with a tender hand. "What's wrong?"

I hesitated. "Do you think… do you think when I'd first met Macar, I should have…"

She saw my eyes were welling. Her lips pursed. "That you should have killed him?" she finished softly.

"I could have." I whispered. "All of this—all that's to come—I could have stopped it. It would have been so simple."

She said nothing. She only wrapped me in her arms and held me there, with the soft sounds of snapping embers crackling in the hearth.

7

TO THE AIRSHIP

XAVIER

The Airship's bell gave three long, resonant tolls as I walked up the ramp with Willow in arm.

The Sky Port's daunting station was packed with cheering Neverlanders. They were here to bid farewell to their beloved, golden-haired queen, who strode behind me, waving to her people.

Queen Anabelle was dressed less splendidly than yesterday at the festival. Today she sported leather trousers and clean boots, her tight blouse and vest buttoned down the middle, her hands hidden in slender gloves. It wasn't very queen like, but I had to admit, it was quite fetching on the lioness.

Willow, in contrast, wore a loose violet gown with the sash tied delicately at her waist to subtly accentuate her growing belly. She couldn't wear anything constricting lately, complaining of discomfort. Only last night, I'd woken to her tossing and turning, throwing off gown after gown and complaining of the heat, despite the chill autumn weather. She'd clung to my Glaciavoker's frosted skin so desperately, I'd lost circulation several times.

Judging from the bags under her eyes now, I suspected she hadn't found much sleep after I'd dozed off. Perhaps our son was kicking more violently? Or perhaps the new weight was a strain on her back?

Willow's tiny crow fluttered around her as we reached the top deck of the ship, and Chai flew to my shoulder in a low croak, nuzzling his beak against my beard. The bustling crew's footfalls vibrated as they and the rest of the passengers rattled the floorboards. Commands were barked here and there and gulls screamed from the towering masts that stretched so high, it was a wonder they didn't hit the station's ceiling. The sails were tied for now, women tending to them up above.

A squeal hissed from up there, so loud and abrupt I cringed and cupped my wolf ears that had grown in response.

Then the women on the masts grabbed the nearest dangling ropes and climbed down to the deck, making room for the several heated balloons that were now expanding between, above, and to the sides of the sails, tied to the ship by nets and hissing to life like newly woken beasts.

From over the rails, I saw our small fleet was inflating heated balloons of their own. They were painted in gold and brown with the Land Queen's emblem displayed proudly.

"Death," I breathed, entranced as I watched the workers make their preparations on each vessel. "So, these are Airships?"

Willow sounded just as mesmerized beside me. "I've read of them countless times in books. I didn't think they'd be so grandiose."

"Cool, huh?" A new voice chimed.

Prince Roji had come between us. A pair of jade goggles covered his eyes as he leaned over the rail and sucked in a strong breath of the crisp, salty air.

His scarlet, feathered hair wavered in the breeze, brown skin glistening in the sunlight and wings stretching long behind him.

"Been a long time since I've flown one of these," he said, rubbing his hands together and grinning like a boy eager to cause mischief.

I frowned. "You're piloting this ship?"

"You bet." Roji thumped my back. "I know the fastest way there, and you won't find anyone better to navigate the storms to come. Just relax and leave the flying to me. Hold in your lunch if you can." He smirked on his way to the helm, and I noticed Willow looked particularly green beside me now.

I offered her a thin smile and wrapped an arm around her waist. "Well," I said, "I suppose if we're to trust anyone with flying us through the sky, it ought to be Sky himself, eh?"

I felt her tremble slightly.

"Don't worry, love." I pulled her from the rail. "Here, come away from the ledge. We can wait in the cabin upon takeoff, to ease your nerves."

She swallowed, nodding. "Y-yes. In the cabin. Inside. Very good."

I guided her through the crowded deck—but nearly tripped over Oliver and Fuérr as they raced in front of us.

"Oliver!" Lilli chased after them, shouting. "Prince Fuérr! Get back inside this instant!"

Oliver flapped his wings in protest, hopping in the air for a spritely moment as he whined, "But we wanna see it fly!"

"Oliver," Lilli warned, weaving through the crowd, then gave up and took to the air with her leathery wings, dodging the flying crew members. "Get back here right now or—"

The children crashed into Jaq's legs and nearly toppled the viper. His armor clattered as he whirled on them.

Jaq grabbed the boys by their shirt collars and lifted them off their feet. "Inside," he ordered. "Everyone's workin'. Bloody feral rats, scuttlin' all over the place under everyone's feet." He slung the protesting children over both his shoulders and nodded to Lilli, who landed beside him panting over her knees and thanked him kindly.

"—Xavier," my brother called suddenly from the crowd. I found Alexander striding toward me from inside the cabin, Matthiel at his side. "We've done a thorough search of the ship," Alexander reported.

"And a secondary background check on the crew members," Matthiel added proudly. "All seems clear. We ought to be ready for departure."

"Well, when our pilots are ready," Alex clarified. "But the Aerovokers we've hired are in position to create a protective air-pocket around the ship so we can breathe easily in the higher altitudes. The air is said to be rather thin up there, so they say it's standard procedure. Roji says the first 40,000 feet will take perhaps twenty minutes or—"

Willow's claws stabbed into my arm, and I yelped in pain.

"4-4... 40,000?" Willow was shaking violently now, azure eyes swimming with dread as her claws dug deeper into my skin.

"Darling," I muttered through clenched teeth, trying desperately to pry her claws free without sounding short. "You'll be fine. Come inside and you'll be... just... fine—"

Ku-KLANG!

The metal roof of the station split apart down the middle, gears and cogs ripping in a *chunk-chunk-chunk-chunk* rhythm, widening the roof's mechanized opening.

"All right!" Roji yelled in a thrill from the helm and cranked back a lever, turned three separate nobs, then turned a new crank five time to the left. He finished with a ceremonial stomp of his feet, and a pound to the helm. "Stormchasers, let's get this girl flying!"

A roar erupted from the Stormchasers among our crew, and the moment they unfastened the ropes tying us to the platform, the ship quivered.

Willow's claws dug into my arm deeper, dragging me down to her height.

The rings of fire under the balloons scorched with a fury, and the ship bumped the platform once, twice, then lifted toward the sky.

Willow screamed and wilted to the floorboards, mercifully releasing her grip from my arm and refastened her claws to the wood, her eyes wrenched open and limbs trembling over the deck.

I sighed. This was going to be a *very* long trip.

OCTAVIUS

"Wow...!" The view up here was incredible, the wind crisp and cold as the Airship climbed over the shrinking cityscape, over Neverland's docks, and even over the *clouds*.

I sucked in a breath and let it out in a laugh. "This is amazing!"

"It is, yeah?" El giggled in her Culatian accent next to me along the rail. She stretched her blue wings as her white cat ears swiveled forward. "It's nice to fly without your wings getting tired."

I rested my chin on my arms, smiling at her. She'd cut her white hair short a few days ago in a cute style, showing more of her slender, walnut neck as the wind ruffled her strands. Her Landish was almost perfect now. She was a *really* fast learner. I was still barely past primary-level Culatian. I needed to catch up with her on that.

Our messenger ravens, Shade and the snow-white Salfwy, were preening each other's feathers between us while cooing and cawing with the occasional wing flutter—

"AAAAHHH!"

A shriek ripped from the encircling crowd in the middle of the deck. "I can't, Xavier—I just can't, oh, please...!"

That sounded like Willow.

I pushed off the rail and headed over, El following me. Yeah, it *was* Willow. She was on her back with her claws dug into the floorboards, breathing hard and looking like she thought lifting her head even an inch would make the ship go crashing back to the ground.

"Lilli...!" She sobbed, wincing and clutching her belly, as if protecting her baby. "Lilli, help!"

Xavier let out a frustrated breath and reached for her. "*I'm* right here. Why do you need Lilli?"

"You don't have wings!" she shrieked. "Lilli! Lilli, where are you?!"

And now she was blubbering uncontrollably. The Death Prince tried to pry his hysterical wife off the floor but failed miserably.

Some of the crew nearby were trying to hide their snickering. It probably wasn't polite to openly laugh at the Death Princess, so they turned their heads when a chuckle threatened to slip out of their mouths and worked to get themselves under control, sighing sympathetically when they calmed down.

Nathaniel shook his head beside me and snorted. "Yeah, that be Death all right. Called it, I did. The poor lass is stuck like a crab to the lad's toe. The wee cave-dweller's fear of heights can always be counted on." He nudged his elbow into Aiden's ribs. "Come on, fluff-fer-brains, cough up the fancy pants vest. I won."

Aiden sighed, but took off his sleek brown vest and gave it to Nathaniel. "Drat. I rather liked that vest… it won't fit, you know."

"Aye, I be thinkin' it suits me just fine," said Nathaniel, slipping on the vest with a huge grin on his bearded face. He didn't button it. Probably for the best, it was way too small to even fit one button on.

The Death Princess was still whimpering for Lilli, and she didn't stop until the bat pushed past me and hurried over.

Willow scrambled to grab every part of Lilli she could manage, almost pulling her to the floorboards herself. But Lilli looked used to it and dragged the terrified woman inside the cabin while Xavier rushed after them.

El came beside me and giggled. "She hates heights?"

"Yeah." I shrugged. "Apparently, all of Death's incarnations are acrophobic or something like that—"

Someone bumped into me suddenly. It was a crew member I didn't recognize.

"Oy, sorry there, mate," the guy said. "Didn't mean ta…" The guy flinched when he saw my face and scuttled away from me. "Y-you're that poison bloke…! Bloods, sorry, Sir, real sorry! I-I…!"

He quickly rubbed his shoulder where he ran into me and looked disgusted, like he was trying to scrub off something gross.

One of his buddies ran over to see what was wrong, then cringed when he saw me. "Shel, Hammond! Watch where you're Bloody goin'! That one rotted off the Leaflites' skin with his own hands in the war! For Gods' sakes, ya could've been dead!"

They hurried to get away from me.

My cat ears grew sourly. *Great.*

Apparently, I'd gained a reputation here in Neverland when we were fighting that old queen. Technically, it was a good reputation. But now everyone knew about my infection Hallows. Most everyone who didn't know me personally was avoiding me, just like they were now on the ship, making a circle around me as they passed by.

I didn't get it. People liked me, didn't they? They keep telling me as much, but they were afraid of me at the same time. What did a guy have to do to be treated normal for once?

I sighed, staring at my hand. *Rotted off a Leaflite's skin…*

The memory made me queasy, remembering her cheeks melting away, her bones poking through, black veins crawling over her. I shivered and rubbed my shoulder. My Hallows was getting so strong, I was even scaring myself. What if I ended up like my ancestor? Like Kael?

A burst of barely-contained snickers made me jolt. Zyl and her brother Roji were not-so-inconspicuously laughing hysterically from the helm and holding their stomachs like they were going to bust open.

"<Did you see her *face?*>" I heard Zyl wheeze in Culatian. I wasn't very good at speaking the language, but El taught me enough so I could understand most of what they were saying. "<Willow actually thought she was going to die! Like we'd ever let that happen on *our* ship!>"

Prince Roji slammed a fist on the wheel and wiped tears from his eyes. "<I didn't think it'd be *that* bad! Oh, Sky, I feel kinda bad, but that was hilarious…!>" They did their own impersonations of Willow's face and erupted in more laughter, stomping their feet.

I twisted my mouth. That was pretty mean of them, making fun of a pregnant princess facing her worst fear like that. I guessed the rumor about Sky's incarnations loving pranks was true—especially when doing them on his soul-sister Death, who was known for her serious nature.

El giggled next to me and snatched my wrist, dragging me up to the helm. "Let's see if Roji will let us fly!"

I stumbled after her, blushing while staring at our joined hands. *Well.* I considered. *At least one person isn't scared to touch me.*

El started chatting in Culatian to Zyl and Roji, but they were going too fast for me to make anything out.

I let them talk and laugh, going to the rail to see the expanse of the city gliding below us smoothly, small wisps of clouds streaking my view. I inhaled a cold gust that blew past and folded my arms over the rail.

Man, this view was so cool.

"Enjoying ourselves?"

My skin crawled at that voice. I glared down the rail, seeing my murdering ancestor was lounging in a net and using it like a hammock, rocking back and forth like she didn't have a care in the world.

Cilia smiled up at me. Her white pupils glowed in her green irises. "My, my. If looks could Cleanse, I suspect I'd be chatting with Nira by now."

"Shouldn't you be staying somewhere no one can see you?" I muttered, annoyed. "Somewhere *I* can't see you, preferably."

She stretched her arms under her head. "Dream was a dear and gave us Sentients rings that can hide our eyes."

"And you're not wearing yours *why?*" I asked.

She shrugged. "I didn't feel like it. Why so concerned, Octavius?"

My eye twitched. "Who told you my name?"

"I listened to what everyone else called you. Your brother's name is Neal, correct?"

My cat ears curled. "You're not allowed to use our names, far as I'm concerned."

She rolled her eyes closed, settling in the net with a sigh. "Of course, of course… Do take care not to fall off, Descendant. I can jump after you and take most of the fall, but I suspect you'll still die from such a height. I'd feel better if you stayed with your winged girl while standing around the edges."

My face screwed up at her. Damn it, she actually sounded sincere. *Tch. Demon bitch.*

"Hey," I muttered, leaning over the rail. "Do you actually think your crazy husband is over there? Where we're headed?"

She peeked open an eye. "Don't ask me. It was the Death Prince and his brother who claimed that."

"But do you believe them?"

Both of her eyes opened now. She looked at the sky. Bloods, she looked… sad.

"I don't know," she said, earnest. "I think I only want to believe them."

She wasn't looking at me anymore. She was off in her head on some thought, was my guess. There was something weird with her expression, though. She just looked so *hopeful.*

I snorted and pushed off the rail.

Demon bitch. I shoved my hands in my pockets, going back to El. *Stop making me feel bad for you.*

CULATIA

8

WHO TO TRUST

MACARIUS

509 YEARS PRIOR

I pushed my spectacles up with a gloved finger, reclining in my cushioned seat with a glass of deep, ruby wine in one hand and a text regarding the Battle of Yarlington in the other. I'd already read this particular text, but it was proving far more entertaining than this blasted party.

I'd found myself a snug little corner by the window, taking rather liberal sips of wine. I'd previously emptied two glasses in hopes of tuning out the incessant chatter of the guests and the lulling quartet in the back alcove.

One of the violins made a hideous *screech* and I grimaced, emptying this highly fermented drink and leaned back in my chair, covering my face with the book.

"I thought you found that text superfluous and drab?" hummed a voice that perked my scaled ears.

I lifted the book from my face and brightened. My blue-haired friend had popped into existence beside me, as was his way. Dramatic rascal he was, his smug grin told me he'd done it on purpose.

"Only because you verified that the battle never happened," I said and thumped the book closed. "So, Dream, what brings you to Roarlord Maron's social? I can't imagine you're here to win the hand of his fair daughter?"

Dream glanced round the ballroom. "Lord Maron? Hm. Perhaps Sir Caldwell moved without informing me."

Ah. He was looking for one of his knights.

"Perhaps Sir Caldwell is under employment with the new Lord and Lady," I considered.

"Perhaps." He was still glancing at the numerous guests—most of whom were adolescent bachelors, such as ourselves. "My word, is that Accursius?" he questioned. "In a Bloody doublet for once?"

I followed his gaze and found my brother Accur standing by the long table in the corner. The spectacle-less face that shared my own visage was chatting with the crowned prince, as per usual, making wavering hand gestures as if extrapolating one of his idiotic plans to woo the fair lady.

"Yes, you have that right," I muttered. "Accur and his bumbling sidekick, Adam. They have a bet, as I understand it. They have Mel running on whomever impresses the young Lady Maron the most tonight."

Dream looked puzzled. "Why all the fuss over the Lady Maron?"

"Her family has only just moved to Aldamstria last week," I explained, then caught a passing waiter's arm and took a new glass of wine from his silver tray. "She isn't spoken for. Her parents have arranged for this little gathering as a 'meet and marry' social, so to speak. They've invited every bachelor, including Prince Adam over there."

Dream's head cocked at me. "You don't sound interested."

"I'm here to humor my parents." I sighed and sipped my wine. "Accur can marry her if he wishes, but marriage doesn't suit me at the moment. Especially with such an odd one."

Dream's nose scrunched, and he scratched his scrawny neck. "Odd?"

"Well," I amended, "I must admit, she's rather fetching, to be sure. But I don't think I've ever met someone quite so… laconic." I chuckled, tipping my glass to him. "I dare say she's perfect for you, Dream. She hasn't the soul for convention. Or propriety. You ought to try your luck."

Dream only shrugged. "I have a wife."

I nearly spat out my wine, gawking. "You… hang on. You're married?"

"Not yet," he said. "But I will be. To someone. I just haven't met her and have no idea what she looks like."

I snorted and relaxed. "If that's your criteria, then you may as well call *me* a married man."

"No, really." Dream's chin lifted earnestly. "See, I've had visions of my future granddaughter. I haven't Seen her often, nor for very long during the visions, but I imagine my wife will have her face. So, I at least have that. I also know her name will be Crysa."

I paused. "Crysa?"

He nodded, pleased. "I learned that bit only a hundred years ago, if you can believe."

"I'm sorry." I set down my glass. "Your wife's name will be *Crysa?*"

"Yes." He smiled. "I think it sounds rather fetching."

I pointed a befuddled finger toward the front of the ballroom. "I don't suppose that would be short for *Crysalette* Maron?"

Dream fell still.

He whirled to follow the path of my finger.

The lovely Crysalette Maron, dressed in an alluring, indigo gown that complemented her luscious, orange locks and black-tipped fox ears, was placed at the front of the ballroom and giving a polite curtsy to Prince Adam… before she hid a prim yawn behind a hand and turned to her parents who stood behind her, conversing with them while ignoring the crowned prince still standing before her. Adam's shoulders sagged dejectedly as he slinked away, regrouping with Accur as the two muttered about their failed attempts at wooing the girl.

When I turned back to Dream, I noticed his face had dripped into pale shock.

Then he laughed.

The young king strode through the well-dressed crowd, not showing the least bit of concern that he was in the midst of a formal party while wearing that same baggy, too-long tunic that was covered in wrinkles and still had that red stain on the right sleeve from our *find the mis-documented piece of history* drinking game last week.

Oh, blast it. The fool was drawing attention at every step. The bachelors surrounding him were giving him a mixture of beguiled and disgusted looks.

Dream, you fool! I pushed to my feet, storming through the mass to get him out of there before he ruined his future and—

"Hello, Crysa!" Dream chimed the moment he stepped in front of the Lady Maron. "I'm your future husband. Our granddaughter will be the next incarnation of Death in the next millennia."

I smeared a hand over my face. *That Bloody idiot!* I bemoaned in silence, rubbing my eyes from under my spectacles. *Very well… it isn't completely over yet, is it? I'll have to coach him on how such things are properly done and try to amend Lady Maron's opinion of him—*

"Well," Lady Maron huffed after several sobering blinks. "I've heard quite a number of proposals tonight, but that is certainly the most unique. Are you per chance the King of Dreams?"

Dream's smile was incredibly wide. "I'm your husband, Crysa, you can call me Dream."

"I see." She cocked an eyebrow. "And were you given an invitation to this event, Dream?"

He chuckled. "No one ever invites me to anything. Except for Relicbloods. Or some of my knights. They have such nice birthday parties from time to time, you'll like them."

"Ah." She laced her fingers together and peered down her nose. "And pray tell, what more do you know of our convoluted and arduous future together?"

He shrugged. "Our daughter will marry the Death King. And our son will be born *after* our granddaughter."

She made a curious hum. Then she turned on her heels to face her father and mother, who were looming behind her to observe each bachelor.

"I have accepted the King of Dream's proposal," she announced. "We will wed once preparations have been made on the soonest Songday."

Dream frowned. "But I've been preparing for our wedding for the past fifteen-hundred years, Crysa."

"Then I'm sure you can wait another five days, hm?" She looped an arm around his and led him out of the ballroom. "Now, do tell me how our son will be born after our granddaughter? And do you mind if our daughter's name is Myra? I'm rather fond of the name, it was my great grandmother's and…"

They disappeared into the hallway, leaving the rest of us in stone cold silence.

That brilliant bastard. He did it. He actually did it!

I glanced at Accur. My twin was shooting me desperate, perplexed looks. And I couldn't stop laughing.

PRESENT DAY

My silver communicator began chirping, interrupting my meal with Sky King Rojired.

I delicately set down my dining sticks and glanced at the screen of projected light. My hidden fangs unfolded. It was that same blasted number. The one the Sky children kept calling from, attempting to contact their father.

"<Blast, who…>" King Rojired's voice rattled in Culatian, his breaths more of an irritated wheeze. "<Who is it now, Garrach? It's been… ringing all damn month…>"

I ignored the caller. The king thought I was his trusted advisor, Sousöl Garrach Venn. He had every reason to believe I was the man himself—my illusion held his bright green wings, his feathered hair and goatee, his sharp chin and hooked nose, his brown skin and thick fingers—but in truth, I had done away with the Sky King's previous advisor when I'd first arrived in Culatia's modern palace. A mere few drops of my venom laced in his morning tea, and he was as dead as a rock in the blink of an eye. I'd locked his corpse in the dungeon and taken the man's image for myself with an 'imposter' Evocation, filled in his role, and this dying king was none the wiser. The old fool had relied on me for guidance for months now. He hadn't a damned clue that the real Sousöl was probably a Necrofera by now trapped beneath this very palace. I'd thrown his loyal guard over the edge just for fun. He was likely scattered to boney bits somewhere in Everland's wastelands beneath us. It was amusing to think of the unlucky shifter who may have witnessed the dispensed corpse crashing to the dirt in a puff of dust and blood.

"<It's more peasants, my lord,>" I said in the king's tongue. Luckily, I'd had many a century to learn Culatian as well as many other languages whilst locked away in that timeless void. I dare say I had the fluent accent perfect by now, which certainly was an advantage for this current role I had taken on as the Sky King's advisor. "<With the absence of the Sky Princess, many vagabonds and common maidens wish to try their luck at pretending to be your daughter.>"

He snorted, clipping his dining sticks over a piece of sliced beef. "<Brilliant… Sky take me, it's… happening all over again. You remember the barrage of imposters… who came waltzing in when… Roji first left?>"

"<Indeed I do, my lord.>" So, it's happened before? What grand fortune. That only made my excuse more believable. I set down my own gilded dining sticks, rising to walk toward the doors. "<Excuse me while I take care of these ingrates, Sire.>"

He nodded his approval, then returned to his meal.

I rounded the corner, making my way toward the palace library. Of course, I wasn't going to answer the call. I let it run its course until it died into silence at last.

"Bloody pests," I muttered and stepped into the library. There were several servants running about, replacing books from their shelves and fetching them for whomever requested them.

I ordered them to leave, wishing to be alone for the call I would make for myself. The winged servants bowed and took their leave promptly before shutting the doors behind them.

Now alone, I dialed the number I wished to connect with. *My, but how far I've come,* I thought pleasantly. It's taken years, but I think I've finally mastered this era's strange, yet wonderfully convenient technology. A damned carrier pigeon wasn't needed. It took but seconds to send a message instead of months. What a wondrous invention.

On the projected screen, a brown, scaled face appeared. The young woman's dark brown hair was braided down one shoulder today, her chosen space of hiding seeming to be some wooden cabin.

"Father," Genevieve greeted, nodding respectfully. She knew of my newest illusion and knew that it was I under this mask. *"I have news."*

"I thought you might," I said to my step-daughter, pacing the aisles of the library and examining each spine. "The Sky children you're following have been calling on quite the incessant schedule. Were the Shadowbloods' assassinations a success?"

Her tone was disappointed. *"No, Father… All agents were caught, due to the Shadow's prophetic Hallows. Two were killed by the new Land Queen."*

I tamed the venom threatening to leak from my fangs. I supposed I should have expected it. It was only a preliminary test of those infecting arrows. Still, hearing the Shadowbloods' powers were strengthening was concerning news.

Why do you fan the flames of our End, Dream? I thought broodingly.

"Does our dearest Land Queen suspect you?" I asked, circling a finger over my aching temple. "Has your position been compromised?"

"It has not," Genevieve said. *"Though, she has yet to trust me wholly. I am kept from meetings with the other Relicbloods. She only brings Sir Linolius and Captain Kurrick."*

My tongue clicked. "At least you're safe, for now. Keep to your role. And if you find our missing demon queen, contact me immediately."

I had lost contact with Cilia months ago. My copies couldn't find her anywhere along the Flowering Trail. I could only hope that she was still following the Shadowblood brothers as ordered. Yet, I had an ever-growing concern.

Claude was with the twins. If Cilia were to meet him… to speak with him…

My fangs grew. I may not have been a Seer, but I fancied myself to have enough foresight to guess that she knew too much. It was likely she's abandoned her leash. With Dream there as well, who's to say he hasn't caught her and told her who she is? What she was?

The memory of those months ago came rushing back, Dream's smug copy standing on the flaming shore of Y'ahmelle Nayû, grinning like he'd won the Gods damned war. But it was only the battle, Dream. There would be many more to come.

"There is other news," Genevieve said from the screen.

"What now?" I asked. It had better be *good* news.

Genevieve hesitated. *"We have taken flight today. We are heading for the Sky Palace."*

Of course, it wasn't good news. I ran a tired hand over my face. "Then it seems my time limit has shrunken once again here."

I had to find Sky's Relic quickly. This damned king was too sick to take me there, but not sick enough to outright tell me where to find the Phoenix of Scarlet. The wait was infuriating… but necessary.

"Very well," I told Genevieve. "Inform me when you are near. I must prepare an escape plan, should it be required."

She nodded. *"Yes, Father."*

The call ended.

I let out an aggravated breath and brushed a hand over the books that were stacked on these shelves. So much was going wrong. Failure after failure, it seemed infinite. Our End was growing stronger while I grew weaker. Cilia's absence meant I now lacked an undead army. That had been my best leverage. *But not the only leverage.*

I could only hope my wife was doing her duty in Neverland beneath us with the schools. Between her and Kael's poisoned arrows, I would need to rely on them a bit further—

The library door creaked open suddenly, and a servant girl bowed her apology.

"<My lord, please excuse the intrusion,>" the girl said in Culatian, her wings lowering in fright. "<There is a man here who is asking for you, and…>"

She was shoved aside by a Grimish man who stormed in, glaring at me with blazing, yellow eyes.

My stare grew livid. "Kael?"

I ordered the servant to leave us, and she scurried out, shutting the door.

I took off the ring that held my disguise and pocketed it. "What are you doing here, Kael?" I demanded, furious. "I instructed you to watch that lion prince in Everland."

"And I did," he said. His stare was cold. Careful. As though he were searching for something in my face that gave away my secrets. "He spoke of some things. Things that I wished to discuss."

I lifted my silver communicator. "You could have called about such things."

"Not this. This was a subject to discuss in person."

Wonderful. "Very well, Kael… Then pray tell, what is so damned important that you couldn't simply utilize this era's miraculous technology?"

"It is about Cilia," he said, the name spoken as a growl.

"Of course it is," I sighed.

Kael lingered there, his gaze wavering between agony and suspicion. Or could that have been… Bloody Shel, it was hope.

"Kael?" I asked after a long moment of silence. I stepped toward him. "What is it?"

He inched away from me. From *me*. Fury boiled hot in my veins, my venom building. *What in Bloods is going on?*

"The prince," he whispered, his fists balling and loosening. "He knew her name. He said she…" His eyes began to well. "She was the demon. The one you have been working with." His teeth sharpened. "The one you refuse to let me meet."

Every scale on my body scorched alive. "And you believed the prince, did you?" I hissed.

Kael kept his distance. "If she is here, Macar, you tell me now. You tell me *now*." His last word curdled with rage. Pain. It echoed through the library, filling the silence.

"This is what you think of me?" I hushed. "You think for even a moment that I, after centuries—*centuries*, Kael—of the suffering we endured together… of the terrors I've kept you alive from… you think I would keep such a thing from my friend? If she was here, you truly think I would say nothing?"

Kael went silent. His eyes reddened with tears. "But the prince knew her name. How could he have known…?"

I sneered. "Did it ever occur to you that Claude was *with* the prince when he left us?"

Realization dawned in his gaze.

I went on, "The rebel leader had the prince. The rebels were with the Reapers. And Claude was *with* the Reapers. All of this happened at the same time. Open your eyes, Kael. Claude sent the prince back to feed you lies. To turn us against each other. If we were weakened, we both would be vulnerable to the Shadowblood. This is what Claude wants, and you damn well know it. Kin of yours or not."

Kael sank into a nearby chair, his cheeks sagged. "Yes… of course. I'm sorry, I… suppose I let my hope weaken my judgement."

"You damn well did." I snarled, but calmed. The flames had been dampened, at least. That was perhaps the closest I'd ever come to watching all of my plans crumble beneath me.

I exhaled and lowered into the seat beside him, adjusting my spectacles. "We cannot afford to form rifts between us, Kael. We've been through too much together. Perhaps… perhaps bringing Claude into our plans was a mistake. I am to blame for your false hope."

"The blame is my own," Kael croaked. "I let him fool me. Manipulate me. I am sorry, my friend. I fear I've lost my mind entirely. After seeing her face in my descendant, I… have grown distracted. And distraction is dangerous."

"Indeed it is." I clasped his shoulder. "Well. Perhaps it is a blessing you're here. It is far easier to acquire arrows and Metaglass in this palace, you can begin production on the next batch with ease."

And this will keep him away from that jabbering prince.

Though, I had to admit this would be tricky. The twins were on their way here, which meant it was more than likely Cilia was on her way as well.

I only prayed Genevieve gave me enough warning when they arrived.

ABOARD THE AIRSHIP

9

A MODERN WORLD

CILIA

Click! Click! Click!

Khol's knitting needles clattered away as the bald, scaled demon king pleasantly weaved and braided his latest scarf. The four of us demons were having tea and muffins while sitting at a round table on the Airship's sundeck. Khol's webbed ears flicked while he hummed to himself, rocking in his chair as if dancing to his own tune as those needles chittered away.

Click! Click! Click!

I grimaced at his current scarf project. It was made of soft, fluffy wool that was dyed a hideous bright green against ugly orange and yellow stripes. Supposedly, this monstrosity was to be mine. Khol had knitted the other demons among our group their own scarves, including himself, as if we were all such jolly good friends and belonged to a cheery little book club.

Miranda sat to my right, the old woman refilling her cup of tea and seeming to have accepted, and promptly ignored, the presence of her neon-purple and marmalade-orange scarf blocking her wrinkled mouth. Hecrûshou sat to my left with his arms crossed, the shark-man glaring bolts at Khol from above his too-large scarf that looked like a dragon vomited blue and brown sprinkles on it.

Khol himself wore an eye-watering yellow and pink scarf, still humming to himself as he knitted away at what was soon to be my annoying 'gift'. Hecrushou's little Bindragon slithered around the balls of yarn on the table playfully, bobbing its cheered head and cooing several *aaahn, aaahn, aaahns* as he coiled himself around one of Khol's knitting needles next. Khol gave a pleasant chuckle and let the dragon stay there as he continued his work, the little serpent dipping his head up and down happily as if he were on an amusement ride.

"Regardless," Miranda rasped as she blew on her steaming tea, resuming our last conversation. "We know that La'Lunaî has recruited Neverland's old queen and Changed her. The good news is that she's still down *there*, and we're up *here*."

Hecrûshou grumbled. "Which will not help us when next we land. It's likely she will be ready to strike the moment we set foot in the mid-realms again."

I delicately pinched my teacup's gilded handle and took a sip. "Perhaps Thörd will agree to join our ranks once we arrive in Culatia?"

Khol piped up cheerfully at this. "Oh, that would be lovely! He's quite strong. I wouldn't have to do any fighting, then."

Hecrûshou rubbed his temple and flicked an annoyed glance at his Bindragon still coiled around Khol's needle. "Yes, you'll be free to keep Aahn company without having to actually *contribute* for once, Bloody pacifist…" With a sigh, he held out his hand to the Bindragon. Aahn cooed and slithered onto his owner's smooth arm, wrapping around Hecrûshou's bicep before the dragon closed its eyes to snooze. Hecrûshou went on, "But that's assuming Thörd will agree to join us in the first place."

I grinned over my teacup. "That will hardly be a problem. Thörd and I have a bit of a… *pleasurable* history. I'm sure he'll join once he knows I'm with you all."

Hecrûshou scowled at me. "And when he learns that we're in Culatia to find your *husband?*"

I waved a hand dismissively. "Still not to worry. I have full confidence Thörd will assist."

Hecrûshou and Miranda grunted their disagreements, but let the matter drop as they fell into their own conversations regarding the autumn winds up here.

I glanced around the deck, noting the many crew members and passengers going about their day. The Clean Ones who walked by us didn't know what we were; that we were Sentient Necrofera who could very easily devour their souls with a snap of our claws. Thanks to Dream's illusions, our white pupils were hidden to make us seem like ordinary shifters. It was odd to have so many people act so calm around us. It had been a while, at least for me.

As the Airship drifted in the sky, I noticed a long, silver pole poke through the fluffy white clouds. Wires and cables were strung from its top and out-stretched sides, sweeping across the clouds toward another pole, then another, and another, stretching all the way across toward a small, floating island in the distance. There were cable cars gliding down some of the wires delivering wingless passengers, most of whom seemed to be snapping photos from their closed-in box as they scooted past our ship.

"Are we stopping?" I asked and perked in my seat to peer out at the floating island. Tall, glassy buildings split from the landmass and pierced the clouds themselves. Though in contrast to the modern city, the smaller islands surrounding us were covered in thick foliage. Crystal-clear streams of waterfalls poured over the edges and misted into clouds. Bird-shifters and feral fowl of many bright colors soared and flapped around the jungle terrain. An electric blue, feral bird swept by the bow of our ship and gave a flighty twitter. Yes, this was certainly Culatia.

Miranda grunted beside me. "It's only a smaller island. I'd wager we're stopping to resupply and refuel."

Khol paused his knitting to hold his needles to his chest in an exuberant gasp. "Oh, I can buy more yarn!"

I grumbled. "Yes, perhaps you can find fewer clashing colors this time—"

"Oh, and I've just finished yours, Cilia!" Khol lunged over the table to throw the hideous scarf over my head, the wool scratching my neck and chin. He preened. "A perfect fit!"

I grumbled irritably.

Craaw!

One of the Reapers' crows swooped down and landed onto our table with a clatter. Atop its back was that ferret I often saw around the ship. The weasel huffed at me as it stretched its long, furry body down and snatched up as many muffins as it could. Then it hurriedly chuffed at the crow as if telling it to go. The crow gave a confirming caw and grabbed an extra muffin in its beak before flying off, a few black feathers drifting down over the table.

I rubbed my eyes. "Does *anything* on this ship make any sense?"

WILLOW

I gripped Lilli's arm with such strength, I heard her wince as we stepped—very slowly—over the center of this stone bridge that connected the Airship docks to the main city waiting on the large mass of floating land ahead of us.

We'd arrived in the isles of *Zing Gobovgo*, which was Culatian for *Frozen Wings*, and were making a supply run on its main island named *Astra Gobov—Lightning Wing.*

Lilli's stiff wings fluttered slightly as I pulled down her arm, accidentally causing her steps to be lopsided. She grumbled, "Willow, if you were too scared to take this bridge, you could have taken the cable cars."

My legs shook under my extended belly. "N-n-no!" I squeaked, my throat tight with fear. "A stone b-b-bridge is far more st… stable than a t-tiny wire…!"

Bloods, the air was so thin up here, I could hardly breathe. It didn't help that I had a small, growing human pressing against my lungs and ribs—and I swore to Bloods, if I didn't find a washroom soon, this baby was going to kick a hole in my bladder.

Lilli sighed. "Honestly… but don't say I didn't tell you so. If your feet swell up from all this walking, I will *not* fly you and little Lucas back to the Airship when next we depart in a few days. We *will* take that cable car."

I swallowed but nodded meekly as I tried to remind myself of all the safety measures this bridge held. It had rails. It had nets underneath. It had been built hundreds of years ago and carried the weight of so many wingless people, yet hadn't crumbled to bits once.

But that doesn't mean it won't start today. I gritted my teeth and forced the paranoia down.

A strong breeze swept past us, sweeping my long, grey hair forward and partially blocking my view. I was wearing my usual earcuff that was enchanted with my 'common Grimlette' illusion. Last I saw of Xavier and Alexander, they'd changed their hair black and their eyes a matching sapphire today, though I wasn't sure where they'd run off to. They'd taken the cable car with the other men while Lilli and I walked along the bridge with the women of our party.

Zyl and El were ahead of us chittering away excitedly and flailing their arms in wide gestures. Zyl's red feathers were disguised with an illusion, like myself, and colored a pale blue, almost matching El's wings. It made them look more like sisters despite the different shades of their dark skin. El had more of a light walnut complexion while Zyl had a dark umber hue.

Bianca, Sirra-Lynn and Rochelle were laughing amongst themselves along the rail and peering down in wonder. *Urk.* I pushed down another wave of fright. How were they bold enough to even go *near* the rail?

Clinging to Lilli's skirts was the little Prince Fuérr. His webbed ears, disguised as brown bear ears, fastened tight to his head in fright as he shivered at Lilli's waist, scared of the bridge's height as well. His fin-like, emerald hair was disguised brown and made to look like mammalian hair with an illusion. He wore a short-billed cap that his aunt, Princess Dalminia, had thought would look 'darling' on him… which it did indeed, I had to admit. He was quite the adorable fake-bear cub.

Dalminia herself walked behind us and chuckled at her young nephew, her own fin-like hair and webbed ears disguised like the boy's. Their scales were hidden by the illusion as well, both looking like ordinary bear-shifters. Her husband, Prince Roji, had worried that his family's natural physique might bring them harm, considering the war between Culatia and Marincia. If they were simply traveling mammals, the Culatians wouldn't think twice if they passed by. Last I saw of Roji and his winged daughters—before they'd left with the twins—they'd worn their own illusions to hide the true color of their feathers.

Little Oliver suddenly flew above our heads and giggled as he whirled circles in the air. He nearly ran into several flying shifters, and Lilli snapped at him to keep close and watch where he was flying.

To either side of Lilli and I were the twins' rabbit-eared vassal, Vendy, and my own green-winged vassal, Rossette. They had been resurrected to fully enjoy and explore this island at their leisure… although, I must admit, I'd asked my scaled vassal, Nikolai, to join Xavier and the men to provide updates and news if anything disastrous happened. I suspected that Xavier had asked Vendy to do the same with me here. The thought would have irked me, yet I couldn't blame him for wanting to keep an eye on me while *I* wanted to keep an eye on *him.*

I hadn't been the target of that assassination weeks ago. Those arrows were meant for him. If any had hit me, it would have been because the shooter missed. *Still,* I considered, *I suppose he has a right to be concerned after an event like that.*

When we finally reached the end of the bridge and stepped onto the solid streets of this modern island, I released Lilli's arm with a long sigh of relief.

"It's about damned time," Lilli muttered, then snapped her gaze to the sky. "Oliver, come down here and stay with us! I don't want you to get lost in this crowd."

Oliver whined but did as asked and touched down beside little Fuérr, who released Lilli's skirts next.

"Thank you," Lilli said and put fists at her sides as she glanced about the bustling streets and wing-filled sky between the towering, glass and metal buildings. "Where shall we start, then?"

Dalminia clapped her hands excitedly behind us. "Oh, let's start with the music district! I want to see these famous electric-based musicians Roji's told me so much about!"

I raised a brow at her and asked, "Do you speak of amplified instruments? Why, you can find those anywhere if given a microphone and speakers, can't you?"

"Not so!" She lifted an informative finger. "He claims there are lutes whose sounds can be altered in many different ways—he says I'll have to hear them for myself to understand."

I hummed, curious. "I thought you said you'd been to Culatia before?"

"Its palace, yes," Dalminia clarified in a shrug. Her false bear-ears flicked. "I've never ventured outside into the cities before. When I came as a child, my father had forbidden it when he was still alive. The only time I'd visited as an adult was the day Roji brought me to his home to request our betrothal.

Obviously, I didn't have much chance to see the city as a whole when we were banished. We'd descended to Neverland swiftly after that."

I brushed thoughtful fingers over my lips. "I'm sorry to hear that… Though, are you sure all will be well when Roji returns?"

"I haven't a clue," she admitted in a hum, cocking her head. "But that isn't up to me, is it? That's something Roji will have to figure out for himself. And I can't say he'll have any luck with that, given how unreachable his father has made himself. Every time he calls his father, this advisor answers and accuses Roji of being a charlatan. It's gotten to a point where *none* of his calls are even being answered anymore."

I grimaced. "How reassuring."

On we went to the music district Dalminia had mentioned. It was indeed a lively place—and incredibly *loud*. Bards littered the streets and balconies at every turn, their speakers blasting different beats and sounds the likes of which I'd never heard. Lilli and I stopped to watch one musician plucking away at the strangest lute I'd ever seen. It scratched and twanged and wavered in strangely harmonious—yet still disharmonious—chords. It was like a dragon's vicious growl singing in a rhythmic beat that made my ears ring.

But more importantly, it rumbled my belly and prompted a strong kick from the baby against my bladder.

"Er…" I touched Lilli's shoulder and held a hand to my stomach. "Perhaps we could find a place to sit and rest? With a washroom?"

Lilli nodded and held a hand over her eyes to shield them from the sun. "Grand idea. I thought the Land realm's sun was unbearable, I didn't think Culatia's would be *worse*."

"Oi!" Zyl called ahead and waved for us to follow her. "There is being good place to eat here! Come, you see, ya?"

I sighed, "I'll take your word about your realm's delicacies over my own any day."

Zyl and El led us to a small, mercifully *indoor* café with cool air pouring from the vents, and I promptly left them to use the public facilities. After relieving myself and washing my hands in the sinks, I stopped to glance at myself in the long wall-mirror along the door. Bloods, my belly had grown larger these last few weeks. I peeked into my gown's open collar and winced at the sight. Dark purple and red streaks had split across my breasts like an angry beasts' claws. Bianca assured me those would fade over time, but how long would that be? How long would I look as undesirable as a sack of spoiled potatoes? I sighed and put a hand on my enlarged stomach.

The baby kicked faintly from inside. *At least it will be worth it, in the end,* I decided with a small smile. It may not have been convenient to have a baby during wartime but, since it was happening regardless, it was at least exciting to think of beginning this new chapter with Xavier.

I just hoped we could provide enough for him when he arrived—

The washroom door *slammed* open, and little Oliver and Fuérr nearly toppled inside over one another fighting to be the first in. But they paused when they spotted me, both blushing.

I set a hand at my hip and pointed toward the wall. "The little boys' room is the *other* door."

"S-sorry Auntie Low!" Oliver piped and grabbed the now confused Fuérr's wrist, dragging him out to enter the *right* door this time.

I chuckled and walked out to join the others at our table—

A new member had appeared beside the others. A very *short* member. The child looked to be about ten or so, his back facing me as he glanced around the café, as though lost. He also had curling, azure hair.

"Grandfather?" I questioned uncertainly, my brow knitting as I approached the blue-haired child. "Is that you?"

The boy—Dream—turned to find me. He was so short, he had to crane his gaze up to look at my face. His azure eyes lit with realization. "Ah," he said in a small voice. It sounded far younger than I was accustomed to. "I thought this might be another shared vision. It seems I was correct."

"But you're in *my* time," I protested. "Usually, I'm in *yours*."

The child shrugged. "This isn't the first time I've Seen your time, Granddaughter."

"But why…" I hesitated, glancing at the many confused faces at our table.

From the chair nearest me, Vendy gave me a twisted expression. "Uh, Highness? Who're you talking to?"

No one seemed to notice Grandfather standing in front of me. And of course, they wouldn't. When I experienced shared visions in *Grandfather's* time, no one could ever see me either. I cleared my throat and told Vendy, "I, er, must make a quick com-call. Please excuse me for a moment."

I hurried out of the café, and my young grandfather followed leisurely. When we were outside and standing in the shade of the building's jade awning, Grandfather hummed. "Your time always fascinates me. I suppose this must be Culatia as well? Are you in the capital isles? *Achrid Tĕgtt?*"

"No, but we're on our way to them… specifically the royal island itself, *Drăcon Ergect.*" I set a hand on my hip. A few passing heads turned my way with perplexed looks, but I ignored them, deciding to let these strangers think me a lunatic. I didn't have these shared visions with Grandfather often, so I wanted to give him my full attention while he was here. "We're taking a small supply and fuel stop in the *Zing Gobovgo* isles for a few days before returning to our route. We're currently on *Astra Gobov,* in the main city. I take it you only ask because *you're* on the capital isles in your time?"

"Indeed," he hummed, still looking about the city and its people. "It seems these shared visions of ours are associated with our precise longitude, latitude and elevation rather than *just* the land's location itself. Since the islands are always in a fixed position to each other, I suppose *Achrid Tĕgtt* in *my* time is currently drifting in the same location as the *Zing Gobovgo* isles in your time. Fancy that."

"Yes, well. What year is it for you, then?" I asked, studying his grossly old-fashioned clothes. He wore a young gentleman's doublet and dress-shirt, the cream-colored sleeves and collar riddled with frills and lace.

The blue-haired child's head followed the passing shifters around us as he answered absently, "It is the year 989 A.B."

I blinked. "That long ago? Bloods, that's over a thousand years back."

His gaze fell on me and he cocked his head. "What year is it here?"

"2104 A.B." I answered.

"I see." He glanced down at my expanded belly. "Ah, you're with child now. This must be Lucas?"

"It is." I hummed and rubbed my belly with a twisted mouth. "He hasn't quite joined us yet… and although we're thrilled for it, *please* tell me we wait a few years before having another, at least? Trying to run military operations as well as political disputes is incredibly taxing already, and Lucas has yet to be born."

"Oh, I haven't the slightest idea about that," Grandfather said. "These visions of ours are so sporadic, it's hard to tell."

I buried my face in my hands and groaned. "Nira, help me…"

Grandfather tapped his chin with a contemplative knuckle, his mood suddenly darkening. "However, this current vision comes at a dire time… it seems I'm in need of your counsel again, Granddaughter."

"Counsel?" I asked. "Again?"

"Ah, we haven't had this discussion for you, yet." The boy reached his hands out as if blindly searching for something. Then he seemed to touch an object I couldn't see, flopped down, and landed on something solid. He looked as though he were sitting in an invisible chair the wrong way, with his legs spread in a straddling position and his arms folded over each other at chest-level. I guessed there *was* a chair there in his time—only felt by him, if I remembered my own experiences when I visited his time. As he floated in the air, he rested his chin over the unseen chair's back.

"While it doesn't happen every time," he said, "we concluded that most of our shared visions seem to arrive before catastrophic or historic events. Often times, we have them when one of us is at a loss for what steps to take next." His body leaned forward while suspended in the air, possibly tilting the invisible chair on its hind legs, and rocked idly. "Given that I'm in *your* time this round, *I* seem to be the one in need of counsel… and given the state of Culatia in my time, I have an inkling I know for what."

I lowered into a nearby seat that *I* could touch, and Jewel fluttered down from my shoulder and hopped onto the chair's metal arm. "What is happening in your time?" I asked.

His azure fox ears grew and folded to his neck. "Sky is dead."

"Do you mean his incarnation back then?" I clarified. "All of us must have died countless times before now—"

"Four," he interrupted broodingly, his eyes growing stale. "This is the fourth time you all have died without me."

There was a hollow resentment to his voice which gave me pause. *That's right*, I thought with a sinking heart, *Grandfather is the only Relic Child to have lived through it all.* By his sour tone and dripping expression, I wagered he remembered each of our deaths as well. Would the *present* Dream still remember?

I shook the thought away and asked, "If this isn't the first time, why does this death matter?"

His heavy gaze lifted to meet mine. "Because it was Sky's father who killed him. And Sky was the last heir the current king had sired." His shoulders sank as he went on, "The rest of you are dead, and your current children are at a stalemate with what to do. Normally when such a heinous act is done by a royal, the other realms' monarchs march against them and force an abdication in favor of the next available heir. But Nă'chul knows we can't force him to abdicate without killing him, which wouldn't normally be an issue, except…"

I finished for him in a sigh, "Killing him will be killing Sky's Bloodline entirely."

He deflated. "Precisely… The council has left the decision to me. But even *I* don't have all the answers. What am I to do?"

I hummed and leaned back in my seat, thinking. "Well, I know first-hand what it's like to live without a Relic Bloodline."

He gaped at me. "You do? Who… who dies? Is it Sky? Is that what's about to happen?"

"It isn't Sky. It was Land, actually, five-hundred years ago. And strictly speaking, she apparently didn't *die*, as we originally thought."

His stare went flat. "She?"

"Land comes back as a woman this round," I explained with a shrug. "I think this is the first time it's happened. Though she was lost for so long, we discovered she was traveling with us for months before she revealed herself. In any case, my time had lived five centuries without a Relicblood. The results were devastating, yes, but life *did* go on for Everland and Neverland."

"Er..." He scratched his head desperately. "What is Neverland?"

"It's the second continent of... oh, Death. Hang on." I leaned forward, realizing something. "You say you're in the year 989?"

He grumbled uncertainly. "Yes..."

"That was before the continent split..." I murmured to myself, remembering my history lessons from girlhood. "And before Land was lost... *and* before Roji's ancestors took over for Culatia..." I snapped my fingers. "Grandfather! Is the Sky King a dragon in your time?"

The boy's brow furrowed so drastically, his smooth forehead grew creases, crumpling the crowned Dream mark there. "What sort of question is *that?*" he demanded. "Of course, he's a dragon. What else would he be?"

I laughed. "I think I know what historic event is about to happen in your time, Grandfather. It's one that you yourself have told me about."

He stopped his rocking, and his fox ears perked. "What is it? Is it something I need to prevent? How do I prevent it—?"

"You needn't do anything," I said, chuckling. "The people of Culatia will soon find their own solution. However..." I drummed my fingers over my chair's arm. *Grandfather told me a Relicblood had to be present for the transfer of power to work,* I thought to myself. Then I said, "If you kill the Sky King now, the Bloodline *will* be lost, and the people of Culatia will not have a chance to bring about the historic event I mentioned. So, I advise you leave the Sky King alive. He ought to be dead soon enough regardless, I should think."

Dream's young face scrunched in disbelief. "If he's to die regardless, then how do we preserve the Bloodline?"

I grinned. "You'll see for yourself soon enough, Grandfather."

The boy grimaced—then vanished into thin air.

I sighed and rose to my aching feet, lowering my finger to Jewel so she could hop on. "Poor Grandfather," I said to Jewel, who twittered in response as I re-entered the café. "It must have been frustrating as Void to be left with that vague answer." I snorted a chuckle. "Finally, I was able to confuse *him* for once."

ROJI

TRANSLATED FROM CULATIAN

"Mavis, get *back* here!" I shouted in Culatian at the fledgling girl who scurried all over the street and nearly tripped a ton of pedestrians. I was lucky as Bloods the three-year-old's wings hadn't grown enough for her to fly off anywhere, but with baby Prylan strapped to my chest in her harness and the diaper pack slung along my back, I was having trouble chasing Mavis down.

She and Prylan were wearing their disguises—their scales and webbed ears looking more humanoid—so I wasn't worried about anyone learning about their mixed Marincian blood, but damn it, if that girl tripped and started wailing, I was *not* in the mood to attract attention today. I'd worn my own illusion disguise to make my feathers more of an auburn color so people wouldn't see that their Relicblood was walking around the streets with them.

Mavis ran into Xavier's legs, making him stagger and whirl in a start. He and his brother, who walked beside him, had disguised their grey hair black, and their eyes were now two matching sets of sapphire instead of their usual heterochromic colors. Probably best, too. After that assassination attempt on them, I wouldn't want to look like myself either.

Xavier relaxed when he saw it was only Mavis, and he bent to catch her shoulder, chuckling while giving her a bearded smile. "<Why don't you stay with us, Mavis?>" he suggested softly in Landish. "<We'll have plenty of time to—>"

Mavis split away like a rocket and hopped to a platform in the street that squirted water in fun little patterns for the kiddies. I groaned as she, and all her clothes and definitely her diaper, got soaked to the bone. I smeared a hand over my face and sighed. *At least she's finally staying in one damned place,* I thought.

I patted Xavier's back in a grunt. "<Not as easy as it seems, huh?>"

Xavier scratched his cheek and laughed nervously. "<Children are certainly… *lively.*>"

"<That's one word for it,>" I said and nudged him in the ribs. "<Better get used to it now. They grow like weeds.>"

"<Ah…>" He looked like he was going to be sick for a minute, but broke into a chuckle as he watched Mavis splash in the squirting fountains like a tiny troll.

Alex commented beside him, "<Good to see their illusions are holding up, at least. The last thing we need is for these Culatians to see Marincian Relicblood hybrids scuttling about.>"

To my other side, Jaq snorted. "<Yeah, that'd be all kinds 'a bad.>"

Octavius hummed as he trailed behind us with Neal. "<*Would* it be bad, though? I mean, I know the king's gone senile and all, but do the rest of these Culatians feel the same way about Marincians?>"

Neal shrugged. "<Who knows. But why risk it?>"

I tilted my head at Neal. "<Exactly.>"

"<Hey!>" Dalen, the twins' resurrected vassal, shouted from a tavern nearby. He waved beside a disguised Nikolai and Hugh, ushering us to join him. "<Let's get a pint! This place is cheap!>"

Matthiel scoffed as he walked over first. "<*Cheap* is neither a concern nor an inspiring sentiment.>"

The others followed after him, but I stayed where I was, keeping an eye on Mavis at the fountains. "<You guys have fun,>" I called with a wave and hefted Prylan strapped to my chest. "<I'm going to get more fuel for the ship. I'll meet you guys at the Howler's Inn downtown.>"

I went to grab Mavis's wrist and pulled her away from the fountains. She was dripping wet, but I figured it was hot enough that she'd dry off eventually on her own. I could worry about a change of clothes later. We were lucky it wasn't a stormy day, though. The summer and autumn seasons were usually pretty clear in Culatia, but the occasional showers still tended to creep in now and again.

After asking around a bit, I found the shop that carried Airship fuel just up ahead. I was almost at the door—

Shouting caught my ear from across the street. It looked like there was a scuffle going on between a trio of shifters.

Two Culatian birds were shoving a web-eared Marincian into a pile of tin drums, the barrels clunking to the cobblestones and rolling aimlessly.

"Get off our island, water-breather!" one shouted and shoved the Marincian to the ground.

His buddy kicked the guy in the ribs. "You can swim fine! Just jump off and slither back to your wormhole!"

Anger boiled, and I was about to tell Mavis to stay by the shop's door, but another Culatian flew down from the skies and started yelling at his fellow winged shifters. This one was a kid in his teen years, wearing a jade school uniform with khaki pants. He'd dropped his pack on the street to confront the two asshats, threatening to call the Footrunners if they didn't beat it.

When they shoved off, the kid helped the Marincian up, and pointed him to the nearest Healing Clinic. He offered to escort the guy in case he ran into trouble, but the fish declined and thanked him before hobbling off that way. The kid rubbed his feathered head, then sighed and picked up his pack, heading across the street to where I was standing.

He blinked when he noticed me. "Oh, a customer?" He hurriedly pulled open the shop's door for me, a smile splitting his dark face. "Come on in! My uncle runs the shop, he'll take good care of you."

"Uh, thanks." I walked in with Mavis in hand and Prylan still strapped to my chest, and he followed me before closing the door behind him. I twisted back. "Saw what you did for that guy back there. Glad to see there are other Culatians who don't hate Marincians."

He shrugged with his head. "Oh, there's plenty of us out there. I'm pretty sure half of Culatia doesn't like what this old king is doing, starting a war with another realm. Most of us are sick of it."

I let Mavis wander around the store and scratched my throat, feeling the coarse feathers there and remembering I needed a shave. "No kidding... Guess everyone's counting on the heirs taking over soon, huh?"

He hummed dully and pulled off a mis-placed item from the shelf and slid it on its rightful spot. "Some are, yeah. There's a rumor going around that Sky himself was found in Neverland. They say he apparently ran off to marry the Ocean King's sister a while back, and that's why he vanished randomly. They think that's why the war started."

I pursed my lips, hesitating. "And what do you think?"

"I think..." He took a minute to consider. "I think it's a load of crap. At least the part about their marriage being the reason for the war."

"Why do you say that?"

"Just doesn't seem right," he said. "I mean, it's the 22nd century! Everyone and their mother are inter-race couples. So what if they're both Relicbloods? The Death and Dream realm did it, and they figured it out. I just think everyone's sticking their noses in other people's business where it doesn't belong. And besides, who cares if the Relicbloods die off? I say good riddance."

I stopped short. "Uh, what?"

"I know, I know," he said and waved his hands dismissively. "It's an unpopular opinion... for now. Just wait, this king is going to keep getting worse and worse to the point where Culatia wakes up and realizes it's better off without any Relicblood. We'll be free from their tyranny—just like the Land realm."

I swallowed, the air suddenly suffocating. "You do know the people in the Land realm were sick of their *non* Relicblood tyrants, right?"

He snorted. "You believe that Enlightener propaganda everyone's obsessing over? Man, you're just as gullible as the rest of them."

Enlightener propaganda? "Wait, how do you know about the Enlighteners? I thought there were only a few of them in every realm?"

"There might only be a few official members, but their crap has been spreading like wildfire up here. My school at the Lysandre Academy put a ban on anything Enlightener related, so we've really seen a difference in how *we* act compared to public schoolers. They're like brainwashed zombies, it's freaky."

"And how do you know *you're* not brainwashed?" I laughed nervously.

"Because the Lysandre Academy values truthful information above all else," he said as if reciting from a textbook passage. "We're taught the unbiased histories of the world and its cultures and know how to spot a politically charged news cast. I'm telling you, what you've been hearing about the Land realm's 'problems'? It's just a lie to get people on the Relicblood's side. They've been feeding everyone that crap so we don't see how much better off those realms are than us. They'd be out of the job like *that*." He snapped his fingers. "Seriously, don't believe what those Enlighteners tell you. If you follow the Shadowblood, you'll be partly responsible for destroying Nirus."

My brow scrunched super low. "Uh… *what?*"

"It's true," he said, like it was the most commonly known fact on this planet. "They and the Relicbloods are going to kill us all eventually. Right now, I just hope the Lightcaster comes to stop it before they cause too much damage."

"Uh… right. Got it…" I cleared my throat and patted my pockets, pretending to look for something. "Aw, damn it. Looks like I left my wallet on the Airship. Better get it before someone from the crew decides to swipe it."

He looked concerned. "Oh. Yeah, better get there quick if you can't trust your crew. Good luck."

"Thanks," I grunted and quickly wrangled Mavis by the wrist before getting the Void out of there. When we were back out on the street, I bolted for the downtown district where the Howler's Inn would be, trying to shake off that creepy encounter. Prylan had apparently fallen asleep in her harness and Mavis started wailing when I didn't slow down to let her look at an outdoor vendor selling toys.

"Sorry, girls," I said through clenched teeth and hustled around the corner. "Daddy's trying to keep you away from lunatics today. Looks like we'll be getting fuel tomorrow…"

10

FAMILIAR FACES

XAVIER

The evening skies loomed over the metallic city as our hover-coach drifted into the rounded courtyard of the Howler's Inn. The lights along the structure's balconies washed out the stars that hung all around us on this floating island, yet there were still so many of them twinkling in that void that they still lit the clear skies like a trail for the Gods. Was Ushar, the patron God of Sky, able to touch those stars? Or did His reach have limitations?

When our coach rounded to a stop at the Inn's entrance and we filed out, a second coach hovered behind us. From that buggy came the rest of our entourage, including my wife. Her disguised, grey hair was tied in a bundle and braided with some strands, her marriage vines clipped to her hair and dangling at her forehead with its diamond centerpiece. She held a hand to her bloated belly and came to stand beside me, sliding an arm through mine in a smile.

"Hello, darling," I hummed brightly and kissed her cheek, still a tad buzzed from the last round of ale our group had shared half an hour ago. "How was your day?"

"Intriguing," Willow said. Her gaze drifted past me as though looking for someone. "Is my grandfather with you? I wished to discuss something with him."

I scratched my bearded chin. "Dream? He didn't come with us. I believe he mentioned something about meeting other Enlighteners with Herrin—"

"As we did," Dream himself interrupted as he strode around the coach on foot alongside his wife, who pushed baby Eryn in a stroller they must have acquired in the city. Herrin and his assistant, Marian, followed behind them.

"Ah!" Willow broke away from me eagerly to meet with Dream. "Grandfather, do you remember the time in 989 A.B. where you sought my counsel?"

Dream blinked at her with disguised, brown eyes. "You've finally started those visions?"

"Yes!" She chuckled mischievously. "Oh, I left you with such a cryptic answer, it must have riled you terribly."

He grimaced. "It did, yes… and you seem all the more proud for it."

She clapped her hands excitedly. "Indeed, I am! After all these years of suffering *your* cryptic nonsense, I had the rare opportunity to give you a taste of it yourself! Oh, you were so distraught, I simply cannot imagine what…"

The two walked inside ahead of us side by side with great enthusiasm, chattering away like that.

I glanced at Chai from my shoulder, who cocked his head at me. "She's having more visions?" I asked my raven broodingly. "Why hasn't she told *me* of them?"

She and I had had a discussion in the past about sharing her visions with me, so why has she resorted to keeping them to herself again? I crossed my arms in a grumble. "She seems to have no qualms discussing them with *Dream…*"

Chai gave a rueful croak from my shoulder.

I sighed. *At least she seems excited over* these *visions,* I considered. *So, I suppose that's an improvement.*

Alexander came beside me then, lifting a brow. "Everything all right?"

I laughed and shook my head. "Fine, fine. Willow and Dream are just off being strange again."

He grunted in understanding as we all entered the crowded Inn.

The lobby was packed with Culatian noblemen and women as well as many visiting lords and ladies from the Land and Death realms—like ourselves.

Alex and I strode to the front counter together, and I folded an arm on the marble countertop as he curled his own behind his back.

The winged steward noticed us and cupped his hands. "Ah, welcome be to you, Howllords!" he greeted in broken Landish. "How can I being of the service?"

"We have a reservation," we said in unison. I spoke separately next. "In the penthouse."

The steward blinked, his wings dipping uncertainly. "*Re?* But, *ye, ye,* Howllords, that reservation is being for…"

Both Alexander and I slipped off the gold rings from our index fingers, which held our illusions. By the man's shocked expression, I took it he clearly saw our heterochromic eyes and grey hair before we quickly replaced the rings on our fingers.

Alex cleared his throat. "You must understand, we have high-profile guests with us. Discretion is preferred, if you would."

The steward shook his head in a stutter. "Û-Û-Ûs! *Ûs* Howllords! I-I not being of the knowing person…!" He hesitated. "But, *ye, ye*… I can no be giving you key to penthouse tonight. Room already taken."

"Taken?" We both clipped, our wolf ears growing. Alex spoke separately in an irritated growl. "Kick them out! We had that room reserved!"

The steward's wings dipped even further. "*Ye, ye,* I be knowing of reservation, but it was being, *ye, ye*…" His head sank into his shoulder meekly. "Canceled…"

I gawked at him. "Canceled? How can you cancel a reservation made by the grandsons of this Inn's owner?!"

He swallowed. "It being, *ye*, unexpected… and this guest is being highest priority—"

"Absurd!" Alex stormed toward the lift across the lobby, and I brusquely stomped alongside him as he shouted. "I don't care who this individual thinks they are, but they can shove out of there! *We* have highest priority!"

The rest of our party saw us and followed in confusion. I jammed the button to call for the lift, and when it arrived, we all filed inside tightly. There was no liftman here, and there was no crank that I was accustomed to using. Instead, a panel of buttons was there. Confused, I clicked the one that looked to indicate doors closing.

Ding! The doors did indeed close.

"Hrm." I experimentally tapped the button at the very top, where the penthouse would be.

Ding! The lift began to rise on its own. No crank or gears needed. Apparently, Culatia had adapted a new method for this device. It was fascinating, but my current mood dampened my curiosity.

When we reached the top floor and the automatic doors slid open, Alex and I stormed through the halls to the penthouse doors with the others shuffling behind us. We threw off our disguises, ready to show this intruder exactly who they'd slighted, and Alex slammed his fist on the doors.

Bang! Bang! Bang!

"Excuse me!" Alex shouted at the doors, pounding again. "We have this room reserved! Shove out, or—!"

The latch clicked from the other side, and the doors were pulled open.

When we saw who was there, Alex and I stopped short, our wolf ears dropping in shock.

An aged man stood under the doorframe. He looked well into his sixties, his Grimish-black hair greying at the sides and crow's feet spidering at the side of his sapphire eyes. His square jaw and broad chin were cleanly shaven, save for the thick moustache above his lip that curled up at the tips.

Alex and I stared in stunned silence at the smiling old man. "Grandfather…?" I began hesitantly. Alex finished for me with a frown. "…Edric?"

"Boys!" The old man laughed brightly and wrapped his arms around the both of us in a surprisingly strong grip for a man his age. "Bloods be good, it's *both* of you…! Look at you—men of your own now, eh?" He released us and shook our hands, chuckling as he looked between the two of us. "Death, it's been ages since I've seen you both at the same time again. We all thought you'd be stuck in each other till the end of time!"

We grimaced. "As did we."

Grandfather Edric took my shoulders to better examine me. "Why, let's get a look at you, Xavier, hm? Seamstress prick me, you've lost weight, *kheh, he!* And you've a well-dressed face there, haven't you? You look more like your father than your brother now, don't you?"

I laughed. "I suppose so. But Grandfather, what are you doing here in Culatia? And on this island of all places?"

"Oh, I was on the islands managing my Inns when all this war business started down below. I thought it'd be best if I stayed above all of that nonsense until it resolved itself. I'm not a soldier like you and your father, I thought I'd let you all handle it." He gave a wrinkled grin and bounced a finger at our faces. "But then your father called to let me know you both were traveling up here and resupplying for a few days at *this* island, so I decided to hop over and surprise you!"

Alex let out a laugh. "Surprise us you did. We thought a haughty celebrity had decided to tread upon our reservation."

"I *am* sorry about the scare, lads," he said and patted our shoulders. "But I thought the reveal would be more exciting that way, yes? Now! I see you've brought an army of friends with you? Please, everyone come in!" He ushered our large group into the penthouse. "Now, do introduce us!" He practically flew to Willow behind me first, who had discarded her disguise on the way here. He took her hands eagerly with a smile. "Ah, our Lady Death! I remember when you were just a sprig up to my knee. Absolutely honored to have you in my Inns—and to have you as a granddaughter-in-law!" He patted both Willow's and my cheeks delightedly. "Lucas told me of your union last year. And about the baby! Congratulations! Oh, I can't wait to meet my first great-grandson…!"

Dream, who had discarded his own disguise and revealed his azure hair and eyes again, chuckled. "That makes two of us, sir."

"Three of us," Crysalette added as she came beside Dream with baby Eryn in his stroller.

Grandfather Edric glanced at the Dream family now, blinking specifically at Dream. "My word, that hair. Are you…?"

Willow gestured to them ceremoniously. "These are my grandparents, the king and queen of Dreams. And with them here is my uncle, little prince Eryn."

"Er…" Grandfather Edric scratched his balding head. "Uncle? *Grand*parents? Not to stare, but neither of you look a day over twenty. And your granddaughter is *older* than your son?"

Dream only shrugged. "These things happen."

Alex and I joined Grandfather's mutter, "No, they don't."

Grandfather's gaze snapped to the rest of our party next, examining faces one at a time. He registered Jaq to the side and clapped his hands. "Ah, I see *you're* still being dragged around with them, Jaqelle!"

Jaq grinned and waved. "Hey, Edric. Long time no see."

Grandfather chortled. "Long time indeed! I'm terribly sorry to hear about your own grandfather in High Everland."

Jaq slid his hands in his trouser pockets. "Master Lucas and his soldiers took care of things. Grandad's ghost set up a vassalship with him, so it's the best option he could have gotten, given the situation."

"I suppose that's true…" He looked at Lilli next beside the viper. "Ah, if it isn't Lilliana! Do you remember me, eh?"

Lilli set a delicate hand at her hip and folded her leathery wings. "Of course, I remember you, Howllord. You visited the twins in the palace a few times, if I recall."

"That I did! I hear you and Alexander here are planning your union soon?"

Alex stiffened beside me. "Er," he stammered, coughing. "We haven't, er, done any *planning*, per se…"

"No?" Grandfather lifted a thick, greying brow. "Well, why not? Your brother isn't trapped in your vessel anymore, you're both well above the proper age, and you're soldiers on a war mission that could mean the end of you before you have a chance to enjoy *any* part of life. Don't you think you should, in a sense… *get on it?*"

Both Alex and Lilli squirmed uncomfortably. "Er, well…" Alex hesitated. "I suppose we could… take that into consideration…"

Grandfather patted his shoulder. "I do suggest it—the life of a soldier hardly sees the same years as civilians… but then, I suppose you're just like your father, eh? He was young and reckless, and while I hated to see him thrust himself into battle with those horrific demons, he always came home, if a bit scathed. The fact that you're standing here today means your parents certainly trained you well, hm?" He paused, then began with a separate thought. "Now, er, speaking of *training*… What are these rumors I hear about you two having… *new* Hallows?"

"Ah," Alex and I said. We each lifted a hand and evoked different Hallows: Alexander evoking a ball of water over his fingers and I evoking a candle-lily made of fogging ice. "Yes, it's true."

Grandfather ogled our creations as Alexander took control of my ice flower before it fell into my palm, and I took control of his water ball before it splashed to the carpet. We pulled the other's creation over to our own hands, our fingers gleaming a bright emerald as our Crests of black diamonds changed into our crowned Ocean marks.

"That's…" Grandfather sounded exasperated, and he plucked the ice flower I had made out of Alexander's magical hold. "That's astounding! Have you any more, or is it just this?"

Alex and I switched to our Dream Hallows next, our hands now gleaming azure lights and our Crests now changing into crowned Dream marks. Alexander created a single copy of himself, the phantom standing beside him. I touched my thumb and forefinger against my lids and re-colored my mismatched eyes into two solid hues of brown for a few seconds.

"Incredible!" Grandfather clapped his hands in a laugh. "I suppose this was what your marks meant, then? We know at last!"

A knock came at the door. Then the muffled voice of Roji sounded behind it. "Hey, are you all in here yet?" he asked, and I heard the faint babble of his young daughters beside him. "I've been waiting in the lobby for hours. The front desk said you guys finally got here."

"Ah, yes we're here, Roji!" I said and hurried to pull open the doors.

Revealed was a rather irked Roji, still in his disguise as he resisted little Mavis who pulled on his arm while baby Prylan was strapped to his chest and playing with his face in amused giggles.

"*Skrii*, about Bloody time," Roji muttered. "You said we get our own room up here somewhere? They wouldn't give me any keys till you showed up."

Grandfather Edric snapped his fingers. "Yes, yes, of course! I shall call for all of your keys right away." He went to the silver com-panel along the wall, pushing a button and ordering our keys.

Roji threw a questioning thumb at the elderly man. "Who's this guy?"

"Our grandfather," I said in a gesture. "He owns these inns. Apparently, he'd come to surprise us."

Roji grunted, not caring when Prylan pushed his cheek comically up his face. "Whatever. I need a drink."

He released Mavis from his hold to let her scurry into the suite. His wife, Dalminia, took Prylan from him as he groaned and found the liquor cabinet in the corner. He poured himself a glass of scotch and chugged it in one gulp, then poured another before removing the ring that held his disguise. His wings and feathered hair drained into their natural, bright scarlet color, and his eyes bled the same hue as he sank into a nearby chair to relax.

Grandfather Edric blinked at the swallow. "Hang on… are you, er…?"

Alexander clasped a hand on Grandfather's shoulder in a hum. "Prince Roji of Culatia. And this is his wife, Ocean Princess Dalminia." Alex nodded to Dalminia, who pulled off an earcuff to reveal her scales, webbed ears, and emerald hair and eyes. Alex gestured to her daughters. "And these are their children, Mavis and Prylan." Dalminia removed their illusion-infused necklaces. Soon, the web-eared, winged girls were fully revealed and scuttling about with fluttering wings.

Grandfather stared and scratched his head. "I… see… my, I wasn't expecting to have four Relicbloods in my inns… er, *seven* with the children, I suppose."

"Eight," Lilli corrected and knelt to Fuérr, removing his enchanted necklace to reveal his scales and webbed ears. His fin-like hair bled to its natural emerald color from under his cap, and his eyes returned to that same green hue as well. Lilli gently squeezed Fuérr's shoulders as she explained, "This is the current reincarnation of Ocean, Prince Fuérr. He's traveling with us as well."

"Ees being nine," Zylveia huffed from beside El and removed her own disguise. She put hands on her hips in a grunt. "Roji being brother of mine."

"Oh," Willow breathed in an afterthought. "Ten, actually. We can't forget about—"

"I suppose this floor is to be ours?" Anabelle's delicate voice asked from the opened doorway. She was accompanied by her usual guard: Kurrick, Linus, and Genevieve. Ana removed her enchanted earcuff to reveal her golden hair and eyes, then stepped inside and held an amiable hand out to our grandfather. "Good day, sir. I am Anabelle Goldthorn, true queen and Relicblood of the Land realm. You have strikingly similar features as the twins—are you a relative of theirs by chance?"

Grandfather looked dumbstruck, stammering. "I-I, er… why, yes. These are my grandsons. Then, the rumors about your return are true…?"

"Indeed, they are," she chuckled softly. "Though, I'm sure you understand that discretion is preferred for all in our party? You see, we're on a mission to meet with the Sky King and stop Culatia's war with Marincia."

Grandfather swallowed. "A-ah… A noble mission it is, your Majesty…! I, er, I'm terribly sorry for troubling you, but I don't suppose I could ask of your, *ahem*, return…?"

Ana smiled. "But of course. Though, it is a rather complex story, so I will keep it brief. When I was a youngling cub, King Dream foresaw a vision of my death—which would have ended my Bloodline—and decided to disguise me as *his* second daughter instead. When the time he'd feared had come to pass, and…"

She relayed her story to Grandfather as they went to sit in the expansive lounge. Kurrick promptly shut the doors and turned the latch while Linus went to the sliding balcony door and drew the curtains closed.

I watched Genevieve storm to the liquor cabinet beside Roji. The viper woman promptly removed each vessel and laid them in a line along the counter, pouring a small amount of each into separate glasses and chugging them one by one.

Roji cocked an eyebrow at her. "Rough day, Sil?"

Genevieve finished her third glass and growled, "I must be sure there is no poison present for Her Majesty to taste." She continued knocking back the row of glasses, and Roji rolled his eyes while taking another sip of his own drink, though this time with a bit more hesitation.

I stepped beside Alexander and chuckled. "Why didn't *you* think to check the liquor for poison, captain?"

Alex shoved me with a shoulder and snorted. "We've no need to. I recruited an Infeciovoker to sense those things. Bloody woman is overzealous and unaccustomed to the likes of Octavius."

"Fair point." I hesitated, watching Sil Genevieve down the last glass in her line up before refilling yet another glass of a specific whiskey. This time, she poured a liberal amount. I grinned. "Or perhaps she's only using the excuse to drink whilst 'on duty'."

Alex frowned. Then clicked his tongue. "Blast, I should have thought of that…"

After three rather relaxing days of gathering supplies and staying in the Howler's Inn with Grandfather Edric, it was time to set sail toward our destination again.

Grandfather escorted us to our Airship at the docking station, dressed in what he called his 'traveling attire' that consisted of a black vest, short sleeved dress-shirt, and a wide-brimmed hat that was curled at the edges. He carried a pack filled with many Storageboxes and spheres of luggage, and he clipped onto the ship's deck with an ornate cane while whistling delightedly to himself.

Willow and I climbed onto the deck behind him. "Are you sure you want to join us, Grandfather?" I asked. "We can't guarantee our arrival will be met without hazard."

He scoffed and waved me off. "Oh, you lot will be all right, of that I've no doubt. We're traveling with *ten* Relicbloods, for Death's sake. And Death herself is here! Hah!" He produced a pipe from his vest's pocket and lit it with a match, taking a few puffs before murmuring in a more serious tone. "Not to mention, if you all find yourselves cast out of another palace, as Lucas claims has become a new habit of yours, I would prefer to be *present* to give your entourage highest priority in any of my inns. A com-call guarantees nothing if I'm not around to watch the staff on site."

Willow hummed. "Very well. I suppose that's a fair argument."

He waved his pipe toward Willow jovially, his moustache lifting as he smiled wide. "And I'd rather like to be here to see the birth of my first great-grandson. Speaking of which, I've a gift for you both."

Grandfather rummaged through his pack and retrieved a Storagebox, setting it in my open palm. "Inside are a cluster of items you'll need for the little one. A bassinet, a crib, a stroller, etcetera… I found a Grimish supplier up here on a different island, to make the nursery feel a little more like home for you both."

I looked into the translucent blue, gel-like crystal and smiled. "Thank you, Grandfather… much appreciated."

Phweeee!

Roji sounded a whistle from the helm and hollered out to the deck. "Ready for takeoff! Everyone brace yourselves—that means *you*, Death!"

Willow glowered. "At least he's giving a warning this time."

I chuckled and took her hand. "Come, darling. Why don't we get you something to eat in the galley?"

I led Willow inside while Grandfather went to chat with Alexander, and soon after we entered the cabin, the Airship began to rumble and rise.

And with that, we were back en route toward Culatia's capital island.

EVERLAND

11

RECRUITING REBELS

CAYDEN

Flies zipped and whined round the three corpses the Seekers had unearthed within the grounds of Roarlord Wales's private manor this drab, morbid night.

Roarlord Wales's partially decayed face stared emptily at the sky from the his sloppily-dug grave, his blue mouth slacked and open, the flies having made a home of his tongue.

The Seekers, dressed in their leather armor with their Shotri holstered and mouths covered by cloths to blot out the horrendous stench of death, hefted Wales's equally dead wife and teenaged daughter beside him, their bodies dropping to the dirt like sacks of spoiled meat.

The Seeker Captain, Garald, knelt to the daughter's head and examined her round face and slender neck, lifting her tangled, stiff hair with a penlight. The captain's hound ears drooped as he rumbled, "Puncture wounds on her neck. The same as her parents." He rose and tightened the cloth on his face, sniffing in disgust before producing a notepad from his leather vest's pocket and scribbled down notes.

I watched my father rub nervous fingers over his scruffy face, murmuring in hushed tones to the captain. "Then, this was Apson's doing after all? Before we apprehended him?"

My lion ears flicked in annoyance, and I muttered, "He simply found signs of a snake bite, Father. It could have been any viper-shifter, Apson is one of millions."

"The prince is right, Sire," the captain rasped, still scribbling in his notepad and scrutinizing the three corpses his officers examined ceaselessly. "It's far too early to say the former Hand is behind this… though, we'd be foolish to rule it out entirely."

Father snarled. "I've no doubt it was Apson! This very thing happened with the last man in his place—with Roarlord Rennegaurd. He and his monster of a son slaughtered a patriotic family who spoke out against their rebellion. Now that we know Apson was one of these terrorists, he's following in his comrade's footsteps. It's a Bloody nightmare, I tell you—oh, I'll have to assign two *new* Hands all over again!" Father threw up his hands and spun to leave, heading back to the palace. "I *must* have more thorough background checks on these men, I swear to Bloods…!"

I watched him cross the yard, his figure swallowed by the evening mist. A fly zipped by my lion ear, and I shook my head to be rid of the pest. *His monster of a son…*

He'd spoken of Linus; of the murders he and his father had been accused of committing. *It wasn't true, though.* I knew that much—all of us knew, in the resistance. Both men had been with us in the meeting the night they were charged of the murders. And all throughout that night, Linus had been with…

My claws grew, and I clenched my coat sleeve. *Linus…* A hollow pit shriveled in my chest at the thought, *Will I ever see you again?*

I felt the same as the night he abandoned me, when his father was executed. It took nine agonizing years to see him again—to learn he was still alive at all. Would I have to wait another eternity this time…?

Captain Garald cleared his throat and turned to me, tugging down his face-cloth slightly. "We'll run what we have to forensics and see if they find any traces of venom in their veins still," he said, straightening dutifully. "In the meantime, I'll interview any servants who may have noticed anything strange. You said you'd noticed Wales was acting strangely the day he vanished, Your Highness?"

I hummed darkly. "It's mere conjecture, but I thought perhaps someone had been posing as him, with an illusion to disguise himself."

The captain nodded and took note of that on his pad. "Do you think it was a member of the rebellion? Or perhaps one of the Reapers?"

I shook my head, knowing full well who it Bloody was, but knew it didn't make a difference. No one would understand the significance of Kael posing as the king's hand. Nor would they believe an Infeciovoker had been walking about the palace halls for months, likely poisoning souls to leave neither a witness nor demon behind. No one from my father's court knew of the intricacies happening around them. They knew nothing of the puppet master pulling their strings. Bloods, they didn't even know his name. *Fools, the lot of them.*

"I don't have a damn clue who it could have been, Captain," I said. "All I know is he had been acting differently. His throat had conveniently suffered a claw wound from a demon and altered his voice, his opinions on court matters had flipped altogether, he had been *hissing* like a cat shifter…"

The captain cocked an eyebrow. "Hissing? Do you think it could have been a snake's hiss, instead?"

I know it Bloody well wasn't, I thought bitterly. But I knew full well I had no proof of the contrary, so I lied and said, "I suppose it could have been."

The captain bowed and put away his notepad. "Thank you, Highness. I'd best find as many servants who are still around, in case they noticed discrepancies as well. Your cooperation is appreciated."

I nodded as he strode into the manor, his men now hauling the three bodies into the emergency wagon that had hovered over on feral horses. I swatted at a passing fly and stomped toward the palace, the soggy, browned grass wetting my boots.

I glanced at the half-dead ferns by a lion statue and spotted the trio of armored Rockraiders who were all too familiar after months of being shadowed by them. They were my assigned honorguard, ordered to stick to me like mosquitoes to a pond to "protect me" from another Reaper abduction… or at least, that was the official excuse. I knew the larger part of Father's reason for keeping so many eyes on me was to be sure I couldn't get near him during his scheming with his generals. The annoying part was knowing it wasn't out of suspicion that I was the rebellion's leader. It was out of fear for breaking my oh-so-fragile emotional integrity which those Reapers so deviously 'shattered'.

Bloody babysitters, they are. I snorted and kept an eye on the trio in the distance, making sure they were out of earshot as I pulled out my personal com from my coat pocket. Father had allowed me access to one in recent weeks—despite the fact I was a grown man who could have otherwise purchased one of my own accord had I not been the son of a tyrannical king. I was able to convince him that a com was necessary for my 'safety', so that I could call my guard if trouble befell me outside of their watch. He fortunately soaked it up like bread in a stew.

After double-checking for any eavesdroppers and finding none, I dialed the proper number to call Fangs Alice. I shielded my mouth with my free hand and used only the audio function of the com, its gears and cogs whirling in a mechanical hum.

Soon, the High Howless's voice fuzzed from the speakers. *"Cayden?"*

"Forgive the suddenness, Honored Fangs," I murmured under my breath. "I don't have much time to report. Wales's body has just been found buried outside his manor, along with his wife and daughter."

She sounded disheartened. *"Good Gods… how long have they been there?"*

"The Seekers are working on finding that out as we speak. But if I had to guess, I would say for the better part of a year, judging from their state. They were killed by snake bites. My Mel is on our dearest cobra behind the curtain."

She hummed. *"I'm inclined to agree… Though, we'll have to wait and see what the Seekers determine. What of progress on your father's assassination?"*

"None, as of yet," I chewed, anger boiling. I kicked at the dead grass and cursed. "Not only am *I* constantly surrounded by these damned vultures, Father has five teams on rotation to protect him. It's my own fault, I suppose… Ever since I attacked him months ago, he's been on full alert in regards to Land's Servant. Though, the delay has given me time to think."

"On?"

"I… should not be the one to kill my father," I whispered, a new light igniting my soul and pulling my lips into a wild grin. "As much as I would love that glory, I believe that honor belongs to my liege. It is her crown rightfully, after all. It should be she who takes it back."

Fangs Alice hummed. *"I see… Then, I suggest you take extra precaution while you wait for her to claim it. I hear from my sons that she and her fleet are en route for High Everland now."*

My pulse skipped a beat. "They've restored the Airships?"

"Indeed. Of course, they'll dock in Culatia first, to settle the dispute between the Sky and Ocean realms. But once that is done, they're scheduled to meet with our armies and storm the capital. Lucas and I are preparing a siege in Timberail as we speak. The Death King is to join us after the battle, should we be victorious—as we should be, given how few soldiers are stationed there, according to our scouts."

"Excellent." I paused, seeing my honorguard trio was striding over. I took a rueful breath, muttering, "I must go. Shel be with you in battle."

I ended the call and stuffed the com in my coat pocket just as my guards came to circle me in their usual formation, following me as I stepped for the palace. I suppressed a groan. *Bloody vultures.*

I crossed into the breezeway and passed several servants, nodding when they bowed in respect. Once reaching the south wing doorway—

A girl slammed the door open, thwacking my nose smartly.

I winced at the sting and rubbed it tenderly, blinking at the young, blonde girl. "Rilla," I said to my younger sister. "Bloods, could you exercise the art of opening doorways more *gently?*"

Rilla scowled at me and dragged a bronze arm under her nose in a sniffle. *Are those tears?* The fourteen-year-old's golden tiara was lopsided, her violet dress wrinkled and stained with what I desperately hoped was wine.

"Bloods, Rilla, is everything all right?" I asked cautiously, reaching for her chin to inspect her face—

She stepped away from me, her glare flicking to my guards, sharp enough to slice the evening mist.

I waved to the guards surrounding me. "Please, some space? I wish to speak with my sister in private."

The guards hesitated, but fell out of formation. They did not, however, step away very far.

I knelt to examine Rilla's face without reaching for her this time. A new bruise painted her forehead, a deep, purplish color.

Father, what have you done this time? Anger simmered, prickling my blood furiously. Father had turned horrifically violent after I first left the capital. I'd come home to find my six sisters and younger brother littered with scars and bruises, and they had doubled in the last few months—Rilla, in particular, fostered the most. I never understood why she always received the worst of Father's abuse.

I brushed delicate fingers over her bruise, rumbling, "Was this Father's doing again?"

She swatted my hand away. "What do you care?"

I froze, dumbfounded. "I'm your brother, Rilla. I care more than anyone."

"Bullshit." Her gaze darkened. "If you cared, you'd *do* something. But no. You're the heir. The only one Father leaves untouched. All you've done is ignore the rest of us—ignore how that man killed Mother."

My chest tightened, remembering how Mother's robes had billowed like sails as she threw herself from my balcony rail months before. My voice scratched hollowly. "Mother... took her own life, Rilla—"

"Because of *him*," she sneered, her teeth sharpening. "My room was right next to theirs, I heard her screaming that night."

Because of HIM? Bloods, so she believed Father's lies about Land's Servant attempting to assassinate Mother... that *I* had tried to kill her.

Rilla's condemning stare was a twisting, rusted blade in my gut. "Rilla," I said, "not everything Father has said is true about that night." I kept my tone to a dim whisper, to avoid the ears of the guards. "Land's Servant was not trying to assassinate Mother—"

"I Bloody know that already," she spat. "Mother was screaming *before* he showed up. I... I ran out to the balcony and saw the Servant break into their room—he was *helping* her. Which is Bloody more than you've ever done for any of us. I damn well hope the Servant wins—and I hope he doesn't see a need to kill *you* when Father's gone, Cayden."

She shoved me aside, then brushed past my honorguard, walking down the breezeway in the opposite direction.

I stared at her retreating back... which seeped with blood through her clothes.

I clicked my bedroom door shut, blowing out a relieved breath when I was finally rid of the guards.

A woman sat at the vanity in the corner. She pulled up the collar of her cream-white tunic and tucked her braided hair over a shoulder as she turned to me.

"Cayden," Revinna, my... *wife*... said. "We're almost late for the meeting. What kept you?"

"My babysitters," I muttered, throwing off my coat and moving to the oil portrait of Revinna and I.

It had been a recent portrait, painted shortly after my return home. Encased in an intricate, golden frame, Revinna and I were splayed in glittering gold and cream garments against a ruby-red void, arms intertwined, our smiles the work of the artist who took certain liberties to fabricate a sense of happiness.

The portrait in this spot before it had been of only me, but it seemed my father was damned determined to remind me he had control of my—and Revinna's—life. I certainly never asked for this surprise marriage, and I know she hadn't either... though, her affection was a growing concern.

I'll deal with that later, I decided, plucking the portrait from its mount on the wall and set it aside. I then carefully peeled back the false wallpaper, revealing the stone brick that was loose within the wall.

I evoked my rock Hallows, a golden light glittering from my fingers, and *pulled.* The stone vibrated and grinded slowly out of its hole. The brick itself was hollow, like a drawer, and it held the items I sought: my Land's Servant disguise. I grabbed my wide-brimmed hat and a dark cloak, then finally placed my face-mask over my eyes and nose.

I glanced in the vanity mirror, checking to be sure the metal bead sewn to the mask, which was enchanted with an illusion rune, had changed my eyes to an olive green, and my hair to a dull brown. The hat hid my lion ears, and I tucked my tail into my trousers.

Then, I rummaged through my vest pocket and plucked out a green hair bead. I stared at the bead in my palm, its glossy surface shimmering in the lamplight.

"Linus..." I whispered, my mood growing heavy. But I set my jaw and laced the bead through a strand of my hair, braiding the end and tying it with a string to keep the bead secure. "My friend, it's nearly time. I pray you use your visions to observe this next meeting. Let our queen know what plans are being made for her arrival."

Revinna turned to me with a frown. "Who are you talking to, Cayden?"

"You must remember to call me Servant when I'm in this disguise," I reminded, humming as I pinched the green bead in my hair. "I… speak to my dear friend, overseas. He is a Seer traveling with the rightful heiress to the throne. He has a bead similar to this one. It links us to his visions."

Her head tilted curiously. "Strange… I thought visions worked best with mediums that were… more *familiar* with the user? How can he see so much from such a small bead?"

My voice was soft. "It was a gift when we were boys. To always connect us, regardless of distance."

"But doesn't it only connect through him?" she questioned. "It's not as if *you* have visions, Cay… er, *Servant*."

"It doesn't matter. He is with the rightful queen and he will relay what I show him to her. That is enough."

Properly disguised, I slipped off my boots and stepped barefoot out to the balcony, hopping onto the rail. Staring down at the grounds, Mother's spiraling figure flashed to memory—

You've already grieved, fool.

I suppressed the memory and turned to Revinna, offering her my hand, which she eagerly snatched in a delighted blush. *Bloods, she acts as though we're running off to a romantic getaway.* She latched onto my waist then. A girlish giggle bubbled from her throat, and I rolled my eyes. *Bloody woman had better not get me and my men killed…* But, as I reminded myself, we could use all the willing recruits we could find. Those of nobility were especially needed to infiltrate this country's political system.

I used my Terravoking through my feet, the soles shining with gold light as I latched myself to the stone railing and walked downward vertically, straining to keep myself and Revinna afloat. She was heavy, but not as heavy as stone, thank Land. Once we were a few yards from the ground, I hopped off and set her on her own feet again, slinking across the grounds and past the gates.

The city of New Aldamstria was still on high alert, curfew having passed long ago, and most household lights were snuffed.

Guards and Footrunners patrolled the streets. Bounty Hunters stalked about for any signs of Wanted rebels… or, more likely, *me.* I could only imagine how much Father would pay for my head—in citizen tax money, no less.

I sidled alongside Revinna through the streets, then had her climb on my back once more as I used my Terravoking to launch us off the cobblestones and land gently onto the roof of a cobbler's shop. We then hopped from building to building, out of sight from the patrolling men beneath us. It took nearly half an hour to reach Henry's armory, and we ducked through the top window in silence.

No one was home, or so it seemed. It was standard protocol to blot out the lights during meeting nights. I led the way down the wooden steps, waving for Revinna to follow me through the armory. The woman would flinch at every sword and morning-star she passed, barely suppressing a frightened squeak when she nearly ran into a rack of brightly glowing swords made of illegal Spiritcrystal. *Well, I suppose they're only illegal to the Grimlings, now.* Here in Everland, Father had made it free for his knights to wield whenever they pleased, Death Laws be damned.

I crossed to the backroom, finding the jade rug in the corner, kicked it aside and stomped the floorboards three times.

There was a pause, and Revinna held her breath while clutching her coat's hood tighter.

I stomped twice more, paused again, then stomped thrice again.

C-clack!

A latch was thrown open from beneath.

Squeak!

The boards lifted on their hidden hinges. Henry's rabbit-eared head appeared from the dim hole, recognizing me.

"M'Lord Servant," he grunted, glancing at Revinna next. "And who's this?"

Revinna nervously cleared her throat. "R-Reeva, sir! I wished to join the cause, in what small way I could. I-if that is all right, of course…"

Henry lifted an eyebrow. "Bloods, woman, the Servant brings you himself and you ask if it's *all right?*" He snorted and climbed down the ladder, leaving the trap door open for us.

I climbed down after him, then helped Revinna… er, *Reeva,* down last. She quietly shut the trap door above her and turned the latch, then followed Henry and me through the dimly lit cellar.

Dust floated in the lamplights that waited on the scattered, wooden tables and several oil lanterns hung from support beams. The dirt-ridden floor was covered in footprints and scrape marks, the crowd of people letting loose their breaths when I came into view.

"Bloods, m'lord!" an antlered man said in relief, patting his chest as though to ward off a heart murmur. "We thought you's was a Hunter up there!"

I chuckled and raised my hands. "Sorry, Nordin, your date with the noose will have to wait another night. On the contrary, I've brought a new recruit."

I saw a slight tremor run over Revinna, and she held fast to her hood as she bowed low. "I-I-I am… Reeva! Pleased to meet you all… I suppose… erm…" She glanced at me helplessly, her dainty boots shuffling over the dirt.

I sighed and shook my head, the long feather on my hat wavering. "You'll have to forgive her stage fright. She's rather new to a life outside the law."

She blushed further and bowed again, lower this time.

Nordin's wife, a goat-horned woman named Guina, let out a ripping guffaw and stepped from the crowd to shake Revinna's hand vigorously. "Pleased t' meet'cha, miss Reeva!" She laughed. "Well then, if you'll be joinin' us, what skills you got what we can use?"

"Uhm…" Revinna swallowed. "T-that is… I suppose, perhaps…"

"Reeva will be another informant within the palace walls," I declared, propping myself against a support beam and folded my arms. "We need as many as we can garner, since Apson is no longer with us here."

Murmurs rippled through the cellar. Nordin eyed Revinna doubtfully. "Issat right?" He said. "And exactly what role d'you play in those pretty walls, miss Reeva? If you don't mind me saying, you look a tad too… *fancy* to be a servant girl." He bent to see her meek face under her hood. His throat reverberated. "Ey now, I recognize that face from the Screens!"

I clicked my tongue. "Damn you, Nordin, spoiling my surprise reveals… very well." I pulled off Revinna's hood before she could protest and announced, "This is Princess Revinna, newlywedded wife of Prince Cayden."

The cellar fell silent. Dust floated in the empty space between them and Revinna, who stiffened beside me.

Guina staggered, blinking. "The… the Bloody *princess* wants to join us?!"

"She can't Bloody be here!" Nordin piped. "She'll report us to 'er husband straight away, she will!"

There were several shouts of agreeing protest—

BANG! BANG! BANG!

Henry slammed his fist on the table. "Shut it! That is *the point* of Roaress Revinna's role." Henry glanced sidelong at me, pausing. "Do I have that right, my lord?"

The crowd's attention was now solely dedicated to me. I chewed on a curse to Henry, then let out a breath.

"Yes," I said. "Her role *is* to report to Prince Cayden, and visa versa. With him being guarded by those vultures, he has little time to speak to me, let alone come here himself." I gestured to Revinna. "Thus, his… wife… has volunteered to come in his stead."

Ah, *there* were the gaping looks. I sighed and added, "Yes, the prince is one of us… he has been with us from the beginning, along with Apson."

"Why in Bloods are we just now hearin' of this?" someone from the back, a man named Lorn, shouted.

Henry lifted a rabbit ear, answering, "You can guess the position the prince is in, can't you? If he's ever caught conspiring to kill his own father, who knows what Galden would do to him. It's only reasonable he didn't want anyone knowing."

"Precisely," I said, thankful at least Henry had taken some thought to come up with that excuse. Henry and Revinna were the only ones here who knew that *I* was the prince. Now I was glad for his quick thinking. "But, given the circumstances," I went on, "the prince is now on lock down, thanks to his father's paranoia—"

"I don't like it," a woman grunted from the middle row. It was Bexie, short for Beatrix IV, a Roaress from the courts. Her long, honey-blond hair wavered at her chin as she shook her head. "I don't like it one bit. How do we know the prince doesn't want his father dead so *he* can be king next?"

Agreeing murmurs spread through the bunker.

"Cayden doesn't want to be king," Revinna said, taking a shy step forward. The crowd hushed as she continued. "He's told me that he always hated his father, but not because he saw him as an obstacle for himself… He believes his family was never meant to be the permanent replacement for the true heir. He even went so far as to stay his blade from his father's throat, only because he believes that such an honor is the right of his queen."

There was silence at first. Then someone snickered, and a roar of delighted laughter erupted.

"Well, I'll be damned!" Guina chortled and thumped a heavy hand on Revinna's back. "Right words, those are, miss Revinna! *Khe, ha!*"

Revinna's cheeks bled a frazzled scarlet. "P-please call me Reeva here. If word spreads to the king that my name was spoken among rebels, I…" She wilted, though the crowd was still rippling with cheers.

From under my hat, my lion ears flicked. I clapped my hands to call for silence. "Enough! Yes, it's surprising. Though, is it truly? Who would despise His Royal Imposter more than those closest to him? Those who see first-hand what monstrosities Galden commits behind closed doors? Miss Reeva has been incredibly brave to come here tonight, given that her life is in danger from doing so." I took Revinna's hand and rolled up her long sleeve. Plaguing her arm were dark, purple bruises and stale claw marks, her once smoothed, bronze skin now puckered and littered with scars.

The room fell quiet at the sight.

"Do not think she is safe for simply being the crowned prince's wife," I said darkly. "If anything, their forced marriage has put her in more danger than she ever cared for."

Bexie piped from the tables. "Forced marriage? What do you mean?"

Revinna cast down her gaze and cupped her hands. "The king… declared Cayden and I married before Cayden had even returned to the palace. Cayden himself hadn't known of it. At least, not until he came back to free Apson's ghost and see him safely to the Reapers."

Nordin blinked. "That was the *prince?*"

Revinna smiled. "Yes, it was. It was a shock when I found out as well, believe you me—"

"Yes, well," I growled, worried Revinna would speak too much and give me away. "*kmm-hmm,* Guina? Perhaps we should show miss Reeva for whom we fight?"

Guina clapped her thick hands excitedly. "Oooh yes, yes, yes! You'll *love* Her Majesty, miss Reeva! She's absolutely breathtaking…!"

Guina pulled Reeva into a chair, then hobbled to the wall where the Vision-screen's gem was embedded. Beside it was a slot with coils and springs, and she inserted a rectangular film-tape, the gears inside whirling.

She quickly turned on the Vision-screen and hopped into a chair beside Reeva, wriggling with delight.

Within the screen of light, a scene appeared depicting a royal ball. Blond and brown-haired nobles were dressed in earthy silks and frosted with jewels, their chatter buzzing over the subtle music playing in the corner.

Revinna cocked her head. "Where is this?"

"Neverland's palace," I explained. "We received this footage from our sister rebellion on the other continent." A grin tugged my lips. "Well… I suppose they're no longer rebels over there, are they?"

The others hooted cheerfully.

On the screen, the dancing nobles suddenly rushed out of the way of four Grimlings. The grey-skinned group were chased by a crazed, teenaged girl with cropped hair, her hands gleaming gold as she made all the potted plants in the ballroom tremble in their soil.

"Who are all *these* people?" Revinna asked curiously.

Henry eagerly came to answer that, pointing to each face in turn, beginning with the bat-winged woman with long, black hair. "Lilliana Tessinger," said Henry, moving his finger to the ashen haired woman. "Death Princess Willow Ember." He moved to the two grey-haired men with mismatched, blue-and-clear eyes. "Alexander and Xavier Devouh—"

"Ember," I corrected in a grunt. "Xavier and Her Highness Willow have wedded."

"Right, right," Henry chuckled. He swiped a book from a nearby table and patted it with his knuckles to show Revinna the title that read *the Legend of the Shadowblood*. "Have you read about the twins, miss Reeva?" Henry asked. "It's a great story. I already knew about it, since my niece Vendy is their vassal, but it's worth a read."

Revinna's brow knitted as she took the book, opening the cover primly. "*The Shadowblood?* What does that mean—"

"There she is!" Guina squealed with excitement, her thick arms dancing as she hopped in her seat and clapped. "Look, look, look…!"

On the screen, the vines the teenaged queen had brought to life were now frozen in place. The screen panned upward to a balcony where a tall woman stood posed and daunting. She was clad in a brilliant gold gown, shimmering with thousands of sequins that dulled compared to her petal-like locks glinting in the chandelier's light. Bloods, her eyes gleamed like golden suns bursting with power, her hands shining as she halted the teenager's vines as though pushing against a feather.

"*I am Annabelle Goldthorn,*" the radiant woman bellowed, her lion ears perked calmly and tail swishing gently at her legs.

The crowd gasped as the marble floor shot up in low, grinding rumbles, forming a lopsided staircase for her to walk down. When she reached the ballroom floor, she stood tall and regal, her gown's countless sequin gleaming in the light, as if dressed in twinkling gold stars.

"*I am the queen of these lands your ancestors have stolen from me,*" my queen announced. "*I am the last Relicblood of Land.*"

Bexie shivered. "Ooooh, it gives me such chills!"

The camera followed Her Majesty as she strode across the marble floor, the lords and ladies making way for her, some kneeling in prayers. She paused when reaching a goat-horned man with dark skin.

My breath died on my tongue, as it did every time I watched this clip. *Linus…*

He was dressed in a fine, cream tunic, his goatee shaped squarely about his brown jaw. He looked shell-shocked, staring at Ana with all her golden glory that even gleamed through the screen. He was on the verge of tears. Her Majesty touched a gentle hand to his wounded shoulder, healing a bleeding gash. He then dropped a knee and bowed his head in reverence.

"Just look at that!" Guina clapped her hands together. "She's used all *three* of Land's Hallows! Bloods be good, and she's gorgeous…!"

Revinna gripped my arm suddenly, the woman's eyes bulging at the lioness on Screen. "Land, it really is her, isn't it…? All this time, I thought it would be a man…"

I slid my arm out of her hold, perhaps too curtly, I admit, but kept my hands shoved safely in my trousers' pockets. "We all assumed the heir would be a man, truthfully. But there is no denying her Hallows, that hair, and that crowned Land mark on her back."

The scene shifted to other footage of Her Grace. They were in a parade now, it seemed, for Death's Festival in the streets of Neverland. The focus began on Her Majesty—

Screams erupted from the crowd, then the view quickly moved to Death Prince Xavier and his brother Alexander. A crossbow quarrel hit Alexander's horse while he dove into Xavier and Willow's open carriage to protect them, and Xavier swiftly produced a shield made of ice to guard his pregnant wife. More quarrels shattered over his ice, and black tendrils slithered around the shield.

What are *those arrows?* I'd seen this footage before, but that question still bothered me. I didn't like those black veins. They looked like poison, as if from an Infeciovoker. *Likely from Kael.* Could he have produced a weapon with his Hallows? Bloods, I hoped to Land there weren't many.

The camera angle suddenly shifted back to Her Golden Majesty, who rose in her open carriage and lifted a single, glowing hand. Two pieces of the road *cracked* apart and shaped into jagged rods at her will. Then with a dismissive flick of her wrist, she sent the pieces flying at incredible speed into the crowd, driving them into two fleeing Neverlanders' heads. They'd been part of the assassination attempt, I wagered.

Henry whistled in awe. "I still can't wrap my head around that strength… and it looked like nothing to her. As easy as breathing."

Bexie held a giddy hand to her lips. "I heard she ripped the fake queen's head off with a single pinky! It was over in a matter of seconds!"

Nordin chortled and slapped a knee. "Bloods, maybe it'll be that quick with Galden!"

Cheers erupted in the cellar, and I clapped my hands sharply to call for silence.

"Yes, we all wish for our battle to end as swiftly as that," I said. "But keep in mind, their old queen had been an adolescent. Merely a child. We oughtn't think us victorious before our queen arrives, and she'll be relying on us to clear a path to Galden when she does. I've just heard from Fangs Alice that Her Majesty is coming with her fleet. But the warriors accompanying her now are from our sister continent of Neverland. They don't know Everland's terrain as we do. I expect to have our troops stationed in the best defensive lines around the city, and to have scouts reporting our enemy's status every evening, starting tomorrow. Nordin, your team will see to this."

Nordin saluted with fingers to his brow. "Aye!"

"And see if you can dig up anything regarding these strange, poison arrows," I added in a thoughtful growl. "I don't like the look of them. They worry me. I want to know how many there are, where they are being distributed, and if there are countermeasures we can take—"

Creeeeaaaaak...

The floorboards moaned above us. The entire cellar froze.

Clunk... Clunk... Clunk... Clunk...

Footfalls pounded up there, dust puffing onto our heads as whoever was in the shop stomped toward the trap door leading down here.

They stopped. Then kicked at the door thrice.

The silence was so venomous, my throat swelled.

They kicked twice.

My lion ear perked from under my hat. *That is the next sequence in the code...*

They kicked thrice once more, finishing the final sequence in our secret knocking code.

Henry and I exchanged a confused glance. He didn't seem to be expecting anyone else either. Hesitantly, he went to the ladder, the rest of us shuffling into the shadowed corners of the cellar.

Henry turned the latch, then very cautiously lifted the door.

A dainty hand shot in front of his face.

"Pardon the intrusion, sir," a young, familiar girl's voice said. "But I'm here to join the cause."

That voice. My brow furrowed. No, it couldn't be her. That was absurd.

Henry awkwardly shook the hooded girl's hand, then sputtered. "I... uh... *Khmm*, all right. How..."

The girl pushed him aside as she climbed down the ladder without permission, balancing a large, crystal ball with one arm while using her elbow and free hand to shimmy down the rungs clumsily. When she touched down, she glanced about the room of dumbfounded faces. Then she pulled off her hood.

A swath of honey blonde hair tumbled over the teenager's shoulders, her bangs tied in a half-tail at the back and showcasing her curled nose, angled crimson eyes and bronze face. She wore a velvet, lavender cloak embroidered with mountain designs sewn with golden thread at the hem. Underneath was a silken tunic with a high-collar and leather trousers, her polished boots caked in fresh mud.

"Rilla?" Revinna blurted before I could open my mouth. She stepped into the light. "Rilla, it *is* you!"

"Hello, Revinna," said my younger sister placidly, not surprised in the least to see Revinna here.

Henry finally clambered down the ladder, and the rest of us circled Rilla with hesitant steps.

"Princess Rilla," I growled, frowning. "*How* did you find us?"

My sister lifted the large crystal ball in her hands. "With this, Sir Servant."

My frown deepened. "What will that do for you? Only Seers can use those."

"I *am* a Seer," Rilla said. Her hands gleamed with azure light suddenly, and images flitted in the ball. Depicted there was… myself, without my disguise. It was eerie to look at my own face without a mirror, moving and speaking. It was from earlier this evening, when I last saw Rilla.

The images faded, and she lifted a sleeve to reveal a Dream mark on her left wrist.

"H… How long?" I demanded, trying not to stumble from shock. My own Bloody sister—a Seer? How had I not known? "Do your siblings know?"

Rilla shook her head, her honey locks bouncing. "My parents kept it from the others. My father thought it a disgrace, to hold the mark of a 'disgusting dream walker'… it didn't matter *which* Hallows I had, the fact it was from the Dream realm was a sin in itself. At first, he thought I was a bastard child that my mother had produced through some kind of affair, but the idiot didn't know that Dream Hallows is given indiscriminately to *any* shifter of *any* family line, unlike the other elements. Either way, he's using me like his own personal war toy. Spying on the Reapers, trying to learn their secrets, beating me with this damned ball every time he doesn't get his answers since I haven't any damned connection with the Grimlings… I'm sick of it—I'm sick of his exploiting—I'm sick of *him*. If I'm to use my Hallows at last, it will be on my own terms and not his."

Nordin let out a trembling squeak and shook his hands in the air. "This ain't right, this ain't *right!* Two princesses want to join our cause? No way in Bloody Void! Somethin's up with this an' I don't—"

"Rilla," I said softly, my hands balling. "Show them your back."

Rilla paused, her gaze shooting at me in surprise. She hesitated, but set the crystal ball at her feet and unfastened her cloak. Then she spun and, covering her front, uplifted her tunic to show her scabbed, still-oozing scars along her spine. They were claw marks. The same as those littering Revinna, my other sisters, my youngest brother… my mother, when she was still alive…

"And who gave you those scars, Rilla?" I asked darkly, anger festering.

"My father," Rilla said in quiet resentment, replacing her tunic and cloak. She gave me a suspicious glare. "How did you know they were there?"

I rubbed my chin. "Your brother told me of them."

She snorted. "Cayden? So, he really *is* a coward… sneaking in the dark and asking rebels to deal with his problems? Did he ask you to help my mother that night, then—?"

I slapped her, her hair bouncing as her head flung away.

"I'll warn you not to speak so poorly of your brother," I clipped, my anger heating to full blown fury. "You should know, I was not there that night. It was your *brother* who helped your mother. Not I."

Rilla's breath caught, clutching her reddened cheek and stared at me in shock.

"Do not think lightly of your brother's work, princess," I growled, calming. "Much like Revinna, he is risking his life by helping us… you of all people know what your father is capable of."

She dropped her gaze indignantly and muttered, "W… *Kmm-hmm!* Well?" She straightened and regained composure. "Am I permitted to join? Or aren't I?"

I looked round the room, everyone scratching their heads and shrugging at me. I sighed. "Well… I suppose we can't simply let you walk out after you've located this bunker, can we?"

The others laughed.

I walked Revinna and Rilla through the dark alleys of the city, heading back to the palace. It was a risk going on foot like this, but I couldn't well carry both of them discreetly—or swiftly, if we met with bad company. For now, walking was best in case we needed to scatter.

"Must I return home?" Rilla questioned in a stubborn scowl, her hood keeping her face in shadow. "I'd hoped to stay in the city…"

"With the way the king keeps a close eye on his children," I grunted. "He will notice you're missing and have the cities searched. And add your apparent abilities which he sees as an asset, I don't doubt he'd tear down every home in New Aldamstria to find you—which would, in turn, risk our troops of being discovered."

She crossed her arms in a grumble. "I suppose you're right… he nearly did as much when you first vanished, in any case. But then, you *are* Father's favorite, so that's to be expected."

I snorted. "Yes, well, I had other plans for that and…" I slowed to a stop, my boots scuffing the stones. I stared at Rilla. She was grinning slyly at me. "Bloods." I rubbed my eyes behind my mask. "How long have you known, Rilla?"

"Since you slapped me," she said haughtily, turning up her nose. "You touched me, and I Saw you under that disguise. Perhaps the next time you decide to sneak off and run a rebellion against Father, you'll think to bring me along earlier?"

I blinked. Then laughed. "Perhaps I will."

Rilla nodded in satisfaction and lead the way back this time, stealing a sidelong glance at me. "How *did* you end up as the rebellion's leader, anyway? You couldn't have started it. The rebellion has been around for centuries."

Revinna hurried beside me eagerly. "Oh, I've been wondering this myself! How did it all start, Cayden?"

I scratched the scruff at my chin. "Well… if you must know, I *inherited* the role as Land's Servant. It is a title that is always passed from man to man. The Servant before me was a man named Gerard." I turned to Rilla next and added, "He was more a father to me than the bastard who sired us, Rilla."

Rilla tapped a finger over her arm. "How did you meet him? I can't imagine he simply visited the palace to have tea with Father?"

I lifted my hands and weighed them idly. "Tea, assassination attempt, it's all the same, really. When I was a boy, Gerard barged into the palace gardens in this very disguise." I tipped my plumed hat. "That morning, Father had dragged me along to have brunch with visiting Roarlords. Not an hour before, he'd beaten me as he often did when I so much as *mentioned* the lost Relicblood of Land."

Rilla screeched to a halt. "He beat *you*? His favorite?"

I grimaced. "Of course, he did. This was perhaps a year or two before you were born, Rilla, when I hadn't yet learned to 'keep my opinions to myself'. I'd only asked him questions of the stories I read, nothing more. That's when he'd ordered the books that mentioned those tales to be burned, then he dragged me to that damned brunch as if all was just peachy with our family." I shook my head. "It was in the middle of our meal that a random rebel soldier attacked Father. Gerard had swooped in and interfered with the attack, stopping the man from killing Father for reasons I would learn sometime later. With guards now surrounding the two, Gerard snagged me and held a knife to my throat, using me as a hostage to run away with me in tow. He only meant to keep me until he was out of sight from the guards. But when he snuck us into an abandoned flat…"

"Why didn't you let him die?" I remembered screaming at the masked man in the plumed hat, the memory flitting behind my eyes. I was angry then. Furious even, my fists were shaking. "It would have been simple! He was unprepared and off-guard! He was RIGHT THERE! Why did you stop your man from killing him?!"

The Servant's voice was curious as he rasped, "You would have preferred he HAD killed your father?"

"Anyone with half a brain would have preferred it!" I thumped onto the floor with crossed arms and legs, my lion ears curled back tight and tail swishing around me. My bruises from the beating earlier still stung and burned. One of father's claws had sliced my arm. "The kingdom would have been better off if Land's Relicblood hadn't died off… we'd all *have been better off."*

The present dripped back, and I sighed. "Well, I'd said some things that I suppose Gerard had found trustworthy. Instead of taking me back immediately, he made me an offer. I could either be tossed on the streets for my father's guards to find me and be on my miserable way, or join his ranks and aid in my Father's death. Obviously, I took the latter."

Rilla scowled. "But why *didn't* he just kill father right then and there?"

"He later explained that if he *had* let Father die that day, an even worse tyrant would have taken his place. At least, until *I* would inherit the throne. But once I did, I would still be an obstacle for the true heir when he… *khmm, hmm,* when *she* returned. Gerard wished to wait for our Relicblood's return before seeing to Father's death. Which I intend to see through in Gerard's absence."

Revinna rubbed her knuckles hesitantly as she asked, "What happened to Gerard?"

I sighed, a pit tunneling my chest to remember. "He was hanged by the Raiders," I murmured. "I was nearly twenty, I think. Our bunker was found during a meeting, and he gave me his garb before ushering the rest of us out. He gave himself up to the Raiders as a normal recruit, and expected me to keep alive the beacon of hope that the Servant represented…" My fists clenched at the memory, and I exhaled hard. "I only pray I've done him well thus far."

Revinna fanned a hand to her chest and offered a small smile. "I should think so, Cayden. Look at your rebellion now—what you've accomplished in your reign. Your Relicblood *has* returned. You'd done what was necessary to see that she surfaced, and you're doing what you can to see that her throne is ready for her."

The thought of our golden queen brightened my mood, and I chuckled at the sky. "You've a point there. And what a beautiful point it is."

ABOARD THE AIRSHIP

12

THE DREAM OF YESTERDAY

KURRICK

300 YEARS PRIOR

*B*reathe. Focus. Listen.

I held my stance and inhaled, sweeping my sword across my chest in a slow draw, sure to keep the angle correct.

Breathe. Focus. Listen.

On the exhale, I swept the sword up in an arc, every movement deliberate and precise. My blindfold was soft against my face, the ambient sounds of the forest filling my lion ears. Songbirds twittered and chirped, the river trickled softly in the breeze, the leaves rustled in a quiet hush.

I inhaled again, drawing my blade straight across.

Breathe. Focus. List—

A loud splash came from the river, followed by several *plunk, plunk, plunks*.

Growling, I drove my blade in the dirt and lifted my blindfold. "Ana, I am trying to…!"

I stiffened. Ana swam in the river with flighty giggles, her hair *not* disguised brown, but glittering its natural golden brilliance. Her walnut skin, darkened by the months we'd spent in the true sunlight, was radiant in the glowing beams that poured through the foliage.

And she was naked.

"Ana!" I cried, ripping off my blindfold completely and stalked to the river. "What in Shel's name are you doing! If someone sees you…!"

"We chose this spot for its seclusion, Kurrick," she said, dipping her golden locks in the water and emerging sleek and dripping. "We've been training here for months, and not a soul has passed through for miles."

"But you… you can't just…!" A rumble poured from my throat, irritated, and I scratched my head vigorously. "At least put your Bloody clothes on! We're in the middle of training!"

She floated on her back, kicked her feet in the water, and hummed, "No."

"Damn it, Ana, I am trying to concentrate! You're disrupting my focus."

She kicked herself in circles in the water, still humming. "Then don your blindfold again."

"That's not the point! Just… just put your clothes on."

"No," she giggled and submerged in the water. She then swam toward the bank where I was standing. She came up for breath at my feet and folded her arms over the grass in a whimsical smile. "Take a rest with me. We've been training since dawn, and who knows when we'll be out in the sun again? The *real* sun, Kurrick! With real plants, real stone, real people…!" She gave a dreamy sigh and rested her head on her arms. "We only get these months outside Aspirre every few decades, Kurrick. Come, let's enjoy them."

I grumbled, "These months out are meant for our training, Ana. *Your* train-ing. We oughtn't waste them with—*hugh!*"

Ana had twirled a gold-glowing finger and sent a patch of grass to wrap round my ankle, pulling me into the water with a large splash.

I cursed underwater, a flurry of bubbles spewing, and emerged in a gasp, hacking. "Blast—*Khauh!* Blast it, Ana…!"

I searched the river for her and found her giggling like a child beside a boulder. Her petal-like hair bounced from her shoulders, even when damp. Her muscular build was becoming more prominent each day, slender arms accented by the shape of her growing strength, and Bloods, her golden eyes glinted like coins in the light.

Damn this girl. My lion ears flicked. Then a laugh escaped me, leering at the youthful teen who chuckled by the boulder.

She saw my hounding stare and hid her giggles behind a hand, shouting playfully as I chased her across the river, avoiding the splashes she hit at me in a laugh.

I caught her by the waist and pulled her in, tasting her throat. She looped her arms round my neck—then drew a string over my head and slipped some-thing around my neck.

I glanced at the gold coin that now glinted from my chest. It was a Shelish emblem engraved into the polished surface and reflecting the sunlight.

"What's this?" I asked, lifting the coin with curious fingers.

"It's for you," she said, her smile spritely as she bit her fingernails. "I found it in the bazaar yesterday. Do you like it?"

I chuckled and brushed my lips over hers. "I love it. Now, what shall we do about your blatant disrespect for your garments—?"

She pulled me down into the water to steal a kiss, the worries of the world bubbling away with my breath.

PRESENT DAY

I weaved through the crowded corridor of the Airship while balancing the steaming plate of steak and cauliflower I'd acquired from the galley. Once rounding the corner, I found Linus standing guard outside our queen's door where last I left him. He flicked me a silent glance and nodded, stepping aside as I rapped my knuckles on the door lightly.

"Enter," Her Majesty's muffled voice called from inside.

I did, closing the door behind me, yielding to a shiver as the draft swept over my skin from the open window. Snow spilled inside and coated the desk where Her Majesty was seated. Her golden locks tumbled over her shoulder when she turned her distant gaze away from the window, then rested her head over her folded arms and sighed.

"You needn't knock, Kurrick," she said.

I inhaled through my nose and straightened. "I've a need to, my lady. Should I catch you at an indecent time, it'd be inappropriate."

She circled a delicate finger over her temple. "I fail to see the impropriety in a scenario I only *dream* of. How long do you intend to keep up this wall of yours?"

Ignoring the question, I strode to the desk and placed the meal in front of her. "I've brought your dinner, my lady."

She pushed it away. "I haven't the appetite."

"You haven't eaten since yesterday morn," I chewed, annoyance budding. "You'll not waste away on your birthday."

She glanced at me sidelong. "Ah, so you remembered after all?"

I muttered, "As if one could forget, when it falls on a holiday. The Grimlings have asked me to extend their good wishes for your *Rae'u Shelic*."

She hummed thoughtfully at that. "Ah, that's right. I nearly forgot one's Day of Life is as cherished to the Grimlings as one's Day of Death…" A new thought seemed to pass through her eyes, and she murmured, "Perhaps I could call Myra, after so long. Do you think it would be appropriate?"

I grunted. "Not only appropriate, but I should think it overdue, my lady."

She chuckled, reaching for the silver communicator on the desk. She tapped its buttons and caused the cogs and gears to warble and whirl. "I suppose you're right," she said. "Come, she'll wish to hear from you as well."

My shoulders locked, stepping back. "She is your sister, my lady. I've no place to converse with royalty so informally."

She gave a disgruntled breath, her eyes rolling. "Oh, will you stop with 'no place' this and 'no place' that? You know well your place is with me—"

"*I am no king, Ana,*" I snapped, but quickly bit back my tone in shame. "I... I apologize, your grace. A subject shouldn't speak his queen's name so familiarly."

"You are *not* my subject." Her nostrils flared angrily. "You have spent the last five centuries with me, if it's proper for anyone to treat me familiarly, it is you. What's happened, Kurrick? Tell me what's changed?"

I affixed my gaze to the floorboards. "You are my queen."

"That never stopped you before."

"Those years are done. You're reclaiming your lands, we both knew it would end one day."

"Then why," she inquired haughtily, "do you still wear that coin?"

My heart jumped, and I smothered the impulse to reach for the Shelish coin around my neck; the coin she'd given me at the river. Where she chuckled under my touch. Where the taste of her lips was as sweet as fresh honeysuckle. Where the day seemed to linger, and for a moment, it felt as if we could remain there, alone and secluded, for as long as we wished.

But we could not.

"You deserve better." My voice scratched. "I would shame the kingdom. I would shame you, my lady."

"Oh, you're on with all that again?" She massaged her eyes. "For the love of Shel, will you call me by name?"

I held firm. "I cannot, my lady."

"I order it!" She whirled, nearly knocking over the chair. "You claim to be my subject? You want to follow my every whim? Then consider this a royal decree. You're forbidden from calling me anything other than my name."

I ground my teeth. "I..." My lips drew into an indignant line. "I cannot, my lady."

She threw up her hands in a furious growl and slumped back to her chair, hiding her face in her flowery hair. "Oh, very well... Keep up this farce, if you wish. I shall wait until you've come to your damned senses."

I hesitated. "My lady..."

"Leave me."

Her cold tone squeezed my chest, and I turned to leave. "Yes, my lady..."

"And Kurrick?"

I paused, hand hovering over the door handle.

"If you knock again," she began, "I will leave the door open at all times. For anyone to see, decent or indecent."

The warmth fled from my cheeks. *Damn this woman!*

"Yes… my lady…" I chewed ruefully, nearly slamming the door behind me.

My lion ears were still curled tight to my skull as I took my post beside Linus, who chuckled.

"My, but her grace knows how to toy with you," the goat said with a grin.

I shot him a piqued glare, snorting. *Damned Seers and their invasive visions.*

"If it's any consolation," he hummed. "I would be proud to serve you, your majesty."

"Do not call me that," I sneered.

"Fine, fine. As you wish… sire." He snorted into amused laughs, his dreads quivering along with his lungs.

"A queen deserves more for a husband," I said. "Better she wed Cayden."

His gaze widened at me, then his laughter exacerbated, the man wiping at entertained tears.

"And what, pray tell, is so damned humorous?" I demanded.

He managed to stifle his chuckles behind a grin. "Her grace isn't… oh, how do I put this? Her grace isn't Cayden's type."

"Type?" I barked, rage flaring. "This is no matter of *type!* Nor even of fancy! Her grace is worthy of any man she deems fit, none would dare refuse her request!"

Ana's muffled voice called from behind the door. "Yet, the man I *have* deemed fit is the first to refuse."

My teeth clicked shut, and oh, but I longed to break Linus's teeth. I stalked down the corridor before I acted on my impulses. "To Void with you, Bloody jester," I spat.

Fool, you are. I struck my brow with gauntleted knuckles. *Such a fool, opening yourself to such ridicule.* Best I returned to little conversing with the likes of that goat. As for Ana…

My neck weighed heavy, the tarnished, Shelish coin dragging it down.

I ripped its string from around my neck and gripped the coin until it dug into my gloved palm so harshly it threatened to tear through the leather.

That girl will learn to move on. I stalked down the spiraling steps and thrust open an unoccupied room, slamming shut the door and unlatching the window. Snow spilled through the frame and dusted the floorboards.

I raised the coin over my head, poised to throw. *She cannot live in the dream of yesterday. For the sake of the Old Kingdom, she will let go. She will...*

My muscles squeezed painfully. The snow bit at my cheeks in the bitter gale, and I felt the coin in my palm, so solid and real, burning through the glove. *I... must let go.*

I lowered my fist and gazed at the coin. Of course, Ana wouldn't move on. She will never... until I have.

But if she believes I have, will it be enough? I drew in a breath before pocketing the coin. If naught else is to be done, its absence should catch her notice.

—The door creaked open then, letting in the yellow light of the hall. That viper girl, Genevieve, peeked in. Her brown scales paled upon spying me inside.

"Forgive me, Captain," Genevieve said quickly, bowing before she turned to withdraw. "I did not realize this cabin was occupied."

Anger brewed at her scaled face. *There is something not right with this girl... blast me, but I will discover what.* I rushed toward her to snatch her arm, her plate clattering.

"Off to make another call, Sil?" I questioned. "I wonder to whom?"

Her fangs grew long, though she kept an even tone. "I wished to speak with the generals of the fleet, across the ships. I thought it best to make certain all were on standby until a plan for docking has been set."

I grunted. "And I suppose privacy was pertinent for this, then? How strange it is. The last call I overheard you make with the fleet had been through these halls, your nerves seeming unfettered with the number of ears surrounding you." My grip tightened on her arm, her plate crackling. "One would question why secrecy was necessary for *this* call?"

She did not flinch at my glare, bones as still as the grave. "It was not necessary, Captain," she said. "I only wished for breathing room from the crowd."

My gaze narrowed further, and she matched it steadily. With a growl, I released her, and watched the snake's every step as she ascended the spiraling staircase, the boards groaning under her weight.

Genevieve, I swear on her grace's name... My sharpened teeth barred. *I will find what you're hiding.*

13

SOMETHING'S BREWING

XAVIER

Cold, white crystals tumbled onto the deck and poured from the dark clouds we sailed through.

I slipped and shuffled through the snowy deck in a violent shiver beside Grandfather Edric, the two layers of cloaks and woolen scarf I wore hardly doing anything for this blasted winter weather.

Some of the crew had taken their meals out here, warm drinks and roasted chicken legs cherished in their huddled groups as they mingled under the snowy sky.

I carried a cloth full of apples, a jar of pickled radishes, a kettle of hot water and various bags of herbal tea—anything I could find that our cooks could spare. Grandfather Edric carried what he could with one arm while his clipping cane occupied the other, his own cloak flicking in the icy wind and his curled moustache gathering flakes of snow.

I was thankful for the warm kettle. The steam was my only source of warmth as another brisk wind pushed me back a foot, the boards having iced over along with the railings. Nathaniel had thrown salt over the deck, and Roji and El have done what they could to tame the weather, but it still wasn't quite enough.

When another gust threw me back, my foot slipped on an icy plank. I would have toppled if Grandfather Edric hadn't thrust his arm out to catch my back. He nearly dropped his load of chicken and grilled asparagus in the process.

"Careful there, son," Grandfather warned. His breath fogged in the chill air, yet he showed no signs of heeding the cold weather. I, on the other hand, shivered and quaked as my wolf ears grew to keep my ears warm with fur. When my teeth started chattering, Grandfather cocked an eyebrow.

"What sort of Grimling trembles so horribly in the cold?" Grandfather asked.

I stuttered, "O-o-one who has *ice* in his soul, G-Grandfather…"

He frowned in consideration. "Hm. Curious. Then, this only came about when you received your new Hallows?"

I nodded in another shiver.

"What of Alexander?"

"H-he isn't af-f-f-fected. He only controls-s ice that already exists. He d-d-doesn't *create* it-t-t—"

"—Your Highness?" Someone called behind me.

With the skin on my face quivering, I glanced over a shoulder, keeping my cloth of food and the kettle of water huddled to my chest. It was Matthiel Inion.

The Howllord wore little more than a thin, ivory cardigan. His raven-black hair whipped past his high cheekbones in the freezing gust that cut through the open deck, yet the blasted man didn't look the least bit discomforted.

Bloody Pyrovokers. I swore to Gods, once Alex and I gained our Death Hallows, *I'd* better get the half that creates fire. Having a soul filled with ice magic in this weather was unbearable.

Matthiel stalked over with hardly a shiver, his grey skin absent of any gooseflesh despite his cleanly shaven chin, sienna eyes looking curiously at me. Even Grandfather Edric was victim to the occasional tremor, though he was Hallowless, so I supposed that gave Matthiel the advantage.

"What's all this?" Matthiel asked as he eyed the load that shuddered in my arms.

My cracked lips shook. "F-f-f-f… for W-Willow…" I gave way to a more violent tremor, some of the water from the kettle spilling and hissing with a wisp of steam onto the deck.

Matthiel promptly took the kettle from my stiff fingers. "Ah, careful! Here, let's lessen that burden." He took the jar of pickled radishes next, frowning. "I suppose Her Highness's cravings have been a bit… indiscriminate?"

My nod came as a rigid shudder. "S-s-she didn't know w-w-what s-s-she want-t-t-ed."

He hummed, moving with Grandfather Edric and me into the warmer, cabin halls. "Well," he said, "I'm glad to see you're going to such lengths for her."

My teeth chattered in reply, still shivering when we arrived at Willow's and my private cabin door.

He handed me back the kettle and radishes, then paused, clasping a relieving warm hand on my padded shoulder. "Don't forget to tend to yourself, hm? She needs you in one piece. Freezing to death would be poor form, I should think."

I trembled there as he walked down the corridor.

Strange… I knew Matthiel still had some loathing for me, in regards to my wife. We'd vied for Willow's favors since we were children, after all, and *I* had been the one to marry her. But now he seemed to have come to terms with it. Still, I wasn't sure how to feel about his helpfulness one way or another.

Grandfather Edric pushed open the cabin door, and I sighed in relief when the small hearth's flames sent a rush of warmth over my pimpled skin, the smoke safely ventilated through the tin pipe leading out of the cabin wall.

My wife sat at her desk by the window. Her long, ashen hair curled to the floor while she scribbled on a ledger in the dim firelight. Her two resurrected vassals, Nikolai and Rossette, surrounded her as if they'd been discussing plans based on her many notes scattered on the desk. Vendy and Dalen were here as well, though they were still ghosts and floating in place while standing over the desk.

My young apprentice, Hugh, was also in his ghost form today and leaning over the papers with a scrunched nose and grown, translucent lion ears. Based on his hard expression, he either wasn't sure what the papers were suggesting, or he was thinking of what else to add to the discussion that hadn't already been broached.

When Grandfather and I entered, everyone glanced up. Willow set down her fountain quill and began to push to her feet.

"D-d-don't get-t up," I insisted while Grandfather and I set down our scavenged items on the table. "We'll bring them t… to you."

She smiled, nodded, and resettled into her chair, rubbing her back in a pained grimace.

Now that I was in a warmer area, I shrugged out of my layers and peeled the scarf off my neck. *Hmm.* It was still rather chilly, despite the hearth.

I plucked one of the empty teacups from Willow's nightstand and refilled it with the kettle's hot water, letting the elderberry leaves drain into the water through the strainer. While that steeped, I brought her the cloth of apples.

"I selected only the best apples," I gloated, smiling while setting down the bundle on the desk in front of her. "Two colors each, split quite evenly down the middle. Just as you like them."

Her lips rolled into a smirk. "You're Deathly set on reminding me why I married you, aren't you, darling?"

"Better to annoy you with affection than have you leave me before our son is born."

"Right good instincts there, son," Grandfather chuckled and unwrapped his findings of chicken and asparagus. "We found the best of what the chefs had to offer, my dear." He clipped over to Willow with his cane to bring her a plate of the meal, setting it beside her on the desk. "I must say, those cats you've picked up certainly are talented. The father knows the proper, nutritious diet for a growing baby, at the least. It's quite impressive. I'm considering offering him a job at one of my Inns."

Willow took the fork and knife he'd provided on the plate and eagerly cut into the glazed chicken. "I suppose that is something to ask Claude," she said. "He is an Infeciovoker as well, so having him on staff would be advantageous for any establishment, given that he can sense poisons and bacteria. And his wife is a Healer, though I'm not sure if you've met her. I think her resurrection may have ended some weeks ago. You said you were Hallowless, sir?"

He curled an arm behind his back. "Please, Edric will do. And yes, no Hallows for me. Lucas inherited his Necrovoking from my mother."

She hummed. "I see. Well, have you been introduced to any of our vassals, sir... er, *Edric?*" She gestured to the crowd of faces—physical and spectral alike—around her. "We've many a ghost with us on this ship. I'm not sure if you've been made aware of which persons have been resurrected versus those who are actually alive."

Grandfather stroked his moustache and inspected Rossette and Nikolai, who were the only two ghosts resurrected here. "No, I don't think I've been introduced properly."

Willow gestured to them. "These are my vassals, Nikolai and Rossette."

Grandfather shook their hands in turn. "Ah, I see! Lovely meeting the vassals of the Death Princess. It's an honor."

I cleared my throat and chimed in beside Willow, "And the *rest...*" I laid a violet-glowing hand on Grandfather's back and evoked my death Hallows, granting him the gift of temporary soul-sight. "... are Alexander and my vassals."

Grandfather staggered backward at the sudden crowd of souls he hadn't seen until now, stammering. "Ah-*ah...!* There were more of you here, then... My apologies."

Dalen's ghost shrugged. "We're used to it."

Vendy grinned and lowered one ghostly rabbit ear. "It's worth it just to see the look on your face."

Hugh looked far too shy to speak, and instead simply waved a spectral hand at my grandfather.

I waved my free hand toward the three in turn, beginning with the rabbit. "This is Vendy, the first of our vassals. She is the niece of a Blacksmith and a brilliant swordswoman." I gestured to Dalen next, whose see-through wings gave a soundless flutter. "And this is our second vassal, Dalen. He is an ex-thief and arms dealer. He and his living brother, Herrin, have been a tremendous help these past years." I ended with the teenaged lion boy, who ducked his head timidly. "And this is Hugh, our latest vassal. He doubles as my apprentice Reaper. His training has been slow going, given all that's happened with our travels and such, but I've had him focus the bulk of his studies on the written etiquettes of reaping until we find a more stable location for him to train with the scythe. I've found a few hours here and there to teach him with wooden blades, but when I'm not available, I've entrusted Vendy to teach him proper form and stances while I've been preoccupied with other matters involving our current mission."

I pushed more of my Hallows into Grandfather's skin under his cloak, letting him see the ghosts for a few moments longer before my magic would leak from his pores, and removed my hand from his back to place it on Hugh's rippling, cold shoulder. "I must say," I hummed. "He's quite the dedicated student. I couldn't be prouder."

Hugh beamed and shrank into the desk bashfully, murmuring. "Th-thank you, Master."

Grandfather peered down at the desk littered with papers and questioned Willow, "Now, what is all this about, my dear?"

Willow tapped a delicate nail over her notes. "We're devising a list of potential disasters that could befall us in the Sky Palace, and forming corresponding strategies."

Grandfather scratched his chin in a nervous laugh. "My, it looks quite… *extensive.*"

"You could say we've developed a depressing penchant for angering other royalty," Willow explained broodingly. "We've learned to prepare for a number of catastrophes."

I went to fetch Willow her tea and examined the notes she and our vassals had accumulated while I was gone.

I rifled through the new notes, scanning them. "Did your father call while I was gone?" I asked.

"He did," she said after sipping her tea. "He and my Mother are to surface to High Everland in the morning to meet with your parents. They plan to secure High Timberail tomorrow evening."

"Remind me where High Timberail is?"

"It's the very eastern coast of High Everland," she explained, circling a hand in the air. "It was the city where I first surfaced."

I grunted. "How fitting."

"I still feel as though we're missing something with this plan," she said in a sigh. "When we arrive at the Sky Palace, who's to say anyone will believe it's truly Roji with us? He's been gone for so long, I can't say I blame his servants for refusing to transfer his calls to the king. Bloods, how many shifters have tried to trick their way into the throne over the years by pretending to be him?"

"I'd wager too many…" I trailed off when I found a piece of parchment nearly buried under the pile, a familiar face painted there with ink and water-color, blue and clear eyes gazing up at me. The words *Praise Shel, for cometh the Shadowblood* were written in bold letters below it.

"What is this?" I asked, carefully peeling out the parchment with my portrait.

Willow glanced at the likeness. "Ah, that's one of the many flyers that were posted throughout High Neverland before we arrived there."

"Why were there flyers of us in High Neverland? No one should have known of us before our visit."

She muttered, "I suspect my grandfather had something to do with it. That particular flyer, though, was given to me by Herrin's new assistant."

"That Seer girl?"

"I believe her name is Marian," said Willow.

I nodded. That had been the girl Herrin and his Enlighteners couldn't find during the months we were encamped outside the capital. Judging from the girl's hideous lacerations on her arms, it seemed the previous queen had indeed cap-tured her, as we'd feared. Had she been the reason the queen found us that day?

"Regardless," said Willow, "Roji's return aside, my real concern lies with your earlier vision. Macarius and Kael may well be in the Sky Palace as we speak. What is our plan if this is true?"

"Apprehend them?" I said. "Have Cilia show herself to Kael?"

"And how will we know—*ah…!*" She winced and pushed a hand to her belly as though our son-to-be had executed a rather strong kick, then com-posed herself again. "How will we know it's them? If Macar is as talented a Decepiovoker as my grandfather claims, I rather doubt he would walk about in his own skin."

I cupped my mouth. "It's possible we'll have to storm the palace by force. Especially if Roji's return doesn't go as we hope. Either way, Roji *must* take over his father's throne. It's perhaps the only way to immediately cease the war with Marincia."

She released a stream of breath through her nose. "Yes… A forced takeover may be necessary. But." She yielded to another wince, pressing a hand on her stomach. "We'll see when we get that far. Now. Let's review the possible sce-narios, shall we? Hugh had thought of a few new items while you were gone, I'd like to keep you informed."

I looked over the list she had written in a ledger, all based on problems we had already run into with previous kings and queens along with a few new additions. "The king attacks us before we dock," I read aloud.

Willow recited the solution that was scribbled beside it. "We have the Death nations' flags up to show we are a neutral party in their war."

I read the next item on the list. "The king refuses to give up his crown to Roji."

"We have Roji appeal to the council to request a forced transferal of power," Willow recited.

"The king has our ships set aflame..."

JAQ

I walked out to the snow-littered deck and let those great little ice flakes hit my scales. *Ahh.* Much better. I was getting sweaty in the cabin, what with everyone lighting their hearths. Warm-blooded jerks. I needed a breather.

I stepped aside to let some of the hired hands pass me on the deck, the blokes messing with the ropes and fumbling with shovels to get rid of this snow. I even saw one winged woman tossing salt over the frozen floorboards for some reason. Maybe it went bad. Did salt go bad?

"Mama!" a small voice whined from the other side of the deck. "Mama, Fuérr won't let go!"

I saw the winged figure of Oliver over there. The little guy was bundled in his thick, wool coat and swallowed in his red-and-black striped scarf. Latched onto his arm, though, was a shivering, hunched over Prince Fuérr.

The green-haired Seadragon was shaking in his boots, keeping low to the floor and looking like he'd drop dead the minute he let go of Oliver.

"Mama!" Oliver whined again, trying to shake off the little prince. "Mama, he's not letting *gooo*...!"

Next to him, Lilli was talking with some of the Airship's personnel, her bat wings draped with velvet wing-warmers.

I grinned and walked over, picking up the tail end of her conversation.

"And you're sure it's no trouble?" she asked the group of women in sleek storm-jackets. They must have been Stormchasers based on the crossbows and quivers of steel arrows strapped to their backs and belts. "He's quite curious. And I would rather he sees what you do in calmer weather like this, than in a dangerous storm."

One of the blue-haired Chasers waved a flighty hand, her wings fluttering. "Ees no problem!" She said in a thick, Culatian accent. "Ees only a little snow. We show him good time."

"And we'll keep 'im close, so don't worry about nothin'," a Landish, brown-feathered bird laughed.

Lilli cupped her hands in delight. "Oh, thank you. We do appreciate—*ahh!*" She winced when Oliver yanked on her wings. "Oliver, please."

"Mama!" He shook his arm again to show that the little prince was still attached to him. "Fuérr won't let go! I can't go if he's dragging me down."

Lilli chuckled and knelt to the boys. "Be nice, darling. Fuérr is only wary of the height. I suspect he finds your wings comforting."

She started talking to the prince in Marincian and reeled him in to her flat chest as if soothing him. The kid let go of Oliver and relaxed in Lilli's arms, shivering just a little less than before as she wrapped her wings around him.

She nodded to Oliver. "Now go on, dear. Have fun. And stay close to them, don't you get lost in those clouds."

"Okay, Mama!" He excitedly stretched his wings, taking off into the sky with the Stormchasers zipping around him.

Lilli sighed as she stared up at them and hefted Fuérr over her shoulder.

I stepped up next to her and scratched my scaly neck. "Goin' on an adventure, uh?"

She flicked her eyes at me, then smiled forward again. "He saw them out there the other day and wanted to see it for himself. He was so excited, I couldn't say no."

"Good for you. He'll learn new stuff doin' new things like that. Should be good for him."

"I do hope so." She stepped away from the ledge.

I glanced over the rail—*ugh*. That's pretty high. Better I stayed more toward the middle of the deck.

I followed Lilli as she sat on the bench that encircled the center mast, keeping Fuérr on her knee, and I sat beside her.

She wore a rose-pink cloak tonight, trimmed with white lace as her fluffy hood wavered in the chilly breeze, stray strands of her silky black hair drifting out in a lulling rhythm. She smelled like flowers again. Now, which one was it this time?

"Lilacs," I said, my grin smug.

She chuckled, looking proud. "Close, but not quite. It's lavender today."

I clicked my tongue. "Can't never tell those two apart."

"I believe that puts me in the lead," she mused. "I have thirty-five points, and you thirty-four. Our draw finally ends."

"Fine, fine, ya cheatin' witch," I snorted. "Ya know I always get the *L*'s all mixed up."

"Indeed, I do know." She was right pleased with herself. "You don't make it difficult by announcing it every time, you realize."

I snorted again, crossing my arms.

Fuérr babbled something to her in Marincian, and she nodded, replied, and the kid hopped off her knee and scurried into the cabin, looking distressed.

"Nature callin'?" I asked.

"Mm-hmm." She leaned back against the mast in a yawn. "I suggested he go to bed early. I don't know how long Oliver will be out there."

I cocked an eyebrow at her. "I'm guessin' you're gonna stay out here till he gets back?"

"Of course." She folded down her hood to let her hair fan out around her slender neck. She was wearing her rose-pink engagement-vines in her hair again.

"Glad you're still likin' the jewelry," I said, pointing to my own head in a gesture.

She gave a blushing smile and fiddled with the glittering vines. "I'm having more trouble taking them off at night." She giggled like a kid. "Alex… well, he's never given me anything like this. When we were young, the most I'd ever gotten from him were elbow pads for training."

I laughed hard. "What a Bloody charmer!" Now I was glad as Void that idiot took the vines I picked out. I was still chuckling when I rubbed my eyes. "Don't worry none, I'll set him straight. Gotta be patient with that one. He don't know nothin' 'bout women."

She sighed and held her cheek lamentingly. "I can't say I know any better about men myself, to be honest. I know he accepted our arrangement officially, so there must be some attraction there, and yet…" She deflated, her wings dipping. "Oh, I don't know. Everything feels so… *awkward* around Alex. I feel like both of us stumble to find any conversation that doesn't involve guard duty. Are we simply a terrible match, Jaq?"

I snorted and waved a dismissive hand. "Aw, don't worry none about all that. You'll probably ease into other things as ya go along. If 'guard duty' is the only thing ya can talk about right now, then talk about it. Try and slip in a personal thing or two. Baby steps."

"Baby steps," she repeated in a mutter. "Right. Very well…" She blushed slightly. "And, er… what sort of 'personal things' are there to mention that we both don't already know about each other? I know what he does all day and he knows what I do. We work together, for Death's sake."

"Well, uh…" I rubbed my scaly chin. "That's, er… huh. All right, yeah, that limits some things…"

She groaned. "Oh, we're never going to reach anything past work mates, are we?"

"You will, you will!" I insisted, shaking my head. "Look—just slip in a few… *suggestive* things every now and then, yeah? Catch him off-guard, have him think about you *without* armor."

Her blush deepened. "I would die of embarrassment."

"You wouldn't have to actually do it. I mean, unless you really wanted to—*ow!*"

She punched my shoulder in a laugh. "I am *not* doing that!"

"All right, all right! So just suggest it. Slip in the occasional lewd mention to get him thinkin' about it."

Her stare flattened. "That is hardly work-appropriate conversation, Jaq."

"Then talk about it during break!" I threw up my hands. "Anything! Bloods, you're just as bad as he is with seducing. I'm gonna have to teach you *and* him at this rate."

She gave me a pointed look, but smirked. "And I suppose you're such the expert to teach either of us, are you?"

"Damn right I am." I flicked a thumb over my nose and winked. "Back home, *all* the ladies wanted to fight with an Everlander's sword."

"Oh, yes," she muttered and crossed her arms. "And I'm sure they all saw more than the tip after you unsheathed the blade, did they?"

I paused and gawked at her. "Did you just…" I ditched the peasant speech and spoke properly. "High Howless! I do believe you just struck me with a *lewd* quip?"

She flushed pink, but grinned. "I can be lewd if I so choose."

"Then why can't you say that sort of thing around Alex? What is the difference?"

"I just… oh, it's just different with you. I don't feel awkward at every turn when we talk, but I could never speak that way with Alex. Perhaps he's just too… *serious?* And besides." She sighed, her wings dipping depressively. "Alex doesn't think of me that way… At least, I don't think he does. It's difficult to tell."

"He's marrying you," I muttered flatly. "If you didn't arouse him to some level, he wouldn't even consider it."

And now she was the purest hue of scarlet. "But he's never said—"

"He doesn't need to say it." I slipped back into my peasant speech to level with her. "Look, Alex isn't the most vocal guy when it comes to his emotions. He's all action. So, *you* have to be all action to get him talking." I lightly punched her shoulder. "Trust me. I've known Alex for a long time. He decided to go through with your arrangement, and when he decides something, it's one Void of a feat to change his mind. When he gave you those vines, he pounded that decision in stone. He knows he's going to marry you soon enough, so he obviously knows you two will eventually…"

Ow. Ow? I swallowed the knot in my throat. Weird. I restarted, "You two will eventually…"

Ow, ow, OW…! I pinched my adam's-apple, swallowing again. What in Death?

"Jaq?" Lilli touched a hand to my forehead. "You look ill."

Bloods, her hand was warm… Normally, I didn't let anyone touch my scales there, where my 'Grimling' scar was puckered. But she already knew about it. She didn't care. So, I didn't care.

"I'm fine," I assured, grinning as she lowered her fingers.

She lifted an eyebrow. "Are you getting motion sickness again? If you vomit on me—"

"I'm fine. You know, this ship ride isn't as bad as the one in the water. It's way smoother. Haven't been sick even once this trip."

She folded her arms, glaring at me suspiciously. "Best not to tempt it, then, hadn't we?"

"Heh, right." I sniffed and rubbed a finger under my nose. "What were we talking about?"

"Alexander and my impending marriage, I believe," she offered with a prim wave.

I snapped a finger. "Right. Anyway, like I was saying: He wouldn't have bothered giving you vines if he didn't want to marry you, right?"

She hummed blithely, fiddling with her vines again. "I suppose. And they are my favorite color. I didn't think he knew, honestly. I expected him to give me the standard, clear diamonds. So, he must have been paying attention?"

My eye twitched. That bastard didn't notice jack shit. That was all me.

"Yeah." I grumbled, grinding my teeth. Well, damn it. I couldn't say anything without making Alex look bad. I went on, "Anyway… with vines, comes a wedding. With a wedding, comes a wedding night. If Willow and Xavier are any indication, Alex is well aware that you guys gotta have at least one night of…"

Death, why was it hard to breathe?

Lilli crossed her legs expectantly. "Of sex?"

—Thump!

What was that? Did someone slip on the deck? Or was that from my ribs?

"Honestly, Jaq," she chided, her cheeks only a slight pink now. "We've already established that I can be lewd if I so choose. Toeing the line is hardly necessary."

I-I can't breathe.

Cawing sounded overhead, and my crow, Bridge, swooped down to my lap, shuddering frantically. She knew something was wrong.

"Bloods, I knew it," Lilli sniffed and rose while her own crow, Dusk, alighted on the bench beside her. She slung my arm over her shoulder. "You *are* ill again. Come, hurry inside. If you vomit on me, I'll—"

"I-I'm fine." I ripped out of her hold and scrambled for the cabin, slamming the door shut behind me.

Don't you dare, Jaq. I clocked myself in the head. *Don't you Gods damned dare…!*

LILLI

"Idiot." I scowled at the door where Jaq had disappeared to. Then I glanced at Dusk from my shoulder. "Well, better he vomits in the lavatory than on me, I suppose."

Dusk fluffed her chest feathers and shook her head.

"I'm sure he'll want some of Claude's cabbage stew," I hummed, drawing up my hood and started for the cabin. "It certainly helped him on the last ship ride, perhaps it will help again here."

I reached for the door. But it swung open on its own.

Alexander paused under the doorway, his mismatched eyes regarding me with surprise.

"Oh," Alex said, glancing over his shoulder into the cabin. "Lilli. Do you know what's gotten into Jaq? He dashed off looking rather green."

I sighed and stepped past him through the doorway. "He's sick again, as he was in the last ship. Don't worry, I'm getting him stew from the galley."

"I see…" He cleared his throat behind a fist. "Er, Lilli…"

I stopped. "Yes?"

"I've done some thinking," he began, hesitating. He cleared his throat a second time. "And considered what my Grandfather Edric had said some weeks ago… I know you expected a union last year, and clearly, it was… delayed. I thought I should try to amend that."

I frowned. "How so?"

"I've spoken with Prince Roji. He's offered his palace as a potential venue, should things fair well when we arrive." Another cough. "That is, if you'd prefer…"

"The Sky Palace?" I clutched my cloak, my wings growing stiff. "I hadn't given it much thought."

"Well. *Khm-kmm*, as my grandfather stated, we don't know when we'll return to Grim… And although Willow and Xavier hadn't bothered with a ceremony, they apparently found it pertinent to wed in Neverland while they were both capable and, well… *alive…*"

There was a strained silence, our breaths fogging in the chilled, snowy air.

"Since we are in times of war," he added awkwardly. "I thought perhaps we could follow their example. You needn't answer now—"

"Yes!" I blurted, wings perking straight up. Bloods, my heart was shrieking with joy. "Yes, I… I would love the Sky Palace as a venue."

Alex exhaled and tugged his lapel. "Good. Very good. I'll… inform Roji, then." He coughed one last time into his fist and strode outside.

"Alex?" I called.

He twisted back. "Hmm?"

My hands clenched, shivering both from the cold and my now surging pulse. *He's all action,* Jaq had said. *So, I have to be all action as well.*

I swallowed the sick knot in my throat, lifted my chin and stepped up to Alex—then pressed my lips against his, holding them there and feeling his soft breath—

He pushed me away, looking shell-shocked. Yet, he kept hold of my shoulders.

"I…" He stammered, his face flushed red. He looked at me, darted his gaze away, then back at me. He sighed, seeming to come to terms with something, and pulled me in to peck my cheek.

"Yes, well…" He rigidly let me go, retreating toward the helm's deck. "Good night, I suppose…" He fled up the stairs.

I drifted inside and gently closed the cabin door, cutting off the bitter wind as I fell back against the door. *I did it,* I realized in disbelief. *Bloody Death, I did it! Oh, Nira, it was so… so…!*

So underwhelming.

I frowned at Dusk on my shoulder, the crow's wings dipping in disappointment. All that build up, all that excitement leading up to it, and then… I felt nothing. Was this how it normally felt with couples? Willow always looked so entranced when Xavier kissed her. So in love.

Perhaps I do need lessons, I considered. I'd always excelled at my Reaper training with the scythe, why did I know next to nothing about *these* things—?

The door to the deck burst open, and a flurry of snow flooded inside.

Oliver came panting in, looking frightened. "Mama! Mama!" He tugged the hem of my coat urgently. "We gotta stay inside for a bit! Don't go out until the storm goes away!"

My brow furrowed. "What storm?"

14

CHANGE OF PLANS

ROJI

TRANSLATED FROM CULATIAN

"There it is, lil Sis." I fanned a hand out toward the cluster of dark cumulonimbi. Sparks of light burst from inside there, making my feathers stand on end. I sucked in a reviving breath and let my soul charge with the distant electricity. "Dragon's Nest… home."

Behind me, Zyl twirled around the upper mast, her wings gliding her feet off the deck as she laughed and stuck out her tongue to catch the snow. "Ushar above, it feels so good to be this close to the storms again…!"

I stretched my wings while keeping the helm steady and grinned wide. "Been a long time since I've seen those clouds. We're half an hour in. Zyl, can you take the helm?"

She swirled down the mast and flicked the snow off her wings before pulling her emerald goggles over her eyes with a toothy smile. "Got'cha, Big Brother. Where're you going?"

"To find Mini and the kids." I let Zyl take the pegs in my place, rubbing my gloved hands together for warmth while trotting to the stairs. "I want to make damn sure they get their illusions ready before we step one talon on any of the capital isles."

I hopped on the stair rail and slid down with my boots, flexing my wings and flying the rest of the way down, my feathers catching the brisk wind.

When I landed on the main deck, one of those Reaper twins saw me and waved me down. It was the short-haired one, Alex. His steps left prints in the snow when he trotted over.

"Roji," he said and cleared his throat before speaking in Landish. "<Lilli has accepted the palace as a venue. That is, if the offer still stands?>"

"<Sure.>" I replied in his tongue and cracked my neck to the side. "<'Course, might want to wait till I see exactly what the situation is with my old man. All of our com calls still haven't gone through to him.>"

He nodded. "<Keep me updated. We'll be prepared for anything that may come.>"

"<Sky, do I hope so.>" I saluted him and went inside.

Bloods, this was going to be hard. And not just with taking Pops' crown. I had a whole Gods damned country to run. A country that might not even want me back. And then there was the question of *how* I was getting it back.

I rubbed my sore neck, yawning on my way through the halls. Up ahead, I saw the gold-haired queen, Anabelle, walking my way. I tucked my wings in to let her pass as two of her guard dogs trailed her as per freaking usual.

"<Evenin' Land,>" I greeted in Landish as she passed. "<Get ready to dock, you hear?>"

She smiled. "<Oh, wonderful. I shall tell the rest of my fleet.>"

We went our separate ways. Then a thought hit me and I stopped.

"<Say Land,>" I began again, twisting back. "<How'd you go about getting your crown back?>"

She was still smiling, her voice soft and sweet. "<I ripped off the old queen's head.>"

I swallowed nervously. "<Ah. Right… Hopefully I won't have to do that with my old man, heh…>"

"<Do let me know if I can help in any way.>"

I tossed her a noncommittal finger and turned my grimace into a smile. "<Yep, sure. Will do. If I need any heads rolling, you'll be the first one I call.>"

She nodded dismally, then went on her way.

I swirled forward and smacked my lips, head shaking. "Bloods, that woman has one Void of a violent streak."

So much for Relicblood-to-Relicblood advice. I didn't want any head-ripping if I could help it. *Looks like this takeover will have to be done Sky style:*

With some good old-fashioned dramatic flair.

XAVIER

Crrr—crack!

I jolted upright, the ledger nearly flying out of my fingers as the explosive burst shook the entire ship. Willow was shocked stiff beside me, her fox ears fully grown, and the others were spooked frozen around us. Grandfather Edric looking to me for an explanation I didn't have.

Crack! KrPOW!

I yelped when the ship jerked to the left and threw me to the floor.

"What in Bloods is happening?!" Willow shouted over the torrent of explosive lightning.

"Stay where you are!" I yelled and fumbled to my feet before throwing open the door and using the walls to steady myself from the erratic tremors. I stumbled outside to the deck, immediately drenched in rain, gusts pushing me left and right, twisters streaming the cloudy terrain like playful dancers at a festival, sparks of lightning brightening the sky.

The ship jerked to the right, throwing me on my back and forcing my gaze up at the suddenly blackened clouds that had only moments before been bright and filled with pleasant snow.

—RrrrrrrrrrAAAGGGGGGGGHHHHRrrrrrrr…!

The thunderous roar crashed and echoed from above, and a shadow rushed over my head and brought gusts so strong, I ducked in a start and braced to keep myself from being blown forward.

Then a monstrous, ten-story high, serpentine *dragon* slithered and soared round our vessel, its scales glinting like powerful bolts of pink and blue lightning spidering in a maelstrom of chaotic fireworks. Bloods be good, it was a Shockdragon.

And Prince Roji was riding it.

"Roji!" I screamed at the swallow shifter while his new pet flew above my head a second time. "What about our plans?!"

From atop his wild mount, Roji looked down at me through emerald goggles. His childish grin was insatiably wicked with thrill as he shouted down, "I didn't like 'em!"

MACARIUS

The Sky Palace's conference room was in a riot. Council members, advisors, and generals alike fought to out-yell each other, though none of their ire was meant for themselves. It was all aimed at the senile king who sat on his hovering chair in front of the several vision-screens that littered the wall behind him, all displaying different faces of his Stormchasers who were stationed in the Ocean realm's frosted capital. The soldiers were awaiting their orders to march. But those of the council were trying to prevent the march in the first place.

"<This *must* stop, your majesty!>" One of Rojired's green-feathered council members shouted in Culatian from his seat along the conference table, where the rest of the members were arguing. "<If we order the march on the Ocean Palace, I fear we will lose unnecessary lives in the process! It isn't worth the risk over an *assumption!*>"

Agreeing hollers were piped around the table. Kael and I, in our winged disguises, carefully sat back in our seats on either side of the sickly Sky King, holding our tongues. There were far too many council members against the marching order, I knew there was no way for me to persuade them otherwise. At least, not without risking a physical brawl.

Rojired hacked into a kerchief and rumbled. <"It is... no assumption, Nugkevf! I saw my daughter in that water-dwelling pit myself...!>"

"<At the same time Death and Dream were visiting!>" Another member shouted. "<It's far more likely she was traveling with them on her own accord!>"

"<If you refuse to stop the march,>" a third member growled, "<We will force your abdication from the throne until your daughter returns—!>"

CRrrrrrACK!

Everyone jumped out of their seats at the burst of thunder, the bolt so sudden and powerful that it shook the very palace itself and flashed through the windowed walls with a blinding white light.

There was silence. Then, in a not-so-subtle build, it began to pour, the windows weeping with a sudden flood of rain. Spurts of light blinked through the blur of water as the storm worsened. Thunder swelled and flourished into a terrifying battalion of frightful crashes and tremendous blasts that cut through the heavy downpour and sliced into the howling gale.

There was a swell of murmurs from the council members as they hurried to the windows.

I would have joined them, but a sudden vibration burst alive from my coat pocket. I hurriedly fished out my silver communicator. It was my dearest step-daughter calling.

I nodded at Kael, and he followed me as I led us out to the corridor, answering the call with a piqued growl, "Genevieve," I began testily. "Is this storm your party's doing?"

"It is, Father," Genevieve replied through the com. She looked rather shaken herself, hidden in what looked to be an empty cabin room on their ship. *"Sky is coming to claim his throne."*

"Bloody Void..." I wasn't ready. I hadn't found Sky's Relic, I needed more time. If Sky could do this much, and Land was as powerful as Genevieve claimed, and the Shadowblood's abilities were strengthening as well...

Venom leaking from my fangs, I turned to Kael. "We must leave."

CILIA

Pots clattered with a storm of noise in the Airship's galley, and the soup Claude had prepared crashed to the floor, splattering his and Mikani's shoes.

The kitchen staff shrieked with fright, proclaiming the maelstrom outside was an ill omen from Ushar.

Or, I thought as my cat ears grew and I stomped out of the kitchens, keeping myself steady on a pillar while I glared round the galley, *a certain Relicblood of ours may have gone rogue.*

The last time an unnatural storm hit, the Sky Princess was to blame. But was it her, or her brother now?

Ah, the Sky Prince's family was still here in the galley eating their meals. Good. I made my way toward the Ocean Princess and her young daughters, the lunging ship making my otherwise straight path jagged and queasy.

"Where is your husband?!" I demanded of Dalminia.

The Seadragon woman sighed, seeming neither frightened of me nor the storm. "He is where you think."

"Then what in Ushar's name is he doing?!"

The woman shrugged, calmly eating her soup. "He does as he pleases, usually. Not to worry. He knows to keep the dangerous play away from the fleet."

I muttered. "How reassuring."

Another crash hit outside, shaking the whole damned ship.

Crrrr-CHRCK!

Our vessel slammed to a dead stop.

Dazed, I rushed to a window and peered outside. We had docked? So quickly? *And in one piece,* came the surprising, yet relieving, afterthought.

My gaze narrowed at the dark clouds outside the window's rain-spattered glass. It seemed the Sky Prince did indeed know what he was doing. Thank Ushar for His son's skill. If not his lack of finesse.

While the other passengers were still collecting their wits, I climbed upstairs to the main cabin, rushing through the halls. Doors were opening, everyone murmuring, shouting, demanding to know what in Void was going on.

I found the Death Princess with her husband storming to Dream and Crysa, baby Eryn wailing in her arms.

"What is he doing?!" Death demanded shrilly, her white hair a tangled mess. "We've spent months devising these plans! This was *not* part of them!"

Dream sounded out of breath, as if the shock of the sudden storm still had him winded. "I should have expected this, blast it... Sky always had a habit of brushing off our careful planning. More specifically, *Death's* careful planning. He always found it amusing."

"Wonderful!" Death threw up her hands, stomping back to her private cabin with one hand keeping her inflated belly afloat and the other pressed to her back in a grimace. "Now we have to expedite everything else!" Her azure gaze snapped to me, and her grown fox ears curled back in a murderous glare. "What do *you* want, demon witch?"

I mused sarcastically, "Forgive me for being concerned with the sudden storm in which the entire ship is in an uproar about. How dare I possess the Clean Ones' trait of rational curiosity."

She turned up her prim nose in a scoff. "Oh, bat off, will you? Do something useful and inform our *helpful* Ancients that we're storming the palace posthaste."

I gave an ostentatiously 'gracious' bow, my sing-song voice dripping with as much admiration you'd find a connoisseur of fine wines giving to the cheapest tavern ale. "Oh, as you wish, your high-Cleanliness."

I stalked past them and stepped out to the icy deck, lunging over the rail. Below me, men tending the docks were far too busy scrambling away from the storm to care that our fleet of ten ships had arrived unannounced without explanation. The city was bright with colorful lights, looming, metal towers with lightning rods and cables crisscrossing every which way that made the city look like a beautiful, sparkling web.

And at the center of the web was its spider: Prince Roji. His scarlet wings and feathered hair sparked with electric bolts, pink and blue zaps glowing all around him as his serpentine steed slithered and swirled in the air with such thrill, it seemed to forget about the world around it.

In the distance, I saw the glistening, glass-paneled towers of Culatia's royal palace.

Kael.

If he was truly there with Macarius, he was surely watching this spectacle. And knowing that snake, he wouldn't want to stay and wait to be discovered.

My teeth sharpened, and I stepped onto the rail, inhaling a deep breath before letting out a high pitched, hideous shriek while pushing my Weight to feel the nearby Fera of this realm. Within a mere few seconds, a black, dripping creature with boney, leathery wings soared down to me. Its skeletal face screeched at me obediently as it bowed, its sharp spine cracking as it lowered to welcome my foot.

I mounted the beast and commanded in a blazing voice, "Forward."

The creature's disjointed limbs lurched and took to the sky, speeding toward the palace. The heavy rain spattered my face and whipped back my drenched hair wildly, the harsh gusts pushing my beast's wings erratically. I'd just reached the city's streets—

A flash of light illuminated the city below me, and I caught two figures hustling through an alley. One had a head of drenched, black hair, which he soon hid under a cowl and ducked round a corner with his hooded companion.

Kael? My pulse thundered in time with the storm.

I ordered my winged beast to land, and once I leapt onto the street, I broke into a sprint to follow where the pair had gone. Though when I turned the corner, I slammed into a crowd of scurrying winged shifters. They were frightened. Confused. Praying to Ushar for this strange storm to settle. There were so many shifters… But where had Kael gone?

The crowd gasped suddenly when every enormous Vision-screen blinked to life in the square. They were all displaying the same image.

And, of course, it was Sky and his Shockdragon steed, whooping and laughing within the heart of the surging storm.

The once frightened screams suddenly turned to stunned silence. Then cheers.

I shoved through the now elated mass, searching for any sign of black hair. Some idiot in a sleek raincoat was standing in my way, and I pushed him aside.

"Ah!" exclaimed the man I had just pushed, his Culatian accent thick. "So this ees Weight that shoved Thörd earlier! What joyous day! Ees being Thörd's beautiful grey-haired kitten! You visit at most fun time, my kitten!"

I snapped my baffled gaze at the man, blinking the rain from my lashes.

Gardener sow me, it was Thörd the Thunderous—Culatia's ruling Demon King. Thörd was a Skydragon shifter with leathery, lavender wings. His white pupils shone brightly against his dark scales from under the shade of his cowl. His once silky lavender hair had apparently undergone a dreading since last I saw him, with but one strand left untouched and braided beside his shaven chin.

"Thörd," I greeted in a rumble, stopping beside Culatia's Demon King. I nodded at him tersely. "At least that's one man we haven't a need to find anymore… Come with me. There is someone else I must find before he disappears."

"That someone ees the returned Sky Prince, no?" Thörd asked, following close behind me with an amused smirk. One of his leathery dragon wings lifted above my head and served as an umbrella while he folded his scaled arms behind his back. His head cocked at me, quivering the lavender braid of hair at his chin. "Why ees my kitten's pupils being the black ones?"

"It's an illusion." I raised my adorned finger to show him the enchanted ring Dream had given me. "And of course, I'm not Bloody looking for the Sky Prince. I came with him."

Thörd's scaly brow lifted. "What news! My kitten brings Thörd such fun gifts to being entertained! Thörd is most joyed."

"Thörd, either be of use and help me find who I'm looking for, or fly off and play with someone else." I shoved another shifter aside, searching the shops along the street. *Still no sign of Kael.*

Thörd's webbed ears flicked. "Who ees kitten looking for so strong like?"

I growled, "My husband."

Thörd held a hand to his heart, his tone pained. "*Skrii* be cruel! My kitten picked another soul to be sharing afterlife with! Why, kitten? Thörd was here waiting—"

"He was my husband *before* I died, you scale-brained idiot," I snapped. "It is an exhaustingly long story, of which I have no time to explain. I must find him before he's taken from me again."

Thörd's webbed ears folded down. "What kitten's love look like? Thörd can find him from skies and push his Weight to locate."

I gave him a narrow look. "Neither my Weight nor yours will do any good. He is a Clean One."

Thörd frowned, scratching his scaled chin in confusion. "But kitten died too long time backward… how Clean One ees being alive?"

"As I said." My tone heated, annoyance burning. "It is a long story. If you find a black-haired cat with yellow eyes, tell me. But do not touch him. He will likely poison your soul."

Thörd looked even more perplexed. "Thörd ask his kitten what she means later. But Thörd will do this for his kitten."

He leapt up and soared overhead, another flash of light sparking from the storm as he disappeared.

Kael. My heart drummed painfully as I stalked the bustling streets. *Do not leave me again.*

15

SOUL OF SKY

ROJI

Ahhh yeah! This was the life!

I whooped and hollered as the dragon under me whirled and twisted between the tall powerlines and tangled cables that swept across the lively city. Colored lights blinked and flashed from vision-screens in the streets, and flying shifters yelped and dove out of my dragon's way.

Then it spiraled downward inside a domed amphitheater where electric music blasted from a live band.

Ah, there's bound to be cameras filming here, I thought with a mischievous grin, *Perfect place to make my return known.*

When I hopped off the dragon and landed on the stage, the music screeched to a halt, and I plucked an electric guitar from one of the musicians and ripped a vicious riff down the neck, sinking to my knees as the distorted notes sang under my fingers. Sky, I felt like a teen again!

The stunned audience suddenly erupted into cheers, the band on the stage laughing in shocked thrill. I let the last note hang on the highest string, tossing the guitar to its owner, who fumbled to catch it by the neck.

I ripped off the nearest microphone and yelled, "*Sky,* it's good to be back!"

More cheers followed me as I remounted my dragon and zipped out of there, bolting toward my old pad like lightning itself. The glass and metal palace was just as I remembered it: Tall, spikey with lightning rods and tangled in a net of cables.

I patted my dragon's neck. "Thanks for the lift, buddy! It's been fun!"

The dragon gave a laughing growl as I hopped off and spread my wings, diving for the palace courtyard.

A flurry of startled screams sounded as I rushed by the servants in the yard, then sped through the corridors, through the ballroom, and shoved open the throne room, where I finally touched down to land, panting with a wide grin.

Pops wasn't here. But a bunch of servants were.

"Where is he?" I asked with a fist at my side.

The servants apparently already knew who I meant, their mouths gaping wide as one of them shakily pointed down the next hall to the left and answered, "C-conference room 3…"

"Great, thanks." I tossed him a two-fingered salute and stalked in that direction on foot. Once I reached the right room, I *slammed* open the doors.

The winged bodies inside jumped.

There, at the head of the conference table, standing in front of a ton of vision-screens that lit up the wall, was my old, sickly father.

Bloods, Pops looked terrible. His feathers were molted and his dark skin was spotted with purple stains, his scarlet eyes sunken and foggy.

The storm still raged outside, and not a damn soul stopped me while I crossed the room, halted before Pops, and put fists at my sides.

"Evenin', Pops," I said. "Long time no see."

Pops blinked at me, dumbstruck. "R… Roji? What in Sky's name—"

"*This* Sky has a problem that needs fixing," I interrupted. "You weren't answering my calls, so I thought I'd deliver the message in person."

He was still staring befuddled at me. "Message…?"

"Stop the war with Marincia," I bent down to meet his eyelevel and gave him a narrow glare. "Or give up your crown so *I* can."

Pop's face turned a blistering red. "You… you have no right to just waltz in here and…!" He fell into a coughing fit suddenly, desperately grabbing a kerchief from his pocket and shoved it over his mouth as the hacking wouldn't let up.

"Option B it is!" I snatched the shiny crown from his balding head and set it atop mine. It fit pretty nice, I thought. I twisted to the crowd of council members, spreading my hands. "Anyone here got a problem with this?"

The room fell silent. Then a burst of thunder shocked from outside, and one of the councilmen laughed. Hysterically. The rest of them joined him, most trying to hide their snickering.

"Didn't think so." I turned back to Pops and shrugged. "Sorry, Pops. Look on the Brightside: you get to retire early. Now…"

I twisted to the many vision-screens that brightened the wall. The feather-headed faces there were all staring at me in shock, speechless as they waited outside the frozen city of *Yu'nn Quisette*. They were in scarlet armor, their shoulder-guards and breastplates decorated with all kinds of medals and fancy decorations, marking them as high-ranking generals or captains.

"Right," I huffed, looking at all the faces with a stern frown. "Which one of you is in charge of our military these days?"

One of the helmeted women lifted a hesitant finger. *"I... I am, your majesty..."*

I clapped my hands, wings fluttering. "Raya! Wassup, girl? Looks like you got a promotion since I was gone, huh? Mind doing me a quick favor and pulling back our troops? We're ending this war."

Raya pushed out a relieved breath. *"Thank Sky..."*

XAVIER

After leaving the docks and taking a cable-car to the royal isles—having had to console my height-hating wife the entire time as she clung to her bat-winged Aide with trembling arms—we arrived at the Sky Palace gates.

Zylveia triumphantly led the way into her towering home, our boots squeaking and pooling with rainwater thanks to her brother's little display earlier. The storm had died in time for our Airship to dock haphazardly, much to Zylveia's frustration when she took control of the wheel as our stand-in pilot, but we still hadn't had a chance to dry off. We were drenched from head to foot, having donned our rubber-like coats too late. My hair was sticking to my neck and my wolf ears dripped to my cold shoulders, and one look at Grandfather Edric's similarly dripping wolf ears told me the elderly man shared my poor opinion regarding our reckless method of arrival. Grandfather muttered something profane under his breath and desperately tapped the water out of his dampened smoking pipe.

Alexander hung at my side fully plated, glowering and refusing to acknowledge that he slipped almost every step of the way. His small squadron marched exhaustedly around my wife and me, Octavius seeming more accustomed to the rain than the rest of us. Dream and Crysalette were muttering amongst themselves, yawning, speaking with Roji's wife in Marincian.

Willow, beside me, was the pure vision of piqued. She scowled so drastically, her brow was riddled with wrinkles, her long hair sopping wet and hot skin steaming the water dry.

"Oltro!" Zylveia called at the front in Culatian, her voice bouncing through the halls. *"Oltrorofv!"*

El came trotting to her side, jabbering in Culatian in suppressed giggles. The two seemed to be sharing a reminiscent moment together, gesturing to paintings, wall fixtures and the like.

Then a wheezing voice sounded from the corridor. "Garrach…!" It sounded painful for the man to speak, as if this pitiful gasp was the loudest his wind-pipes could produce. "Garrach!"

Zylveia's wings fluttered at the voice, and her smile fell before she stalked to the sickly old man who rounded the corner in a hovering, mechanical chair.

"*Papa!*" She said, her face scrunching into a scowl as she set her hands on her hips, blathering at full speed in their tongue, as if scolding him.

"Sorrowed Death," I murmured to Willow under my breath. "Is that the Sky King?"

Willow's saddened tone confirmed it. "His illness has taken its toll."

The withered old man's gaze flicked in our direction, noticing us. Willow and I took our cue and stomped our dripping selves over to meet him.

I spat out a wet strand of hair from my mouth. "Where is he?"

Rojired's expression sagged with unspeakable exhaustion, clearly know-ing whom I meant. The sickly man sighed and gave a feeble nod down the hall.

"He is… being in… conference room," he said in stilted Landish. Then he squinted an eye at Willow. "You be ones to… bringing back daughter…?"

"Yes," chewed Willow, pleasantries abandoned. She curtly gestured for Zylveia to lead us to the conference room.

As I followed them, I twisted back to see Rojired shake his head, looking solemn and depressed. Then the elderly man hovered his lethargic chair in the opposite direction as we went on our way.

After several minutes of exploring the wide corridors, voices could be heard from a partly opened door. Zylveia pushed it open, letting us file inside.

Prince Roji—no, *King* Roji—was swirling his father's crown with a lazy finger. The headpiece revolved round and round like a trivial plaything. The new king was reclined over a chair in the conference room, kicking his crossed feet while he spoke with King Ninumel of Marincia on a large vision-screen.

"<Yeah, I've already called back my Stormchasers,>" Roji assured in Ninumel's watery language. "<Don't sweat it, bro. This war's as over as my dad's feather-modeling days—>"

"<Daddy!>" little Mavis exclaimed in Marincian suddenly from her moth-er's coattails behind Willow and me. The hybrid fish-bird shoved past us and flew into her father's lap rather ungracefully. "<Daddy, that was fun! Do it again! Do it again!>"

Roji chuckled and ruffled her scarlet, feathered hair. "<Maybe later, Mavis. Daddy's got some things to talk about with your Uncle Mel.>"

Mavis looked at the scaled man on the screen, one of her webbed ears flicking up.

Ninumel's face creased with an interesting combination of confusion, horror, disgust, and intrigue. "<What is that thing?>"

"<That *thing*,>" Roji's wife huffed and strode in front of the screen, holding her younger daughter in her arms. "<Is your niece.>"

The Ocean King's scales drained Deathly pale. "Dalminia?! <Rin be blessed, is it really you, sister?!>"

Young Fuérr ran beside Dalminia with wide, emerald eyes, and his little arms reached for the screen as the boy began to cry. "*Papa!*"

"*Fuérr!*" Ninumel's attention drifted from the rest of us and fixed solely on his son. The man was practically sobbing now, speaking with Fuérr, Dalminia and Roji only. They were discussing family matters.

I caught Roji's attention and gestured a silent question of 'should we leave?'. He nodded his agreement, and we left the family to their reunion.

Back out in the corridor, Willow muttered, "I'm still going to kill him for that storm."

"Darling, please," I chided. "Think of the baby. *I'll* kill him."

I started through the corridors, tapping into my mental connection with our vassals. "Dalen, Vendy, and Hugh? Please sweep the palace grounds for any signs of Macarius and Kael. If they were here before we arrived, there's still a chance they're here now."

Dalen's voice fuzzed in my thoughts, *I'm on it.*

Me, too, Vendy affirmed dutifully.

Hugh's nervous voice stammered last, *R-right away, Master!*

When the connection ended, I felt a tad more at ease. According to Kael and Dream, Macarius was only a Somniovoker and a Decepiovoker, so the likelihood that he'd have soul-sight was all but impossible. Having ghosts as scouts would be advantageous here. *Unless he had the foresight to get soul-seeing masks,* I considered broodingly.

Alexander rolled back a plated shoulder at my side. "We'll search inside. Octavius, Neal." He threw his head at them, tossing a signaling hand. "Keep watch with them here. The rest of you, stay together and search the quadrants. Keep your coms in hand. If you see anything—*anything*—inform me immediately. Do not engage, and for Death's sake, do not separate. You have less a chance of being poisoned if you're together."

Jaq, Lilli and Matthiel saluted with fists to their chests, then withdrew down the corridor with their glowing scythes drawn.

I nodded to Alex and watched as he searched our current hall, opening doors and inspecting the rooms one by one.

The others stayed clustered together, Willow and I taking the lead as we cautiously moved through the halls, Neal and Octavius guarding our flanks.

"I should think with that storm," murmured Willow, her fox ears alert, "they would have had plenty of warning to flee."

"Warning or no," I said, "There's still a chance they stayed. I don't wish to take any chances."

She hummed low. "I'm sure my grandfather shares your sentiments…" She paused, turning to look about the group. "Hang on. Where has he gone?"

I craned to look myself, seeing the young king was nowhere to be found in our herd. I glanced at his rust-haired wife. "Crysalette, where is Dream?"

Crysalette hefted her fox eared baby over her shoulder, patting his back. "He went to search on his own. He promised a swift return."

"I'm sure he did." I rubbed my lids. "I only hope he knows what he's doing."

MATTHIEL

"Any sign of the hostiles?" Alexander asked from the com screen I held.

I didn't slow my pace in the corridor beside Lilliana and Jaqelle, shaking my head. "None, Captain. We'll search the north and south quadrants next."

He nodded, growling, *"Keep me updated."*

I saluted with a fist to my chest. "Yes, Sir."

The call ended, and I hooked the com around my ear, in case I needed to contact the captain quickly without the screen… normally, this duty would have been assigned to Lieutenant Jaqelle, but he'd been a bit distracted since we arrived—for whatever reason—so the duty fell upon my shoulders instead.

To my right, Lilliana murmured, "What are we expected to do if we find the snake and his pet Infeciovoker? It's not as though we can apprehend a poison-spewer."

I grunted. "The captain instructed us not to engage, so I suspect we simply report his whereabouts while staying out of reach." I pried a finger into my visor's slit and wiped a drop of sweat from my lashes. Death, but this helm was sweltering. I glanced at Jaqelle to my left. "What say you, Lieutenant? Any plans if we meet the hostiles?"

Jaqelle tossed his head to the side, his gaze strangely locked onto the windowed walls. "If we find them, shoot them with Shockspheres and lock them in a room."

I muttered, "Ah… Yes, Sir…" *As if it will be that simple,* I thought flatly.

This was a most peculiar, modern palace. The ceilings were incredibly tall on every floor. The winged staff and guards flew freely through the metal buttresses and decorative archways, which looked more like open tunnels made of reinforced, polished steel that left a mirror-like shine in the many chandeliers' bright lights.

Jaqelle still stared out the long windows, as if mulling over a thought.

"You have concerns for the plan?" I asked.

"Huh?" Jaqelle's head snapped to me, his thoughts seeming to dissolve. "Oh, uh… No, that's the best we can hope for right now. But something tells me they're already gone."

"And what tells you that, then?"

Jaqelle rubbed a finger under his nose and sniffed, thankfully doing away with his ridiculous, pauper dialect and taking the matter seriously. "One would think with that storm Roji summoned," he said, "That they had plenty of warning to flee. I think it more likely they've taken shelter in one of the main islands in the city."

I scowled at him. "You don't think they would simply leave the Sky realm altogether?"

"I don't think so, no." He pushed up his eyeglasses from inside his visor's slit. Honestly, that man needed to invest in a pair of eye-lenses for this line of work. Jaqelle went on, looking at his messenger crow, Bridge, who was perched on his forearm. "Macarius is supposedly after the Relicbloods' Hallows, isn't he? If he is half as dedicated to that mission as Queen Ana suggests, I doubt he would abandon everything and leave without another plan in mind."

I grimaced, my own crow, Paschal, fluttering in a shudder. "Fair point."

"While that does make sense," Lilliana agreed, "nothing disproves he's going about a new plan in a different, *safer* country, Jaq."

He denied a reply, once again glaring out the windowed walls as we patrolled the corridors.

Then, up ahead, I spotted a familiar face. A young man stood at a dividing segment of stone between the glass panels, his bronze fingers pressed against the window sill as the crowned, azure Dream mark centered on his brow gleamed. King Dream's eyes glazed as though having a vision, then blinked into focus, his blue fox ears grown and draped to his neck.

"King Dream?" Jaqelle called, approaching the young king. "Any visions about the hostiles?"

His Majesty's tone was unusually gritty, as though haunted. "Macar is no longer here," Dream said and drifted down the corridor, his mind seeming elsewhere. "But, I fear, not for long…"

We all watched him disappear up the spiraling staircase, murmuring nonsense to no one.

I pulled the com from my ear and called Alexander again, the device's gears whirling into action as the screen of light projected before me, the captain's face illuminating.

I saluted with a fist to my chest. "All clear, Captain," I reported, speaking louder to compensate for Lilliana and Jaqelle's sudden conversation behind me. "We've spoken with King Dream. He's had a vision of the hostiles fleeing the premises."

Alexander's head bobbed thrice. "Very well. Keep vigilant. There may be others tied to him whom we're not familiar with."

"Yes, Captain." I returned the com to my ear and turned to Jaqelle and Lilliana. "The Captain wishes us to…"

"Should honestly see the nurses, I say," Lilliana huffed, poking at Jaqelle's breastplate sharply. Both soldiers had abandoned their helms, which were now tucked under their arms, and Lilliana brushed her sweat-and-rain drenched locks back. "You still look seasick from the trip."

"I said I'm Bloody fine, woman," Jaqelle scoffed, rubbing his eyeglasses on his tunic's exposed hem to clean them.

"And those are another thing," she clipped, grabbing his eyeglasses. "These could be a safety hazard. You have every means to buy eye-lenses, so why do you insist on wearing these while on duty?"

"None'a your damn business, that's why." He snatched his eyeglasses, reverting back to his annoying, pauper dialect. "Shove off, will ya? I've been fine so far, anyways."

"You were all but blind in Tanderam without them." Her weight shifted to one side, a hand on her hip. "Jaq, you're being unreasonable. If you want to die just so you can keep looking like a peasant—"

"That ain't why, now shove off already!" he hissed, both Lilliana and I drawing back when his fangs unfolded threateningly.

What in Death is wrong with him today? And here I thought he enjoyed being called a peasant… perhaps the threat had him on edge.

Jaqelle calmed and adjusted the straps of his gauntlets, muttering, "There's no more immediate threat here, so… you may as well go check on Oliver or somethin'."

Lilliana fluttered her wings, looking ripe to snap at him, but she held her tongue and flew off, weaving through the overhead traffic of flyers at the arching ceiling.

Jaqelle watched her leave. And an all-too familiar, pained gaze overtook his features.

Ah, I thought, *so that was it, eh?*

"That is a dangerous road, Lieutenant," I warned.

He glared at me, squinting an eye. "What do you mean?"

"Nothing," I said and lifted an eyebrow toward the path Lilliana had flown. "Though, might I offer some advice? It may be best to say something *before* she weds Alexander."

He scowled at me so fiercely, his fangs dripped with venom. "Piss off, Matt." He said nothing else and stalked brusquely toward the north quadrant.

Nira help that man. There was still a chance for him, more than I ever had... If only he wasn't an idiot.

"Ah!" A girl's voice chimed behind me, making me jump. "Ah—um, S... Sir Matthiel...!"

I cringed, recognizing that Marincian accent. *Bloods be good, it's that stalker girl!* Bloody Death, was there no escape?

"S-Sir Matthiel...!" She called again, sounding bashful.

I drew in a slow, preparing breath, then inched my gaze back.

There she was, her thin pig-tails falling over her tanned shoulders, black hair ridden with countless, colorful hairpins and one bear ear perked in my direction.

"Miss Lëtta," I greeted through clenched teeth, sure to keep my tone patient. "I see you're still set on following me without explanation."

"U-um, well..." She blushed, scratching her head as though nervous. "I-I have a reason, but you were always busy with others, so I... I did not want to intrude. B-but I wanted to ask you something!"

My shoulders locked and I cleared my throat, guessing what it was. "I'm very flattered, Miss Lëtta, but I'm afraid I'm really not interested—"

"Will you teach me how to sew a soul into their living vessel?" she blurted.

I clicked my teeth shut. "Oh." I looked left. Then right. Blinked at her. "That's all?"

She nodded vigorously and clasped her hands. "I-I still can't do it, and I feel so ashamed... I am studying under Land's Tailors, but I can't help our own patients. But *you* can. Without being the Shadowblood. Please teach me? I want to help our patients as best I can."

"Oh," I hummed lightly, rubbing my shaven chin thoughtfully. That's right, I'd almost forgotten she was a Necrovoker. "I suppose I could try a lesson or two, when I'm off duty. Though you must understand, even *I* have difficulty with the Evocation."

She loosened her lungs and bowed. "Thank you...! I'll mostly be in the palace's west wing infirmary, that is where Mistress Sirra has settled. When you have time to teach me, please come and let me know there. Thank you!"

She bowed a second time and giggled, rushing back the way she'd come and hanging a sharp left down a different corridor.

All she wanted were lessons? I chuckled, then burst into laughter. Why had she taken so long to ask for something so simple? Bloods, was I really that intimidating?

I started toward the south quadrant, cheered now, but thinking it may be best to check for potential threats that may yet be lurking, just in case. Still, my mind was buzzing with lesson plans.

OCTAVIUS

"All right," Alex announced to Neal and me, the three of us standing guard outside Xavier's and Willow's sleek guestroom doors, all of us still fully plated with our helms' visors down. Our messenger ravens were all perched on our shoulders, and Alex pulled off his helm, tucking it under his arm and waved a hand at us. "Everyone's declared the palace clear for now. But I still want the dungeons checked. You both, go down there and inspect each cell, in case they've decided to hide there as a last resort… if all is clear there, you can find yourself a place to rest for the night, and I'll keep watch till morning with Jaq, Lilli and Matthiel."

I scratched my head, cat ears growing. "You sure?"

"I need my team rested and vigilant while we stay here," he said, "The Airship was an isolated location with little chance of threat, but we know for a fact the person wanting us and our charges dead had been here at the capital. I can't have you all falling asleep while on duty, so after checking the dungeons, get as much rest as you can tonight. It might be the most you'll get these next weeks… Perhaps even months. We'll have to alternate shifts as well with our members, so we'll decide the day and night shifts first thing tomorrow."

I nodded, massaging my sore neck while glancing at Shade from my shoulder. "O-okay…" I wasn't really looking forward to searching a freaky, dark dungeon, but I guessed it was best to be sure someone wasn't waiting to slit our throat while we slept.

Neal and I started down the hall, Shade and Ace croaking low in some conversation.

"Ah, and Octavius?" Alex called, stopping me. "When next you see El, would you ask if she'd be interested in a position on our squad?"

My brow furrowed. "I… guess I could ask, yeah. But can she? I mean, she hasn't formally graduated as a Reaper yet."

"Yeah, she has," Neal cut in, scratching the stubble under his chin, Ace bobbing his head while climbing down to Neal's forearm. "She was one of my students back in Neverland, remember? Once the war was over, I signed her apprentice papers *and* graduate papers in one go. Wartime gives certain allowances in these things, so it's all official."

I gawked at him, throwing open my visor. "Wait, wait! I just realized—*you* haven't technically graduated either, Neal! How are you allowed to sign papers like that? How are you allowed to *have students* when you're not officially graduated either?"

Alex hummed. "Actually, he is."

"What!"

"Before we set out for *Y'ahmelle Nayû* to find Xavier's body," Alex said, waving hands in a gesture, "Neal was formally introduced to Mistress in High Drinelle. From there, she ran him through a series of tests, which he passed, and after learning he was your brother, she declared him fit enough to be knighted. Her only requirement afterward was for Xavier and me to teach him the Creed. So, Neal has been knighted for over a year now and is authorized to train and graduate apprentices of his own."

"Why in Bloods didn't I know about this?" I demanded, glaring at Neal. "What the Void was *I* doing during this?"

"You were out with Dad and Connie, remember?" Neal nudged my side with an elbow. "Catching up or something. So, no worries about El coming aboard. Go ahead and ask her. Actually." He cupped his mouth in thought. "Why don't we find her now, yeah? She'll probably know the way to the dungeons… and who knows? You might find yourself a place to sleep, if you ask nice enough." He winked at that.

I flushed. "Um, I don't think…"

He shoved me forward. "Aw, go on! Try while you can, right?" He snickered as we both made our way down the hall. "Might not get another break in a while."

Behind us, I saw Alex hide his snort behind a hand, but his shoulders still shook with a chuckle while his raven, Mal, fanned its wings to keep steady there. The captain gave me a grinning nod of encouragement, and my face burned, stiffly shuffling down the hall beside Neal.

Great. I slipped off my helm, shaking my damp hair. *And now I have a new Bloody thing to be nervous about.* I wasn't sure which was worse, making a move that huge with El or looking for killers in the dungeons.

Neal's and my plated footsteps clattered through the enormous, arching hallway, a few winged shifters flying overhead with cleaning supplies—some with crossbows large enough to fit full arrows instead of the smaller bolts you usually saw—and most of them staying off the floor where we walked. Land, it was almost like they forgot there *was* a floor.

We kept along the outer wall, which was mostly windows stretching from floor to ceiling, separated by stone columns every few panels. This palace was weirdly modern, with metal trim and bright chandeliers, and I could even see crisscrossing cables outside through the rain, the floating islands dotting the cloudy terrain. So, all those islands were basically giant Levi-stones, huh?

Shade suddenly gave a croak next to my ear and hopped off my shoulder, flying to a curtain rail overhead. He perched next to a snowy, white raven, and the two fluffed their feathers and clacked their beaks on the rail. *Salfwy.* If she was here, then where was…

"Tavi!" I heard El hiss from behind a leafy plant. She leaned into view and waved at Neal and me, still hushed. "Over here!"

Neal and I walked over, and I scratched my nose. "There you are—"

"Shh!" She shoved a finger to her lips, then pointed to the partly opened door she was standing in front of. "*Lov'plect…*"

"Family sickness?" I slowed when reaching the door, peeking through the crack.

Roji and Dalminia were in there, Zyl standing next to them with a serious scowl on her face, and their baby daughter in her arms. Little Fuérr stood by his aunt, one emerald eye squinting at a sickly old man who sat in the center of the room. Roji's older daughter, Mavis, sat on his knee.

Is that the old king? Roji's dad?

"<So… this is what you've done in… your absence?>" the old man wheezed in Culatian, every breath sounding painful. Luckily, he was going slow enough for me to understand. His brown, pocked face crinkled in disgust when he glanced at Mavis. "<Making these… *hideous*… things?>"

"<Those *things*,>" Roji snapped, "<are your granddaughters.>"

"<They are… half my blood,>" the old man paused to go on a hacking spree, swallowing before continuing, "<But look at these… half-fish goblins! Feathers and scales? Webbed ears? I suppose they—>" More hacking. "<—grow gills… and tails in the water? Disgusting…!>"

"*Oi!*" Zyl barked from the corner. She handed the younger hybrid to Dalminia and stalked to the old man, yanking Mavis up, the three-year-old giggling and fluffing her feathers as she latched onto Zyl's neck. Zyl sneered at her dad. "<They're not disgusting, pops! Mavis is adorable, and cute, and sweet, and a little weird, and a troublemaker, and, and…!>" She let out a groan, which turned into a growl as she turned her back on him. "<They're *dragons*, Pops. We got dragons with scales just like them, you've seen hybrids with feathers and scales before. They're *my* family, and yours, too, and I ain't going to sit here and listen to you bad mouth my family.>"

Roji went wide-eyed at his little sister for a minute, as if surprised. Or touched? Either way, Roji, shook his head. "<Now, we're not going to cast you off or anything Pops, but if you're going to keep staying here, you've got to get used to my family. And I don't want to hear any…>"

El tugged Neal and me away from the door as she hissed in Landish, "Come on. Let's leave them alone, yea?"

I stammered, "Y-yeah. Right…"

Neal grimaced when we were out of earshot again. "Bloods, that sounded rough."

El hid her nervous smile behind a hand, her white cat ears dropping. "Yea. But it's not a surprise. Roji and Zyl haven't been home for years, Roji even longer. *Skrii*, this is the first time in a long time the whole royal family has been back."

"Land…" I murmured as Shade flew down from the curtain rail and nestled on my head. Salfwy landed on El's shoulder, and I scratched my cheek before starting again, "Oh yeah, Alex says there's a position on the royal guard for you, if you're interested."

One of her cat ears perked. "The royal guard? Like what you do?"

"Yeah." My smile faltered. "I mean, we're going to be super busy until the immediate threat is gone…" *Half of that threat being my ancestor.* I scowled, but went on, "We don't know when things will calm down again, but I guess Alex thinks having more members on the guard will help everyone take shifts so we can rotate sleep and meals."

"So…" She bit her lip, her lemon-yellow eyes flicking sideways at me. "I'd be working with you?"

I blushed. Neal nudged me in the ribs encouragingly, and I swallowed. "Um, I mean… I can ask Alex if we can take the same shifts, I guess, but I, uh… I don't think I can guarantee anything."

She gave a toothy smile. "But it's the best chance I'll have, right? If you're going to be busy for a while, then I have more chances to spend time with you if *I'm* busy the same way."

"I guess that makes sense." Gods, my face was burning. Did she have to be so blunt? I shook my head and stammered, "W-well, anyway. Do you know where the dungeons are here? We need to search it for threats before we can call it a night."

She nodded and walked ahead down the hall. "Yea. It's this way, I'll take you there."

She led us through the palace, and Bloods, it was a super complicated path. We took five different lifts down several different floors, turning corner after corner, climbing down another *three* floors on stairs this time until the carpeted halls turned into stone-floored cellars with narrow passages, cobwebs dressing the wooden framework as feral rats scurried at our boots.

"Sorry for the long walk," El said ahead of us. "The dungeons aren't actually *in* the palace itself. It has its own area underground, but this passage leads there from the palace."

We eventually stopped at a huge, wooden door. It was dusty and splintered in some places, the iron hinges rusted over.

El looked at the door with a scrunched, white brow. "There should be guards here..."

Thump!

Something slammed against the door from the other side, rattling the loose hinges.

Neal glanced at me nervously. "What was that?"

Thump! Thump!

There was a long pause between the three of us. Then, slowly, we all leaned an ear against the door—

CRACK!

The door burst open, throwing us back.

Skririririrriii!

A dripping, screeching demon suddenly leapt out and spread its boney wings, screaming as it pounced right for me. I stumbled on my back, scrambling to find my scythe-sphere—

El whipped one of her throwing scythes right through the Fera's sticky chest. It gave a horrified shriek, dwindling into a pitiful whimper until the thing slumped over, dead, and landed on top of me in a squishy thud.

"Eugh!" I gagged while shoving the thing off me and shuffled to my feet, my plate now covered in static I could feel with my Infeciovoking. "Gross, gross, gross..."

The black tar on its body hissed away and revealed the corpse underneath.

When his face was cleared, El gasped. "Oh, *Skrii*..."

"W-what?" I panted, dusting off my armored legs, which prickled with germs now. "Do you know who he is?"

"Who he *was*," El corrected as she looked at the winged dead guy's decaying face like she'd puke. "This was the king's Hand..." She flicked her yellow eyes at me uneasily. "It was Garrach."

Neal's brow furrowed. "The guy who Zyl and Roji kept getting their calls blocked by?"

"No way," I sputtered. "I mean... look at this guy!" I jabbed a gesturing hand at the body. "He looks like he's been dead for months! Roji was on com with this guy like, last week!"

El shook her head. "Then it *wasn't* the real Garrach."

"Great..." I stepped over Garrach's corpse and peeked into the dimly lit dungeon, plugging my nose. Bloods, it reeked in here. There were flies zipping around and, from what I could see under the low-lit lamps, on the moldy ceiling soggy pieces of *people* were scattered on the stone floor, massive blood stains splattered and soaked in like it was part of the decoration. Some of those pieces were still wearing armor, too, raggedy flesh and splintered bones sticking out of gloves and grieves.

I thought I'd be sick, swallowing as I looked back at El and Neal. "I-I think I know what happened to the guards..."

Neal peeked over my shoulder and reared back in disgust. "Eugh. Looks like they were Fera food."

I rigorously scratched my head and pulled out my com, calling Alex. The captain's heterochromic head appeared on the screen of light, growling, *"Find anything?"*

"There was a Fera in the dungeons," I reported in a grimace. "It's dead now, though. El says he was the king's Hand, the guy Roji and Zyl were intercepted by on the com for the past few months." I shrugged. "I guess that means it was really Macarius on com with them?"

Alex looked disturbed by the news. *"Perhaps... Any immediate threats down there, or was it just the one Fera?"*

"Just the one." I glanced around the dungeons again to be sure. "Looks like it had plenty of meals for the past few months, but it's all clear now."

He hummed darkly. *"Very well... if there are no other threats, I'll send Jaq and Matthiel down there while you all get some rest for the night... and stay alert."*

"Right. Will do." I ended the call with a sigh, turning to Neal and El. "He says to get some rest."

Neal stretched his neck to the side. "Like I'll be able to sleep after that."

I grimaced. "Yeah... good point..."

ROJI

TRANSLATED FROM CULATIAN

"All right, Mavis." I opened the arching doors into an expansive bedchamber, Mini and I waving ceremoniously. "This is your room now, little Sky Princess."

Mavis peeked in from behind Zyl's leg, her little wings fluttering. She didn't move.

"Don't worry, sweetheart," Mini said, crouching to ruffle her feathered hair. "We'll get it all prettied up, just for you. But it'll take some time, so be patient, all right?"

Mavis's webbed ears flapped for a minute, then she latched tighter on Zyl's leg, announcing, "I want to go with Auntie Syl!"

Zyl stiffened, widening her stance as if hoping Mavis would slide off. "Eh?"

I chuckled. "But you have your own room, sweetheart. All to yourself."

Her grip on Zyl strengthened. "*Pleeeeease?*"

I rubbed my neck and glanced up at Zyl. "Well, uh… Guess that's up to Auntie Syl."

Zyl blushed, but muttered, "Uh, I guess it's all right… for one night."

"You hear that, Mavis?" I said, lifting a finger. "One night."

Mavis gave a victorious giggle and let go of Zyl, grabbing her hand instead and dragging her down the hall. "Sleep over, sleep over…!"

"Heh, all right, all right," Zyl yawned, starting to follow Mavis.

But before she got too far, I caught Zyl's shoulder. "Hey, sis," I began, hesitant. "Thanks."

Her face twisted. "It's just one night."

"No, I mean for earlier." I shrugged, my grin falling thin. "What you said to Pops. About my kids being your family."

She sniffed the air indignantly. "Yeah, well, they are. Pops better get over it soon."

I laughed. "Well… thanks. It means a lot, sis." I looked at the towering ceiling, its old design still the same as it was before I left, nostalgia hitting as I sucked in a reviving breath. "And Sky, it's good to be back. I've got you to thank for that, too."

Zyl's wings twitched as she tried to hide her proud smile. "It's good to have you back, Big Brother."

"Sleep over!" Mavis cried and pulled Zyl's arm so hard, she had to lunge down. "Sleep over!"

"All right, all right," Zyl laughed and followed after my daughter, eventually taking the lead to show Mavis where her room was.

Beside me, Mini slid a hand on my back, hefting little Prylan over her shoulder. "Mavis has gotten quite attached to your sister, hasn't she?"

I chuckled. "Yeah. Mavis reminds me of Zyl, actually, when she was that little. I used to play with her just like that, too…"

"That's not fair!" I remembered a tiny Zyl yelling up at me from the hallway floor, jumping up as if hoping to reach for the chandelier where I sat. "I can't fly yet…! That's cheating, Roji!"

"We never set the rules, now did we?" I laughed, the echoes bouncing through the halls.

I heard her grunt down there—and I nearly fell off the chandelier when she fluttered her tiny wings so fast, she actually got off the ground. But she was getting really high, and her wings looked ready to give out.

"Zyl!" I called down, panic setting in as I hopped off to soar to her. "Don't get too high—!"

Her wings gave out, and she went spiraling down, her feet hitting the floor first as a pained wail erupted from her lungs.

"Zyl!" I landed and scooped the screaming girl up, folding my wings around her. "It-it's all right, it's all right! I got you, sis…"

Sky, her ankle was all mangled, her face drenched in tears as she hiccupped between sobs. Each cry was a knife in my stomach.

"It's all right, Zyl," I hushed, leaping up and flying at full speed to the infirmary. "It's gonna be all right…!"

The memory faded, and I sighed.

Mini hummed beside me. "Roji? What's wrong?"

I shook my head. "I was just remembering something. Did I ever tell you my sister broke her ankle once?"

Mini's emerald eyes widened with interest. "Did she?"

"Yeah." I rubbed a finger under my nose. "She was trying to chase after me before she could fly and ended up falling really far. Nearly killed me when she started screaming… Pops slapped me for it later."

A small smirk tugged at her lips. "And did you deserve it?"

"Heh, yeah. I guess I did. But remembering that just reminds me of now. When she drank all that Yinklît Gel and slept for weeks and… she still doesn't have all of her Hallows back because of it."

"And you feel guilty for this?" Mini guessed, a webbed ear folding down in question.

"I should have stopped her from drinking it in the first place." My stomach churned, feeling sick. "I was right there, sitting next to her. I could have done anything—slap it out of her hand, tell her to stop, *something…*"

Mini took my hand gently. "Roji, you couldn't have known what was in those drinks. What's important is that you were there for her afterward, when she needed you."

"But why does it feel like I'm only there for her *after* these things happen?" I asked, the sickness burning deeper. "I just… I just don't have an excuse. Here she is, my little sister sticking out for me and my family, and what am I doing for her? Why can't I be there for her when she actually needs me?"

"All you can do is try, Roji," Mini hushed. "Now why don't you give me the grand tour of our new home?"

"Ah… yes, where are my manners?" My smile was thin, but I gripped her scaled fingers and led her through the hall. "Come, my queen. I think you'll particularly be interested in the pool—"

"<Sky,>" a small voice piped in Marincian from my feet. Then something tugged at my still-damp tunic. "<Sky, I want to talk to you!>"

I craned down, finding a pair of large, emerald eyes glaring up at me with a stern expression, though the young face it burdened just made the Seadragon look cuter.

I switched my speech to Marincian. "<Fuérr, didn't Mini just put you to bed in your own room?>"

The little Seadragon's webbed ears flapped, and he brushed aside his translucent, emerald hair. "<I can put myself to bed, I'm not a baby. But I want to talk to you, Sky.>"

I grunted while crouching to his level, my knees popping. Bloods, I had *not* planned to feel like an old fart at thirty-four. Maybe I shouldn't have done that knee-slide stunt with the guitar earlier. Didn't think that one through. "<Sure, Ocean,>" I said to Fuérr, cupping my hands to show him he had my attention. "<What's on your mind?>"

"<I want you to teach me Culatian,>" he huffed, lifting his scaled chin. "<Or Landish, whichever you think should be first. I'm tired of everyone talking gibberish. If they're not going to speak the standard Marincian, then I'm just going to have to learn the other languages. My tutors at home had said it would be important anyway, since I am Ocean, and it is always expected of Ocean to know all languages.>"

I licked my lips, surprised. "<Huh. Well, sure, Fuérr. Let me know when you want your lessons and I'll see what I can do… though it might be better if I just hire tutors for you while you stay here.>"

He glanced up to think on it, then nodded once. "<Okay. That will work, too. Thank you, Sky.>"

His boots squeaked when he spun on his heels and marched back to his room four doors down.

Mini laughed when the Seadragon clicked his door shut. "It seems Mavis isn't the only one warming up to a relative, hm?"

I grinned. "I guess not… now, where were we?"

She balanced Prylan on one shoulder and looped an arm around mine. "I believe you were showing me this fabled 'pool' of ours?"

"Ah!" I snapped my fingers. "Of course. Only the best for my queen."

EVERLAND

TIMBERAIL

NEW ALDAMSTRIA

16

WELCOME TO THE NEST

TAYMEN

The snowy ground trembled under my armored boots.

I had to squint to see the sloshing, black lines of soldiers that flooded down the horizon, the Grimling militia marching down against the sun-set backdrop that stung my pupils the longer I looked.

Bloods, there's so many of them. My arms shuddered, vision blurring through the tiny slit of my helm's visor, my grip rattling over my heavy sword. I debated using my Somniovoking to put myself to sleep so I could get out of doing this, but decided that might be too risky. What if the Reapers noticed I was still alive and skewered me while I was sleeping?

Or worse, what if the Noctis Golems got to my sleeping soul before I could create my protective barrier in Aspirre?

There were only so many of us dream walkers still in Timberail. Everyone else had been hauled off to jail, since anyone with a Dream mark was considered a traitor to Everland. Since my Da was a Rockraider, he was able to pull some strings and keep me from being locked up—but now I wondered if I would have been better off? Putting up barriers all over the city's subconscious parallel with only a handful of Somniovokers in our arsenal was *exhausting...* And as the line of Reaper soldiers crept over the snowy hilltop in front of me now, I sure as Land would rather be shackled in a safe, cozy dungeon than out in this death trap.

"D-D-Da?" I shivered, lungs shaking like a busted radiator.

Da stood beside me with his sword in one hand, Shotri in the other, holding his stance with the rest of the Raiders who squeezed around us. Timberail's coast only had two hundred men handy. We even had to drag some civilians out to stretch around the city's perimeter—barely.

Shouts and proud cries boomed from the Grimlings as they closed in, leaving tracks in the snow along the barren hill. One wolf-eared woman on feral horseback darted from side to side at the front line and shouted orders at the Grimish soldiers, her polished armor gleaming like ice against the hot sunlight. A different man copied her, taking the other half of their militia and shouting words of confidence.

And at the head of the charge was a horrifying demon, covered from head to foot in spiked plate, his black cape rustling in the wind and showing the crest of Grim.

Land's Blade, it's the Death King's Eyes!

"Da…!" I swallowed. Only Da's bristly chin was visible under his helm next me. "Da, w-we have to submit! There's too many of them! And that's Lucas *Devouh*—"

"Taymen, shut your Gods damned mouth," Da snapped. I saw his grip tighten on the hilt. "I didn't raise a damned coward. You're a Bloody knight and this is *our* home. No corpse-raisers are going to set a claw on it."

Bloods. I didn't even think about corpse-raisers. How many did they have up there? My bladder was throbbing now, and I regretted that last pint I'd chugged before formation—

"For honor!" Lucas Devouh bellowed, raising his long-staved scythe over his head, the blade glinting in the sunlight and glowing a faint blue.

"FOR HONOR!" the entire militia roared behind him, so loud my stomach quivered and the piss came right out of me, leaving a warm trail over my thigh.

"For Death!" the Lord's voice clapped.

"FOR DEATH!"

"For the Mother!"

"THE MOTHER!"

His horse pounded a small beat into the snow, and as it reared, the Lord screamed in Grimish, *"MU NECROS NESCHALI YETTEK!"*

The air ripped with an incomprehensible wave of war cries, then they swallowed the hill whole, their white cloaks and silver armor barely visible in the white blanket of snow.

I swear to Gods my heart stopped.

Our captain hollered a cracked *charge!* and row by row, the other Raiders pushed on—and I let out a bleated squeal when the row behind me shoved me forward, my helm spinning over my head and blocking my view.

"I-I can't see, Da!" I screamed in the new blackness, wheezing hot breaths that blew right back at me in this bucket. "I can't—!"

Pffwwa—BRRRUMMM!

Something exploded out there, a wave of heat hitting my right side as my legs burst with pain, the ground vanishing under my feet before my gut lurched sick, flying, *falling*, then my spine hit the freezing snow and my head cracked into something—

Blackness.

… Land, my ears were ringing…

There was something over my face, my breath was muffled and blowing back at me. And *Bloods*, something smelled like shit.

The ringing dimmed a little, and I swore the ground was rumbling. Were those screams?

I groaned and peeled off the tin can over my head—oh, it was my helmet. My eyes had trouble focusing on the white and red terrain, smoke pluming all over the place, sticking to my lungs. I sat up, but my stomach lurched and I heaved over the snow, puking my throat raw. I hacked painfully, wiping off drool. What in Land happened to me…?

I rubbed my eyes, blinking through the smog.

I froze stiff.

"Da…?"

Da's helm was halfway off his head. His head was halfway off his neck.

"Da!" I shoved the mass of slumped bodies off him. "Da…!"

Da didn't move. He didn't blink. His greasy brown hair was damp with sweat and stuck to his scarred jaw; his skin burnt away at some places. His throat was wet with blood, the opening at his neck crusted over.

"No, no, no, no, no." I hugged him, squeezed my eyes shut. *Not Da too. Not him.* I didn't have anyone left. "Da…" My chest shook. "*Da…*"

Shouts pierced my still-ringing ears, jerking my eyes open again. It was hard to see through the tears, but I saw a wolf-eared man a few yards to my left, barking orders.

I rubbed my eyes dry to clear my view. Then went cold.

Lucas Devouh's sapphire eyes were bright against the snowy hill. His once ice-silver armor was now a slick, dripping crimson.

Watch your head, watch your insides. Of all the times to have a nursery rhyme pop into my head from childhood, it had to be now. *Else they ride with the Death King's Eyes.*

I glared at Da's murderer, the black-haired demon pacing the field of bodies like a beast hunting for more prey.

Death and cinder, steps like tinder.

His boots crunched over the snow, so close I could hear each step over the constant ringing in my ears. The battlefield had shifted into silence, nothing but crackling embers from old explosions sounding, the smoke thick and black between the High Howllord and me.

Comes Lord Lucas, the terribly ruthless.

One of his grown wolf ears flicked in my direction, and his head snapped my way.

I ducked under the mass of bodies surrounding me, hugging Da with shivering arms. After a few minutes, I dared to peeked my head up, my grown lion ears draped painfully low.

The Terribly Ruthless had turned away and continued surveying the field. My heart thudded softer, and I let out a breath.

"I'll make this right, Da," I whispered, kissing Da's brow. "I'll get our home back. I promise."

I'll kill him. I crept over the bodies, sneaking away from the snowy graveyard while rubbing my eyes raw. I reached the edge of the battlefield and ran for it, dragging my feet as fast as I could in the snow, glaring over my shoulder. *I'll make sure not even your corpse-raising friends can resurrect you, you dirt crawling son of a bitch—*

I collided into someone and fell back into the snow, a puff of white powder dusting around me. Panicked, I looked up, cringing at the towering woman who stood over me.

But I paused, my brow furrowing at the lady who peered down at my face. She wasn't wearing any armor, just a delicate, violet smock that ruffled gently in the crisp breeze. Her bronze skin was warm against the frozen backdrop around her, and her cropped, blonde hair was woven with small flowers of every color. She looked so serene, standing like a hollow shell over me, like an angel sent from the Father God… except her neck bore a hideous, vine-like scar that ran across her throat like a choking necklace.

And her pupils were a bright, glowing white.

The woman stepped closer.

"Wh-who…?" I shuffled back in the snow. "Who are you?"

She crouched beside me to examine my face. Then her eyes glided down to my neck, where my Dream mark was showing. A soft, haunting purr sang from her lips. "I am Syreen."

—she *drove* her clawed hand into my chest, the icy pain cracking through my ribs, and she ripped out a dripping, red mass that stained her fingers.

"Welcome to my Mistress's nest," she said in her ghostly voice, her face slowly fading from view until even the wet snow became nothing more than a faint memory.

17

GHOSTS OF THE PAST

LUCAS

SEVEN YEARS PRIOR

T^{ck!} My dart hit the black and white board with poor accuracy, barely landing in the 18th zone. I clicked my tongue, taking another swig of whiskey from the glass on the nearby table in Alice and my private cabin on this ship. I'd lost count of how many glasses I'd had today. My son's memorial service ended hours ago, but I'd begun drinking long before then. The cabin swayed more than it should, and I nearly stumbled before catching myself on a chair's arm.

I grumbled and choked down another swig, *clacking* it on the table before throwing another dart.

Tck! It landed on the 4th zone.

Tck! I threw the last one, which completely missed the dartboard and *thunked* into the delicate wall paper.

Bloods, but I was terrible at this game. Or maybe it was the drink. *Oh, what does it matter?* I lamented in a dismal sigh.

I dripped into the chair like a soggy towel, the leather creaking under my weight as I turned to the vision-screen on the wall.

"*... still continues their hunt for the young lord on the surface,*" the reporter announced, the screen panning to a canyon where Reapers and Footrunners scoured every nook and cranny of those blasted rocks. "*Due to the lack of a body and the eyewitness report of Her Highness Willow, Death King Serdin has declared the boy dead. The royal family held a memorial service for the young lord today, and...*"

A new recorded footage was shown. It was of Alice, Alexander and myself, standing at the front of the black-stone slab that was my son's memorial. A crowd of friends, family, and supporters lined the royal cemetery in thick blocks. Serdin and Myra stood on the other side of us with heavy heads, Daniel beside them. Willow had declined to leave her chambers for the service. Not that she'd left them all month after the attack, but Serdin had at least hoped she would make an exception for this… occasion.

While we were all a sullen mess, Alexander was perhaps the worst sight. Unkempt despite the servants' efforts to tame his shaggy hair, disengaged from everything and everyone, staring emptily as if a soulless shell.

The reporters noticed. The view zoomed on my son's despondent face, the woman reporter murmuring her commentary on what she thought must have been running through Alexander's mind. As if anyone could know what that blasted boy was thinking in these circumstances.

"Bah!" I threw my glass at the vision-screen. It phased through the screen of light and shattered against the wall before sprinkling to the floor in a dripping mess, the reporter still blabbering on. "My son isn't dead, you blathering peacock!" I slurred to the screen. "We'll find him! We'll Bloody find him…!"

I sank back in the chair, squeezing my temples hoping to snuff out the swelling pain—

Panic shocked through my blood like a barbed arrow, jolting my spine erect.

"Barrach?" I called in a slur, stumbling to my feet. The cabin swayed drastically and I gripped the chair's arm for support. That venomous panic still thrummed through my soul in a sharp echo, the sense that danger approached still choking my pulse. It was a familiar feeling. One that only meant my messenger raven, Barrach, had sensed something was amiss outside on the docks.

Craw!

I whirled to the window. Barrach himself had perched on the sill and was pecking his beak against the glass feverishly.

Then shouts burst through the ship's halls. I could swear I heard my wife screaming commands from the upper deck.

—Shhh-thunk!

A black, boney hand sopped up to my window and stuck to the glass, causing Barrach to fly off in a vicious screech.

"Fera!" I scrambled to find my coat, cursing that I'd carelessly thrown it on the carpet earlier. I nearly tripped on the damned thing but rummaged through its pockets and found my glowing scythe-sphere.

CRASH!

The slug-infested beast shattered the window and dripped inside, its skeletal head giving a guttural bleat. It had horns on either side of its squirming skull, perhaps the remnants of a bull shifter.

I pressed the rippled sealing rune on my sphere and let my weapon melt into my long-staved scythe, the olium and Spiritcrystal solidifying in a hissing *clash* once it was fully formed.

The Fera sloppily charged for me, and I ducked away before its horns caught my chest. I heaved and sliced at the beast's chest.

Snap!

My blade found purchase on its NecroSeam, and the thing dropped at my feet in a clattering thunk, its blackened soul hissing away from its decayed skin and vanishing in the air.

My drunken head rolled to the side and I nearly toppled over the corpse, but I leaned on my staff for support. *Fool, Lucas,* I thought bitterly as Barrach soared through the shattered window and perched on my shoulder with ruffled feathers. *This was not a grand time to have drenched my sorrows in spirits.*

"Nathaniel," I said, speaking through my vassal's mental connection. "I've just killed a Fera in my cabin. How many are left on the deck?"

My vassal's voice fuzzed through my thoughts. *Yer wife killed the rest up here, Da'torr. But one dragged yer son overboard.*

That was enough to shock me sober. "WHAT!"

Aiden's found him already, he assured. *He's flyin' him back now.*

"Is he injured?!" I quickly threw open my door and stormed through the halls, shoving crew members aside and climbed the steps toward the upper deck. "Does he need a Healer?! Bloods, Nathaniel, I've already lost one son, I can't afford to lose another…!"

I flung open the door that lead to the upper deck. But paused.

It was eerily quiet up here, despite the number of people standing about. Corpses from the Fera littered the deck, and there seemed to be no sign of any more. Near the main mast were Aiden and Nathaniel. Aiden didn't glance my way when I came out, his brown and red wings stiff as granite and his brown skin flushed pale as his ghost, were he not resurrected. Nathaniel's bear ears were pulled down to his thick neck, and he caught my gaze for a mere second before reverting his attention back to my wife and son who appeared to be the center of everyone's focus.

Alice's long braid was frazzled and swinging over her shoulder as she crouched over my son's slumped figure, her fur coat from earlier abandoned along with her chained dual-scythes off to the side. She looked haunted while she hovered over Alexander, who was curled on the floorboards and shaking like a rabid feral. The young teen was soaked to the bone, his shaggy grey hair stuck to his face as he clutched his head as if in pain. The boy was whimpering.

My eyes snapped to the pool of water around him, fury boiling at the blood that swirled within it, draining from my son's back.

"What happened here?" I boomed, stomping toward my bleeding son. The crowd surrounding him parted to make way for me, and I snapped at them. "Don't just stand there, you dimwitted fools! Call for the ship's Healer! Immediately!"

Several crew members squeaked in affirmation and scurried into the cabins. I crouched beside my wife and examined Alexander's panicked expression. His eyes were shut tight, sharpened teeth gritting and grown wolf ears curled tight to his skull. He was whispering to himself, so quiet only my own grown wolf ears could hear it.

"Don't," he seethed, his muscles twitching. "Just… wait. I can't… get enough time to…"

"Alexander?" I hushed and clasped a hand on his shoulder.

The boy flinched and his mismatched eyes flew open.

My soul shattered with such blissful agony, it thundered through my ears in the swelling silence. Alexander's mismatched eyes were in the wrong place. The boy staring up at me now was my first son.

The son I had lost.

"Y-you're…" he whimpered, his voice squeezed with fright. One of his wolf ears perked as he registered my face, as though straining to remember. "F… Father…?"

"Xavier…?" I whispered hollowly, my throat loosening a joyous sob. "Xavier…!" I cupped his face, searching his mismatched eyes through stinging tears, and pulled him close for an embrace. "You're alive…! Seamstress be praised, you're *alive*…!"

Xavier's chilled skin trembled in my hold. "F-F-Father…"

—His heterochromia switched places. Now I held Alexander, who had not seconds ago been Xavier.

"Father," Alex shuddered in heavy pants, looking at me through his wet bangs that stuck to his nose and cheeks. "W-w-what's happening to us…?"

The breath left my lungs, the silence returning save for the lulling hush of the lapping waves. "What in Bloods…?"

PRESENT DAY

The smoke had thinned along the coastline of High Timberail, my boots sinking into the snowy beach as I gazed out at the ocean.

The waves reminded me of that day on the ship—the day my son's soul was discovered inside Alexander.

And I'll see them again soon, I thought, a swell of cheer simmering under the sorrow from today's dark events. *Both of them. Separated...*

The day was drawing to an end, the echoes of this morning's battle still fresh with the fallen bodies of the enemy. We had taken few casualties on our end. But every loss was to be mourned. Even those of our adversaries. Reapers bustled through the town to carry out their duties—there were souls to be freed, prisoners to be questioned, citizens to crosscheck...

"High Howllord," an armored, scaled man with webbed ears came beside me and saluted. He shouldered a sharp trident over his scaled plate and announced, "We've secured the coast, as was asked of us by King Ninumel. Is there anything else you need of our knights?"

Now that the war between Culatia and Marincia had been resolved, both kings had agreed to see through our agreement and offer a number of their knights to our cause here in High Everland. Marincia's Wavecrashers had helped secure the coastline while Culatia's Stormchasers patrolled the skies for enemy flyers.

I nodded to the Wavecrasher. "We'll need you all to man this city when we march on the capital. If our plans don't go as we wish, we'll need to sustain our territories in the event of a retreat."

"Aye, Howllord." The Wavecrasher saluted again, then trotted off to shout orders at his fellow Ocean Knights.

I gazed back at the lapping ocean again before walking along the beach—

"Lucas," a gruff voice rasped to my left. "Are the ones we brought not enough?"

I whirled, my breath catching to see a helmed man in black plate staring down at me from atop a large, leather-winged Flamedragon. His mount had marbled grey-and-red scales, a narrow head and a long, pointed snout filled with serrated teeth that were hooked at an angle. It wore black armor over its spiny skull, hindlegs, barbed tail and clawed talons which were attached to its wings. Overall, the beast resembled a slender, thirteen-foot bat.

The rider's ebony armor glistened in the reflected light of the sun against the snow, accenting the intricate designs on his plate and silken cape that billowed in the breeze. When he lifted his visor and craned to peer down at me with clear, white eyes and a smug grin, the silver skull-crown hugging his helm glinted.

I let out a laugh. "Sire! You've surfaced already?"

"Just in time to catch some of the excitement in the geysers," the Death King chuckled and dismounted his Flamedragon, patting the creature on the neck.

The beast gave a guttural coo and opened its jaw to let loose a calm stream of red fire at its feet. The snow melted to reveal the sand beneath, and the dragon heated those grains as well before curling atop them and licking its wing-talons with a forked tongue.

The Death King removed his helm and tucked it under an arm, clasping hands with me. "Lucas, good to see you," he said with a grin. "You've gotten old."

I guffawed. "As have you, my lord. I see you brought a few resources from Grim on your way up." I nodded to the Flamedragon waiting patiently on its heated bed of sand. Serdin's messenger Songcrow, Locke, flapped onto its snout and gave a low whistle, preening his feathers. My own messenger, Barrach, flew into view and alighted beside him, croaking and screeching in a new conversation with Locke. I turned back to Serdin. "I take it the fire breathers helped in securing the Surfacing Port in this city?"

"—Both them and the Bonedragons," a new voice said from behind Serdin.

Another familiar face approached us from atop a horse-sized, wingless dragon covered in bones. Its steps clicked and clacked with its makeshift armor, and when the rider—my old bat-winged friend, Daniel Tessinger—dismounted, I clasped hands with him and thumped his back. "Daniel! Bloods be good, how long it's been. You're looking more wrinkled than the two of us combined, eh?"

"It shows how much more mature I am than you both." Daniel scoffed. Then his moustache pulled back in a mixture of delight and caution. "As for how long it's been, I suppose that had been your intention, hadn't it, Lucas?"

"Yes," Serdin muttered with resentment. "If I'm to understand it, our delayed meeting was by your own design."

I hesitated, guilt sitting heavy in my gut. "Yes, yes… You're right. I… do not deserve forgiveness for keeping it from you, my lord."

"Yet, my forgiveness you have," sighed Serdin. "What's done is done. Let us put this behind us and think of the future now, hm?"

I exhaled, though my heart was still heavy. "Yes, my lord."

"Oh, dash the 'my lords' and 'sires'," he yielded to a grin as he took my hand with a firmer grip and reeled me in for a strong embrace. "It's Bloody good to see you, my friend."

I chuckled, patting his shoulder as we broke away. "And you, Serdin." I nodded to the bat next, exchanging a laughing embrace. "Daniel, I hear my son has given your daughter her engagement-vines at long Bloody last."

"So I've heard!" Daniel's smile shinned as bright as the surface sun. "Lilli looked so delighted, last we spoke. Is Alexander thrilled as well?"

I made a point to mask my wince. "Ecstatic."

Begrudged was more like it. Alexander barely spoke of his impending marriage, and any mention would cause him to end the call swiftly.

Serdin snorted, a smug grin tugging his lips. "Yes, a new marriage is quaint. But Lucas and I, Daniel, have a far more important event to look forward to. We're to be grandfathers in one short month."

The reminder stretched my smile so wide, my cheeks went sore. "Indeed we will! And they're naming the boy after *me*, I hear." I patted Serdin's shoulder in sympathy. "Sorry, Serdin. Perhaps their next son will hold your name."

Serdin snorted. "He'll have my hair and eyes, as well as my Hallows. You can have the name."

The three of us shared another hearty laugh.

"*Khm hmm.* Well." Serdin cleared his throat and scanned the watery horizon of the beach. "I suppose we ought to get to business. I see you've claimed the coast. What have you planned next?"

I nodded for them to follow me across the snowy beach, their Flame and Bone dragons following at their heels. "Alice is reviewing the plans with Fangs Lastings as we speak," I said. "Come, they're meeting in the old Raider Station in the central district."

Serdin hummed. "Very well… ah, but before I forget, Lucas." He fished into the Storagebox that was clipped to his leather belt, reached for the shrunken items held within it, and pulled out a book which grew to its proper size when it entered the outside air. "You asked to see this."

I took the book titled, *the NecroSeam Chronicles, volume one.*

My smile vanished. "Ah… this was the book you mentioned?"

"It was written by one of my mother-in-law's scholars. She calls him an Enlightener, as I understand it."

I read as I walked, plucking my reading glasses from the hidden pocket in my cloak.

A dripping, skeletal creature leapt from the water and hooked its claws into my shoulder, one passage read from Alexander's viewpoint, *yanking me overboard and dragging me into the water with a cold splash. My pained curses bubbled in the dark waters, my shoulder burning as the creature still had me hooked, and it dragged me farther into the water's depths toward the shrouded floor.*

"Bloods," I murmured, flipping page after page. "This was the day on the ship when we discovered Xavier had been tethered to Alexander. It's so… accurate."

Serdin hummed. "Myra tells me the Enlightener who scribes these stories uses a third-party Seer to show him the narrator's memories of every event. Supposedly, this is why each scene is so vivid. It's quite fascinating… He even has a few chapters in *our* perspectives, and we haven't even met him."

I cocked an eyebrow. "How could he get visions in our perspectives from so far away?"

"I suspect Willow and your sons may have provided some sort of medium for the Seers he uses. Myra tells me it's not uncommon. Although, in your case, it may be more likely that you yourself had given him a few items to use as a medium when he was with you all in New Aldamstria."

I scratched my beard. "I've met this author?"

"According to his books, he's the younger brother of your sons' winged vassal." Serdin leaned over my shoulder to flip to a different chapter in the book, then pointed to an emboldened name and read aloud, "Herrin Tesler?"

I frowned, trying to recall a face, but only his elder brother came to mind. "I… vaguely remember the name," I murmured. Then shook my head and thumped the book closed. "Bah, I'll read from the beginning when there's time. I think it best to focus on the present at hand."

"Couldn't agree more." Serdin clapped both Daniel and my shoulders. "Now, where is Alice? Myra had gone to meet with her and I suspect they plan to call Willow about the baby. I for one wish to see how she's progressing."

"That would make two of us," I chuckled and walked out of the snowy beach beside the two, taking to the streets that bustled with Reapers and Landish rebels. "They'll be with Fangs Lastings, then. Come, we can see if there's been word from our spies in the capital as well."

18

PREMONITION

ALICE

"We've secured Timberail," I reported to Henry, Cayden's trusted contact within Everland's capital. "We estimate the invasion will begin within a month. Be sure the Servant is informed."

The rabbit eared man grunted from the screen. *"Would if I could, Fangs. He's gone silent for a month."*

"Silent? Death…" If Cayden hadn't met with Henry in so long, he must be under too much surveillance in the palace. I licked my lips and asked, "Can you inform him by other means? He must know the schedule. It's imperative your men and ours are on the same clocks."

"I understand, Fangs." He scratched the stubble at his chin, pensive. *"Maybe there's one way. It's a risk, but it may be the best chance we got."*

"How much of a risk?"

"More than I'd like," he admitted. *"But you're right. This next fight will hopefully be the last. If we're going to make a move, it's got to be now."* He took an apprehensive breath. *"I'll go to the palace on an arms delivery. If I can find either Cayden, his wife or his sister and tell one of them about the schedule, maybe we'll get away with it."*

I paused, my brow knitting. "The prince's… wife? And sister?"

"They joined the rebellion," Henry explained. He sipped from a steaming, cracked cup and hummed. *"Apparently, the king's been a worse asshole to his kids than to the rest of the country."*

"I see… Very well," I said. "Inform whomever you can there. So long as it reaches Cayden, that will suffice."

I ended the call in a sigh, rubbing my temples.

Fangs Lastings stirred from his place on the back wall. "Do you think the Servant will know in time?"

I scoffed. "I have the utmost confidence. We will proceed as planned—"

"Alice!"

I whirled at the bubbly voice. Under the now opened doorway stood a tall, black-clad woman with wavering, azure-and-grey streaked hair. A silver crown rested atop those flowing locks, and her toothy smile was stretched from ear to ear.

"Bloods be good," I chuckled, striding over to embrace the woman. "It's been too long, Myra!"

"Yes, it has!" She slid out of my hold and clasped my arms. "Serdin and I just arrived. I'm glad to see the siege was successful. You Fangs have done a splendid job."

Fangs Lasting blushed from the wall, dropping to a knee with a fist to his chest. "Thank you, Your Majesty…! I-I hope your Surfacing was met with little complication?"

"Hardly any," she reported with a flighty wave. "Daniel and Serdin were able to dispose of the handful of Raiders waiting for us. Our guards were hardly necessary, especially since we brought a flock of Flame and Bone dragons with us."

"Wonderful," I said. "Where is your husband, then?"

"With yours, I should think."

"Ah. Should we find them?"

She hummed blithely, her eyes glazing for a moment as her Dream mark gleamed. "No need. They're on their way here."

Ah. She must have had a vision of them. "How convenient," I said.

She clasped her hands excitedly. "Now—I *must* know how you've been! I read of your sons' strangeness, but what was it like for you and Lucas these past few years?"

My shoulders locked. *Starting with that right away?* I exhaled, massaging my eyes. "It was admittedly hectic… Roden, could you grant us some privacy?"

Fangs Lastings coughed awkwardly and sidled out. "Ah—yes, of course…" He bowed and shut the door behind him.

I sank into a nearby chair, decompressing. "I have to wonder, Myra." My nails clicked the untreated desk idly. "I understand why Serdin came along, and even Daniel… but you're not a warrior as we are. Why have you come?"

She went to the window and peeled back the tattered curtain, her tone whimsical. "Curiosity. There hasn't been a war since I was a girl. How could I not come to see?"

"War is not a damned theater show, Myra," I said, piqued. "Honestly. You could be hurt."

Myra inhaled a deep, calming breath, and released it in a smooth stream. "Actually… I've come to ask you to hold your troops here for a time."

I stared at her. "What?"

She kept her gaze to the snow outside. "Stay here with your army. If for only a little longer than you planned. When our children arrive with reinforcements, I pray you wait even then."

"They'll be months before arrival," I protested. "Not to mention, in case your memory has left, we're to be grandmothers soon. It's one thing to bring yourself here, Myra, but a *baby*?"

"All will be well, when they join us," she assured. "But please, take more time when they do. If you move to the mountains when you plan, the Raiders will find you. And you will not be prepared."

My lungs filled with ash. "You've had a vision?"

"I have," she lamented, facing me with arched brows. "Though, future visions hold many outcomes. All are faint now, but the clearest of them will not end well. Pray, change your course now. It may give you the time you need to change the outcome."

I brushed a thumb to my lips, deliberating. "How clear is this vision of yours?"

"It's faint," she admitted. "But I still worry, Alice. Please."

My wolf ears lowered, tail curling round my waist. *A faint vision is not the most likely to happen.* It would be a risk, going in as she says… Yet, expecting the outcome will give us the advantage. Enough to change it at the last moment, when we would need it most.

"I'm sorry, Myra," I concluded, rising. "We will move out as planned. But we'll double our scouts and defenses along the way. Will this change the outcome?"

Myra touched my wrist, her Dream mark gleaming azure, and her eyes went stale. After a moment, she sighed. "It's grown dimmer, at the least. The outcome where you live has gained lucidity."

"Then that is what we'll…" I trailed off, noticing the door was parted slightly.

Half of a bronze face peeked behind the door, one curling ewe horn scraping the frame.

"Ah…" *That girl we found in Drinelle.* What was her name again? "Milann," I remembered aloud, striding to her. "This is no place for children, dear. You should be with Yulia."

Milann ducked her head when I peeled open the door. She looked from me to Myra. Her gaze clung to Myra, her grip tightening on the scythe-sphere she held for comfort.

"Ya look like her," Milann blurted, pointing at Myra's curious face. "Ya look like the Missy Reaper! But... but you're taller. And your hair's all blue."

Myra pushed a considering finger to her lips. "Hm? Do you mean my daughter?"

"Milann!" Yulia's voice hollered from the halls. "Oh, Milann, what have I told you about disturbing the High Howless?"

Yulia's lovely visage appeared under the doorframe and scooped up Milann, the Dreamcatcher puffing. Then Yulia's gaze caught Myra standing there.

"Your Majesty!" Yulia gasped, bowing low. "Forgive the girl, she was under my watch... It was I who strayed in my duties."

Myra hummed and bent to match the ewe's eye-level in Yulia's hold. "Apologies not needed... Let's have a look at you, then."

Myra touched two delicate fingers to the child's brow, her Dream mark gleaming.

"Ah," Myra said after a long silence. "How interesting..."

Myra scooped the child out of Yulia's hold and walked off, the Death Queen's bubbly voice bouncing through the halls. "May as well spoil you now, mm? Perhaps you'll help me prepare for the new one on the way. Tell me dear: what flavor of ice cream is your favorite?"

I glanced at Yulia with a questioning scowl. She only shook her head.

YULIA

I walked adrift through the halls, confused with the Death Queen's sudden custody of Milann and distraught over what I was to do with myself now that my charge had been lifted.

"Ah, Yulia."

I turned, finding Lord Lucas walking from the other direction. With him were two men. One was bat winged with black hair and a thick moustache; the other had ashen hair and quartz-clear eyes, a crown engraved with skulls adorning his head.

My face warmed, and I hurried to bow. "My lord...! Your Majesty...! The-the Death Queen has just left with the ewe girl, my lord, you've just missed her..."

Lord Lucas scratched his thick beard. "The ewe girl? Odd... though, it does sound like Myra to wander off with a child of strange backgrounds."

His Majesty Death muttered, "I'd bet my ears she went to buy sweets for her."

"She did," I agreed, nervously placing my hands at my skirts. "They've left for ice cream."

The bat winged man—could this be Lord Tessinger? —let out a sharp laugh. "Ice cream! With all this snow! Sounds like your wife if ever I heard, Serdin."

"Yes, it does." His Majesty sighed and pinched the rim of his nose. Then he paused, glancing at me when I lifted my face. He blinked, as if stunned for a moment.

By habit, I glanced away, keeping my face turned downward.

"Erm… Forgive me, Howless," His Majesty began, suspicious. "I don't suppose… are you the widow of Lord Vivelle?"

The sound of my forced-upon family name was a knife in my ears. "Yes, my lord…" I said softly. "But I do prefer Yulia, if I'm to beg your pardon…"

"Of course, of course," he hushed as he cupped his mouth in thought. "Forgive me. I'm only puzzled how I'd yet to meet you. You were the one Dream came to me about some twenty years ago, was it?"

"Twenty-one," I whispered, the air growing chilled. I barely noticed my claws were digging into an arm I hadn't realized I held. "The twins were barely into their first year when Lord Lucas came and…"

—My scream split painfully, his thrusts reopening sores from last night. If only I could squeeze my eyes tight enough, if only I could grind my teeth hard enough, if only I could force myself to sleep, I wouldn't need to feel him—

"Thank you." I had to force the words through a swollen throat, swallowing. "For sending Lord Lucas. I am… truly thankful."

"—You ought to be thankful I don't toss you with the rest of the lot." He grabbed my long hair and shoved my head down the cellar door, his lantern flashing over the numerous women's corpses rotting on the dirt floor. The skeletal beast he had chained down there feasted on its latest meal, his former wife, her bones crunching and splitting—

"Well," His Majesty's lips stretched into a warm smile, though his look was concerned. "You're very welcome… are you all right, Howless? Your ears have grown."

My fox ears folded to my neck as I tightened my grip on my arm, trying to stifle the tremors. "Yes, Sire. Forgive me, I… struggle to forget, at times…"

Lord Lucas grasped my arm tenderly, his voice gruff yet quiet. "Perhaps you'd fancy to join the queen on her sweet excursion?" He cleared his throat, his bearded smile gentle. "I fear what Her Majesty is plotting with the girl. Be sure she doesn't spoil that child too much, eh?"

I returned the smile faintly. "Yes, my lord." I bowed and took my leave, hearing Lord Lucas give a long, disheartened sigh behind me.

Upon stepping out to the snowy streets, I breathed in a calming breath and laid a hand on a nearby railing covered in icy powder. I let the snow chill my fingers, melting under my palm. It was cold, but it was precisely what I wanted: a distraction. A reminder of where I was; that *this* time was real and *that* time was long behind me. Perhaps joining Her Majesty Death wasn't wise at the moment. She was King Dream's daughter, so it was more than likely she may ask similar questions that her husband had asked. *Best not to tempt it*, I decided.

"Yulia?"

My attention fizzled, and my head snapped up. Jimmy was there, his throat swallowed in a navy-blue scarf while his elk antlers collected a thin layer of snow. His gloved hands were stuffed in his coat pockets as he tossed his head in a gesture. "Got a minute?" He asked.

I cleared my throat and strode toward him, discreetly wiping my snow-wetted fingers on my cloak. "Yes?" I asked when meeting him.

"We found more Dreamcatchers in a few of the jail cells here," he explained and threw a thumb over his shoulder. "We need to set them up in the Howler's Inn here, but like with the other times, we can't get them clearance without you signing them off."

"Very well," I said and nodded. "Lead the way."

"It's over in the southern district," he said while he walked ahead. "Would probably be faster to catch a porter, but since the siege is still pretty fresh, there aren't any around to give us a ride. Hope you don't mind the walk."

"I needed a bit of fresh air regardless," I hummed.

He frowned at me. "Something happen?"

"The King and Queen of Death have arrived. His Majesty meant no harm by it, but he brought back a few… crude memories that I'd rather not relive."

He looked surprised. "You have a past with the Death King?"

"Of sorts. This was the first time we'd formally met, but he'd heard of me through *our* king."

"Why would King Dream…" He paused. Then fell quiet. "Oh. Right, guess that makes sense…"

I shot him a sharp look. "*What* makes sense, exactly?"

"Well, I mean, I guess it was Dream who told the Death King about your husband, right?" He asked. "And I'm guessing that's why he sent Howllord Lucas over here to lop off his head and all?"

I stopped short, my boots crunching into the snow. "You… know of that…?"

He scratched his nose in a shrug. "Yeah, the Howllord mentioned it—"

"Seamstress Cleanse me." I stormed ahead as my fox ears curled back, tail swishing furiously. "That was *not* his past to unveil."

Jimmy fumbled to keep at my side, rubbing his neck. "Uh, sorry… I don't think he meant anything by it. I guess it was pretty traumatic—?"

"If you plan to question me as His Majesty Death had just done, I shall find the Howler's Inn on my own." I kept my irked gaze forward. "*I* will decide when to share my past, thank you."

He staggered behind a foot, then cleared his throat. "Uh, r-right... sorry."

I breathed in through my nose and shut my eyes, shifting the subject as I calmed, my fox ears receding. "Now," I sighed gently. "Tell me about the new Catchers. How many were found?"

He didn't question the redirection and answered, "There were about four dozen crammed in each jail. It's not a very big town, but it's still a lot considering there's probably hundreds more either hiding out or long gone before things got sticky."

I laid my hands over my skirts. "I suppose we'll have to post notices in this city's Aspirrian parallel if we successfully overtake it tonight. Though, I fear we'll need a better strategy to pick out the pretenders this time around."

Thus far, in every city the Reapers had taken siege, we Dreamcatchers had a battle of our own to wage with the local Somniovokers who sided with Everland's king. There was a surprising amount. Most of those were typically Rockraiders who happened to double as dream walkers, but there were a number of normal civilians who they'd recruited to defend their Aspirrian parallel after the physical town had been conquered. The difficult part was not the battles themselves, but sorting out which Somniovokers were truly with us and which were playing as spies. The last problem had caused us many casualties among the Brotherhood.

Jimmy rubbed his goatee thoughtfully. "You said King Dream's daughter was here, right? Can we ask her to use her prophetic Hallows on anyone we take in to see if they're the real deal?"

I paused. "That... could work, actually. Her Majesty has both Somniovoking and scrying abilities, we've yet to find any dream walker with both elements to help with this dilemma."

"Perfect." He grinned. "Looks like we have ourselves a plan for tonight—"

"Sil Yulia!" A shrill voice shouted from across the road. It was a woman Catcher I recognized as Sil Eileen. Her blonde hair was tied in two braids that fell over her shoulders and bounced hectically as she ran over to Jimmy and me, panting over her knees. "Sir Jimmy...! Come quickly, there's an emergency with one of the Catchers we found in this district's jail!"

"What's happened?" I asked, alarmed.

"It's the man's daughter," Eileen explained. "She went into Aspirre to search for a way out before we arrived, and she hasn't woken since!"

I exchanged a determined nod with Jimmy. "Show us where she is."

Eastern Timberail's jail was indeed a bleak and moldy dungeon. When Jimmy and I arrived in the cell Eileen led us into, it was a struggle to push through the murmuring crowd of our fellow Catchers. Most were familiar faces we'd rescued throughout the campaign, but there were a few others I didn't recognize. They must have been the newly rescued from earlier today.

At the back of the crowded cell sat a grey-skinned man with black rabbit ears. Clearly a Grimling. On his lap, cradled in his arms, was a similarly rabbit-eared Grimlette that could only be his daughter. She looked perhaps sixteen, her pale face dusted with dark freckles while her black hair lay in a raggedy mess over her shoulders, sleek with grime and sweat just as her prison garb was.

On her exposed shoulder was an azure Dream mark that gleamed brightly, showing that her Hallows were active.

"Move!" Eileen shouted and had the crowd make way for Jimmy and me. "Sil Yulia and Sir Jimmy are here! Give them space!"

The Catchers fell back immediately, nodding to us in respect. I'd grown accustomed to their treatment of us lately. I supposed they thought us key figureheads among the Dreamcatchers in this war, since we were the first two walkers among the front lines when Her Highness Death stormed Tanderam Prison in the deserts. Supposedly, our names had been echoed within Aspirre since then. It was more than daunting to have so many people look up to us, but if it eased their nerves, we supposed there was naught we could do but strive to keep earning the respect they gave us.

Jimmy knelt to one side of the man and his daughter while I crouched on their other side. Eileen stood a distance behind me, worriedly peering over my shoulder as I examined the Grimlette. "Were you travelers from Grim?" I asked the father.

He nodded shakily, his black rabbit ears draped down his neck. "W-we'd only just surfaced on holiday when the war broke out. We tried to descend back home, but they'd blocked off the surfacing ports and rounded up any of us with Grimish hair."

Jimmy pointed his chin at the girl. "How long's she been asleep?"

"Two days," answered the father, wiping at tears. "Sh-she went into Aspirre to look for a way out—I tried to tell her to wait for me—but she hasn't woken up since. I can't find her in Aspirre anywhere. I-I don't know if she got lost or if one of the Noctis Golems ate her soul...!" He fell into a sobbing fit, clutching his daughter tighter.

I clasped a hand over his and hushed, "Her Hallows are still active. Had she been eaten by the golems, her mark would be dulled at the least."

"But where is she?" He pleaded desperately. "Why won't she wake up?"

Jimmy's voice was gritty. "That's something we intend to find out. Eileen." He flicked his gaze up at the awaiting woman. "Call for a Healer and get as many Brother and Sister Catchers down here as possible. Have them join us the minute they show up. We don't know how many enemy dream walkers are in this city's parallel, and I don't want to risk being outnumbered for too long if they've captured her soul, or if we run into any Noctis Golems on the way."

Eileen saluted and ran off to do as asked. I turned to the rest of the crowd and said, "All of you, please, join us in the parallel if you have the energy for it. We must find her quickly." I spoke to the father now. "I suggest you stay here in the physical realm to watch after her body. You'll need to give the Healer details on what's happened."

He nodded, his answer a strained sob as he held his daughter tenderly.

I glanced at Jimmy, who nodded. With that, we both leaned our backs against the moldy wall and evoked our dream Hallows onto our own chests, blue streams of light flowing from our hands and seeping into our skin as we drifted to sleep.

I awoke in Aspirre soon after closing my eyes. Now, my soul sat along an isolated brick road that floated within the black abyss of the Dream realm.

I turned to my right and found Jimmy was only now appearing on the same strip of road. His soul began as strings of azure light that swirled and wove into existence until they solidified into his more tangible, antlered form. When his eyes snapped open, he found me and rose, as did I, meeting him midway on the road. Soon, the dozen other Catchers from the jail cell appeared on their own zipping strings of light, and one by one, they fell into a determined block behind us, weaving themselves extra space on the road with their glowing Hallows. They then wove themselves fox-masks, as was part of the traditional Dreamcatcher's garb to hide their faces. Jimmy and I wove our own fox-masks to match them, but his had an elegant, red design running down the right side of his mask while mine had a blue design curling down the left side of my mask. This was Jimmy and my usual formation, so the others could identify us over the mass. Somehow, they preferred knowing which ones we were.

I evoked my Hallows and wove a translucent blue barrier around the whole of this area, knowing it was surely the missing girl's subconscious zone. It would help keep out the golems upon our return and mark the zone so we could find it again.

The girl couldn't wake unless she was brought back here, where her body lay in the physical parallel.

Now that her zone was protected, I led the knights off the isolated road, weaving myself a pair of azure wings to fly over the empty abyss before landing on the next strip of road. Jimmy and the others followed suit, and we hopped from road to road.

In the distance, I found the center square of Timberail's Aspirrian parallel. Parallel cities were the approximate locations that directly corresponded with the physical world. This particular parallel consisted of a few small buildings and a block of cobbled road that hovered suspended in Aspirre's blackness.

Flying with our makeshift wings, we touched down two roads before the isolated city. I crouched over the edge of the bricks under my bare feet and overlooked the terrain, holding up a fist to signal everyone to halt.

"Everyone, send out scouting copies," I said and evoked my blue Hallows, spreading my fist out to an adjacent road beneath me. Several fox-masked copies of myself were woven into existence in a stream of light, each holding the same wings I still had, and each of them flew off in different directions toward the city.

Jimmy did the same with his copies, and I glanced back to be sure the rest of our group followed our example.

Jimmy called back to them behind his red-marked mask, "Spread out and find the girl. And keep an eye out for enemy walkers."

They all gave confirming grunts before I hopped off the road and flew into the city, ducking behind one of the buildings. I peered around the corner to inspect the square.

Jimmy's masked face came beside me and peered over my shoulder. "I don't see anyone," he grunted. "Weird. Usually we find at least a few dozen walkers around."

"True," I murmured and slowly crept from around the building. My hands gleamed azure as I wove myself a thin rapier, the curling hilt wrapping around my knuckles in elegant swirls. "Those against the Reapers, come forward!" I shouted into the square. My voice echoed in the silence, and my heart drummed painfully loud. It was a risk coming out in the open like this, but we found that this was the easiest way to find our adversaries.

There came no answer.

Jimmy shuffled out to the street next, as did the rest of our party, though hesitantly. They each wove themselves weapons of different types, whatever brought them the most comfort. Minutes past in the silence, yet still, the city lay still and eerie.

Jimmy muttered, "Maybe we did get them all in the physical realm—"
HSHHHHHHhhhhhhhh...

A hissing wave of sound swelled from somewhere within the square. It sounded like sand grains sloshing against stone, its echoes bouncing about the small city and deflecting its point of origin.

"The Shepherd save us," I whispered and raised my rapier in a guarding pose, my fox ears growing. "There are golems in the town?"

Jimmy's elk ears grew, and he growled, "Any walker in here must be dead already for them to have gotten through their barriers—"

A scream split the quiet air like a rusted knife through paper. It was coming from the second floor of a building across the square.

A gargling roar trumpeted then, and from an alley came a black, sandy beast. Its form shifted and tumbled with no clear definition, sloshing toward the sound of the scream. At times, it took the form of a slithering serpent, at others, like a skeletal beast with four limbs. It was as if it struggled to remember what shape it was supposed to be, slinking at incredible speed toward the building.

"Death," I breathed in a shiver, then sprinted for the scurrying golem with my rapier raised, changing its silvery blade into a long, wide shepherd's crook. "That could be the girl up there!"

The golem sloshed against the building's door and flailed against it with sandy claws, screeching hungrily—

I swung my crook round its neck and yanked the creature away from the door. Then I quickly evoked my Hallows and created a translucent blue shield between the golem and me. "Back, beast!" I growled behind my mask.

The beast shrieked and charged for me, and I shoved my shoulder against the shield to keep it back, my bare feet sliding over the cobbled road and scraping painfully. I shouted to the others, "Everyone, get inside and help the girl! There may be more!"

Jimmy led the way inside, and once I was sure everyone was in, I heaved an exerting grunt and poured more Hallows onto my shield. The glass-like edges stretched and widened, and I smoothed the shield into a single, translucent dome around the golem, trapping it inside. The beast shoved its sandy body against its cage and clawed in an enraged howl, but it only caused cosmetic scratches. With the golem contained, I hurried inside and shut the door, weaving a new barrier over it to keep any more golems out.

Another girlish scream split from the upper floor of this building, and I rushed up the steps, using my temporary wings to help give me lift—

A new golem shrieked into view on the stairwell and sloshed down to charge at me. I flattened against the wall to dodge its bite, but it swiped a sandy claw at my shoulder and cut a large gash there. I yelped and clutched my dripping shoulder, but bit down the pain and shoved my shepherd's crook straight into the golem's granular chest. I wove its edges into sharp, hooked points while it was wedged inside the thing, then leapt up and yanked the golem down the stairs under my jumping feet. The golem was sent crashing down below. I quickly wove a new, translucent barrier within the stairwell and formed a wall to keep the golem down there, then rushed up the steps again.

When I reached the upper halls, I found the other Catchers in the throes of battle with several more golems. It was a frenzy of sand and flashing azure light, and I pushed my way into the mass, ducking and dodging and flying over golems until at last I reached the final room in the hallway. Its door was splintered and cracked apart, leaving naught but wooden shards along the doorframe.

I rushed inside and found the fox-masked face of Jimmy. He was carrying a black-haired girl with rabbit ears in his crimson stained arms and struggling to kick back a straggling golem. The girl was missing an arm, her ragged shoulder gushing with blood as the grey-skinned Grimlette shivered in Jimmy's hold.

I hooked my sharpened crook into the golem's sandy back and swung the beast away from them, using my Hallows to weave a domed barrier around it.

"We got her!" Jimmy shouted to the Catchers outside in the hall. "Fall back!"

Affirming hollers came from the others, and Jimmy took the lead by leaping out the nearest window and using his temporary wings to soar out of the city. I flew beside him, glancing over my shoulder to see the others form up behind us.

"—Yulia!" Jimmy yelled, getting my attention—

A flying golem rushed for me from the abyss, nearly invisible in the surrounding blackness, but its hissing grains alerted me in time to dodge. It came for Jimmy next, but with his arms occupied by the Grimlette, he could only duck and dip chaotically to avoid it.

I let out a vicious snarl and hooked the beast by the throat, flinging it far, far away until it was nothing more than a fading memory within the abyss.

Yet then, a light blinked into existence where it had been.

I squinted at the tiny speck of light, watching in confusion as it radiated wider. Golems didn't gleam, not that I'd ever seen. What was happening?

The gleam brightened like a star, and I could swear I heard the faintest squeal of agony as it bloomed—and then winked out entirely.

Yet in that light's absence, there came another. It wasn't nearly as large, but it was perhaps the brightest glow of azure I'd ever seen in Aspirre. But unlike the first light, this one was shaped like a young boy. The boy held my gaze in the distance, his gleaming shepherd's crook jingling like bells. Then he nodded, and floated away, his figure swallowed by the darkness.

I stared after where he'd left. "What in Nirus…?"

"—Yulia, come on!" Jimmy shouted, snapping me out of my distraction. "We're almost there, and we have company!"

I whipped my gaze ahead of him. Swarming like invisible insects in the distance, rising behind the translucent barrier we had set around the girl's subconscious zone, were hundreds of golems. Bloods be good, the open town nearby must have attracted more than usual.

"Everyone!" I called back and swept my sharpened crook in a determined ges-ture. "There are too many to keep back! Put up your barriers and push through! Our priority is bringing the girl to her zone and returning to the physical realm!"

"Aye!" They shouted back, and one by one, they wove themselves protective bar-riers that looked like glass bubbles, and they all floated forward at incredible speeds toward the girl's subconscious zone. I wove one for myself, then another for Jimmy and the girl, since his arms were full.

The golems splashed into us in a shower of pelting sand, blocking most of my view as the blackened grains bounced off my barrier and skittered away like a torrent of rain—

My bubble rumbled and shook when I hit the zone's barrier, shattering both at once as I, and the Catchers around me, dropped onto the isolated roads suspended in the abyss.

I threw my glare at Jimmy. "Wake her!"

Jimmy's hands gleamed azure as he touched the girl's brow—and they both disappeared.

I evoked my own Hallows, my hands shining blue.

Hhhssssssshhhhhhhhhaaaaaaaaaww....!

A flurry of golems came screeching onto the road on either side of me, closing in. I quickly brought my glowing fingertips to my brow just as they collided in a shower of sand—

I gasped awake in the jail cell, my pulse thundering.

The golems had disappeared along with Aspirre. Jimmy sat against the wall beside the Grimish father and daughter, and the other Catchers were all waking up in heavy pants. I checked my shoulder, the one that had been snagged by a golem, but the cut was gone. I should have known it would be, wounds made to your soul within Aspirre never remained in the physical realm. But the searing sting still clung to my memory and played tricks with my mind. I supposed that piece of my soul had yet to heal while back in my vessel. Hopefully it wouldn't take too much longer.

The Grimlette was coughing and gasping for breath in her Father's lap, shivering and clutching her arm—which was still in one piece and not ripped off her shoulder as it had been in Aspirre.

"Fehn!" cried the father in a joyful sob. He squeezed his wakened daughter fervently. "Thank you! Thank you...!"

I exhaled and pushed to my feet, Jimmy doing the same and brushing himself off. "You're quite welcome," I said and offered the father and daughter each a hand. "Now, I'm sure you're both overdue for a bit of hospitality. Come, we've room for you both in the Howler's Inn, courtesy of its founder."

They gladly took my hands and let me lift them to their feet, leading them out of the cell.

On the way out, Jimmy leaned close to my side and murmured in my ear, "It looks like we have a lot of work ahead of us in the Golem department. Should I round up a few Brothers and Sisters to start work on a new barrier to keep them out?"

I nodded, assuming he was lowering his voice to not upset the father and daughter. "Do so immediately," I whispered back. "We cannot allow those beasts to run rampant with so many souls here needing sleep. I'm surprised the civilians have survived this long *before* we arrived."

He shrugged. "They might have had a few dream walkers hidden in town to protect everyone, like these two. Don't worry. I'll make sure we put up a strong barrier tonight. In the meantime, keep everyone awake."

"Understood."

Once we exited the jail, I watched Jimmy hurry eastward toward a cluster of other Catchers, and I led our rescued guests to the Howler's Inn.

There was much work ahead of us indeed.

19

NEW RECRUIT

CAYDEN

C lack!

I slammed the now empty glass of whiskey on the gold-dressed table, swiping another glass from the passing servant's tray and chugging that halfway.

My lion ears twitched at all the chatter in the ballroom, the palace guests buzzing with carefree fervor as the brass quartet played a bold tune from their designated corner.

"Damned foolish," I muttered bitterly, swigging the last of the whiskey. I hit the empty glass over the table in a clatter. My eyes flicked to two women beside me. My *wife*, Revinna, and my teenaged sister, Rilla. "He shouldn't be celebrating," I said. "They've lost Adrial to the Reapers."

Young Rilla sniffed and turned her nose up, glugging her goblet of lemonade. She was too young to drink spirits, but from her indignant posture while clacking down her goblet, you'd think she were a middle-aged alcoholic. Her curly blonde hair cascaded down her back and was dressed with a row of baby-blue ribbons and bows that matched her frilly gown. She'd covered her latest bruises—curtesy of Father during their secretive sessions where he tried to exploit her prophetic visions—with makeup and powder, as she usually did.

"I say it's a show," Rilla huffed. "In our last session, he had me show him the outcome of the Reaper's march on Timberail to the east." She smiled wickedly and cackled. "It went *horribly* for him."

I grimaced. "I thought as much, given that I heard his screams from outside the door and had to interrupt before he chucked the crystal ball at you again."

Rilla shrugged. "Would have been worth it just to see the panic on his face. But thanks for keeping an ear to the door like I asked." She flicked me an olive-eyed glance of appreciation and flushed slightly. "I… don't trust him not to kill me if left alone, so… thanks, Cayden."

I gripped her shoulder with a stale smile. "That's why I'm here, Rilla… but you really think he's putting on a show? The very idea of a ball seems ludicrous after two losses in the same month."

Beside Rilla, Revinna swirled her wine delicately, her expression even as she gazed upon the amiable crowd. She wore fine, violet silks today to play the part of her new role as a princess at this royal ball. Her marriage-vines glittered from her hair and forehead in the colorful chandeliers' lights overhead, her honeyed hair braided with various other jewels that complemented the tiara adorning her head.

She stole a sidelong glance at me as she kept a forced smile for the crowd and murmured under her breath, "Is this not a good thing for your cause, Cayden?"

I snorted. "Oh, it's Bloody fantastic for the cause. But this behavior, when facing such a devastating loss, is madness. You'd think he'd be panicking." I slumped into my chair, my lion tail swishing angrily as I shifted my glare to my father.

Across the marble floor, Father spoke with two men in hushed tones. He wore his crown messily today, his blond hair greasy and frazzled.

The men with him were his newly assigned Hands. One was a spindly man with a hawkish nose and long, orange wings, his skin a Landish walnut. His name, as I recalled, was Roarlord Nerran, my father's replacement First Hand after Apson had been executed. Last I heard of Apson, his ghost was safely delivered to High Howllord Lucas and had formed a Bloodpact with him. The news had eased my nerves, but only so much. There were still concerns left unanswered.

The man who'd posed as Roarlord Wales, whom I'd outed as Kael Treble, had vanished since our confrontation. He claimed he'd left to speak with someone regarding Cilia… It had been a risk to give myself away so recklessly, but it seemed luck had been on my side. Since Kael disappeared, Wales's true body was discovered outside his manor, buried poorly in his yard. The Lady Wales was found with him along with their adolescent daughter, their corpses pale and festering with squirming maggots.

The Seekers determined the cause of death had been snake bites. They found their limbs swollen and blistered, traces of venom in their long-dried veins. If this Macarius man truly was a snake shifter, I had no doubt he was behind the murders. But, of course, my father blamed Apson for the family's death. Apson was, after all, a viper with venom. Nothing would convince Father otherwise.

Wales's replacement was Roarlord Houzer, speaking in whispers to my father and Roarlord Nerran now. Houzer had forward-curling bull horns and a thick, wide-set nose. All three, I noticed, held the same, grave expression. From what I understood, these men were headmasters of the Lysander schools in separate districts here in the capital.

Perhaps Father IS panicking, I considered in silence, my grown claw tapping the drinking glass with small, rapid clinks. *Is this why he bothered throwing this soiree? To hide how poorly his war was fairing against the Reapers and my rebellion?*

I sighed and folded my arms over the table, wishing another servant would come by soon with another drink for me.

It had been months since Mother's death… since she had tossed herself off my balcony. I supposed if she hadn't done it herself, Father would have seen to it eventually. She merely wanted that choice for herself, since he'd taken everything else from her.

"Khmm, *hmm*," a clearing throat rumbled behind me. "Good evening, Your Highness."

My lion ears jolted stiff at that voice. Slowly, I inched my gaze back. A burly rabbit-eared man with dark skin stood behind me, holding a long parcel wrapped in a velvet cloth.

"H… Henry?!" I hissed. Revinna and Rilla whirled at the name as well, and in a panic, I shot my gaze round the crowd. There were a number of eyes focused on Henry and his grimy, Blacksmith's overalls, their murmurs buzzing with questions. I turned back around to face the table and chewed, "What are you *doing* here, you foolish bastard? Do you want us both hanged?"

"I'm just here delivering that Crystal sword you ordered, Your Highness," Henry said painfully loud for all to hear. When I inched my gaze over my shoulder again, I saw the man smirk and hold out the wrapped parcel in an ostentatious bow. "For your… *assassination* problems."

My lion ears picked up the newly accepting chatter from the surrounding crowd of eavesdroppers. Henry's excuse seemed to give them understanding enough to leave us be and mind their own affairs once more.

Brilliant plan, Henry, I commended in silence. I supposed I hadn't had a chance to sneak away in some time—neither had Revinna nor Rilla.

I relaxed slightly and faced him again, taking the wrapped sword and unveiling the hilt. With an inspecting eye purely to keep up the act, I partially slid out the glowing blade and hummed. "Ah, yes! Thank you, sir. This looks to be as brilliant as my recommender claimed. Your reputation for quality craftsmanship certainly holds true." After another glance around the crowd to be sure we lost the extra ears, I grabbed his bulky shoulder to reel him in and murmured under my breath. "Is there word from Fangs Alice? Is that why you came so blatantly?"

Henry lowered one long ear and nodded. "She says they're planning to march on the capital in another month. Her Majesty Land is scheduled to arrive by Airship then."

"Brilliant! Tell the others in town and have a line of defense prepared. We'll want to give them a clear opening into the mountains if we can afford to." I shoved him forward. "Now, get the Land out of here before the eavesdroppers get curious again. If none of us can come find you, assume we'll all be ready within the palace on the Day of Revival."

Henry grinned and bowed low, then spun on his heels and strolled out of the ballroom.

I turned back to Rilla and Revinna with a wild smile. "We three have much to prepare for, it seems."

TAYMEN

The endless blackness lurched and swayed around me, like a gelatinous river squeezing and bubbling over a piece of driftwood.

I thought I heard people talking, but it was all muffled and dim. I think my eyes opened, but all I could see for now was an orange, flickering blur. Maybe a fire?

I tried to move, but what little muscles I could still control were numb and tingling, and a slosh of bile gurgled in my gut. I was pretty sure I groaned, but that could have been one of the blurry people talking around me.

"Hey, the new recruit's awake," one of the muffled voices blubbered like cottony fuzz in my ears. The man's tone cleared up as he went on, "Mistress? Hey, yeah, the new kid's waking up finally. Might want to come down and Mark him."

I felt a croak blister up my throat. "Wha…?"

The man's face finally solidified when I squinted my eyes into focus, the snowy world around him still swimming a bit, the stars streaking in the night sky.

"Mornin' sunshine," the man said and flashed a disease-ridden set of crooked, yellow teeth. He was bronze-skinned with dark brown hair, a wiry goatee framing his chapped lips. He was holding some kind of half-chewed meat with a splintered bone sticking out, completely raw with blood still dribbling down his fingers. He ripped off a piece with his sharpened, crooked teeth, some of it getting stuck in one fang as he chewed heartily and said, "Ho' waff yur beau'y sweeff?"

I was too busy staring at his eyes to answer. Instead of normal, black pupils, his were white and *glowing*. Like tiny balls of white fire burning against his brown irises. They were so freaky, I looked down to get a hold of myself.

Then I saw what kind of meat he was eating.

"Ah—hah—ah…!" I jolted back and scrambled on all fours in the snow to get away from him, pointing a shivering finger at him. "Th-th-that…! That's a *hand!*"

The crooked toothed man was tearing into the soaked flesh of a dismembered arm—a *shifter's* arm, with pale fingers and muscle and nails and bones and…

The bile from before gushed up my throat and splattered on the snow in a painful retch, my stomach shuddering another gag.

When my stomach finally settled down—

My vomit pile suddenly blackened and turned into millions of tiny, squirming maggots. I barely had time to yelp before the maggots slithered over the snow and onto my fingers, crawling up my arms and shoulders and neck and chin like hungry worms until they funneled back into my mouth and poured down my throat again, choking me, and latching back into my stomach where it started.

When I could breathe again, I let out a disgusted, rough scream, wiping my mouth in heavy, frightened pants. "Wh-wh… what in Land just… *Hrrrmph!*" I gagged again but clamped a hand over my lips to stop the puke from coming back.

The white-pupiled man still eating the arm guffawed. "Aw, you'll get used to it, kid. The sickness goes away after the first day."

"F-f-first day of what?" I croaked, hugging my shoulders in a shiver. I was naked in the snow, except for a pair of boxers. "W-where are m-my clothes?"

He shrugged. "You'll get new ones, no worries. Mistress La'Lunaî wants everyone to look uniform, so we know which of us is which when the fighting starts."

"What are you…"

A hissing growl sounded behind me.

I spun so fast, my vision took a second to catch up. Crawling in the snow and dripping with black sludge—the same gross, squiggling worms that came out of me earlier—was a skeletal *thing* with glowing white eyes. I screamed and shuffled away from it. The demon cocked its disgusting skull at me, sniffed my bare toes, then bleated a disinterested growl and crept on its way, joining the hundreds and thousands of other creatures like it in this valley. There were a few clusters of shifters in the mass, lounging around and goofing off, as if they weren't surrounded by monsters who could rip them apart.

The man behind me muttered between chews, "Might want to scooch over a bit, kid."

I gave him a twisted, desperate look. "What?"

The ground shook suddenly, and a shadow fell over me—

Something as big as a mountain *crushed* me so deep into the snow, I hit the dusty ground underneath and *cracked* every bone, *squished* every muscle, and *popped* every organ in my body flat. The sheer agony would have had me howling, but my throat and skull had been turned into pancakes along with the rest of me. My lungs were pulverized.

Finally, whatever had crushed me lifted up—like some enormous, rocky foot—and my bones squirmed with black worms to reform themselves in painful, tear-wrenching pops. When my lungs reflated, I gasped for breath, coughing while I waited for my mangled arms to crack back into place along with my skull and ribs.

Crooooooaaaa!

An earsplitting roar trumpeted above me, and my head snapped up in a painful crick, my spine still in the middle of reforming.

A towering mountain with legs stalked through the blackened mass in the valley, shaking the ground with every step and carelessly crushed any demons unlucky enough to be caught under its massive feet.

It was a Stonedragon. And in the distance, I saw several of them walking through the valley, all covered in the white powder as they stomped slowly around the swarm of demons, minding their own business. Cluster after cluster, the demons were crushed under the dragon's heavy feet, but like me, the creatures only glopped back together after it left as if nothing happened.

Like me? I raised my shaking hands, watching as my broken fingers slithered with black tar and cracked back into place. "I-I…" My voice quivered, and I swallowed hard. "I'm… a Necrofera, aren't I…? A demon? Like—like from the stories parents tell you to make you behave?"

The man behind me cackled. "You're pretty sharp, kid. You remember your name?"

"My name?" I strained to remember, but now that I thought about it, I couldn't remember *anything*. I hit my head furiously, knowing damn well I should at least know my Bloody name. "It…" I said, straining. "I-it's… Taymen?" That sounded right.

"Good start," the guy—another Necrofera? —commended with a nod. He tore into his raw, shifter-arm and chewed thoughtfully, gesturing with the dismembered hand. "The rest should hopefully come back over time. No telling how long, but rest assured, it'll come back. Anyway, welcome to the horde."

He swept the arm around the valley of demons. "Most of us are mindless animals right now, but every now and then we get other Sentients like you and me coming around."

"Other Sentients..." I looked around the valley, paying better attention to the humanoid shifters that were scattered in their own clusters in the blackened mass. We were in our own cluster of shifters apparently; I didn't even notice all the people around us until now. Some were laughing and sharing a meal of fresh, shifter corpses while some were bare-ass naked and screwing in the snow, moaning like they weren't out in the open.

"The name's Jace," the man with the arm greeted and pounded at his chest. "I'll be watching after you and the rest of our designated squad, along with my lieutenant, Syreen."

Jace nodded to a woman I didn't notice had been sitting on a log on the other side of a nearby firepit.

I froze when I registered her face. "H-hey! You're that girl...!"

The woman, Syreen, barely turned her head to look at me, but it was like she was staring into space instead. She didn't say anything and went back to watching the fire like a mindless doll.

Jace laughed. "Syreen was your recruiter. Don't expect her to say too much, she's not really the chatty type. The others say she was some kind of queen in Neverland before this, but she can't really remember too much yet. I'd leave her be if I were you though. You don't want to know what happened to the last guy who tried to talk to her—"

"Hello there, new recruit," a little girl's voice chimed behind me suddenly.

I whirled and found some web-eared kid staring up at me with emerald irises and white pupils. She put fists at her sides. "Welcome. I am your Queen, La'Lunaî of the Southern Seas."

I blinked and looked at Jace to see if this was some kind of joke. Jace only crossed his arms.

"Uh..." I said and turned back to the little fish girl, La'Lunaî. "Look, miss—uh, *queen,* or whatever... I don't really know what's going on, but I should probably get out of here and—"

A crushing weight slammed me backward several feet, and I yelped, landing on my back in the wet snow as the weight pushed my bones like some invisible mountain, ribs cracking painfully.

"You misunderstand, little one," La'Lunaî sang as she loomed over me. With her this close, that same weight crushed me tenfold and pushed me farther into the snow. She lifted a scaled finger and touched it to my forehead. Then a black slug wiggled out of her knuckle and slurped into my skin, digging deep like a viper sinking its fangs into my brain, and I let out a pained howl. "You belong to me, now," she said. "And as my newest pet, you're not to leave these feeding grounds until I give explicit permission. Understood?"

I wheezed for breath, that worm in my brain wriggling harshly at the command and locking my muscles in place. "Y… yes…" I found myself squealing thoughtlessly. It was like my jaw was moving on its own.

La'Lunaî lifted a finned eyebrow. "Yes, *what*, pet?"

"Y-yes, Mistress…" I nearly puked again, but swallowed it. I wasn't really sure where the name came from, but it was yanked out of my mouth like a disgusting slosh of acid.

Satisfied, La'Lunaî—Mistress—stepped back and the crushing weight disappeared. I gasped a strained wheeze and rolled to my stomach in a sickened hack. My head throbbed wildly with that black slug, like it was making a cozy little nest for itself in my skull.

La'Lunaî smiled and nodded her approval. "Very good, pet. Now, I expect your nestmates will see you well fed, yes?" She turned to Jace and that quiet girl, Syreen.

Jace lifted his half-eaten shifter arm and grinned. Syreen only nodded.

"F-f-f…" I stuttered, staring at that gross arm in Jace's hand. "Fed…?"

Syreen rose from her log by the fire and knelt to the discarded corpse that I only now noticed was lying there. It looked like a man's body, missing its arms and one leg, a bit of his skull and brains…

Crack!

Syreen shoved her hand through the corpse's back, making me flinch as a solid *snap* sounded. When she pulled her hand back out, she was holding onto a pale, screaming ghost.

She walked forward with the frantic ghost still in her claws, and I shuffled back.

"W-what are you doing?" I demanded tightly.

Syreen said nothing. She stepped beside me, grabbed my chin and wrenched it open, then *shoved* the screaming ghost down my throat. I gagged and gargled, trying to push her off, but she was like a boulder, still cramming the slimy, cold soul into my mouth. She clamped my jaw shut and held it closed, staring at me placidly.

"Swallow," La'Lunaî barked.

My throat obeyed, and the soul's screams vanished into nothing. Syreen finally let me up and I exhaled in disgust.

"There," La'Lunaî chimed pleasantly. "You'll grow accustomed to the taste. I expect you to feed whenever the opportunity arises. I need my horde as strong as Cilia plans to make hers—"

"Pardon me, madam," a woman's voice suddenly cut in. "You wouldn't happen to be the queen of these beasts, would you?"

La'Lunaî turned, and I craned to see who was talking.

It was some random viper woman. She had brown scales and frizzy, walnut hair with some grey streaks running down the sides. Her smile displayed the two small fangs at the front of her teeth. Accompanying her were two thug-looking teens around my age, one carrying a mirrored sphere and the other carrying a long metal box.

Mistress La'Lunaî cocked her head hungrily. "Clean Ones? Ooh, my but you've stumbled into the wrong nest, haven't you?"

Mistress leapt for the woman in a heartbeat and shoved her hand through the viper's chest.

But it phased through without touch. Like the woman wasn't even there. Like a ghost, but with color, and one that even Mistress couldn't touch.

Mistress blinked. "What in Bloods…?"

"Forgive my rudeness," said the viper woman with a humble curtsy. "But my original is conducting business elsewhere at the moment. I've sent a copy here to negotiate with Queen La'Lunaî instead."

"Copy?" Mistress scrunched her brow. "Ah. You must be a dream walker."

The woman smiled. "Indeed."

I blinked, remembering the name 'dream walker'. Had someone called *me* that in the past? *I think… I think I was one of those,* I thought while touching my neck—where my Dream mark was. *Yeah, that felt right. I was a Somniovoker.*

"And your cohorts?" Mistress asked the viper woman, eyeing the two thugs beside her. "Are they phantom copies as well?"

The woman gestured to the two thugs. "They are as tangible as the mountains surrounding us, I assure you. Consider them part of our negotiations: willing recruits who wish for the prize of immortality that you so generously offer."

The two thugs said nothing, but they both nodded, not a hint of hesitation on their hard-set faces.

"However," the woman added, "I would ask you to wait a moment longer before recruiting them to your horde, your majesty. I've more gifts to bestow." She paused, her eyes flicking to Syreen beside me suddenly. She curtsied and hummed, "Oh, my. Then the rumors were true after all. We wondered where you'd disappeared to after Land's Relicblood disposed of you, Queen Syreen of Neverland."

Syreen's lion ears flicked in question. "Do I… know you?" the quiet girl hushed.

"Briefly," the viper said. "Your reign was rather short. But I didn't expect to find you here in Everland's valleys. My name is Lanyce Lysandre, Headmistress of the Lysandre Academy and its various international schools across the realms. As a Necrofera, I don't expect you'll remember much of me, if you ever do at all."

Syreen looked away, as if lost in a deep thought now.

Lanyce Lysandre cleared her throat and addressed Mistress La'Lunaî again. "Regardless, your dark grace…" She turned to the brute with the metal box expectantly.

He opened it dutifully, and she waved a hand toward the contents: some kind of Metaglass arrows and knives and swords filled with what looked like squiggling, black veins. "My first gift, on behalf of my husband, are these newly developed weapons of war."

Mistress folded her scaled arms in a huff. "What use have demons for weapons other than ourselves?"

"Ah, but these are no ordinary weapons, your grace." Lanyce grinned.

The thug holding the box plucked the knife from inside and—

He drove it into his own chest.

The thug gave a pained grunt and dropped the box, the rest of the weapons falling to the snow as he collapsed. Black veins spewed from the knife and crawled over the guy's limbs like spiny weeds. Patches of his skin started to burn away in a nasty simmer, his cheekbones poking out, and soon enough, a black mist hissed out of his pores and evaporated into air. Then he was soul-sucked dead, his blood painting the white powder around him.

The second thug bent to pick up the arrow and sword his dead cohort dropped, not even looking at the new corpse bleeding at his feet.

The viper woman smiled at Mistress La'Lunaî. "As you can see, these weapons are imbued with a rare form of Hallows that was once thought extinct." Her smile twisted darkly. "Infeciovoking."

Mistress's webbed ears perked with interest. "You found a poison spewer? Outside of Cilia's bloodline?"

"Oh, our source is the very man responsible for instilling that Hallows into Cilia's line." She chuckled like she was bragging. "Her husband crafts these poisonous tools for us himself. They affect both the vessel and the soul, making wonderful close-distance *and* long-range attacks against pesky enemies who like to resurrect the dead… enemies such as, say, an army of Reapers?"

Mistress La'Lunaî rubbed her chin in thought. "I suppose you've had some informants tell you of my predicament, then?"

"My daughter is risking her life to spy on the Reapers. Your name was spoken often among their group." She looked at the still-standing thug on her right. "As for my second gift… We've brought you something that may give you some… leverage against your rivalling demon queen."

Mistress clapped her hands like an excited child as the thug lifted the mirrored sphere he held and slid open the lid, presenting a gleaming pile of glowing lights inside.

"Your dark grace," Lanyce began with a low bow. "I give you the cherished memories of Demon Queen Cilia of Everland."

CULATIA

20

HORRORS

KAEL

500 YEARS PRIOR

My angel's silken hair poured through my fingers like a soothing river. Each stroke left crimson streaks.

Her darling cheeks, once rivaling the warmth of Grim's Flamedragons, was now cold and worn; a ghost of her fire long dampened, her soul's brimstones long cooled. I held her so, so gently to my breast, rocking over the floorboards as I always would when she needed me.

This night, it was I who needed her.

"I'm sorry." The claws of my whisper raked and ravaged my throat, praying for an answer.

Yet she was as silent as the surface skies. Her breathless lips were half parted, green eyes which once were full of love and life and all that was just under the watch of Nira were now as stale and dim as the Seamstress's wrathful Void.

Her open neck still dripped and drenched my arms, pooling red around us, yet I cared not. I held my angel fast and I held her with a tenderness I had shamefully withheld since the day we'd wedded.

"I'm to blame," I croaked, rocking her. Merciful tears blurred her scattered pieces and torn, naked flesh from sight. "I should have been here. I… I should have…"

My eyes squeezed shut, spirit collapsing, cradling her sweet, beautiful head. And wept.

"Cilia…" My breaths shivered. "Cilia, forgive me. Nira Cleanse my soul, forgive me…! I love you. I love you, please, let this be a dream. Let Iri have me punished with this dream; I-I see now. Please…"

She still gazed up at me with those soulless eyes. Silent. Still.

"I love you…"

"—Kael," I heard Macar call from the front door of our home, his banging frantic. "Kael, I know you're angry, but I must insist you listen to reason…!"

The creak of a door hit my ears, and Macar's voice faded into silence. I kept to my rocking, holding my angel's head close, whispering to her.

"Kael," Macar's tone was so soft, I could barely hear it. "What… what is this?"

I rocked her steadily, whispering. "I'm sorry."

"Kael, snap out of it!" Macar seized my arm and ripped me to my feet, gagging when he found her beautiful head in my drenched arms. "Bloody Land, Kael!" He swatted her out of my hold, her skull *thunk, thunk, thunking* to the smeared floor.

I screamed and reached for her, but Macar shoved me back, slamming me to the wall. "Get a hold of yourself, Kael!" he shouted, striking my cheek once, twice, three times. "Be calm! Tell me what's happened!"

"I-I came…" My lungs splintered with a wheeze. "I came home and… and Cilia—my angel—my angel was tending to a roast, and I… I felt a child within her. A child not of mine, I… I called her a whore. I called my darling such horrible things… I-I left to calm down, and once I returned, she… s-she was…" I collapsed into Macar's chest, sobbing, a squeal pushing through my raw throat.

But something fizzled when I touched his scaled arms. The static of his blood pulsed in my soul. It was a familiar static that I could swear I'd felt… recently.

I shoved him back, my cat ears curled. "*Your* blood…!" My breaths crackled. "It was your blood…! Why did that child have *your* blood, Macar?!"

Macar blinked under his half-moon spectacles. "What are you on about?"

I grabbed his tunic and slammed him against the wall, roaring, "The child she bore had your blood! The very blood in your veins, Macar!"

His face went stale with shock, then his expression sagged as if understanding. "My blood?" he asked, hushed. "Or my twin's?"

My grip loosened. "Accursius…?"

Macar pushed up his spectacles, exhaling solemnly. "I… caught them some time ago, in his chambers. I confronted her after, and she claimed Accur had threatened your position in the infirmary." He rubbed his eyes. "At first, I didn't believe her, but… I decided to investigate myself. I sent a copy to spy on them one night. I overheard him threaten her—threaten *you*, Kael. With Accur being Adam's Hand, he has every authority to cast you out."

Tears blurred my vision. "H… how long…?"

His head shook. "I only discovered it some months ago."

"Why hadn't you said anything?" I demanded, shoving him. "Why hadn't *she*…!"

"She asked for my help," he said softly. "And asked that I stay silent… at least until Accur was exposed. I was on the verge of a breakthrough tonight, yet…"

His haunted gaze swept across the spattered home. On the wall, where I had found my angel's head hanging by her hair, the words still read hot and bright: *Your failure's payment.*

Her dismembered limbs were still scattered about the floorboards. Her mutilated heart was still wedged against her naked groin. Her head—my angel's head—had rolled to one cheek, soaking in the sticky crimson.

Macar grabbed my shoulder suddenly, his look wide as though realizing something. "Kael," he said, "where is Caleb?"

Blinking tears, I whispered. "Caleb…?" Panic speared my blood and I ran to my son's bedroom, throwing open the door. "Caleb!?"

There was silence, the stink of wax and sulfur lingering from the long-snuffed candle by my son's bed.

I stumbled to the thin sword mounted on our wall and sprinted to the snowy streets outside, screaming, *"Caleb!"*

—I saw a cloaked figure move from the shadows ahead. Over the figure's shoulder was a young boy, gagged with a cloth and arms tied behind his back, his green eyes spotting me and wriggling desperately.

"CALEB!" I bounded for him, readying my sword.

The hooded figure's head snapped to me.

Adam? I stumbled on a snow mound, the shock of whose face I gazed upon so jarring, I fell to the cold powder. Adam's golden locks bounced from his tanned cheeks as he ran into the nearest alley and disappeared with my son.

PRESENT DAY

The rain drizzled outside this flat's window, the busy streets of Culatia's capital buzzing with hover-carriages, horses, winged and grounded shifters alike below us.

"Three weeks of this rain," I rumbled, watching many large vision-screens blink and flash on the wall of every tall building, the screens of light partially blocked by the metal bones of our building's scaffolds. The poles dripped with the relentless torrent of water, overflowing the gutters. "Is there ever a time it ends?" I asked Macar.

Macar did not answer. Behind me, the voice of his step-daughter fuzzed from the screen of light projecting from his communicator, it's strange cogs and springs gyrating in a gentle hum.

"Security is still far too thick, I'm afraid," his daughter, Genevieve, reported. The window behind her hissed with rainwater, much like our own in this loft. *"The new Sky King has his guards marching the hallways, the ballrooms, the gardens—every damned inch of the palace grounds... were we to strike now, I fear we'd be filled with arrows before stepping a toe across the bridge."*

Macar tapped a ponderous finger on the metal desk before him. "And you've been sure to stay away from Dream's prophetic touch, I hope?" he asked her.

"Of course, Father," she said, hesitant. *"Though, I'm finding it far more difficult to make these calls with the Land Queen's lumbering pet slinking about my shadow. I can scarcely find a moment to break away."*

"Then do take care, dearest daughter. And alert us once the river of guards runs thin."

She nodded, and the screen dissipated.

Such strange devices this era has created... From what Claude had explained when he was still with us, these communicators were the updated renditions of the vision-gems Macar and I knew from our era. Though, the Culatians had toyed with the gems. They'd fastened wires, coils, cogs and gears about the things and found some way to project the images into the air through some magic with mirrors.

In our day, one only needed to gaze upon a gem's fragmented surface to see what its other half revealed. No technology, no strange magics, simply the mineral itself and nothing more, as the Gods Bloody well intended.

A knock came at the door, startling me while Macar tensed in his seat.

"M'lord," a muffled voice called from behind the door. "It's Drestel, m'lord."

"Ah!" Macar rose and folded his arms behind him. "Come in, Archchancellor."

A man entered and uplifted his rubbery hood, his scaled wings dripping water.

Macar strode to the newcomer. "What news from your school, Drestel? Have your students given an answer?"

"I should think they're your students, truly," the dragon grinned. "The descendant of Loran Lysandre may well be considered a founder himself."

Descendant. I stilled my tongue before a scoff escaped. Loran had been Macar's father, not his ancestor. I wondered if Macar would ever care to correct this in his schools. Though, I supposed the likelihood of them believing one could be over 500 years old was slim indeed. And Macar needed to be believed by all who followed him.

"You know well they wish to see the Lightcaster succeed," Drestel went on. "They care for this world just as we do. And all have accepted your call to arms."

"Wonderful!" Macar patted Drestel's back, chuckling. "And do be sure to remind them of the age minimum. No child under fifteen has any business in such a dangerous time."

"Of course, m'lord." He bowed, and threw his dripping hood over his head once more, and started out the door. "I'll remind them swiftly."

The dragon left, and Macar tapped a finger over his arm in thought. "Perhaps I ought to see how the other schools are faring," he said to me. "I worry for the students in Everland, with the war raging so."

I grunted. "Last I saw of that king, he sent a draft notice to all boys of age. I think it likely most of your students in his kingdom have been called to *his* war."

"Not so," Macar contradicted, his smile proud. "Before I left, I was sure to make arrangements so that all students of the Lysandre schools were immune to those drafts. They remain a neutral party." He paused, then amended, "so long as that fool hasn't broken his word."

Macar pulled out his communicator once more and fiddled with the buttons. *Thnk—Squee!*

A winged man flattened against our window, startling me. His lavender dragon wings stretched wide to keep himself steady. He peered at me through the glass with slender, tinted goggles. The dragon's scaled face twisted as though disappointed, then he pushed off our sill and flapped to the next window beside us, and so on until he was done with the building, and flew to the streets below.

This stormy kingdom and its strange people. To think these birds lived here willingly, shrouded in darkness and exploding clouds, constantly drenched— yet, all here seemed to enjoy it.

I sighed, staring at my false reflection in the window, my disguised brown hair and unfamiliar, sagging face looking as drained as I felt. *This is no place for me*, I decided. Better I spent the rest of my days in Grim… There would be no need for these disguises there. I could hide my Hallows, live freely as I pleased. Or perhaps I should venture to find my descendant again? The one who shared my angel's face… the one who may well house her soul.

I'd been a fool to let that conniving prince toy with me. I was sure Cilia was still here among us, yet I knew she must have been in my descendant. Lady Mikani had been so much like her…

I leaned a fist against the cold window, snuffing that immature hope. *If I wish to see her again,* I reminded, *and live freely, I must first ensure there is still a world for either of us to live.*

Determination rekindled, I pushed away from the window.

CILIA

I hid under the shelter of metal scaffolds, the city's many vision-screens blinking bright against the stormy night.

Despite my efforts to keep dry, the gutters overflowed with water and dripped through the scaffolds' cracks, splashing into the puddles at my feet. The storm drains did their due diligence, yet little could be done about the flooding.

I was ripe to find drier shelter when a winged dragon landed beside me and adjusted the tinted goggles over his eyes.

"Thörd can no find his kitten's mate," reported Thörd. Culatia's demon king cocked his scaled head. "Is Thörd's kitten being the sure one he here?"

"I'm damned sure of it," I chewed, stifling my fire before it erupted. "Macarius must have him disguised with an illusion."

I'd feared as much, but if by chance his guard had slipped while Thörd was out searching, I thought perhaps there was still hope. It seemed I had thought wrong.

We crossed the busy street to the cable-car station, taking a car to the seventh island where Thörd resided. Climbing the electric towers and avoiding the crisscrossing cables, we found the others already waiting in his rounded roost.

The roost's interior was dressed in modern styles of furniture, bright colors of crimson and yellow draping the walls, save for one which was a long window that stretched from floor to ceiling, the storm billowing outside.

A vision-screen was lit along the wall. The faces of the new Sky King and his web-eared wife and daughters were shown there, sitting in cozy chairs across a hostess as they gossiped over where the royal family had been for the past few years.

"*‹Oh, you didn't know?›*" Roji questioned in Culatian, leaning forward in his seat with his legs crossed and shifting his weight to one lazy side. Roji had shaved since last I'd seen him, his modern, jade clothing sleek and cleanly pressed while jagged bolts of silken lightning were woven into the trim. His jeweled crown decorated his feathered, scarlet hair, and around his neck was a pair of teal goggles with platinum, wired frames that shifted when he explained, "*‹My old man banished me from the islands back then.›*"

The hostess sat in shocked silence, stuttering, "*‹B... banished, my lord? But why?›*"

"*‹He didn't like my choice of partner,›*" chuckled Roji, throwing an arm around Dalminia, who was dressed in a similar jade attire, though it looked odd on her since it matched her emerald hair and eyes. "*‹But Mini and I didn't care all too* *much. We settled down for a while in Neverland, and had these two treasures along the way.>* "Roji ruffled the feathered hair of the infant in Dalminia's lap. *"< This little one is Prylan. And that big girl sitting all by herself and behaving is Mavis. >"*

Mavis giggled, her webbed ears fanning proudly while her wings fluttered shyly.

The hostess seemed at a loss for words, her stare perplexed at the little goblin children. *"<A... ah... How precious... So then, Sire, I suppose with this union, you hope to strengthen ties with Marincia and...>"*

I snorted and strolled across the tower's spacious room with Thörd, the dragon stretching his arms over his head and grinning. "All being the happy ones in Thörd's roost, yes?" Thörd greeted to the three Ancients who had waited for us here. "Thörd not remember last time so many Ancients being in one place, yeah?"

Miranda and Khol knelt at a low-lying table with smooth edges while Hecrûshou stood at the windowed wall with crossed arms. His little Bindragon coiled around one of those arms playfully. Miranda and Khol were both enjoying a strangely serene vision of tea drinking at the table, both adorned in Khol's latest knitting creations.

"Oh, you're back!" Khol exclaimed pleasantly and smiled at us like a feral pup who'd awaited its master's return, his webbed ears flicking happily. Along with his knitted paraphernalia, he had apparently taken Thörd's suggestion of "make yourselves at home" and found what seemed to be *all* of Thörd's blankets and throw pillows, and had bundled himself in a snug cocoon. He set down his handle-less teacup like an excited child, his bald, scaled head glinting off the overhanging light as he hurriedly retrieved a pile of *more* knitted creations and presented them to Thörd. "I've finished your gifts, Thörd!" Khol announced brightly. "I've already made so many for everyone else, I thought it only polite to make some for you."

Thörd guffawed and gladly took Khol's ugly gifts. "Monk fish still ees being the strange one! Thörd thanking you for gifts."

Khol clapped his hands in delight and went back to sipping his steaming tea.

Miranda's wrinkled face scowled at Thörd, the old woman grumbling, "The last time any of us gathered like this, it was to dispute territory... Is it wise to live among the Clean Ones so carelessly, Thörd? If Culatia's Reapers were to find you, I dare say your immortality will come to a Cleansed end."

Thörd wafted a dismissive hand at her. "Ees being the okay thing! Clean ones not know much of us. And Thörd not get asked why he always wearing these." He tugged on the goggles that hugged his head. "Clean Ones not seeing Thörd's eyes are being the white ones. So, Thörd can do what Thörd wants."

At the windowed wall where his clothed trident rested, Hecrûshou grunted. "Yes, well, while we thank you for hosting this ridiculous social, I'm far more eager to learn what fruits your excursions into the city have labored? Any sign of the cobra and your husband, Cilia?"

My mood fell like a boulder cracking down a mountain. "No sign," I reported, shedding my rubbery coat and threw it on the floor where Thörd had done the same for his. "Anything of interest happen in the palace?"

"The same as before," Hecrûshou strode to join the rest of us at the small table, though like myself, he did not sit. His Bindragon, however, did uncoil itself from around his arm and slithered onto the table with a curious *aaaahn?* Hecrûshou rumbled, "I still worry what's become of La'Lunaî and her new pet... Wherever she's disappeared to, I'm sure she's plotting our demise."

Khol choked on his tea, shivering despite the hot drink in his fingers and the layers of blankets wrapped around him. "B-b-but she won't find us up h-h-here will she?" Khol squeaked. The little Bindragon on the table cocked its head at the bundled demon and slithered onto Khol's head in a consoling coil above the layers of blankets, sighing a soft *aaahn.*

Miranda drew an impatient, nasally breath through her hooked nose. "I hardly think La'Lunaî is brave enough to come near us with a fleet of Reapers surrounding us."

Thörd uplifted his goggles and gave a toothy smirk, pounding his chest in a grand show. "La'Lunaî not come to Thörd's islands! She know water fish not good match for thunder dragon!"

Thörd's proud laughter seemed to ease Khol's nerves, and the weaker Ancient chuckled meekly as Aahn curled his long head in front of Khol's face curiously.

"For all our sakes, Thörd," I sighed, gazing out the crying window, "I hope you're right."

21

CELEBRITY APPEARANCE

ROJI

TRANSLATED FROM CULATIAN

"A… Ah…" The station's hostess, Fallia, stammered, forcing an awkward smile as she looked at my web-eared, winged daughter. "How precious… So then, Sire, I suppose with this union, you hope to strengthen ties with Marincia and set a new standard between the Ocean and Sky realms?"

"You bet," I said, sure to give the cameras a proud smile. "Though, that was just a perk that came with it. Obviously, Mini and I married because we wanted to, it just so happened that it could help unite our nations."

"Oh… I see." Fallia's surprise turned into a warm smile, and she stole another glance at Mavis, who sat in her own chair kicking her feet, her tiara crooked over her feathered hair. "Princess Mavis, was it?" asked Fallia.

Mavis flicked her emerald eyes at the hostess, one webbed ear perking her way.

"How old are you, then?"

Mavis's scaled cheeks blushed, and she silently held up three fingers.

Fallia laughed. "Three! Oh my, how grown up you are. And how do you like your new home, your highness?"

Mavis spread her hands. "It's *big*!"

That prompted laughter from the studio audience. *That's my girl.* I was worried about bringing her and Prylan at first; worried they wouldn't be accepted, with their mixed scales and feathers. Though, Culatians were used to dragons, I guessed. Maybe not Seadragons, but dragons nonetheless. And setting this standard was the reason I agreed to bring everyone on this interview. One way or another, the birds of Culatia were going to learn how ridiculous their pre-conceived perceptions of Marincians were.

In the midst of her laughter, Fallia flicked her eyes over my shoulder, probably to read the prompt sign I knew someone was holding behind Mini and me. Fallia's brow scrunched suddenly at whatever she'd read. She took a hesitant breath, then shook her head and looked back at me. "And how did you both meet, if you don't mind me asking?" She asked, her tone pleasant, but hiding a strange bitterness that seemed to be aimed at whomever stood behind us.

I heard a scoff behind me and twisted, seeing the man by the gear-warbling camera clutching a now crumpled sign in one hand while the other was raised to a com that was hooked to his ear, muttering, "Stick to the Bloody prompt, Fallia."

I caught Fallia discreetly pulling her com out of her ear and set it aside on the small table beside her, politely crossing her legs while Mini answered her question.

"There was a hurricane in the western seas those years ago," explained Mini in our language, pulling her braided, green hair over a shoulder. "The residents of *D'rofaux Nayû* were in danger of losing their homes if the storm wasn't quelled. But for a hurricane, one must tame both the winds and the seas, and so our Wavecrashers were to be deployed there, as well as your Stormchasers. My brother Ninumel was tending to a fiscal crisis in Marincia's capital city, and so I volunteered to oversee the efforts in *D'rofaux Nayû* in his stead. Equally, Roji was sent with the Stormchasers by his father."

Fallia rubbed an intrigued finger over her lips. "How wonderful! One could say it was fate, then?"

Mini laughed. "It certainly seemed that way. It was odd, being raised to believe a whole race of people were so different from our own, only to discover they were much like ourselves."

I heard the background man hiss behind me, calling for Fallia's attention, which he didn't get. Instead, Fallia ignored him and kept her eyes on my wife, curious as she asked, "Could you elaborate on those similarities, your grace?"

"Of course." Mini weighed her scaled hands. "In Marincia, we often favor focus and diligence over leisure. But that does not mean we never have leisure of our own. We enjoy games and competitions just as the Culatians do, and we also don't believe work and play should mix. There is a time and place for everything, as my father would often say."

"Yeah," I added, "It's a complete myth that Marincians are boring worka-holics. When I first got to *D'rofaux Nayû*, we were three weeks early to prepare for the storm. We still had preparations to make, so I told the Stormchasers to get their business done first before going off and enjoying themselves. But while we were thinning tree canopies, I saw this woman swimming off the coast with a few Wavecrashers, playing a game and laughing. It wasn't at all what I expected. My whole life, people kept telling me how stuck up and serious Marincians were. But there was Mini, splashing around like any of us Culatians, having a good time."

"I invited him to join," said Mini, chuckling. "I spoke Culatian, since my brother never cared to learn and I was typically his translator. But I was quite surprised when Roji not only declined the offer, but did so in Marincian. He even told me, "No play for us till the work's all done" so fluently, I was admittedly startled."

I grinned. "She wasn't expecting me to know all the same languages. I mean, as Sky, it's my job to represent our realm in front of the other royalties. If I wanted to make us look good in front of my fellow Relicbloods, I figured learning all of their languages would be a sign of respect."

"Indeed, it was," Mini agreed.

Behind Fallia, I stole a glance at my lil' sis, Zyl. She was with El in the back of the studio, the two giggling and sharing grilled octopus skewers as they whispered to themselves.

"Fallia!" that same man behind me hissed louder. I inched back in time to see him flapping a rolled-up packet of papers in her direction, the gesture terse.

Fallia's expression locked with fake ignorance, her talons growing long and piercing her leather chair's arms.

"Go on and ask," I encouraged, crossing my legs expectantly. "Clearly, your producer wants you to ask something uncomfortable. May as well spit it out, before he starts molting."

Laughter sounded from the studio audience, and Fallia chuckled along with them. But her laughs were nervous.

"I, er…" Fallia cleared her throat, hesitating. "Very well, Sire… Regarding Princess Mavis and Princess Prylan…"

I braced, clamping my teeth shut in case the question forced anything impulsive out of me.

She took a breath, then asked, "With their mixed blood, does this mean their Hallows is weakened? Just as Death Princess Willow's had been?"

There it is.

The studio fell deathly silent, waiting for my answer.

I let out a slow, calm exhale and folded my arms. "First of all," I began, "I've been to war alongside Death these past months. I've traveled with her, fought with her, and have found nothing *weak* about her or her Hallows. So, no. I don't think my girls will have a problem kicking someone's tailfeathers if they ever needed to. And Mavis is already pretty good with a bow. If they turn out as fierce and strong as Death, I'll be more than thrilled."

A cheer from the applauding crowd, and Fallia laughed as if relieved, clearing her throat. "How wonderful, Sire! Now, speaking of the Death Princess, how far along is she in her pregnancy?"

"She's got another three weeks, last I heard," I said, propping an elbow on the chair arm. "End of the month, around the Day of Storms."

"My, that's close!" Fallia fanned her dark collarbone. "She and her husband must be excited?"

"Yeah, they're pretty stoked. Her husband's been running around all over the place, preparing."

"Do they know the sex yet?"

"Oh, they've known since they found out they were expecting. We were traveling with a bunch of Seers, King Dream himself, even, so they confirmed it was going to be a boy way long ago."

"Do they have a name picked out?"

I rubbed my nose, humming. "I think they settled on *Lucas*."

This seemed to surprise—or confuse—Fallia. "Lucas?"

"After the prince's father."

"How strange…"

I frowned. "Strange?"

"Well, it's just that…" She struggled for the right words. "I'd heard that the captain of Prince Xavier's guard, Sir Alexander, has a father with the same name. I only thought it was a strange coincidence."

"Coincidence?" My brow crinkled so low I felt the skin pull. "How is it a coincidence if they're twins?"

The audience went dead quiet.

"H… hang on…" Fallia looked perplexed now. "Sire, are you saying Xavier Ember is the twin brother of Alexander Devouh?"

"Duh," I grunted. "I mean, they don't exactly *look* identical right now, but their weird eyes are kind of hard to ignore. You really didn't know?"

"Well… no," she admitted. "We've only seen Sir Alexander on the Screens in passing, we haven't seen the Death Prince at all yet."

"But how didn't you know who Princess Willow was married to?" I questioned skeptically, rubbing my temple. "All the Reapers in this country knew straight away. The two have been engaged for damn near ten years. And then there was that whole thing with Xavier disappearing after that assassination, him coming back out of nowhere, their marriage *and* heir announcement…" I couldn't help but laugh. "Sky, it'd be harder *not* to know at this point."

Fallia flushed and twirled her feathered hair. "Most of us up here aren't Reapers, your grace… We have little need to keep up with Grimish gossip, not to mention we were far more concerned that you'd returned and claimed the crown." She straightened bashfully and wiggled in her seat. "*I'd* personally heard of the Devouh brothers, of course—the *Shadowblood.* There have been flyers and books… although, I haven't read them myself yet, I've still heard the stories. I didn't realize the Death Prince was the other Shadowblood."

I hunched over and tapped a finger to my chin. "I guess he hasn't really left the palace since he got here… Hm. Might have to drag him out of those walls to make an appearance sometime."

"Well, since we're on the subject!" Fallia fumbled in her seat, scooting to perch on the edge as her wings perked. "Is it true the brothers have gained all of the Dream *and* Ocean realms' Hallows? Just as the Relicbloods have them?"

I tossed a hand. "Yeah, that's all true. Seen it myself, and Bloods, they've even surpassed the Relicbloods in some cases."

The audience rang with fervent murmurs.

"Then!" She held her breath. "Do they have *Sky's* Hallows as well now?"

I rubbed my neck. "Not yet. We're still working on it, we're just making sure certain, uh… parties don't interfere."

"Do you mean the Lightcaster?"

My feathers went stiff as rocks. "How do you know that name?"

"It's been the buzz of the rumors, your grace," said Fallia. "The Shadowblood and the Lightcaster—oh, it's so very exciting…! When will the brothers have your Hallows, then?"

I shook my hands in the air. "I really can't give out that info. You'll just have to wait and see."

Fallia exhaled dejectedly, but perked again with a new question. "Then, were the Shadowblood brothers the reason you decided to return, your grace?"

I shrugged. "Eh, not really. You can blame *that* one over there for that." I pointed at Zyl from off-set.

Lil' sis froze mid-bite of her octopus skewer when the cameras turned her way, her brown shoulders locking.

I gave a toothy grin. "My lil' sis came looking for me. And she found me. When she told me about the war with Marincia, that pretty much convinced me to come back. But honestly, it was mostly because the previous queen of Neverland had poisoned her with Yinklît Gel. She's still getting her Hallows back, but there was no way in Void I was going to let Zyl go off on her own again after that. I gotta look after my lil' sis, you know?"

A studio personnel pushed Zyl onto the set, and Fallia guided her to a chair beside me. Zyl was still as rigid as a board when she lowered into the seat, blushing as she swallowed the rest of her octopus.

"Princess Zylveia," Fallia began eagerly, "What happened to make you poisoned?"

"Uh…" Zyl stared wide-eyed at the cameras. "I drank some wine at a party. Apparently, it wasn't wine… so, now I don't have much access to my Hallows." She lifted a finger, and a tiny spark sputtered out. Zyl sighed, depressed.

The audience swooned sympathetic *awwws* in response, and I saw Zyl's eye twitch in annoyance.

I put an arm around her shoulders. "Don't worry, sis. Keep up with that medicine, and you'll get your Hallows back in no time."

Zyl's tone wasn't so enthusiastic. "Um, yeah…"

Sis… Damn it, it was my fault she didn't have her Hallows; my fault she was poisoned. If I'd at least told her to stop, maybe she'd have…

I sighed. *It doesn't matter.* What's done is done. But there was no way—no way in Bloody Void—I was going to let anything happen to my little sister again.

Anyone who comes near her will be my new target practice.

22

SPIRIT PARENTS

ALEXANDER

"*You'll just have to wait and see,*" Roji explained in his interview, his face glowing bright from the vision-screen displayed on the wall of our room inside the Sky Palace.

I grimaced, glancing at Xavier and Grandfather Edric behind me. "Bloods, that was bizarre. The Culatians weren't aware we were brothers? Do you even remember such a time?"

Xavier didn't reply. Neither did Grandfather Edric. The two weren't even looking at the screen, and given their frantic scrambling about the nursery we were preparing, I doubted they'd even heard me.

"No, no," Xavier said to Grandfather as he flapped a paper manual in a sharp gesture. "The instructions specifically say part C should latch onto part D."

"Bah!" Grandfather grunted and fiddled with the pieces of the crib they were attempting to assemble. "I don't need Bloody instructions! I married a batty woman who ran a line of luxury furniture."

Xavier grimaced. "You also divorced said woman."

"Yes, well," he grumbled and took a puff from his pipe, stroking his thick moustache. "I never said it was an enjoyable marriage… Nevertheless, I know what I'm damn well doing, son. This generation is always given the answer so readily, none of you know how to think for yourselves anymore."

I walked over and overlooked their partially assembled construction, humming. "Shouldn't you have the servants do this in the first place?"

Grandfather scoffed. "Servants! Hah! You think those bumbling fools could do any better?"

"Grandfather," Xavier and I chided. Xavier rubbed his dark lids and sighed. "You oughtn't call the hired help fools, honestly. They're in the position they are because of their skill with such things."

Grandfather took another puff from his pipe with a disapproving mutter. "You're all too Bloody soft these days… When I was your age, it was the servants who were thankful to be under our employ, not the other way around. And for another thing…"

Grandfather prattled on, and Xavier glanced up at me with tired, heavy eyes.

Bloods, he looked exhausted. His long, grey hair had been tied in a hurry; tangled strands having fallen loose at his shoulders. His silken, black shirt was only buttoned to his exposed chest.

I lifted an eyebrow. "When was the last time you slept?"

"Slept?" He laughed. "How can I sleep? There are far too many dangers that have sunk their fangs into my dreams every Gods damned night, it's a wonder I get *any* sleep these days."

"What sort of dangers?" I asked.

"For one: How do we expect to bring a *baby* to a warring nation?" he challenged. "Bloods, the whole idea is ludicrous! Part of me absolutely wishes to aid Father and Mother down there, but now all I can think of is my son meeting an arrow—or a Flameglobe bursting at our ship as he falls out of his crib and breaks his undeveloped neck—or, or…"

He flattened his back over the floor and cupped his face in a groan. "Death, and that's being optimistic… What if we lose him during the birth? What if all this work and excitement and fear—what if it's for naught?"

"It won't be for—"

"What if something happens to Willow during delivery?" He smeared his hands down to his bearded chin and moaned helplessly. "Even if the baby arrives safely, what if I lose Willow? I-I can't do this alone, if something happens to her, I—"

"Now, now!" Grandfather interrupted with a soothing tone. "Calm down, son. It will all work itself out in the end, you'll see. All you can hope to do is be prepared for anything."

"And in any case," I said and yanked Xavier to his miserable feet. "We have several Seers who tell us all will be well. Not to mention the army of Healers we have on hand, one of which will be your son's Spirit Mother."

Xavier snapped out of his foggy mood. "Bianca…! Bloods, I forgot to ask her!"

I pinched the rim of my nose. "Of course, you forgot… Have you informed Lilli of her role, at least?"

"Actually, er, no." Xavier knuckled his temple. "Bloods, but I can't recall the last time I've seen either of them. I haven't even asked Jaq to be Spirit Father."

"Then let's get going, you damned fool! They need to know before the birth in order to hold the ceremony of your son's *Rae'u Shelic*." I grabbed his arm and dragged him out of the nursery, leaving Grandfather Edric to his fiddling with the crib.

Xavier fumbled behind in protest, "But—I—*now?*"

"Yes, now. What if Willow goes into labor early?" I pulled out my communicator, the screen of light blipping to life in front of me as I ordered it to call Jaq.

When the viper's face appeared on the screen, he pushed up his glasses. *"All's good on this end, Captain,"* Jaq reported, sidestepping through whatever corridor he traversed to make way for a block of patrolling Stormchasers. *"No sign of that cobra or Tavius's ancestor."*

A groan sounded from off-screen, Octavius muttering, *"Can't you just say his Bloody name?"*

"Yeah," agreed Neal's voice to Jaq's other side, snickering. *"He's my ancestor, too, ya know. Could just say 'the Trebles' ancestor'."*

Octavius groaned again, and I saw half of his face creep onto the screen, the man massaging his eyes.

"Jaq," I said, "you're needed in the west wing's infirmary in ten minutes."

Jaq's face scrunched, and he scratched at the orange-tinted goatee he'd been growing since we arrived at the Sky Palace. *"Why?"*

"Just meet me there." I hung up and called Lilli next. "Lilli," I said, "Meet me in the west wing's infirmary in ten minutes."

She blinked out of whatever distraction had her attention. *"What?"* she questioned, alarmed, and I saw El and Matthiel peer at the screen intently from behind her. *"What's happened?"*

"Nothing's happened," I assured. "It's a minor issue."

"Regarding what?" Lilli demanded, flexing her bat wings. *"Is Willow having her baby—?"*

"Ees being my order?!" A feather-haired woman behind Lilli squeezed half her face into view, nearly pushing Lilli out entirely. The woman's green feathers were crinkled and messy, her large eyeglasses speckled with diamonds embedded in the rose frames, making her face look bigger than necessary, perhaps a fashion trend in this realm. *"I ask those Alchemists to be making nice perfume for wedding, and I ees telling them to be the quick ones!"*

My boots squalled over the marble floor when I halted, and Xavier bumped into my back. *The wedding!* Bloods, I'd nearly forgotten! The woman on screen was the planner Roji had hired for us: *Soûsül* Vivati.

"And since we ees having you on com, Howllord," Vivati clipped, shooting Lilli a rueful glare, *"Maybe you tell fiancée how big important ees to be going to tailor! She need being sized for nice gown, and we ees only having three weeks before ceremony, but she not listen!"*

Lilli rolled her eyes, muttering, *"As I've said, can it not wait until I'm off duty? You can take Oliver to be fitted in my stead if you wish, I'll follow some other day when I'm free."*

"Ees big important, Howless!" cried Vivati. *"We not be having much time and I have job to be looking after, and…!"*

Lilli circled a prim finger over her temple, ignoring the planner who prattled on, and addressed me again. *"Honestly, though. Is Willow having her baby?"*

"Not yet," I assured, "It's related, I suppose. Just meet me in the infirmary with Jaq."

"But I'm looking for Jaq now," she said, irritated, her bat ears growing and swiveling back as the planner chirped on. *"He isn't answering his com and I haven't seen him in weeks. I haven't even seen him on patrol routes."*

I frowned. "He answered his com swiftly when I called just now. And he was *on* patrol with the Treble brothers. He should be heading for the infirmary now, in fact."

She bristled. *"He answered YOU? That Bloody bastard!"* The call ended suddenly.

"Er…" I rubbed my chin, glancing at Xavier, who stared at me in question. "Odd… Well, in any case, that should gather the three of them in one place. Bianca should be in the infirmary now."

She was usually there when I visited, at least. Though, if Vivati had hired her Alchemists for something regarding our wedding, I wondered how she was taking it…?

I shuddered. I hadn't intended for Bianca to be involved in *planning* the wedding. Damn that nosy woman. Why did Roji hire us a planner to begin with? I knew it wasn't Lilli's idea, she was bothered by the woman more than I, and was none too happy with it either.

Why are we even doing this? I wondered dismally.

The whole thing seemed to be a pain for both of us. Lilli had seemed distracted lately also, our marriage seeming at the bottom of her priorities. Not that I blamed her, with everything that's happened. But then, if it wasn't a priority, should we wait until it was?

Or. I bit my knuckle. *Should I call off the marriage altogether?*

No, don't be an idiot. You've already caused such a fuss, this would make everything worse. Lilli expected a wedding, and I'd promised her one…

"What's all this about the infirmary?" Willow's voice bounced through the hall behind us.

Willow stepped down the stairway with a tender hand to her massively swollen belly, her ashen hair bundled in a tangled mess. She was as disheveled as her husband, but she still remembered to wear her marriage-vines which glittered from her forehead.

I sighed, casting aside my dilemma for another time. "Xavier has neglected to inform your son's Spirit Parents of their role," I said, gesturing for her to come along. "Care to join us to amend this?"

Willow strode beside Xavier and looped an arm around his, humming, "We haven't assigned the Spirit Parents yet?"

Xavier murmured, "Apparently not. I'd completely forgotten."

"As had I," she agreed, the pair following me through the halls to the west wing.

Bloods, did I hope the news staved off whatever contempt Bianca might hold for me when we arrived. I'd have to be sure to apologize about Vivati's order. Yes, perhaps that will work. It damned well wasn't my idea to involve her and her Alchemists in these things. If she should be annoyed at anyone, it ought to be Vivati.

In any case. My lips tugged into a smile. *At least it's another excuse to visit.*

BIANCA

"Good, Vio," I praised the lizard woman as I walked by during my inspection, lightly shaking a vial of my latest, bluish tonic along the way.

Bazil strode at my side, the skinny Barkdragon creaking with every bow and bend its wood-like limbs made. His back was patched with new sprouts and fully blooming flowers of all sorts that I'd planted months ago, just things I knew I'd need pretty often.

We Alchemists were sharing the infirmary room with the Healers and Medics, so we were all wedged in one corner where our tonics wouldn't be much of a potential danger if a mixture didn't go right.

In the other corner, Matthiel was teaching Lëtta how to tether a living soul back into its breathing vessel with a temporary NecroSeam. I couldn't really hear what he was saying, but the girl's bear ears were perked with so much intensity, it was a wonder they didn't rip off her skull. Through my goggles, which I'd had Matthiel enchant with a soul-seeing Evocation since Xavier was always so busy lately, I saw Sirra-Lynn's ghost float over Lëtta's shoulder curiously. Sirra watched the teenaged nurse attempt to create her own temporary NecroSeam in a string of purple light that spewed from her fingers. Lëtta tried to stitch the awaiting soul working with them to its sleeping vessel, but the thread of light didn't stick. Lëtta's bear ears dipped depressively, but Matthiel gave her some encouraging words and she tried again more determinedly.

I hummed thoughtfully and tapped my goggles with a nail, an idea hitting me. *Maybe Matthiel could help me with that poison-arrow cure,* I considered. I'd been working with Octavius on the experiment, but so far, nothing we did helped my remedy Hallows fuse with any soul we tried to Heal. *I can't touch a soul,* I mulled and twisted my mouth. *But a Necrovoker can…*

I wiggled my nose excitedly, one of my rabbit ears lifting along with my grin. *All right,* I decided. *When Octavius gets here for today's session, we'll give this new angle a try.*

I walked down the row of my busy Alchemy students who were all mixing the same concoction as their newest assignment, nodding and offering help when they needed it. Red already mastered the mixture, so he was helping the others along, too.

But my attention snapped to two Alchemists ahead of me, who were chit-chatting while grinding herbs—herbs that weren't part of this assignment.

"An' I dun think Rosemary will be good wiff the rest o' it," the squat elk, Rob, argued with his taller, fatter guildmate, Harri.

Harri scoffed and took a pinch of rosemary from the many bowls of flower petals and spices I didn't authorize for this assignment. "Fine," Harri said. "Make your weak bouquet, then. See if the Howless doesn't gag at the scent you've tarnished at her wedding—"

"What are you two doing?" I barked, making them jump. Bazil sniffed at their coats with his long snout, his throat making soft creaking noises.

They both whirled and balked at me through thick goggles. Harri yelped, "M-Mistress Chemist! This—er, that is, we were just…"

"Not completing today's assignment," I said. "What are you goofing off with?"

Rob tugged at his lab coat's collar. "W-We got a request from a lady this mornin', askin' for an order of aromatic oils and potpourri…"

My rabbit ears dropped, one eyebrow lifting beneath my goggles. "For what?"

"For Sir Alexander and Sil Lilliana's wedding," Harri explained sheepishly, slipping off his pointed, uniformed hat and wringing it nervously. "Their wedding planner made the request… She offered a fair pay, so we couldn't say no… though she, er, didn't quite have an exact request for *what* scents to use, so we're working with whatever we have…"

He shut his trap when he saw my glare. But I loosened a breath and snorted. "Fine. Whatever pays, pays... and Alex likes peppermint. Might get a good tip for it."

They quickly grabbed a handful of peppermint grinds they'd already prepared in a separate bowl and tossed it into their concoctions, starting up the burners.

I sighed and strolled down the counter again. "Just get back on assignment when you're finished, all right?"

They nodded vigorously, dumping the ingredients in their beakers and poured in the carrier oil. The pleasant scent perfumed the air as I continued on, shaking my vial idly with Bazil striding at my side.

That Bloody idiot. So, Alex was still set on marrying the Howless? Getting a planner to make arrangements, even... I guessed it was all official now. It was feeling more *real* by the day.

I shook the vial faster, my stomach twisting miserably.

Damn it, why did it *hurt* so much...? Every time he came to visit, he still had that look on his face—that hope, like he wanted me to say something; to slap him and demand that he call it off, or... *Or did I just* want *to do that?* What if he did want to go through with it? But then why did he still come to see me with that stupid smile and warm laugh and...

Oh, stop getting your hopes up, you Bloody idiot—!

The cork popped off my vial, foam exploding from the rim and drenching my glove. *Crap!*

My guild members heard the noise and whipped their heads my way in a start. I rushed to the sink to rip off my gloves and rinse my hands... and of course, who would show up first except my first mate, Red?

"Boss?" Red asked, pulling down his face mask as his brown nose scrunched, large goggles still fastened over his eyes. "You all right?"

"Just fine," I mumbled. "Just wasn't paying attention."

"That's the sixth time this week ya weren't payin' attention." He folded his arms. Those goggles of his were giving me a judgmental look. "What's eatin' at ya?"

I finished rinsing and shut off the faucet, then peeled down my goggles in a grumble. "I said I'm fine."

He sniffed and leaned against the counter. "It's that Howllord, ain't it? Rob and Harri were talkin' about him, and ya always get ticked after he's mentioned."

"Red." I sucked in a slow breath, calming. "Like I said, I am fine—"

"Bianca?"

I jolted.

"Ah, good," Alex's voice called from the infirmary's open doorway. "You're here after all."

I spun on my heels, blushing. That stupid, adorable smile was stretching his dumb, pretty face.

Alex stepped inside, clad in armor as usual. His plate clanked noisily as he sidestepped his way around the Healers, nurses and Alchemists to meet me. Behind him, a disheveled Xavier and Willow followed.

When Alex neared, he patted Bazil's head and sniffed the air, looking surprised. "Is that peppermint?" he asked.

I muttered, "Uh, yeah… Your planner hired two of my Alchemists to make something fragrant for your wedding." I squeezed my arms for comfort, but pretended I was just crossing them casually, trying not to sound hurt. Pretty sure I failed. "I told them what you liked. Better tip them well for that, hear?"

I saw his shoulders tense. That look came on his face again, and he coughed behind a fist. "Ah… yes, very well… I am sorry for that. I was only just informed Vivati asked you all to do that. It was neither Lilli's nor my intention, to, well…" He cleared his throat, his gaze slipping to my Barkdragon for a split second before he started again. "Regardless—*kmm*—that's not why we're here. There is something you and Xavier should discuss."

He stepped aside to let Xavier walk in front, the father-to-be scratching at an ear. "So, Bianca…" Xavier began, "with the baby coming so soon, I realized—"

Alex jabbed him in the side with an elbow.

Xavier rubbed at his ribs and started again. "*Alex* realized… I'd forgotten to ask you something."

I cocked my head. "What is it?"

He and Willow shared cheered smiles, and Xavier explained, "Well… you and Jaq have been the closest friends I've had for a very long time, and, well, you see… I wondered if you would be a Spirit Mother to our son—?"

I let out a squeal and yanked him in for a hug. "Yes, yes, yes! Oh my Gods, *yes!*"

Clattering footsteps rushed through the door then as Jaq, Octavius and Neal came panting inside, alarmed.

"Who screamed?!" Jaq demanded.

The three men's eyes flicked all over the room, their scythes in hand. But they relaxed when they saw us. Looking confused, they put away their weapons and walked over.

Jaq's look narrowed at me. "Did you scream, Bianca?"

I bit my nail, still giggling like a kid, but nodded. "Sorry, I just got really excited!"

"Why?" he asked, looking at the chuckling Xavier and Willow for an answer.

Xavier cleared his throat. "Jaq, I've something to ask you, if you'll accept."

"Uh… Accept what?" He scratched at his scaled brow.

Xavier thrust an offering hand his way. "To be our son's Spirit Father."

Jaq was silent for a minute. Then his voice cracked. "Really?"

"Yes, really," Xavier said with a grin. "Who else do you think I'd choose?"

"I just… I didn't really think…" Jaq's eyes glazed and he rubbed a lid from under his glasses, dropping his peasant persona and laughing. "Yes. Absolutely, yes. Of Bloody course I'll do it, I-I'd be honored, mate."

Octavius cocked his head at the viper. "Jaq, are you crying?"

"Of course, I'm Bloody crying." He pulled Xavier in for a strong hug, thumping his back and sniffling. "I'm going to have a Spirit Son…!"

"Me too, me too!" I squealed, grabbing Jaq's arms and jumping so much I was getting dizzy.

Xavier and Willow laughed, and Alex cracked a smirk off to the side.

"*Jaq!*" a new voice clipped from the doorway. "Where have you been?"

I twisted and grimaced. It was *her.*

The High Howless stomped into the infirmary, clad in armor with her helm tucked under an arm and her bat wings dipping and ducking to avoid the crowd. She stalked past Octavius and Neal before halting in front of Jaq.

"Why aren't you answering my calls?" she demanded, stabbing a furious finger at his chest. "And where have you been? I swear to Bloods, Jaq, if you're avoiding me, you had better tell me the reason—"

"I'm just busy!" he snapped, but retracted. Then he shoved past her to head for the door. "Neal, Tavius, come on! We're still on duty."

The Treble brothers exchanged an awkward glance but followed Jaq nonetheless—

"Wait!" I snagged Octavius's arm before he left. "Can Tavius clock out early?" I asked Jaq. "I thought of something for the experiment that I want to try, but I need him to do it."

Jaq gave me a puzzled look, but a quick glance at Lilli seemed to make him flinch and stammer. "Uh—s, sure, whatever. Neal, come on!"

Neal grumbled a complaint as the two ducked out in a weird hurry.

Lilli's bat wings flared and started after them. "Jaq, don't you dare run off without…!"

"Actually, Lilli," Willow interrupted, making the bat pause. "Before you leave, I wished to ask something of you."

Lilli's feet were still turned toward the door, but her bat ears swiveled to Willow, and she asked, "Oh… yes?"

Willow placed her hands on her huge belly and smiled. "You've been much the sister I never had, and I'm ashamed I'm asking this so late, but… I want you to be a Spirit Mother to our son."

What! I almost groaned out loud, but stifled it just in time. *Her too?* Gods damn it, is there anything she won't take from me?

Octavius winced beside me, and I realized I still had a hold of him and was crushing his arm so much, it pinched his armor to his skin. I let him go in a glower.

Lilli's stupefied face fell as she stared at Willow, looking ready to tear up. "Nira, but I… Yes! Of course. I would be beyond honored."

They shared a hug, and Lilli held a hand to Willow's belly, feeling the baby kick and laughing in delight, talking with the couple like no tomorrow…

I turned to Alex who stood off to the side. He was already looking at me and jolted when I caught him staring, scratching his neck to play dumb. He coughed behind a fist, as if about to say something to me, but kept his trap shut. Then he shuffled out quick as a feral weasel.

Alex, I thought with a growl, blinking to get rid of the annoying water stinging my eyes, *I wish you'd just make up your mind…*

I sucked it up and spun on my heels, tossing my head in a gesture at Octavius. "Come on, Tavius… Let's get to work."

"Uh, right," Octavius said meekly and followed at my side. Bazil came creaking over at my heels again, and Octavius gave the Barkdragon a friendly pat on the head.

I pulled on my goggles again. The few ghosts who were floating around the infirmary came back into view through the enchanted lenses, and I strode toward the translucent figure of Sirra-Lynn. The ghost woman was still looming over Lëtta's shoulder while Matthiel gave her instruction about forming a thicker NecroSeam for the living soul that sat over its vessel between them.

"Sirra?" I asked, getting the ghost's attention. "Mind if we start a little early today?"

Sirra was the soul who volunteered to be our test subject for this experiment. Octavius wasn't too happy about it at first, but Sirra was pretty stubborn— and a great help. This whole thing wouldn't even be possible without a soul to experiment on.

Sirra turned to me curiously, then noticed her son beside me. "Oh, Tavius. You're done with patrol already?"

Octavius shrugged. "Guess so. Jaq was acting weird, so I don't think he was actually paying much attention."

Matthiel snorted and paused his instruction with Lëtta to murmur, "He's working through a few things at the moment. Hopefully, the idiot will make a decision sooner rather than later."

I put fists at my sides and looked at Matthiel. "Howllord, think you can take a minute and help us out? I got an idea that I want to test out."

Matthiel's brow furrowed, and he stood up. "I suppose... We'll continue this tomorrow, Miss Lëtta. You're progressing well."

Lëtta sighed dejectedly, but nodded. "Thank you, Howllord... I'll try harder tomorrow." She slunk away with the living ghost she had been practicing on, the two chatting as they left the infirmary.

Matthiel tugged on his lapel and looked at me. "What is this idea of yours, Doctor?"

I led him, Octavius and Sirra's ghost over to the counter we usually did this experiment on, opening the upper cabinet to pull out the rack of vials I'd filled with my latest attempt at the soul-cure. That was the current name I was calling it. The vials were plugged with cork wedges, the liquid radiating slightly with a greenish-yellow glow in the glass.

I plucked one vial out of the wooden rack and handed it to Matthiel. "Can you try infusing this tonic with a soul-touch Evocation?"

Matthiel lifted an eyebrow. "Soul-touch? Imbued to a *liquid?*"

"Bear with me," I urged. "The problem we keep running into with this cure is that none of my remedy Hallows—or even any *physical* medicine—can actually interact with a person's soul. We can only affect the vessel. But it makes sense, since Healers have never been recorded as having access to a soul before. But Necrovokers *have.*" I gestured to the vial in his hand. "So, I'd like to try combining the elements to see what happens."

Matthiel scrutinized the tonic, then took a thoughtful minute to think on it. Then he shrugged. "Very well. Let's give it a go, I suppose." He evoked his death Hallows in a small sliver of violet light over his extended finger, then unplugged the vial and experimentally stuck his finger—and stringy Hallows—into the glass. The violet lights poured into the greenish-yellow liquid until it bubbled and fused with the tonic, making it glow a light, subtle lavender.

Matthiel hummed as if surprised. "Fascinating. It actually did something."

"Great!" I snatched the newly lavender tonic and nodded to Octavius. "Tavius, we're ready."

Octavius grimaced uncomfortably like always, then reached out to his mom's ghost and evoked a tiny stream of his infection Hallows onto her soul. Black veins crept from his hand over her wispy shoulder, spidering wildly and digging so deep, Sirra gritted her intangible teeth and seethed in a wince. It was only temporary, though. Octavius was always sure to use the smallest amount to make sure it would fizzle away before it could do any actual damage.

"Slowly…" I hushed to myself while tipping the vial over Sirra's blackened shoulder, the lavender tonic creeping toward the rim. "Steady…"

Blip!

Hsssssssssssss!

A single droplet hit the infection.

We all stared at the veins, holding our breaths.

Shhhhhhhh…

The veins started to boil.

FWISH!

A bright, lavender flash shinned from where the droplet hit the infection, and in a matter of fleeting seconds, the veins bled the same light purple color and started to disintegrate. When the last of the veins turned lavender and peeled off of Sirra's newly cleaned shoulder, we all let out a gasp.

"IT WORKED!" I squealed and squeezed the life out of Matthiel and Octavius both. "It worked, it worked, it worked!" I ran out of the infirmary and bolted down the hallways hopping ecstatically and shouting, "XAVIER! WILLOW! IT BLOODY WOOOOOoooorked!"

EVERLAND

23

STOLEN TERRITORY

ALICE

With silver-gauntleted fingers, I gripped the reins of my Bonedragon and pulled it to a stop before the rocky ledge of the mountain path. The spring wind ruffled the grey braid over my shoulder as I peered through the slit in my visor, overlooking the bustling city of New Aldamstria which waited far beneath us. Everland's royal palace stared at me from the other side of the enclosing mountains. The sturdy structure was set flush against the rocks and towered over the town at a safe distance from where the peasants and working classes resided in the bowl-like foot of the mountains.

A shadow soared over me, and one of my wolf ears swiveled to Serdin as he landed his Flamedragon on a rocky pillar to my right. My husband clattered to my left on his Bonedragon as it halted beside mine. A portion of our troops, both rebels and Reapers alike, waited behind us on this particular mountain path. We had more along other paths to the east and west flanks of the city, and several more who should be moving through hidden tunnels below us with the help of Henry and rebel troops within the capital.

Myra rode a dappled grey and white mare, clopping solemnly up to the ledge while sharing her saddle with that little ewe girl, Milann. The blue-haired Queen of Death wore no armor, having agreed not to join the main battle along with her father's Dreamcatchers and instead resigned herself to watching after the girl.

I flicked my gaze at Myra and grunted, "Well? How does our future fair at the moment?"

Myra's bronze face pulled into a hollow grimace. "Several possibilities show success and survival. Several show defeat and death." She crossed her arms gently over the little girl sharing her saddle. "It all depends on the choices you make while in battle, now. But I can't See which choices connect to which outcomes."

I set my jaw, wolf ears curling back determinedly. "Then vigilance will be key." I peered up at our black-plated king. "My liege? On your word."

Serdin nodded, then glanced at his wife through the slit of his visor. "Darling, if you would?"

Myra took her cue and trotted over to a bend in the pathway. She was heading for a separate team of Decepiovokers who had been waiting half a mile down behind the cover of rocky pillars. It took her some time to reach them, but once her blue-haired figure trotted up to them, the group became a blur of radiant azure light.

Then, from the mountain peaks came phantom figures, conjured by the illusionists. It began with one black-armored figure riding his steed of a winged Flamedragon, his scythe raised high above his head menacingly and a silver crown glinting from his helm. The detail was difficult to see from a distance, but if any scouts were to look through a spyglass, they would see that this was, no doubt, the Death King.

Next, behind the phantom version of Serdin came block upon block of armored Reapers in glittering silver armor, the sunlight hitting their plate and sending blinding reflections like mirrored water as they poured along the mountainside by the hundreds, then thousands, until the rocky wall was draped with them like a shining curtain.

To anyone close enough to notice, most of their figures were only half-done, the backs barely even fleshed out and holes appearing in their sides, but from afar, it was enough to alert the commoners in the city.

We'd hoped that by attacking during daytime—with a show—we could warn the civilians of our coming and scare them into bunkers and hiding. We would have preferred to keep this battle out of residential areas, but their king refused to leave the safety of his mountains. So, we had little choice but to take the battle to him.

With our decoy army now in place, I glanced at Serdin beside me. The apprehensive Death King exhaled with a sharp nod and settled his Flamedragon along the stone pillar it was perched upon. I glanced at my husband to my other side, who mimicked Serdin's gesture on his Bonedragon.

"Right," I grunted. "All that's left now is to wait."

CAYDEN

Revinna and I stood vigilantly outside the private room Father had trapped Rilla in for their latest Scrying session. I had a lion ear pressed against the polished, wooden door, listening for any violent tones that might erupt, my tail swishing anxiously. If Father began yelling, I would have to burst in and grab Rilla, as I've had to do so often over the months.

Revinna had her own lion ear to the door beside me, biting a gloved knuckle nervously. In truth, she hadn't a reason to be here, but I supposed it was best that we three kept close until we knew when the Reapers would invade with the rest of my rebel army. We only had Rilla's vision to keep us informed of any attack *prior* to its occurrence. If the battle started without our knowledge, it may put us at a disadvantage to help the effort—

The shouting started from inside. Clamorous bangs and thunks and glass shattering burst next. I was three seconds from breaking down the door before it was shoved open on its own.

My very red-faced, *livid* father shouldered past me and screamed down the corridor. "GUARDS!" His grown lion ears were curled so tight to his head, you'd think he'd been born with them glued to his skull. "GUARDS! Send for my Hands and my generals *at once!*"

He stormed off around the corner, still shrieking commands in a frenzy.

Rilla walked out of the room then. She held her large crystal ball and wore the widest grin on her face I'd ever seen. "It's begun," Rilla declared in a wicked giggle, showing the image of the silvery, glinting army of marching soldiers within her crystal ball. "The Reapers are here."

HENRY

"Come on, men!" I shouted while distributing sword after lance after axe after Warhammer, the other rebels running to the booth outside my shop in a frenzy before scurrying back to the streets to push back the Raiders. "Hurry and get out there! We need these southern districts locked down and boarded up *before* the Reapers get here to help keep this territory!"

When I was down to the last claymore left in stock, I grabbed it and hopped over the booth, dodging a Footrunner who charged for me with a lance and drove my plated shoulder into his chest. He was knocked back into a stack of crates which cracked into splintered pieces.

Across the street, I spotted a rebel teen hacking aimlessly with his axe at a Raider. The poor amateur was only swinging at air. The Raider laughed at him and raised his heavy sword over the boy's head—

I sprinted over and stabbed into the Raider's open armpit. The guy's corpse dropped between my feet and the boy's, and I knocked on the kid's copper helmet. "It'd probably be easier if you actually hit the guy next time!" I said over the chaos.

The kid nodded vigorously. Bloods be good, he'd pissed himself, there was a dark stain running down his pant leg. I grumbled a sigh and shouted, "Get inside, kid! You won't be any good to the cause if you die from shaking nerves!"

The kid wiped at his tearing eyes and sniffed, nodding again before ducking into my shop for safety.

I snorted and craned to look up at the southern mountainside, one of my rabbit ears lifting. The silver glint of the Reaper's armor still glittered up by the peaks. Fangs Alice let us know in advance that those shining soldiers were only decoys, but I wasn't sure if it would be enough to lure Galden's troops up there. Turns out, it was more than enough. There were only a few patrolling Raiders left here in the lower cities, the rest of them had dropped everything and started scrambling up the mountain paths to get to the 'Reapers'. Little did they know the real soldiers were stealthily trickling down to us from the narrower paths and through the hidden tunnel we'd made for them over the months.

Don't celebrate yet, I reminded in a grunt and hustled down the streets. *This plan to claim territories in the city will only work if WE set up the welcoming party first.*

I ducked into alleyways and hopped over flour sacks, noting the progress our men were making on creating a sturdy, stone fence around the southern districts. So far, it looked good. We'd assigned all Terravokers to form solid blockades from the cobbled roads, and thousands of labor workers offered their help, too.

I ran up to one section of the original wooden fence. A group of Hallowless rebels were struggling to keep it from collapsing under the Rockraiders who shoved against it on the other side. Growling, I evoked my rock Hallows on the stones at their feet and stretched them against our side of the fence for added support.

But at the same time, two Raiders scrambled up to the top of the fence, drawing their Crystal swords. I couldn't get to my claymore in time. At this rate, they would break through our defenses—

Screeee!

The echoing screech made everyone's ears perk. From the skies, a swarm of what looked like huge, armored bats soared over the districts and spit fire onto the enemy soldiers. The two Raiders scaling the fence above me were scorched by one of the creature's fire breath and fell back onto their side in agonized screams.

The bats—*no, those were dragons, weren't they?*—perched on the perimeter of tall buildings beside the fence and served as fire-breathing sentries, warding off the intruders. After squinting, I noticed those dragons were ridden by armored Reapers.

"—Are you Henry?"

I wheeled around in a jolt, looking up at whoever just called my name.

Staring down at me was one of the dragon riders, having landed his mount next to me on the street. Unlike the other Reapers, this one wore black armor, and clinging to his waist was an azure-haired, un-armored woman. Squeezed between them was a little girl with sheep horns who was cradled by the woman like a loving grandparent.

"Aye," I said over the clamor on the other side of the fence. "That'd be me."

"Uncle of a girl named Vendy?" he asked next and slid off his mount to stand on the street. He helped down the azure-haired woman next and took off his helm. "Vassal of my son-in-law and his brother?"

"Son-in-law?" I blinked at the guy. Now that his helm was off, I saw his ashen hair and colorless, white eyes. One of my rabbit ears dropped. "Gardener sow me! Your Majesty Death!" I bellowed a laugh and bowed to him and the woman, who must have been his wife. "And Your Highness Dream! It looks like we've pretty much secured the southern districts with your help. I'm sure my queen would be appreciative."

"She was," the Death King said frankly. "We'd spoken with her some hours ago on com. She's to arrive with her fleet as well as the Sky King's Airships within the next three days. If we can keep this territory secured until then, those extra troops should be enough to advance further into the capital."

"Great!" I laughed, putting a fist to my side. "We'll do our best to keep these districts, rest assured."

CULATIA

24

PAST MISTAKES

DREAM

506 YEARS PRIOR

White flakes dusted my cheeks as I stood under the stone archway to the balcony outside the palace ballroom. The scent of ice was eerily serene compared to the stink of death inside.

Two men stood on the balcony with me. One gripped the hilt of a dripping, thin sword; the other gurgled from that very sword being lodged in his throat. The dying man, King Adam's chief military general, Accursius Lysandre, swayed limp into the arms of his murderer: his own brother. Accursius's breath choked as the sword was shoved farther into his throat. The snow speckled red around them.

Accursius's killer gave a low chuckle. "For all your precious foresight, you never were the brighter half, brother... I suppose we each have our *talents*." He grunted and ripped the sword upward, slicing open his brother's neck and kicked him to the ground. The snow fell lightly over the body like a soft veil.

"Macar...?" I whispered.

He turned to me, and I shuddered. Something had changed in that stare. Behind his blood-splattered glasses, his eyes were no longer wide and curious, eager to learn the mysteries the world had to offer. His lust for knowledge had curdled into lust of a different sort.

He smiled like a lunatic. "Ah! Dream, my friend. I wondered when you'd arrive for the show." He kicked his twin's boot with a grin. "What do you think? I dare say I've finally gotten the best of this brute. Perhaps it wasn't the most graceful of executions, but I think with practice, grace will come more naturally."

I stood in silence, my bones numb to the freezing snow and gentle breeze that batted against my robes.

Macar frowned. "Dream? Are you that amazed?"

"Macar…" My lungs quivered painfully, tears hitting as I realized I'd made a grave, *grave* mistake. "What have you done…?"

"What have I done?" He laughed, using his tunic to wipe blood from his spectacles. "Why, I'm doing precisely what I swore to do when you knighted me, Dream." He replaced the lenses on his nose and his lips split with a fang-filled grin. "I'm doing what's necessary."

The snow drifted onto the balcony in silence.

It swirled in the air between Macar and myself.

It coated the stone rail and dusted the curtain that fluttered in the crisp breeze behind me.

And it blanketed the scaled skin of Accursius's bleeding corpse.

"Necessary…?" I whispered, my voice shaking as I stared at Macar in horror. "How is this necessary…? How… how is *any* of this necessary?"

Macar simply shrugged as the spattered blood on his spectacles dripped over his scaled cheek. "This is the most efficient way to protect us, Dream."

"Protect us…" Through my grown fox ears, I could still hear the clang of metal echoing inside the ballroom—the place where bodies littered the floors; the place where Kael battled with the Death King.

Anger sharpened my teeth, and the nauseating twist of complete, utter failure churned my quivering stomach as I thrust a hand toward the ruffling curtain that blocked the gore hiding within the ballroom. "What protection do you speak of?!" I shouted, tears blurring my vision. "This is *not* what I'd meant…! You've brought *death* to all of these shifters, Macar!"

He stepped toward me while brandishing the crimson-stained sword he'd used to kill Accursius, giving the blade a thoughtful gaze. "Better this small bunch than *all* of us…" He grinned, his long fangs showing. "Don't you think?"

He drew nearer. I backed away behind the curtain, stumbling over a shifter's corpse, landing on my back inside the ballroom. The clamor of Kael and the Death King's battle was piercing in here.

Macar followed me inside, his excited smile sickening. "In the grand scheme of things, I'd say this is a worthy price to pay."

I shuffled back. "Macar… Please…"

He smiled cruelly and raised his sword. "Do not fret, Dream. You'll thank me when next you're born…" He chuckled like a madman. "For, you see, there *will* be a 'next' waiting for you in the end, after I'm done."

He thrust down his blade, and I braced in a terrified yell, throwing my arms over my head—

I felt my Hallows suddenly pour out my soul, draining through my fingers as a bright, blinding flash shined from the pouch where I kept the Orbs of Azure. Though I could hear Macar scream furiously—his startled snarls accompanied by Kael's own hollers behind me—I could see nothing through the thick veil of the intense light, my eyes watering in pain as it swelled and enveloped everything around me.

When the light dimmed at last…

Macar had vanished. Kael was nowhere to be found as well.

The only lives left in the ballroom were little Anabelle, who sobbed over her fallen birth-father, the boy who watched helplessly behind her, and Death King Ysthavon who had lowered his scythe in confusion to find that his opponent had disappeared before his eyes.

But he and Macar hadn't simply disappeared. With my prophetic Hallows blazing in my Third Eye, I Saw that I'd sealed them both away in Aspirre—trapped them inside physically, like a timeless prison cell.

I stared at my hands, blinking back dumbfounded tears. How long have I been able to cast an Evocation like that? A seal that traps others in Aspirre? My Soul-Father never mentioned such a gift…

Perhaps it isn't a gift, I considered darkly. It had been enough to save us in these dire moments, but how long would the seal last?

How long before our deaths returned…?

I wheezed for breath, crouching on all fours as I quaked over the marble floor that pooled with red puddles, staining my trembling fingers.

"Iri…" An agonized squeal pushed up my throat, my undignified sobs echoing in the suddenly silent ballroom. "Father… forgive me…"

HUGH

PRESENT DAY

I swept my crooked, oaken blade to the right, then the left. Right then left. Right then left. Right then left.

Bloods, my arm hurt.

Master Xavier nodded his approval as he paced around me. "Very good, Hugh. Widen your stance. Keep your knees bent."

Something shocked my blood, and my feet slid wider on their own, knees bowing before my mind had a chance to give the command.

Master winced. "Ah, right… I suppose that sounded like a demand. Forgive me, Hugh, I'm still not accustomed to training a vassal. I'll, er, take more care with how I word your instruction."

My reply came as a pant, my sore legs wobbling. "It… it's all right, Master. Perhaps it will force me to do what I should."

"Which contradicts the point of following instruction." He breathed through his nose and scratched the groomed beard at his chin. "The goal is to teach you self-discipline. How are you to push yourself if you allow your muscles to skip the mental work?"

"Yes, Master," I said, swallowing another wheeze before continuing my exercise. *Right then left. Right then left. Right then left.*

Master was dressed formally today. Over a soft ebony, long-sleeved dress shirt hugged a silver vest with black embroidery along the buttons. Clipped over the middle button was the chain of Master's pocket watch, which he opened to note the ticking time, slicked back his grey bangs as his diamond marriage stud glinted from his left ear, and slid the watch back into his vest pocket with a sigh. His boney finger tapped restlessly over his side.

Then he announced, "I think that's enough for today, Hugh."

Thank Land! I dropped my arm in relief, rubbing the screaming bicep.

Master nodded toward the door. "Why don't you prepare for tonight's event?"

"You mean Sir Alexander's wedding?" I asked, tucking both my oaken scythes under an arm and cringing at my own sweaty odor. A bath was certainly needed before I attended a formal occasion.

"Yes," he agreed with a smile, smoothing back the grey hairs over his lip. "Wear something appropriate. I'm expected to be there early, but I hope to see you among our small crowd?"

I saluted with a fist to my chest, letting a chuckle slip. "Yes, Master. I won't be late."

"I should hope not." He grinned and waved me off with a dismissive gesture.

I trotted out to the palace corridors, slowing at a more leisure pace to stare out the glass walls of the Sky castle. This modern architecture was incredible; sunlight spilled through the walls in golden beams and gave life to the dust floating through them like orange glitter. This was one of the few days where Culatia's skies were void of storms. During the last month, there hadn't been a single day like this, the cityscape in the distant islands sparkled in the sea of fluffy clouds and brilliant sunlight.

Bloods, I thought, *this realm was beautiful in its own, modern way.* The metal and glass towers lined with crisscrossing wires and cables were nothing like the solid-stone buildings I'd grown accustomed to in Neverland.

And if it wasn't for Master, I considered, *I never would have seen such sights.* I pressed my hands to the glass, a wash of sadness hitting. *Sy would have never allowed it.*

It hurt to think of Sy. I knew she hadn't meant to kill me, it was my fault for having rushed in front of her strike, but part of me felt betrayed; betrayed that she hadn't seen me in time, as I'd trusted her to; betrayed that she truly was out for blood, rather than the good of our fair country; betrayed that Master had been right. And I… had been so terribly wrong.

And I paid the price for my mistake. I gazed solemnly at my hands—hands that were temporarily filled with blood, thanks to Master and Sir Alexander. It was a challenge to remember I was a corpse. Here and now, I was as alive as Master himself, fully functioning with my soul sewn to my beating heart, but it wasn't permanent. Many a day have I spent as a ghost. My true form, now.

All because of Sy.

The pain returned, and I pushed off the window. I knew I should forget my sister and what she'd done to me. But I also knew she was still out there somewhere, her soul likely rotten and Changed into one of the very demons I was being trained to kill.

Sy, I lamented in silence, *I pray we don't meet again. I may well be forced to return the favor.*

"You're brooding again," a girl's voice piped beside me suddenly.

My skin jumped along with my legs, but I relaxed when seeing the rabbit-eared face of Lady Vendy. Her two brown braids fell over her dark shoulders, which were dressed in silken-yellow sleeves that matched her formal gown. It was unusual to see Lady Vendy in a gown, but even in those rare times, like now, she still wore a belt with her Crystal sword sheathed at her hip. She may have been attending our *Da'torr's* wedding, but she would never be caught unprepared for an unexpected conflict.

Lady Vendy put a fist at her side and lifted a rabbit ear. "Still hung up on your sister?"

I blushed and mumbled, "Well, yes… What am I to do if we see her again as a demon? Will she even remember me? They say the Necrofera lose their memories when they Change. Will she still be my sister anymore?"

Lady Vendy gave a one-shouldered shrug. "Don't know. But if we see her again at all, she'll probably be controlled by that little girl Sentient. Our demons keep talking about a possible army she could be building down in the mid-realms somewhere."

I sighed dismally and fiddled with the oaken scythes tucked under my arm. "Master speaks of the possibility as well. If that battle is anything like what happened in Neverland's city, we could be in for more than we can handle, if we don't prepare enough."

She grunted. "Yeah. And if it comes to that, can you do me a favor and *not* run off on your own?"

I winced, remembering that had been the reason for my death in the first place. "I *am* sorry for that, Lady Vendy... I should have listened to you and Master—"

"Yeah, you should have." She folded her arms with a piqued scowl. "I failed a direct order from my *Da'torr* because of you. I was supposed to guard you, and because I couldn't keep up, you died. Now it's my Bloody fault you're dead. So, thanks."

My lion ears grew in shame. "It was no one's fault but my own. But I promise I'll listen this time. You have far more experience in combat than I, Lady Vendy—"

"And that's another thing." She poked at my chest so hard, I had to take a step back. "Will you stop calling me 'Lady Vendy' and just keep it to 'Vendy' already? It's way too formal. We have the same *Da'torr* for Land's sake, we'll be stuck with each other till they both die. Do you seriously expect to keep calling me 'Lady' this and 'Lady' that for another century? Or even longer if we get a new *Da'torr* afterward?"

"I..." I paused, my lion ears perking as I realized the implication of that last question. "Are you saying you'd... follow me during our afterlives?"

Her rabbit ears shot up and her cheeks flushed the slightest shade of pink. "I-I don't know! I'm just saying it *might* happen, not that it...! I mean...!" She snorted and stuck up her nose before pivoting the other way and stomping off. "You'd better take a shower before *Da'torr* Alex's wedding! You smell like a feral pig!"

She stormed off in a huff, and I couldn't help my now elated smile as I strode the other way in a daze.

25

TREAD WITH CARE

XAVIER

Once Hugh left the training room, I turned to the young man who'd appeared suddenly in the corner without the boy's notice.

"Is it time, then?" I asked Dream, strolling toward the azure-haired king. "I scarcely think I've seen you in weeks. You being here now must mean something is happening. Are we off to Sky's Relic?"

I certainly hoped so. Alexander and I had been patient as he requested and waited a whole Bloody month. Since we hadn't seen any sign of Macarius or Kael, I thought it was safe to proceed as planned.

Still, Dream seemed hesitant. "I wish we had more assurance." He rubbed his knuckles, then stuffed his hands in the pockets of his stained, orange sweater. "Yet I also don't wish to delay your Blessings. My daughter tells me Serdin and your parents have infiltrated Everland's capital and are keeping the southern districts on lockdown under Reaper territory. Ana *must* be there to provide support, as do you and Alexander as the Shadowblood. Which means, much to my disliking…" He sighed. "I suppose it's time to take you to the Phoenix."

"Grand!" I said and clapped my hands. "With Mother and Father's initial siege a success, we can get both this *and* Alexander's wedding over with and leave for Everland tonight!"

"Ah, yes," Dream murmured, as if only now remembering. "The wedding. A fine break from the outside dangers that seek to crack our protective bubble of frivolous distractions."

Death, but the young man's usual, blank expression was pulled into the darkest glower today, his brow creased drastically low as if his thoughts threatened to burst from his skull. He hadn't bothered to tame his grown fox ears, his teeth sharpened and ready to tear out the nearest throat that dared come near.

I found myself sidling back a step. Dream had been absent lately, true, but something had visibly changed over the weeks.

Dream started out to the corridors, and I followed behind cautiously.

"Dream," I risked, "we've looked everywhere. The castle grounds, the city, the skies… They're gone. I find it more likely Macarius fled Culatia altogether."

His red-rimmed eyes offered me a sidelong glare, then he turned forward and continued on, ignoring me.

I hurried after him. "If you'd just consider that neither Alexander nor I have had a single vision of Macarius during our stay?" I grabbed his arm. "I'd say that's a favorable omen if ever I…"

The moment my fingers touched him, my point of view flew away, my eyes un-focusing as I adopted another man's perspective.

His horse halted with such force, he was thrown off the blasted saddle and flew straight into a prickly, snow-dressed briar, white powder coating his now tussled hair like a poorly tailored wig. His skin whined with shallow cuts; his ribs ached with mild bruises.

Worse yet, he'd gone and torn his knitted cloak! His beloved Crysa would never let him hear the end of this. She'd spent a month on the project. Fool he was for having worn it on a hunt, relaxing though the event had been.

"Dream?" He heard his friend call from outside his entrapping briar. The voice sounded farther away, though the narrator couldn't tell exactly how far since his friend's visage was cloaked by thorns and the veil of night.

Grunting, he brushed the twigs and soggy snow from his head and began his crawl out of the thorns, crafting his exit with his already scraped hands as he brushed each branch aside—

One of the branches moved under his grip. Bloods, that was no branch, it was a feral serpent! He swiftly dropped the snake, the now angry thing uncoiling and whipping for his too-near neck.

But a scaled hand shot betwixt the snake and himself, the serpent's fangs sinking into the intruder's palm.

Macar sighed and lifted the snake that was now stuck to his hand, prying the creature free and offered it a disapproving gaze.

"Stay your jaws, comrade," he muttered, "You could say we're merely visitors."

The feral serpent hissed, and Macar returned the gesture in kind before tossing the creature into the snow, where it slithered away.

Macar brought the light forward to look me—him—over. "Did she strike you?" Macar frantically patted the pockets of his warm coat and fished out several vials, pushing up his glasses to better read the labels. "I haven't any antivenom save for my own poisons. If you would see me bring you to Kael, don't you dare hold your tongue, or I'll rightly drag your corpse back to your wife. Best to let her scold your ghost than I."

Dream chuckled at his friend's rather Grimish sense of humor, pushing to his feet and scowling at the tear in his knitted coat. It was so large, he could fit three fingers through. "I'm afraid the only folly I'm to be scolded for is my lack of care for Crysa's creations."

Macar laughed at that.

The vision melted away, my own point of view returning.

My fingers still gripped a very livid Dream's arm. His fox ears were curled so tight to his skull, I feared they'd rip. He'd Seen the same vision.

No, to him it must have been a memory.

"You…" I loosened my grip, a thought coming to mind. *Perhaps I should question him now?* I'd been silent as Crysalette advised—waited months—yet I still couldn't forget that first vision I'd had of Dream and Macarius. Perhaps it was time to pry for some Gods damned answers.

"Just how close were you and he?" I asked. "And why are you so obsessed with finding him?"

"Do not underestimate that snake," Dream snarled—*snarled!* "You've seen but an ounce of what he's capable of. Take it from an old man who's spent half a millennium searching for the splint that would rectify his broken judgement." His jaw clenched, breathing deeply through his nose to calm himself. "If there is but one truth I am certain of," he said, "Macar is still here. He is waiting. And I know he is watching."

He strode out, but paused under the doorway. "Fetch your brother, Xavier," he said, "I will meet you both at the colosseum."

His retreating steps soon fell into silence.

DENIAL

KURN

I steered Clover to the Sky Palace's observatory tower, gently pulling on the crow's neck-feathers to guide him there. The crow dipped and fluttered with a straggled caw, my weight becoming increasingly too heavy for the small scavenger.

"KURN'S DEFENSIVE ENERGY LEVELS LOW," announced the robotic, female voice in my thoughts. *"NANITE POWER AT 3%... RECHARGE SUGGESTED."*

I patted Clover's head apologetically. "Terribly sorry, my young friend. Once I find enough Shockvials to re-power my nanites, you'll hardly notice me on the way back."

Clover cawed in a pant, not understanding me.

He landed within the open, stone windowsill of the observatory, and I hopped off to scuttle down to the floor and rummaged through all the boxes and drawers and shelves that were scattered about the rounded room.

"There must be *some* of those lightning-vials up here..." I muttered under my breath, skittering onto a desk and stretching up to a shelf on the wall. "This is the Bloody Sky realm! Ringëd was always on about how these blasted vials were made up here by the Stormchasers, why is it so hard to find any?"

I pushed aside a row of books and tunneled behind them. Then I found a bag waiting at the end of the long shelf. When I pulled it open, eureka! An entire stash of Shockvials were hidden within. The trapped lightning sparked and snapped inside the Yinklît-coated glass tube.

"Finally!" I exclaimed, eagerly setting my paws on one of the lovely vials.

At the touch, the lightning within slowly leaked out of the metal prongs on either side of the glass tube, and the nanites in my blood sucked the power thirstily. When they were fully charged, and the vial empty, I closed the bag again and grabbed it with my teeth, hauling it down the shelf to bring with me. You never knew when you'd need to charge up again—

Voices echoed from up the spiraling staircase at the entrance door. *Blast!* If I was caught thieving these vials, I was sure to never hear the end of it from Ringëd. If he knew I could drain these power sources, then he'd know that *I* was the one draining the battery from his communicator all these years. What if he made me skip a meal as punishment?!

The footfalls clanged and clattered over the metal stairs as the shifters approached. Panicking, I hid behind the tunnel of books and peeked over their bindings to see who it was. "And you can see the other planets in our solar systems with this thing," a man's voice explained. "It's pretty cool. I figured you guys would be into it, since you're both bookish types and all."

Three bodies entered the observatory. The first was the scarlet-winged Sky King, Roji. Behind him were two other winged bi-pedals, a male and a female. Ah, Marian and Herrin! The ones called 'Enlighteners'.

"We prefer 'scholars', thank you," Marian huffed as she scribbled down notes in a ledger.

Herrin went to the enormous telescope at the center of the observatory and peered through the eyepiece curiously. "Wow… you can even see the farthest planet in the system with this thing…"

I blinked, my round ears perking straight up. *The farthest planet?*

Why, that was my planet's communication-relay base! They could see it from all the way out here on this primitive planet?

I abandoned the sack of vials and snuck down to the floor, scurrying toward the telescope.

HERRIN

"Space travel?" I asked skeptically, staring through the palace observatory's enormous telescope and seeing the vast, black expanse of outer space filled with shining stars and colorful planets. "You think that's possible?"

I looked away from the eyepiece to glance at Roji, who was grinning.

"You bet it is," the Sky King said smugly. "You should talk to some of our top astronomers. They've got a fool-proof plan to take a ship up there to test it and everything. Culatia's science studies are the most advanced in the world."

Marian took a turn to look through the telescope this time, breathing, "Amazing…" She ruffled her brown-and-red wings excitedly and looked at

Roji. "Do you think there's life out there, just like us? And—oh, what if they've already mastered this 'space travel' and passed right over Nirus? We never would have known!"

Roji rubbed his chin. "Mmm, well, there's actually been a few claims of 'visitors' coming to Nirus from other planets. Most of them are rumors, but someone *did* snap a picture of something pretty suspicious some years back, but it's still pending a certification of authenticity." He went to a bookshelf and pulled out a thin text titled, *Visitors From Afar?* He walked back to Marian and me and flipped to a specific page before showing us. "See? Hard to tell from the fuzzy quality—it was taken with a low-tech camera—but it definitely looks like a person walking out of some weird, floating transport."

The transport he mentioned was pictured as a metallic blur with flashy lights speckling all over its shiny walls. There were other pictures to go along with it, one showing the undercarriage of the transport which was totally flat and didn't have any Levi-stones, so the thing was definitely floating by some other means that was foreign to our tech. The other picture showed a close-up of the stranger walking down the ramp.

Marian pointed to the third picture curiously. "Look, he seems to be holding some sort of little creature."

"Creature?" I asked, squinting and turning the book at a different angle. "Huh. Kinda looks like... some kind of feral animal."

I flipped the page. There were more pictures of the same stranger and the animal, almost like the person taking the photos had followed them in secret and snapped whatever they could. One clearer picture showed the guy was wearing some kind of suit and tie, almost looking like a butler. Another picture showed a close-up of the animal, and...

I stopped short, looking at Marian. "Uh... does that thing look familiar to you?"

Marian blinked back at me with a pale face. "It... it looks just like Ringëd's..."

We finished in unison, "Ferret?"

Squeak!

We all turned at the small squeal of metal.

It came from the telescope. Something had accidentally moved the eyepiece. And that something was a long-bodied, round-eared weasel.

Kurn.

The ferret was laying on its belly along the telescope and peeking into the eyepiece. A sack of Shockvials was clutched in one of his front paws. When the ferret snapped its head up and noticed us, he froze.

No one said a word.

Then Kurn freaked out and fumbled to the floor, the sack of Shockvials he'd held tumbling loose as vials rolled out around him. He quickly stuffed them all back into the sack, then scurried toward the stone windowsill—where one of the Reaper's crows was apparently perched. The ferret skittered onto the crow's back and snickered urgently at the bird. It flew them out in a hurry, leaving us gawking after the pair of ferals.

LILLI

Sousül Vivati laced another white-and-pink speckled bloom in my braided, black hair, finishing the row that trailed the left side of my head over my dangling engagement-vines.

"These being called stargazers," the wedding planner said in her heavy accent, adjusting the parasols above Willow's and my head in the palace gardens to save us Grimlettes from the harsh sunlight.

I'd heard Culatia's storms sometimes strayed from the islands, but Nira, I wished someone had told me the sun was hotter in this altitude than anywhere else on the blasted planet. The air was still rather chilled, though nothing compared to Grim, but the springtime here felt like Everland's summers. Even Willow was batting a fan at her face like a madwoman, her maternity gown already forming sweat stains.

Her Highness Zylveia, however, sat basking in the light stretched on her back over the stone bench beside Willow with her wings spread lazily. Her crossed legs bounced up and down as the woman sucked on an icy treat.

"I think ees *much* fitting!" Vivati went on, pinning up a loose strand of my hair. "These flowers being type of lilies, grown here in Culatia. Ees fun thing, no? Lilies for Lady Lilli!"

"I see," I hummed absently, combing Oliver's feathered hair while he sat indignantly at my knees, shaking his rubber, 'crystal' ball and watching the blue glitter tumble within is watery confines.

Across from him sat Fuérr, the little Ocean Prince chittering in Marincian while lying on his stomach and poking at Oliver's rubber ball, hypnotized by the storm of glitter.

Oliver wriggled under me, ducking his head when I tried to comb his feathers back into place.

"Oliver, please," I sighed, "Could you hold still for only a moment?"

"Why do I gotta wear this, Mama?" Oliver whined, tugging at the buttoned collar of his long-sleeved, snow-white tuxedo and grimacing.

"Speak properly, darling," I reminded gently. "As practiced."

He groaned, but complied and restated, "Why *must* I wear this, Mother? It's too hot!"

"I'm sorry, darling. It will only be for a little while today. Be patient for me, please?"

He grumbled, but raised no further protest, returning to shaking his rubber ball across from Fuérr. Fuérr reached for the ball, asking for a turn in Marincian. I was sure Oliver hadn't understood the Seadragon's words, but his body language seemed to register, and Oliver handed over the ball.

"Mama," Oliver began, but stopped himself and amended, "Mother… Where's papa?"

I rubbed my lids, knowing Oliver meant Jaq. I wasn't sure at what point he'd taken to calling the viper 'papa', but I'd assumed it had to do with Jaq's presence in Tanderam with us.

"Jaq is… busy working, darling," I said, hoping my worry hadn't leaked through my tone. "I'm sure he'll be around shortly." *One of these Bloody days,* I brooded to myself.

Oliver curled his wings forward in a pout and blew out a grumbling breath.

I held a hand to my eyes and blocked the glaring sun, our parasol barely shielding the harsh light. It didn't help that the palace's glass-and-metallic design amplified the glare tenfold. Whose idea was it to build such a modern menace? If Jaq were here, I'd venture to bet he'd have quite a few words to describe the architect and…

My breath faltered, stomach twisting sick.

"Lilli?" Willow asked beside me, pausing her frantic fanning to look me over.

I jolted. "Oh—er, yes?"

"Are you all right? If you'd been a Seer, one would think you had a vision."

I forced my lips to pull into a small grin. Though, I couldn't keep it for long. "I wish it were a vision," I sighed.

Willow folded the fan and set it on her lap before plucking one of the four glasses of chilled lemonade from the table, taking a sip, then pressing its cold surface to her sweaty brow. "Lilli," she said, gesturing with her glass and causing the ice to *clink*, "we've searched the grounds thoroughly for the last month. Wherever Macarius and his poisonous tool went, you can rest assured they won't interrupt your wedding."

"My…" I suddenly remembered why we were here. "Oh! Yes. The wedding." That's right, Alexander and I were to wed in a mere hour. I'd nearly forgotten.

Willow squinted an eye at me. "What's claimed your thoughts, then?"

"I'm not sure."

She cocked an ashen eyebrow at me. Blast, but the woman could read my face too easily.

I rubbed my knuckles over the skirt of my silken, rose-pink gown. "I... I suppose it's Jaq," I admitted.

Willow's expression skewed quizzically, and Her Highness Zylveia's head turned my way. Willow questioned, "Jaq?"

"He hasn't spoken to me since we arrived at the Sky Palace," I said, "not a single word."

"He's been quite busy, hasn't he?" Willow commented. "Last I recall, he is your fiancé's chosen best man. Such a role comes with many responsibilities."

"But it's more than that." I insisted. How could I explain? "I've seen him passing the halls with Octavius and Matthiel, and the moment he sees me approach, he turns right around without them. Oh, Willow, if you could just see the *look* on his face..."

"All right, all right." Willow kept an even tone. "Let's humor the thought that he's avoiding you. Why does it matter?"

"I don't know!" I groaned, burying my head in my hands. My bat ears grew alongside the festering pit in my stomach. "What if I've done something wrong? And if I have, how do I amend it? What if he..." *Blast, don't you dare weep, fool.* "What if he never speaks to me again? What if I've hurt him beyond repair? What have I done, Willow?"

"W... well." She sounded forcefully calm, as if trying to keep me from panicking. "Have you asked Alexander?"

"This isn't about Alexander."

"Honestly, Lilli, is this really so important right this minute? You're to wed in only—"

"Have you not heard a thing I've said?" I cried, panicking despite her efforts. "Willow, what if I've *hurt* him? What if he's suffering be-because I..."?

"Lilli." For a moment, her azure gaze turned contemplative. "I don't suppose... do you think you might, er..."

Willow winced suddenly, gasping while clutching her enormous belly.

My own worries dissolved. "What's wrong?"

She released a steady stream of breath, then relaxed. "I'm fine. He's rather active today." She gave another gasp of pain, and both Zylveia and I rose in a start, nearly knocking over Vivati.

"*Skrii!*" Zylveia cursed, her scarlet wings stiffening. "Ees Death baby the coming one?!"

I offered Willow a cautious hand. "Perhaps you should see the Healers? You're due any day now, aren't you?"

"Three days." She winced again, and I took her arm as delicately as my nervous hands would allow.

"Three days is soon enough," I said, "come, let's see you to the Healers."

"I'll be fine." She waved me off, walking the path herself. "Though, perhaps I should find my husband. I could use his coldness for a moment."

I hesitated. "I can accompany you?"

"You, Spirit Sister," she called back, waving a hand at me. "Have a wedding to attend. Go on. Best you don't dally."

I bit my lip. Would she really be all right? Perhaps I should insist…

Zylveia snorted before I could decide and stalked to Willow's side. "I help find Death Prince. If baby the coming one, you not want to be by self, eh?"

Willow exhaled, her head shaking. "Oh, very well. Come if you wish, but I tell you, we will not be met with any surprises today."

They withdrew from the garden and disappeared inside those glassy walls, the reflective glare of the sun blinding my view. Dusk, who was perched atop the flight-feathers of a metal phoenix sculpture, gave a low croak and ruffled her feathers, head dipping solemnly.

"Well, well, well!" Vivati chimed and clapped her hands happily. "Ees almost being the time! Come, come! We go to ballroom now, I ees needing to check the catering and food—"

"I'll meet with you there shortly," I interrupted, waving a dismissive hand at the planner while taking up the folded fan Willow had left behind on the table, flapping the refreshing air at my sweat-coated neck. "I'd like a moment to breathe… but could you take Oliver and Fuérr with you? I don't want either of them overheating in their suits out here, I should think the ventilation will be better for them indoors."

"Yea, yea, ees no problem, miss bride!" Vivati took the boys in either hand, chittering excitedly to them as they all went inside… leaving me alone in the gardens at last.

Vivati, I thought in a sigh, *for all your constant nagging, you're quite a good sport for tolerating me.*

I lowered back on the bench, taking the parasol to keep this blasted light from searing my skin. Though, I supposed I couldn't complain too much. This had been the first day the skies were free of storms since we arrived. It was admittedly quite beautiful… Willow had said the good weather was an omen for my wedding.

My wedding.

What was wrong with me? I've dreamt of this day since I was a girl: the day Alexander and I would have our union…

Shouldn't I be excited? Nervous? *Something…?* I just felt so bored with it all.

Dusk jolted from the phoenix sculpture, her head snapping to the west end of the garden. Our bond pulsed with a sting of thrill and uneasiness as we both watched the blond figure and his own companion cross the cobbled path.

Jaq!

The viper was dressed in pressed trousers and a silken dress shirt, but he hadn't bothered to button the collar. His sandy locks were tied in a short tail, though his wavy bangs were loose and sloppily tossed about his scaled cheekbones, slim eyeglasses resting low along his nose.

He looked despondent, crossing the garden with stale eyes stuck to his boots, posture slouched and hands stuffed in his pockets as he kicked at a loose stone. Even Bridge looked downtrodden from atop his shoulder.

I rose from my bench and started toward him. "Jaq?"

He froze mid-step, spotting me. His face wrenched into the most disgusted sneer, then he spun on his heels and retreated the way he'd come.

"Jaq!" *Not this time, damn it!* I spread my wings and leapt up, soaring with rushed speed and landed in front of him. "Jaq, what in Nira's name is wrong?" I demanded.

His teeth gritted, fangs grown long and unfolding as he hissed, "Who said anything was wrong?" He turned and hurried the other way.

"Jaq, please!" I grabbed his arm. "Why are you avoiding me? What have I done—?"

"Will you mind your own Bloody business?" he snapped, black eyes cold. "And don't you have somewhere to be, *Howless?*" The last title dripped with contempt.

The sickness churned, loosening my fingers from his sleeve. Now he wouldn't even call me by name? Death, I *have* done something terrible.

He scoffed and started away again.

I caught his shoulder, tighter this time, and shoved him against a breezeway pillar. "Will you just stop!" I shouted. "Not a month ago you could tell me anything and everything, yet now the very sight of me disgusts you? Have I said something? Done something? If you wish for me to stop calling you a peasant, I will, but Gods damn it, I will not have you ignoring me!"

His initial shock took a moment to dissipate, then his brow furrowed. "What? I don't care if you call me a peasant."

"Then by Nira, what is it?" I pleaded. "I can't take this anymore, Jaq! There are things I can't even speak to Willow about, I'm going insane keeping it all crammed in my skull!"

He snorted. "That ain't my problem."

"I know!" I slammed a fist on the pillar, exhaling a softer breath. "I know. I'm sorry. But I can't keep this up, Jaq. I don't feel like myself anymore and I…" How did I describe it? Blast, I hadn't the proper words. What was wrong with me?

Jaq wouldn't look at me, and he mumbled, "Don't you have a wedding to go to?"

"I don't care about a Bloody wedding!" I growled, bat ears growing. "Just tell me what's wrong!"

He muttered, "Give me one good reason—"

"One." I pointed to Bridge, who'd flown off his shoulder and alighted on a nearby branch, then I ripped off his glasses. "I helped you when you couldn't see worth a damn in Tanderam. You trusted me to tell you if our messengers were the ones to be killed next. You could have thought me a liar to save your heartache, but you didn't. Two." I gestured toward the palace, where I'd left Oliver in the charge of Vivati. "You're the only other person Oliver actually listens to. He asks after you more than anyone, you should know. Three." I cupped my hand over his forehead, feeling the hidden bumps of his 'Grimling' scar. "I will *never* forgive myself for this scar. *I* was meant to bear it. Yet instead, you do. Four…" I dropped my hand. "I've seen too much of you. Too much in the darkest times, and you're the only person on this Gods-forsaken planet who's seen the same for me. I can't lose you over some ridiculous jest I might have made, good intent or no. Now please." Nira help me, why did it hurt so much…? "What have I done?"

His jaw locked, and he squeezed his eyes shut. He took in a slow breath from his nose and—

He snatched my waist and pressed his lips against mine, his fingers entangling my hair. The shock sent that sickened knot right away, my pulse burning hotter than I've ever dreamt…! I hadn't the breath to gasp, mind growing numb, limbs threatening to follow—

He ripped free, his eyes red and glassy.

Then he snatched his glasses out of my stiffened fingers and brusquely made his retreat.

I was frozen where I stood, gasping for breath, that knot returning twofold as I watched him vanish inside.

Oh, mournful Nira.

I squeezed my chest, fearing it would erupt the way it throbbed with such anger, such violence…

And such wonderful, beautiful *bliss*.

27

THE PHOENIX OF SCARLET

WILLOW

I gritted my teeth and kept a hand to my swollen belly when that same wave of heat clenched my back and stomach like a tight belt, slowing my pace through the palace corridors.

Zylveia put fists at her sides and cocked her head at me. "You being sure Death baby not being the coming one?" she asked.

"As I've said," I muttered, "he has another three days. I'm only dehydrated."

She gave a disapproving hum. "If you being the sure one…"

I sighed, walking ahead of her. "If it will cease your doubts, I'll find Octavius or Claude and ask for a second opinion. How does that sound?"

Zylveia was oddly silent behind me, offering no reply.

"Zylveia?" I turned around to look.

She wasn't there anymore. "Zylveia?" I called again.

The Sky Princess was nowhere in the arching halls, though I noticed belatedly that there were, in fact, *more* shifters crowding the place now than there had been a moment ago. Where had these people come from?

They were all rushing here and there, most congregating out to one particular archway leading outside, shouting frightened cries. It was raining outside now. When had that happened? Thunder clapped from the windows, servants I hadn't recognized bustled out that one archway and followed a single, brick path toward some sort of colosseum that was suspended on its own piece of floating island connected by railed bridges.

"E-excuse me," I called to a passing shifter, reaching for her, "Where is everyone go…?"

Her image passed through my fingers like mist, the woman sprinting on her way as if she'd neither heard nor seen me.

What in Bloods? Was this a vision?

My fox ears grew, guessing what was going on, and I followed the current of racing shifters through the open archway. As I suspected, the pouring rain didn't touch me. It phased through my skin as if I were a ghost, the wind brushing my long hair and bell far gentler than the gusts that threatened to rip the trees of their roots. If this was a vision, there was only one way to find out.

I kept a keen eye on the faces rushing about, following the path most traveled. Bloods, it seemed the entire country was here. But where was the one face I expected to find? *Grandfather, if you are here again, I pray you tell me what this is about.*

I followed the current of winged shifters along the path, fox ears curled and gaze deathly determined.

ZYL

TRANSLANTED FROM CULATIAN

"Where you going?" I asked louder in Landish. Willow was walking so fast, I had to trot to keep up with her. How could a pregnant woman move so quick? *"Hello? Why you ignore Zyl?"*

What in Sky's gotten into her? She just dropped everything and started walking to the colosseum. We were already crossing the bridge to the isolated island, her fox ears swiveling all over, her sightless gaze scanning the land for something.

There was a soft, blue glow under her dress, where I remembered her Dream mark was. I saw it there the time we shared a dressing room in that crazy queen's palace in Neverland. Was she having some weird vision? It was like she couldn't even see me anymore.

I scowled and folded my hands behind my head. Ah, whatever. If she couldn't see *me*, there was a good chance she couldn't see a cliff if she fell off it. Probably best if I followed her in case I needed to catch the psychotic pregnant woman. At least until she snapped out of the vision.

We walked all the way to the open-air colosseum, its towering walls filled with stone benches that dipped tier-by-tier and met at the center, where the floorless arena waited like a gaping mouth that had swallowed the cottony clouds. Several stray platforms floated in the gap, connected with chains and anchored to the arena's stone ledge.

I flew up to perch on a metal statue, watching Willow from above. Her tiny crow fluttered next to me, chirping like she was just as confused as I was.

Willow started babbling to herself now. I scrunched my nose, straining to listen, but she kept saying 'grandfather', 'grandfather', and stuff like that. What was she Seeing?

I watched her for another few minutes, enjoying the warmth of the sunlight and kicking my feet, watching the clouds... *ugh* this was boring! How long was this going to take?

I fished into the leather pouch at my hip, taking out my scarlet, glass ocarina and twittered a few notes of *The Winds of The Storm.*

—*Zzzzap!*

A spark hit my fingers, making me gasp. *Was that... was that my lightning?* I stared at my hand, focusing.

Zzzap, snap!

Ha, *ha!* A shock! Sky be praised, my Hallows were coming back! Just as Bianca said they would if I drank enough of her disgusting tonics. Gross as they were, at least they were working. I was starting to think I'd never feel that sweet electricity again.

I happily kept playing my ocarina, testing out my Aerovoking while I was at it. The wisps of wind wove in and out of the holes as my fingers commanded, *Bloods* did I miss this—!

Movement caught my eye from the other side of the circular arena, and I paused. Was that the wolf twins over there?

Actually, I remembered belatedly, *wasn't Roji supposed to give them Sky's Blessings or whatever today?* So, the twins were already here. But where was Roji?

I rubbed my chin, having a thought. Technically speaking, wasn't *I* a Relicblood of Sky? *I* knew the Call; *I* could wake up the Relic... And, since my Hallows were back, even if just a little bit, maybe I could give them the Blessings instead and give Big Brother a break? And Void, maybe the Relic could give me *all* my Hallows strength back?

I stole a glance back at Willow. For the most part, she seemed half aware of her surroundings. At least, the surroundings that mattered, like the solid stone benches and the railings on each tier. *I'll just keep looking back to watch her.*

I grinned and, looping my ocarina's lanyard over my head, I flew to the twins.

"All right, wolf twins," I said in Landish, touching down with a toothy smirk. *"I here first, so I can give Call!"*

The brothers exchanged a curious look, shrugging. Both nodded, and Xavier gestured for me to lead the way.

My lips stretched wider, and I hopped up the steps. *"Come, this way! We go to the Sands."*

They didn't complain as they followed. After walking them around the ringed colosseum, I brought them to the top row, right in front of the hour-glass-shaped, stone tower that loomed over the whole structure. I found the ladder and climbed up, making sure they were still following under me. Sure, I could have just flown to the top, but this was really to show them how *they* could get up here. My excitement bubbled the farther up we got, heaving myself up each rung while humming the song I'd played earlier, my ocarina swinging from my neck as if dancing.

Strong gales rise
With our demise
Beat your wings to its great cries

I paused my singing, swinging on the rungs to check on Willow down below on the other side of the colosseum. She seemed fine enough, so I kept climbing and went back to my song.

Faster still
As the hail does spill
Best keep pace before you're killed

By the winds of The Storm

I reach the top finally and perched on the edge of the open hourglass structure. I smiled at the scarlet sand grains that glittered in the hot sunlight, remembering the times I'd come up here with Roji and my father. I ran my fingers through the glittering grains, sighing. *It's been too long, old friend.*

The twins climbed to the ledge beside me, staring at the sands in awe. Heh, I didn't blame them. The Sands were too beautiful not to be stared at.

"*This ees being the Sacred Chalice,*" I said in Landish. It didn't sound as cool in their language. I swirled my hand through the scarlet grains. "*And these being the Eternal Sands.*"

The brothers looked confused, and I grinned, bringing the ocarina to my lips and drew in a breath.

Then I played *The Winds of The Storm.*

The sand began to gleam scarlet, and dark nimbus clouds began billowing—

Then a *crack* of lightning exploded from the sky, jagged strings hitting the Chalice, and a glass feather appeared from the sands.

Crack, crack, crack!

Strike after strike, the lightning erupted over the grains, forming a glass feather each time. The pieces swirled in the cutting gale and clinked together in the new whirlwind.

And in the midst of my playing, the Phoenix of Scarlet opened its gleaming, electric eyes.

WILLOW

After crossing the long, railed bridge, I stepped onto the ring of land that floated amongst the dark clouds. Rain pelted the stones around me yet passed through my semi-tangible self as lightning streaked the skies. A vicious screech cried from within the nimbus, causing the audience around me to duck their heads in fright.

Being that I was, for the most part, incorporeal, I stepped along the rows of stone benches which stretched in a disc shape round the open-air colosseum—which had neither a floor nor a safety net, but instead opened into the clouds beneath. Small platforms floated within, all chained together and anchored to the arena's stone ledge.

Another crash erupted from the skies, lights blinking, the crowd gasping and screaming. One woman cradled her winged toddler and began sobbing. What exactly was happening here?

Crrrack!

An enormous bolt shot at the copper spire above our heads. Then a single, blue-and-red winged man swooped out of the clouds, drawing back his bow and loosening an arrow at his scarlet-haired pursuer. The second man, wielding a bow himself with sparks of lightning spewing from his hands, had red, leathery wings flapping strong against the gale as he took his challenger's arrow in the shoulder and loosed his own projectile. But he missed and released a vicious snarl that only those in our section could hear before the two soared to the other end of the colosseum.

But as they passed, I caught a glimpse of the feathered man's face. Despite the navy-blue shade of his wings and hair, I could swear he looked just like…

"Roji?" I murmured, watching the two battle in the storm, entranced by the frightening scene.

"—You picked one Void of a day to visit this time, Granddaughter," a tiny voice said under the howling wind.

I had to crane my neck to see the child that stood beside me. He was no taller than my waist, the small thing wrapped in his heavy, soaked cloak and sporting a pair of large goggles that protected his eyes from the water. I spied a drenched strand of azure hair stuck to his forehead, which held a crowned Dream mark.

Ah hah! There he was. No wonder I'd had so much trouble spotting him. Just like in our last shared vision, he looked no older than ten, his voice higher than I was accustomed to and his little size all but swallowed by the crowd of taller adults.

Then I was right. Grandfather's presence meant this was a shared vision between us, like the previous times.

"Grandfather," I said, "What is happening here? What year is this?"

"It's still the year 989 A.B." His small voice was strained, almost frightened, like so many others here. "And Sky King U'lbric is being challenged for the crown."

A blinding strike ripped across the sky, provoking screams from the horrified spectators. Then a haunting cry pierced through the roar of the storm. The next flash of light displayed an enormous, blackened silhouette of a creature with the largest wingspan I had ever beheld.

Though I couldn't fully see the beast behind the clouds, I could guess what it was. "Grandfather, is that…?"

"The Phoenix of Scarlet," he answered. "Our challenging swallow demanded it bear witness to this duel."

"Bloods be good," I whispered, the hidden Phoenix letting out another shriek before the clouds grew black once more. "They allowed so many to see the Phoenix?"

"Allowed?" Grandfather sounded perplexed, craning his round face to look at me behind those large goggles. "Why wouldn't they be allowed to see the Phoenix?"

My brow furrowed. *Still the year 989…* This must have been a time before the Relics were lost. Before Grandfather hid them from the world. Which meant this was the event that I'd warned Grandfather about in our last vision together. This was the night Roji's ancestors overthrew the Skydragons—

My belly swelled with pain suddenly, and I doubled over in a sharp wince.

When next I blinked, the storm had changed.

The crowd was gone. There was nothing left save for the empty colosseum, though the rain still pelted the benches—and myself. I was tangible again, susceptible to the weather. *But hadn't it been clear before I entered the vision?*

Another swell of pain, more intense this time, and I grasped the metal railing for support. I clutched my belly, seething. Jewel twittered furiously next to my trembling hand.

Dearest Death…! This pain…!

My legs lost their strength, and I lowered to the stone benches. My thighs suddenly felt warm. I glanced down, seeing my gown's skirts had a trail of what seemed to be water soaking through, forming a triangle among the dark spots where the rain had hit the fabric.

"Oh, Bloods." I let out a pained cry when my belly pulled in agony again, and I turned to my panicking messenger. "Jewel…! Get… Get Xavier…!" I yielded to another cry as Jewel sped off toward the glassy palace. But something caught my eye at the top of an hourglass-shaped tower. Scarlet, glass feathers were swirling in a twister, clinking together, lightning shrieking over the tower and blowing up red sand. *The Phoenix…?*

Standing on the ledge of the tower was Zyl. She danced with her ocarina, her feathers swaying with whatever melody she played, the sounds swept up by the winds. And standing beside her were… the twins?

Yes, that was most certainly them. I could see Xavier's grey hair whipping in the breeze, donning a black doublet while his brother wore white beside him.

White?

The last I saw of Alexander, he'd worn black for his wedding this morning… and didn't Jewel fly in the opposite direction? That was unlike her. She'd sensed Xavier before in the past, or at least his messenger. Why didn't she sense him now—?

I screamed as the pain radiated at my belly again.

I focused on my breathing and tapped into my mental connection to contact my vassals.

"Rossette," I wheezed, wincing at another round of pain. "Nikolai… Something is wrong—*argh*…!"

28

COLD FEET

ALEXANDER

Rain pelted the window outside, streaks of light bursting from the dark clouds that had appeared out of nowhere. The sunlight that had only moments prior basked the islands in its rays had been swallowed entirely.

Good riddance, I thought with a snort. I was growing sick of that blistering sun. It was far worse up here than it'd been in the Land realm below.

I glanced at my silver pocket watch, staring at the second-hand that ticked away, and clicked it shut.

"Have any of you heard from Jaq today?" I asked the others who were still dressing in their pressed suits.

From the room's corner, Dalen only shook his head, but Octavius shrugged from the open windowsill.

"Not since this morning," reported Octavius, "and even then it was for like, two minutes."

Neal buttoned his tunic, agreeing. "We were on our way here and then he up and ditched."

"He's experiencing a… rather difficult dilemma," Matthiel muttered, fiddling with his collar-string. "He claims he only needs some time alone to, well, sort through it all. Best we left it to him, I say."

I glanced at my watch again, stifling a tremor. Truth be told, Jaq's absence wasn't what had my nerves so wracked. Bianca was also missing. I'd looked in the infirmary and the lab, asked her guild members and pupils… Where was she? Could she not at least grant me one last meeting before I followed through with this?

I stuffed the watch in my ebony coat pocket, wolf ears growing. Why did I even wish to see her now of all times? I'm promising myself to another woman today. I shouldn't care if I see her.

But gracious *Bloods*, did I. I couldn't do this. I wanted—*needed*—Bianca to burst through that door and stop me from making this horrible mistake. I needed her to slap me and demand that I come to my senses. I needed her to…

"Please," Mother Maria's voice itched in my ears again. The memory of her blood-ridden face flitted to mind. *"Take care of my Lilli…"*

My wolf ears curled, and I damn near struck a hole in the wall.

Damn it, Mother Maria. Why was I the one to watch you die? Why was I the one to drag you out of the fire? Why was I forced to stay there, soaking in your blood, watching your soul leave to the Unknown…?

Octavius suddenly perked from the window—then he scrambled to open the silver frame's latch. Rain poured onto the carpet, and Octavius stepped back as El, dressed in a loose, formal gown with her snowy hair decorated with jeweled pins—now soaked through—flew in and perched on the windowsill beside him, ruffling her pale-blue wings dry.

"Have you seen Zyl?" She asked Octavius with her thick Culatian accent, yellow eyes puzzled as she tried in vain to ring out her damp gown, her cat ears flicking droplets.

Her white raven swept in beside her, greeting the rest of our ravens which were scattered about the chamber, now croaking up a storm.

Octavius frowned at his lady friend. "Zyl? Shouldn't she be with you?"

El fluffed her wings and gave a disparaging hum. "I was supposed to meet all of them in the garden, but they weren't there. Then this storm came out of nowhere."

I closed the window and stared at the rain that applauded over the glass, rubbing my newly shaven chin. "This storm *was* rather sudden," I said, "but I assumed such was the norm for this realm?"

El shook her head vigorously. "Storms don't come so suddenly like this. Not unless an Imbrivoker is doing it."

A knock came at the door.

I went to open it, grumbling, "What Imbrivoker could cause such a large…" I pried open the door and stopped cold.

Lilli stood under the doorway. She was wrapped in a slender, rose-pink gown with a thin layer of chiffon that flowed to her ankles in graceful ruffles. Her black hair was pinned up, save for two strands which fell straight at either of her grown bat ears, beautiful white-and-pink flowers lining one side of her head.

I found myself lost for breath. Dearest Death, she was absolutely *stunning*. Her sharp, orange-brown eyes were painted with black liner and maroon powder, her pale cheeks dusted with a subtle rose color that matched her luscious lips.

"Lilli," I said, fumbling for something to say to my soon-to-be wife, "you look… well."

She cast her gaze away. "Oh… Thank you."

I cleared my throat behind a fist, the nervousness returning. "Have you seen Zylveia by chance? Her Aide is looking for her."

"She's escorting Willow to find Xavier, last I saw," she said. Her voice was oddly… cheered? Depressed? I wasn't sure whether she was ripe to laugh or weep.

"I suppose you're, er, ready for this afternoon's events?" I asked, more to fill the silence. Death, when did it get so hot in this palace?

You can't do this, you Bloody idiot, my thoughts shouted as my hands balled, stifling a tremor. *Call it off. Call it off now, before—*

"Actually." She clutched her thin fingers. "I wished to speak with you for a moment. Privately?"

"Ah… I-I suppose." I swallowed, but stepped out into the hallway, clicking the door shut behind me. *Call. It. OFF.* "—what is it?" I asked in a rush, my throat tight.

She blushed under her powder. "I… I-I'm not sure how to say this, but… something's happened. Well, I suppose it was there for some time, but I hadn't understood exactly what it was until now. But I'm finding that I'm not quite… oh, how do you word it? I'm not so much in control of my mind, as my mind is already made up on its own and I can't help how it wills itself anymore."

My look dripped in confusion. "Er… I'm not sure I follow."

"Please, forgive me." Her hands shook as she reached for the sparkling engagement-vines that dangled from her hair. "I have someone to find. But I only wished to tell you…" She inhaled deeply. "Alex, I don't want to mar—"

"Alex," Xavier called suddenly from behind Lilli. "Dream wishes to meet us in…"

My brother paused when he spotted Lilli. He gave her a bearded smile. "Oh. Why Lilli, aren't you an absolute vision today?" He had an afterthought, then asked, "Have you seen Willow? I'd hoped to check on her before Alex and I went off."

Lilli blinked at him. "She went to find you. You didn't cross paths on your way here?"

Xavier scratched at his neck. "I haven't seen her since this morning."

"Oh, dear." Lilli brought worried fingers to her lips. "She wasn't feeling well when she left. Perhaps she went to the Healers after all?"

"—I'm afraid you won't find her there!" a voice shouted down the echoing corridor, several footfalls hammering toward us.

King Dream was leading a pack he had apparently acquired, Jewel fluttering at full speed by his head.

With him was Grandfather Edric, Anabelle and her guards, Nikolai and Rossette, Vendy and Hugh, little Oliver and Fuérr with that pet Bindragon of Hecrûshou's coiled around Fuérr's arm, Claude and Sirra-Lynn, Mikani and Ringëd…

And carting a bag of medical tools with a determined look creasing her brow was Bianca.

Bianca shoved her way to the front, glancing at me for only a heart-fluttering second before turning to Xavier.

"Dream had a vision," she told my brother, her rabbit ears perked straight up. Octavius and others came out of the room behind me as Bianca went on, "Willow's at the colosseum, off the grounds. She's gone into labor."

Xavier paled, his voice in a panic. "*Where is that Bloody colosseum?*"

"Dream knows the way," Bianca assured, lifting her bag of tools. "Don't worry. We've got five Healers here to handle the delivery, and there's no way in Void I'm going to let anything happen to my Spirit Son."

"Hurry now!" Dream hollered as he sped ahead to lead the way. "We've no time to spare!"

Xavier rushed at his side, firing frightened questions at the young king as the rest of us tried like Death to keep pace.

But I noticed Willow's two vassals were sputtering for breath behind the pack.

"W-wait!" Rossette called to Xavier, though he was too far ahead to hear, and her wings seemed to have given up.

Nikolai looked just as exhausted, as if the fish-shifter had just run a marathon. "ees… ees zomezing not right! *Da'torr* say… say not right!"

I grabbed Nikolai's scaled arm. "What's not right?"

"She not know," he panted, shaking his head. "But she say… say she see you two there now!"

"We'll be there as soon as we can," I assured.

"That is not what he means!" Rossette contradicted, flying in front of me. "*Da'torr* claims you and your brother are *already* there!"

My boots screeched to a halt. "Excuse me?"

HERRIN

Marian, Roji and I stared at the picture of the ferret in the space-visitor's book, all squinting at every angle.

"Can't be Kurn," Roji disagreed with a scrunched nose, his scarlet wings fluffing in a scoff. "This one doesn't have food stuffed in his face."

Marian breathed in awe, "But look at the markings on his fur. They match quite exactly, don't you think, Archchancellor?"

I scratched my feathered hair. "It really does look like him… but then, maybe a lot of feral ferrets have those markings?"

"And anyway," Roji said, "wouldn't Kurn have told Ringëd something about being from space or whatever? He's a 'supposed-to-be' ferret shifter, they chat all the time."

Marian's wings lowered as she gave the Sky King a flat look. "He *has* told Ringëd about being an exiled emperor from another planet. Have you read any of Master Herrin's books?"

Roji snorted and went to one of the rounded windows and slid it open. "Why should I? I've been traveling with everyone, so it just seems kind of pointless to…" He spotted something out there suddenly, and his feathers went stiff. "What in *Skrii?*"

He hopped on the sill and flew out, leaving me running to the window to see what the problem was. All I could see was the colosseum next door.

Wait, there were people there.

"Oh, crap!" I hopped out the window myself, spreading my wings and calling behind me, "Marian, hurry and bring your notes! And-and a pen! I think the Shadowblood is about to get Sky's Blessings!"

"What!" Marian grabbed her satchel from the floor and flew out beside me, both of us soaring after Roji. "Void take me, we'd better not have missed it!"

29

ELECTRIFIED

XAVIER

I raced along the stone-and-metal bridge alongside Dream, far ahead of the group, storm clouds sparking with light as the winds blew strong and ruthless.

Willow…! Gods have mercy, I prayed she wasn't alone. With this storm, anything could go wrong.

"Is she outside in this weather?!" I shouted at Dream.

Dream puffed next to me. "She was when last I Saw. We need to get her into one of the colosseum's lodges before the storm hits—"

A bolt of lightning crashed down from the sky, thunder rupturing after.

Then, from within the veiling clouds came a terrible, haunting shriek.

I skidded to a stop as a colossal silhouette flickered in the building nimbus, a hidden creature with an unspeakable wingspan spreading its wings.

The Crest on my left hand began to gleam, the purplish light swelling as the winds strengthened.

Then one diamond shone scarlet.

"What in Death?" I looked at Dream, whose face dripped with horror when the second diamond shifted scarlet next.

Dream's voice wavered, perplexed and disturbed, "The Phoenix…?" He turned his gaze to the sky, where three figures were soaring down from the observatory. One, I noticed, was Roji, his red wings unmistakable. Dream's tone thickened. "If Roji is up there, who is giving the Call and *why*?"

"Xavier!" Alexander called behind me. He came panting from the back of the group, having fallen behind some time ago. "Xavier, we have another problem!"

The last, middle diamond on my left hand—and Alexander's right—gleamed scarlet the moment he clasped my shoulder.

And the world slammed into darkness.

The screams rose to a crescendo, a discordant choir in my ears.

My lids cracked open—or, one did. The other refused to comply, my right eye shrouded in blackness permanently.

Through that one eye, patched and spotted though it was, I found myself facing the stones, coated in blood. Was it mine?

"Alex…?" I heaved the name, lungs crackling. The screams kept at a constant ring, the sky shattering in jagged fractures, like a glass bubble breaking away and raining down upon the chaotic mass of shifters. In the broken fragments' places were nothing but dark patches.

"Alex?" I called again, dragging myself over the ground and groaning. My leg was broken… no, it wasn't there at all. The ripped-up stump slid over the stone and left a messy trail as I crawled forward. "Alex…!"

I turned to my left—and stopped crawling. There was a body slumped there, half its face exploded from the back. The intact half stared distantly to the shattering skies with one, white eye, the black Crest of three diamonds showing under the knuckles of his right hand.

I screamed, crawling for Alex, but each inch darkened my vision. Then all I knew was blackness once more.

… Looks like you don't have much time to waste.

I floated in the abyss beside Alexander, newly whole and beholden to the winged, scarlet Skydragon weaving around us, its scales sparking with its own, electric light.

Take my Blessings, said the dragon, its voice crashing and rumbling like thunder. Have fun with them. I'll do what I can with the storm…

I awoke to the cold splash of rain and the vicious *crack* of thunder.

Thunder that crackled from my soul.

ZYL

TRANSLATED FROM CULATIAN

Yeah, baby!

My lightning sparked from my fingers as I trilled them over my ocarina, giving the Phoenix its Call by playing *The Winds of the Storm*, feeling the wind and the rain and the biting snow thrash inside me again. Sky, I missed my Hallows!

In the midst of my playing, I peered at the twins beside me, both beholding the colossal Relic of Sky that loomed over the colosseum.

Its glassy feathers solidified as the Eternal Sands rose from its sacred, stone chalice. Every lightning strike that came from the storm melted the scarlet grains to form each new glassy piece of the Phoenix. The Relic's enormous, red wings stretched as wide as the arena itself, every flap bringing a strong gale and sparking with red, electric bolts. Its shining eyes watched me play the Call on my ocarina, its thunderous shriek vibrating my soul in divine approval.

"Zyl!" Roji's voice cried from the skies. I saw his scarlet wings hustling through the storm, his voice ripping as he screamed, "Zyl, *get away!*"

I lowered my ocarina, my mouth twisting. "Away from wha*huchhhgt....*"

My throat went numb, a cold shock slitting across it.

I dropped my ocarina, the glass breaking on the stone floor of the Chalice, dark droplets spilling over the pieces. Something tasted rusty, warm liquid draining from my lips as my legs lost feeling and the Chalice's ledge rushed out from under me. My skull cracked when it hit the edge of a stone bench far below. Now, I found myself staring up at the maelstrom, the Phoenix wailing a haunting cry.

Above me, Xavier's chuckles curdled and twisted into deranged laughter. The dripping dagger in his hand quivered along with his lungs.

What...?

"*Thank you for your generous service, Your Highness Sky,*" Xavier called in Landish with a cracked smile. But that didn't sound like Xavier.

Both Alexander and Xavier stood atop the Chalice, the twins suddenly *changing.* I watched with fading vision as Xavier's features suddenly dripped away, his mismatched eyes bleeding brown and his skin growing scales as his grey hair faded brown with blond streaks.

Son of a...

The thought slipped away as quietly as the storm's rage that fell silent in my muffled ears.

ROJI

TRANSLATED FROM CULATIAN

"ZYL!" I screamed, watching my sister collapse. One of her limp arms dangled over the open arena's ledge below. *"NO!"*

I landed beside her, my hands shaking as I reached for her empty, stale face.

"Zyl…?" I scooped her up so, so gently, sweeping my wings around her, keeping out the thrashing winds. My voice cracked. "Sis…?"

She didn't answer. She only stared at nothing, her open throat spilling fresh blood. My chest squeezed and threatened to heave up my insides, tears blurring her face.

"Zyl…" I held her tighter, a squeal ringing from my throat.

I was too late again. Always just… too late…!

My lungs crackled with static, the pain sparking hot. I laid Zyl's body on the ground—then bolted into the sky and raced for Zyl's murderer, my throat ripping a scream as my hands splintered with lightning, shooting at the cobra from the ledge of the Chalice.

The snake threw a hand up—and deflected my bolt with a simple flick of his wrist.

My wings spread in shock, staggering. *What in Sky?*

The snake now had bright scarlet hair; his eyes lightened to an electric-red. He stared at his sparking hands in satisfaction.

"This…" He laughed in Landish, testing the sparks as they brightened over his palms. Then he ripped his tunic down the middle to gaze upon the crowned Sky mark that gleamed from the center of his scaled chest. *"This power! Hah, hah…! Incredible!"*

From the stones below, Zyl stared at me with empty eyes, her throat split open and flooded with blood. My nostrils flared, feathers shaking.

"You…!" I dove for the scaled bastard, my hands spewing with electricity. *"You rot in Void, you fucking worm!"*

I threw my lightning at him—

The bolt bounced off his hand and shot back at me, burning my wings so intensely, I screamed, spiraling down and stumbling to the benches beside Zyl's body. My muscles twitched, skin snapping with sparks. *What the Void…?* I rolled to my stomach and wheezed, still yielding to spasms. Was I just electrocuted? *But I… I'm an Astravoker.* We didn't *get* electrocuted.

Did we?

The bastard's laughter pierced the storm's howls, ringing my pounding ears as he climbed down from the looming tower.

"Arrrgh…!" A woman's scream ripped out, catching the snake's attention along with his black-haired lackey behind him.

The two walked off toward the scream, leaving me alone with Zyl's drenched corpse.

I crawled to my sister, wrapping my stinging wings around her again, and sobbed. "Zyl… I'm sorry…"

30

HE WHO WILL BRING THE END

WILLOW

"Arrrgh…!" My claws scraped the stone bench, pain heating my swollen belly and nearly breaking my back. My screams rivaled the crackling thunder. *"Ahh!"*

"What's this, now?" a voice drawled above me.

When I looked up, I found a scaled face with scarlet hair and eyes inspecting me musingly. "Why, if it isn't our dearest Death Princess!" A red-haired Macarius said brightly. "Oh my. What a surprising turn of events. I see you and that Shadow-half have been busy, of late."

I barred my teeth, trying in vain to stifle my screams and pulled myself up to sit, crawling away.

Macarius followed me at a leisure pace, chuckling. "Did we catch you at a bad time? Well now, what a conundrum: do I take you, or the child you're about to deliver?"

I shrieked and tried to throw my fire at him, but it was doused by the torrent of rain. *Damn it!* I bit down another shriek of pain and evoked my Infection Hallows instead. Black veins littered my palm and licked between my fingers in warning.

I snarled, "Come near me, and I will melt the flesh from your bones!"

He kept to his laughter, his newly scarlet hair damp and sticking to his scaled cheeks as he raised his hand, fingers sparking with electric bolts. "You misunderstand, lady Death. I haven't a need to come near."

His palm burst with a jagged bolt of lightning—it struck my limbs, burning my skin, my throat blistering with an agonized cry. *I-I can't move…!*

My muscles twitched and yielded to spasms, another pained breath heaving from my lungs.

"Macar, stop…!" A new voice yelled over the storm.

My imprisoning bolts mercifully ceased, and I wheezed, clutching my ever-tightening belly. Through slitted lids, I caught a glance of the man who'd interrupted. *Bloody Nira!*

Standing with clawed fists, his back to me as he faced Macarius, was a black-haired man. His cat ears were curled tight to his skull. At first glance, I thought it was Claude, but when his head craned to me for a brief moment, I saw the younger face of Kael.

Macarius scowled at his murderous lackey. "You're in the way, Kael."

"You mustn't bring the mother any more stress than she's already suffered," Kael said, sweeping a protective hand in front of me. "Stop this now. You have what we've come for, we are done here. To take Death is one thing, but her child has no part in this."

He's… defending me? I thought in disbelief. *Why?*

Macarius scoffed. "I think it prudent to take both. Why, with Death's child, she'll be far more inclined to bring us to the Willow of Ashes. Consider it insurance."

"A child is not insurance!" Kael's tone hardened. "For Nira's sake, Macar, we've done what was planned. Leave the mother be. We will… find her another day." He gazed at me, eyes swimming with emotions far too complex to pinpoint.

Crrrack!

Kael was engulfed in a blinding flash, the bolt so powerful, he was thrown off his feet and *slammed* into an upper level of the stone benches, twitching from the ground in stuttering groans.

Macarius spat venom and sneered, "Worthless wretch, softened by that descendant of yours… If I'm to save the world myself, then I shall."

His hands sparked again with lightning, striking me as my limbs burnt and shuddered, my screams fracturing—

DRRRRRRRRRRKOW!

A new, ear-splitting bolt ripped over my head suddenly. It was so powerful, it made the hairs on my neck spark straight up as it streaked over me and *crashed* into Macarius, throwing the cobra onto his back.

Heaving gasps, my head snapped to the source of the new lightning. A shadow-haired man charged for us at incredible speed, his bare feet swept by the billowing winds themselves, his hands sparking with static as bright as his scarred, mismatched eyes.

My husband leapt over me and, when Macarius fumbled to his feet, Xavier slammed his electric hands into the cobra's chest in a vicious scream. Sparks glowed around his pale skin with divine brilliance, throwing Macarius farther back, the cobra nearly tumbling over the ledge of the open arena's center before he took control of the winds and hefted himself back on steady land.

Xavier kept a belligerent stance in front of me, his wolf ears curled and face contorted with such fury, I hardly recognized him.

"How *dare* you," he snarled, so booming and curdled his voice sounded of thunder. "Touch my wife again, and I'll send you to Everland below without a head, snake."

He's received Sky's Blessings, I realized. He must have gained the creation half of Astravoking—

"Ahh!" I gasped in pain, clutching my throbbing belly as another contraction swelled.

Xavier's head whipped to me so suddenly, I thought his neck would tear a ligament. "Willow?" He knelt and took my hand, looking me over. The various, bubbled burn scars speckling my skin brought back his rage. "That bastard is *dead.*"

Macarius laughed, inciting a blazed glare from my husband.

"Why, if it isn't the father!" The cobra's laughter zapped with static. "Come to the aid of his mate and pup? How lovely... I see you're enjoying our new powers as well." His scaled face gleamed in the light of his electric hand. "But I suppose you've only been granted half of them, haven't you? Such a *pity.*"

His last hiss brought a large crack of lightning, and Xavier braced.

—But a new figure rushed in and *snatched* the bolt with his bare hands.

Alexander, gripping the stringy, wild lightning, released a crackling shout and the bolt rippled in the opposite direction, splashing over Macarius with a thunderous explosion and sending the cobra flying into the arena's benches several levels up.

Alex turned to his brother, then nodded to me. "Get her inside," he said. "I'll keep him busy."

Xavier returned the nod, scooping me up with a delicacy fit for a prized antique. "I won't be long," he told his brother, and carried me with hastened steps through the rain.

ALEXANDER

I watched Xavier carry his wife up the colosseum's steps, away from us. Hopefully, the others would be waiting for them in the closed balconies—

A crackle heaved from the snake behind me, and I twisted in time to catch the bolt of lightning he'd thrown, the static latching onto my fingers and sending a strangely invigorating shock through my blood.

Scowling from an upper-level railing, Macarius dismissed the bolt, letting it fizzle between us. His newly scarlet eyes were fixed on me, the snake pushing up his eyeglasses.

"Bold of you to give up your advantage." Macarius's tone was edged with annoyance. "You'd have had twice the chance of walking away alive if you didn't choose to fight alone."

"You forget," I said, "Necrovokers are rarely alone."

In a new flash of light, my father's vassal, Nathaniel, stepped beside me with a wide cutlass clenched in his fists; my mother's vassal, Aiden, flew down with an arrow nocked on his bowstring, wind twirling threateningly between his fingers.

Joining them were Willow's vassals, Rossette and Nikolai, their Hallows bursting from their raised palms. Dalen flew down beside them next, his Crystal daggers raised to his face in a boxer's stance. Last to arrive was Vendy, who skidded into view at my side with her glowing sword drawn and ready.

Hugh was the only vassal absent. Xavier had told the boy to watch over Willow and provide updates for when he joined me again. And a wise decision it was to leave him out of the fighting. Hugh was progressing in his training, but he was nowhere near ready for any combat yet.

Macarius pushed up his glasses and offered a scant glance at the vassals surrounding me, unfazed. "I suppose you think me outnumbered, then?" He lifted his hands, his smile crooked as the wind thrashed about, tussling his drenched, scarlet hair. "You mistake the number of those who care for our future."

The colossal Phoenix gave a ripping shriek above.

Then from the storm's shadows, figures appeared and slinked to Macarius's side, all cloaked in rubbery, white coats and slim-fitting masks.

Bloods, how many were there? Everywhere I turned, five more seemed to crop up with each new flash of lightning, as if they'd been standing in the benches all along, camouflaged until now—

A winged woman threw herself, and her saber, at me from above. I ducked low, preparing to counter…

But a black-haired woman flew between us, her wedding gown rippling in the gale, bat wings stretched as if to block my assailant's view of me, and the sound of clashing metal pierced my wolf ears.

Lilli heaved my female attacker away, kicking her sternum so hard, the woman was thrust back several feet and carried off by the storm.

Behind me, more figures stepped into my peripherals, and I found myself surrounded by members of my team. Matthiel was here with his long-staved scythe. Neal, Octavius and El were poised with their throwing weapons.

Most surprising was Claude who stood with a poisoned sword he'd coated in black veins.

Lilli, still dressed in her wedding gown which I noticed she'd ripped at the hem, slipped beside me with her scythe blades at the ready, surveying our enemies with a startled, yet piqued eye.

Everyone was here, save for one. *Of course, my damned lieutenant is the only one missing at a time like this.*

"Where is Jaq?" I growled to Lilli.

Lilli's bat ears dipped at the name, as did her wings, but a thought seemed to fly through her eyes so quickly, it barely lasted a second, and her wings lifted again in determination. "I'm sure he'll notice the giant phoenix and investigate."

I grunted. "Fair point."

Macarius gazed at our team, his scaled lip turned up as if disgusted, then he spotted the Treble family and grinned so wide his fangs unveiled.

"Why, Claude!" the cobra chuckled. "What luck that we'd meet again here of all places. And what timing. Now you can see what fruit our labor has yielded."

Claude's infectious veins strengthened on his thin sword, the black tendrils slithering like worms and blotting the steel. He had nothing to say in return, it seemed.

Macarius turned to his cloaked followers and called, "Some of you may remember dear Claude, yes?"

A few rueful murmurs from the cloaked figures came, the woman who'd rushed me spitting.

Macarius continued, "Yes, Claude left us to aid our End. He has chosen to bring us all—our families and friends—to our deaths."

Angered sneers hissed from the figures.

Claude snarled, "How long do you think it'll be before they all find out Dream's prediction wasn't for you, Macar? You think they'll still follow you if they know *you* were the one he Saw bringing our End?"

Macar lifted an eyebrow. "Saw?" He chuckled, walking up the steps of the colosseum with his hands folded behind him. Then his gaze caught something past us, and his smile dripped wider. "I wonder, what have you been telling them, Dream?"

I kept my stance firm, but craned back.

Dream stood there, soaked all the way to his bare feet even though the rain didn't seem to hit him, and the wind didn't thrash at his azure hair.

Macarius scoffed and thrust a hand at the fox. "Still sending your copies to greet me, Dream? Why the evasion? Too much of a coward to face me with your original?"

Dream offered no reply, his gaze sunken.

"Where are you hiding, then?" Macarius jerked his hands in random spots throughout the colosseum, bolts striking the benches and crumbling bits of stone. "What's wrong, Dream? Don't you wish to see my destiny fulfilled at last? To see that your prediction has finally come to pass?"

More bolts sparked from his hands around us. Even his followers were scattering to safety. My team huddled for cover, Rossette casting her own Astravoking and creating an electric, protective web around us.

Macarius screamed, "This is what you wanted for me!" He struck the observatory tower in the distance. "How many nights did you spend planning this day for me?!" He struck a metal spire, the sparks zapping long after it faded. "You told me *I* was to be the one that saves us! That *I* was destined to stop the Shadow from killing us all!"

My panic paused, brow furrowing at Dream's copy. *What?*

Macarius sent a final, surging bolt at Dream's copy, the flash blinding me and sending static snapping at the hairs on my neck, the thunder crashing like cannons in my ears as the colosseum quaked, whole chunks cracking out of place and crumbling down to the Everland continent below.

My feet dipped when the stone surface under me began to grind out of place. Hesitation abandoned, I yelled, "Move up!"

I used my new Astravoking to grab Rossette's electric safety net and tore it apart, allowing me to lead my team off the crumbling stone. We found refuge on a still-stable section of benches three rows above.

"Why did you abandon me?!" Macarius screamed, the sound like thunder, his eyes fixated on Dream's copy. "Do I frighten you so?! *I* was willing to do what was necessary! And look at you now—pampering our deaths! The very ones you warned me would shroud us in the shadow they were destined to cast upon the world!"

What in Bloody Death? I glared at Dream's copy, perplexed. Dream was still silent, his gaze saddened.

"Why did you crawl to them instead?!" shouted Macarius, "Why turn to the ones you spent a thousand Bloody years knowing would End us all?!"

That WE would End us…? I turned to Macarius, a hollowness growing as I spotted a bare patch where his tunic's collar had been ripped in the very center of his chest. And there, I did not find a Dream mark. I did not find a crowned Sky mark.

Instead, I stared at a tri-leaf of three black diamonds.

The same Crest that rested under my knuckles.

"He… has the Crest…?" I hushed, the words drowned by the howling zephyr.

XAVIER

I rushed my screaming wife into the enclosed lodge at the top level of the colosseum, the one in which Hugh had reported the others were waiting.

I thanked Nira they were. The moment I stepped in and slammed the door with my foot, Willow shoved herself out of my hold and grabbed a nearby chair for support, clutching her back and howling in pain, startling the messengers and Hecrûshou's little Bindragon who'd gathered in here for shelter.

In the center of the room, Bianca saw us and her rabbit ears perked straight up, shooting to her feet. She helped me bring Willow to the cluster of pillows and plethora of towels she and the other Healers—Ana, Sirra, Rochelle and Lëtta—had set up for her.

Bianca and I lowered Willow down, my wife letting out another crackled scream as she clutched her belly, her claws tearing her gown.

"Breathe!" ordered Bianca, placing a conical stethoscope against Willow's belly and listening intently. "As we practiced."

Willow's following breaths were stuttered, but she did her best to comply between screams.

"You're doing wonderfully, darling," I hushed and clutched her hand tenderly, evoking my soul Hallows to give her a tactile illusion of numbness, hoping it would ease her pain.

As the violet lights leaked from my fingers and seeped into her skin, her breathing deepened, relaxing, though only slightly, her cries muffled.

Now that she was settled and being tended to, I kept hold of her fingers and examined the room. It was more crowded than I'd expected.

Hovering over us was Ringëd and Mikani. Ringëd's feral ferret, Kurn, scuttled at his feet with concerned huffs.

Suddenly, my brother's messenger, Mal, piped up from his place among the cluster of messengers in the corner. He fluttered and screeched wildly, looking panicked. The raven rushed over to Bianca's medical bag and tried to pry his beak inside—

"Woah!" Bianca hurried to push his beak away. "Easy there, Mal! Some of those things can stab you if you aren't careful."

Kurn and Aahn hobbled beside Mal, then. The ferret patted the raven's wings in assurance while the Bindragon slithered over to Bianca's medical bag. Aahn deftly evaded her swiping hands as he slipped inside the back and plucked out some sort of pouch with tinkling vials hidden inside, his long body coiled around it. With his prize now in hand—or, er, in *suckers*—Aahn slithered back to Kurn and Mal. My brow furrowed when the ferret chuffed frantically, and Mal obligingly lowered his wing to let Kurn and Aahn climb on his back. Mal flew to the door and perched on the handle, pecking his beak against the metal and croaking frantically.

The ferret turned its head at Ringëd and panted at the feral human urgently.

Ringëd's brow furrowed. "You sure, Kurn?"

"What is he saying?" I asked.

"He says they need to go outside to help the others," Ringëd translated, rising to open the door.

Mal and his two passengers flew out in the rain with the pouch of vials in tow, then Ringëd shut the door again.

I frowned at him. "You're not going to stop him?"

Ringëd shrugged. "I gotta hand it to the little guy. I saw him do some real damage back in Neverland while riding the messengers. After that, I'm inclined to believe him when he says he can help."

Gazing out the window with frightened flinches at each bolt of lightning were Grandfather Edric and Hugh. Beside them, staring out a different window, were Kurrick, Linus, little Fuérr, and Oliver.

Dalminia and her winged, web-eared daughters were here as well, standing beside the rust-haired Crysalette in the corner. Crysalette came to Willow's side across from me with baby Eryn in her arms.

"Keep pushing, dear," Crysalette encouraged her granddaughter, balancing Eryn in one arm while she tucked a strand of Willow's ashen locks behind her grown fox ears. Crysalette gasped at the burn scars that patched some spots of Willow's grey skin. "What's happened?"

"Macarius has his Sky Hallows," I growled, teeth sharpening to see the scars my wife now fostered. "That bastard is a dead man."

"Xavier," Dalminia called from the corner. She hesitantly made her way to me, asking little Fuérr to watch over her daughters, and her webbed ears flicked with worry. "Did you see Roji? Out there?"

I shook my head. "I could barely see anything ten feet away, the storm is too thick."

"But if that snake has Sky's Hallows now," she began, voice shuddering, "who's blood did he spill to gain it?"

My jaw locked. That was the question I'd set aside while I was focused on my wife. Now that she was safe, Dalminia's question brought back the concern.

My silence made Dalminia's teeth grind, her scales growing prominent over her skin. "Are you going out there again?"

"Yes."

"Then I'm coming with you," she said. "If Roji is out there, I will find him."

Ana rose to her feet and came to join Dalminia. "As will I."

From the window, Kurrick's lion ear twitched in her direction, and he unfolded his arms to stride at her side, nodding.

Ana's second guard, however, stayed by the window, Linus touching the glass with a stale gaze, his Dream mark gleaming from his shoulder.

"The Sky King was not the one to fall," Linus said, hushed. "It was his sister. Zylveia is… dead."

Silence swallowed the room. Even Willow's breaths were suppressed as she processed the news.

Ana's golden lion ears grew, and she started for the door, tapping a finger to the communicator hooked to her ear. "Genevieve, gather the fleet," she ordered. "Tell all ships to rendezvous at the colosseum and surround its walls. And load the cannons."

Ana let her hand drop and ripped off her gloves. "Come, Linus," she said with a jerk of her head, and Linus joined her and Kurrick without complaint. She stopped before Dalminia, nodding. "We will find Zylveia and your husband. Linus will show us the way."

"I'll waste no time, my lady," confirmed Linus, saluting.

"Thank you," said Dalminia while brushing her tears aside. Determination brightened her glare as they all stepped out to the rain.

Willow screamed in pain—then a puff of fire spilled from the hand that I clutched, and I released it in a startled wince. As I shook the fire from my hand, Mikani knelt beside me and took Willow's flame-spouting hand instead.

"Probably leave the fire-holding to another Pyrovoker," Mikani grunted.

"Er, right…" I cleared my throat, rubbing my neck—then my head twitched suddenly. Then again. And again. Then my eye twitched, and an arm muscle next. Bloods, I was so full of energy, I couldn't sit still.

I jumped to my feet and began pacing, trying like Void to stop the twitching muscles. They wouldn't cease.

Ringëd cocked an eyebrow at me as I hurried by him for the twelfth time. "Jittery there, dad-to-be?"

My neck twitched, then a shoulder. "It, er—I just need to expel some of this energy, I suppose."

Crysalette frowned at me. "Dream was never so… twitchy when I went into labor."

"I—I think it—it's—the new Hallows," I stuttered, head snapping violently. "I just—feel like I've swallowed a thunder bolt. Darling?" I spun on my heels and looked down at my wife, a foot tapping restlessly. "I've left Alex alone long enough, I think. Will—will you be all right—without me?"

"Of course not, you... *Arrgh!*" She focused on her breathing. "Idiot. But I want you to kill that Gods damned snake anyway—*Aaah...!*"

"At your command, love." My attention twitched to young Hugh. "Keep me updated if anything changes."

Hugh nodded from the window, and I stepped out to the rain once more.

The storm winds hadn't dwindled in the slightest, the Phoenix of Scarlet still shrieking and soaring circles above the arena, sparks of electricity snapping from its feathers so strongly, I could *feel* the static in my soul—

My feet hit a slumped figure hiding behind a stone pillar, and I nearly fell over him. The soggy wretch was curled in a ball, hugging his knees. His azure hair was sopping wet and stuck to his jaw, fox ears glued to his neck.

"Dream?" I called over the storm winds.

Dream murmured something, but his throat was so strained, I couldn't make it out.

"What was that?" I asked, crouching to better hear.

"I'm sorry," he whispered, burying his face in his knees. "I'm sorry. I'm sorry..."

He kept to that mantra, shivering.

What in Bloods? I shook my head, refocusing. There wasn't time for this. Alex needed me. I hurried down the steps, sprinting to where I last left my brother. Or, had I left him the other way? *Blast it, what does it matter?* The colosseum was a damned circle anyway.

I rounded the stone benches, my bare feet splashing in puddles. It was cold as Void, but *Death* I need to let out this electric energy any way I could. I'd abandoned my shoes back on the bridge to let my new Hallows breathe from my feet as well as my hands. Keeping it in only started the twitching again, so now my steps left trails of glittering static behind me.

"Xavier!" someone hollered from one row higher.

It was Jaq. His long, sandy hair was drenched along with his buttoned shirt and pressed trousers. He hopped over the rail and landed in front of me, lifting a hand to shield his eyes from the torrent of water. "What in Death is going on?!"

"Too much!" I said over the wind. "Where have you been?"

He rubbed his shoulder. "It, uh... doesn't matter! I saw this giant ass bird come out of nowhere and figured I should check it out! And of course you're in the dead center of it, Bloody lunatic! What'd you do now?"

"To summarize," I said, my head twitching now that I'd stopped running. "Alex and I have our Hallows. As does Macarius."

Jaq spat rainwater—or was it venom? —to the side. "When did that bastard get here?"

"Death if I…"

Two winged figures soared over our heads suddenly, both of us ducking. I watched the bird shifters fly a short distance ahead and join a huddle of people. They were *our* people: Dalminia, Ana, Kurrick, Linus… the flyers had been Herrin and Marian.

And in the center of them all was Roji, cradling his limp sister, her head pressed to his chest. Her open neck dripped with blood, but the rain washed it down her torso, draining over the stones and staining Roji's arms.

He quivered there in the rain.

And wept.

31

HARD TRUTHS

ALEXANDER

Sparks burst from Macarius's hands, each strike accompanied by a splintering scream.

"I know you're out here, Dream!" cried Macarius. "Face me! Do not insult me with any more of your damned copies!"

I watched from under Rossette's new electric net as Dream's copy fizzled into vapor.

Dream. Anger burned with the growl vibrating my throat. *Why does Macar think WE will bring the End?*

After everything Dream has put us through, after everything he's told us—where was this coming from? Why has he said nothing of—?

Macar let loose one last bolt where Dream's copy had been, then whipped round, his fingers leaking blue light as the Crest upon his scaled chest changed into an azure Dream mark. His image split into several copies. The copies scattered, and the original turned to his cloaked subordinates and snarled, "Deal with them! I've a coward to pull out of hiding."

The cloaked followers sprung for us—

Crrrack!

A powerful bolt of lightning hit Macarius's back, causing the cobra to stumble.

Then a scarlet blur flew through the storm and *slammed* him to the ground. Roji raised his electric fist, his face wrenched in pure hatred.

"You killed my sister, you son of a bitch!" Roji cracked his fist at the snake's face—

Macarius's hands burst with their own bolts and threw Roji back several feet.

But Xavier sprinted into view and caught Roji, steadying him. Xavier nodded to me before turning back to Macarius. With my brother came Roji's wife, Dalminia, her hands fogging while gripping a long trident made of frosted ice. Ana stood beside her with two enormous stone swords that glowed with golden light, and Kurrick and Linus stood at her flanks.

Bringing up the rear was my lieutenant, Jaq. *About Gods damned time.* At least the idiot found *one* of us in this mess.

Beside me, Lilli's bat wings perked and she hushed, "Jaq—"

Roji shot for Macarius again, and Xavier rushed to assist.

The colosseum burst into chaos as Macarius's cloaked followers sprang for the rest of us.

That winged woman from before flew at me with her saber, and I plucked the spheres from my neck-chain to draw out my scythes in time to deflect, our blades clashing noisily. I evoked my wind Hallows and *pushed* a strong gale at her wings, sending her spiraling back and smashing her into the edge of a stone staircase.

"Alex!" Lilli suddenly called beside me, kicking back a foe of her own. "There's something I need to tell you! About the wedding!"

"Now?!" I grabbed one of the natural lightning bolts that shot from the clouds and sent it crashing onto a cluster of Cloaks on the far end of the arena.

"There may not be another chance!" She said, desperate.

Oh, Bloody Void. Granted, there may not have been, but… *no, wait.* If this was our last chance to say anything, should it not be the truth? Gods damn it, I didn't want to die keeping this lie.

"All right, fine!" I shouted, cracking my hilt over a woman's temple. "But I need to say something first!"

"I really think *I* should go first!" She sliced her blades over a man's chest and felled him, turning to me. "I'm really, really, *really* sorry about this but—"

"I don't want to marry you!" I paused. We had said it in unison. I blinked dumbly at her. "What?"

"I don't want to marry you, Alex," she repeated.

"W… well, I…" I flinched when a man shot an arrow at me in the distance, and I quickly used my Aerovoking to fling a cold gale at it, thrusting the arrow back, striking the man square in the chest. With that settled, I frowned at Lilli again. "Not that I'm complaining, but *why?*"

She grabbed my shoulder and hooked a strong kick at a new assailant behind me. "I'm in love with Jaq."

My gaping worsened. "Jaq? What in Death are you…" *No,* I realized, *this makes sense, now.* Jaq's absence, Lilli's fondness and then obsession with his coldness… I stammered, "But I… Then… Well, does he know?"

"I haven't had a chance to tell him," she panted, stealing desperate glances at him in the distance.

"Then what in Bloods are you doing here, woman?!" I pushed her toward where Jaq was fighting. "Tell that idiot before either of you are sliced to shreds! He's the one who picked out your vines to begin with, anyway!"

She yielded to a laugh, then kissed my cheek. "I will. Thank you, Alex… for everything."

She spread her leathery wings and flew off. I grinned after her.

Well, that was simpler than planned. I chuckled. *Now, to find Bianca—*

An arrow whistled past my nose, and I threw a countering gust at a second one. *Right,* I thought, remembering my priorities, *Live first, THEN find Bianca.*

—another arrow shot from behind me and shattered over my arm. Shards and glass splinters dug into my skin, the large ones drawing blood, and I grunted. Then from the wounds sprouted black tendrils that latched onto my skin and dug deeper into the gashes, yanking a scream out of me.

"Death!" I stumbled into a stone bench and tried to crawl away from the festering poison, but it was already hooked onto my shoulder and crawling up my collarbone. "They brought those damned arrows again?!"

The tendrils were spreading quickly, biting into my soul around my arm and shoulder, and I rolled off the bench, hitting the flooded floor in a pained cry.

"Hang on, Howllord!" A voice said above me.

I ripped my gaze up. A young man in a lab coat and overalls rode atop the slender, woody Barkdragon that I knew belonged to Bianca. The man was the Mistress Chemist's assistant, Red. Red rode a rather frightened Bazil, wearing large goggles over his eyes and was covered in belt upon belt that housed hundreds of tiny vials with violet liquid.

The black tendrils on my arm surged and pulled another yelp from me, and Red quickly plucked one of his vials off his belt and popped off the cork stopper with his teeth. He drained the vial's contents onto my wounds, and the violet-glowing liquid seeped into my skin soothingly. The black veins hissed in protest as the light swallowed it whole, then dissipated into nothing, the pain receding until it was only present in the original, physical gashes.

I panted and nodded to Red. "Bloods, thank Gods your guild mistress developed that."

"I know, right?" Red grinned, raindrops speckling his large goggles.

Craaw!

A scratchy croak came from above—then my messenger, Mal, swooped past my head. On his way, I briefly spied the ferret and Bindragon riding atop the raven's back, and from the Bindragon's suckered body dropped a pouch which I caught in a flinch before the three soared off again.

When I opened the contents, I found the same vials of the soul-cure that Red had used on me.

"Huh," said Red, "Well, that worked out. The other guild members have tons more all around the arena, too. The boss told us to distribute them to you all. We brought everything we made over the month, so be careful and try not to get hit too much."

I strapped the pouch to my belt by its drawstrings. "Understood," I said. "Be careful yourself. And for Bloods' sakes, if anything happens to that Barkdragon under you, your mistress will likely kill you herself."

Red's brown face paled slightly, but he still grinned. "Understood."

JAQ

What in Bloods did I *miss?*

Xavier and Roji were having a lightning battle with that other snake, who now had the same hair as Roji, Zyl was dead, there was a huge monster-bird flying circles above us—

A winged guy in a white cloak came at me with a dagger in hand, and I hopped back from his swing, throwing my chain-scythe at him, slicing him at an angle over his torso. The guy fell like a bag of wet, dripping bricks.

AND there are now random people trying to kill us! Who were these guys, anyway? I kicked at the guy's fallen dagger, picking it up and scrutinizing it. It looked like the blade was made out of Metaglass. Inside writhed a festering knot of black veins that poked and hammered the inside of its Yinklît-coated cage.

"Aw, great," I muttered and belted the dagger, keeping a more vigilant eye on any projectiles that shot through the air. "They brought those Bloody infection-weapons with them."

Matt was slicing his staved scythe at a Cloak beside me, his black hair drenched and clinging to his face in a tangled mess.

He shoved his Cloak back with the butt of his staff and shot a glance at me. "Rude of you to show up at the last moment, Lieutenant! What kept you?"

"Things!" I spat venom to the side—the glob smacked a Cloak in the eyes and she screamed, clutching her lids. *Whoops.* Ah, well, guess that works. Still, I should be more careful. Didn't want to do that to a teammate.

"'ey!" someone shouted from one level above us. It was one of Bianca's antlered guildmates, Rob. His eyes were hidden behind huge goggles and he tossed Matt and me several fist-sized pouches. "The Mistress Chemist told us t' give e'eryone a ration o' the Soul-Cure! Jus' in case!"

Matt and I exchanged a look, the pouches we now gripped clinking with small vials inside. I shrugged and hollered up, "Thanks, Rob!"

Rob saluted lazily and ran off, probably to give more of those pouches away.

"Well," Matt said as we tied the pouches to our belts by their drawstrings, "that certainly was wise of Dr. Florenne to prepare so many vials before this."

I snorted. "Trust me, it's rarer when she *isn't* wise."

A round of *bangs* pelted from the left suddenly, and I turned in time to see one of the Cloaks was firing Shockspheres at me. I dodged and jerked back, but my foot slipped over the edge of the arena—and I screamed when toppling over, flailing as the wind rushed up along with my panic, Matt reaching down and hollering one second too late.

—my stomach lurched to a sudden stop when someone wrapped their arms around my chest my from behind, and I heard the *whoosh* of wings flapping.

"Bloods, thanks, mate!" I called to whoever held me. My eyes were too focused on the storm clouds sloshing under my kicking feet to look. "*Please* don't drop me!"

"We wouldn't want that, now would we?"

My hairs stood on end, knowing that melodic voice anywhere. I groaned, "Aw, Death!"

I dared a look over my shoulder. Lilli's face was too Bloody close to mine, the bat tightening her grip as she lugged me back up toward the open-air colosseum.

I snapped my head forward again, my scaled ears pounding. *Damn it!* Why did she have to save me of all people? *Well…* came an afterthought, *aw, screw it!* I couldn't hold this in anymore.

"Lilli, I-I'm really sorry about earlier!" I called over the gale. "I just—I couldn't help it, all right?!"

Lilli sighed next to my ear, like static rolling over my scales. "Jaq."

"No, I gotta say this!" I shouted, my ribs thundering so hard it hurt. "Alex doesn't deserve you! And-and I don't either, and I shouldn't have done that without your permission and everything! I just… *Gods*, I can't stop thinking about you, all right?!"

"Jaq."

"And I mean, everything you said earlier, every Gods damned thing, was right, and that's why—"

"Jaq, will you shut up?" she snapped. "I love you."

"—why you can't marry Alex, and…!" I stopped cold, craning to look at her, but half her face was outside my glasses and blurry. "You… you what?"

"I love you, Jaq," she said again, and *Bloods* was it numbing to hear her chuckle. "I'm not marrying Alex."

My eyes bulged so wide, I had to blink out the rainwater that smacked them. "Really…?"

"Really." She giggled again, and drew her face to mine—*Wait!*

I quickly turned the other way before our lips met, and she breathed in surprise.

"What's wrong?" she asked, startled.

"It, uh…" I cleared my throat. "Well, I'm still on an adrenaline high from fighting and I've still got venom leaking in here, so I, uh… I don't want to kill you."

"Oh." She kissed my cheek instead, making me grin so wide, my scales hurt. It was a welcome hurt.

32

BROKEN STRINGS

CILIA

The storm raged over the colosseum as I crouched over a pillar that towered just outside the arena. My perch was slippery from the thrashing rain, but I couldn't look away from the glorious Phoenix soaring in the clouds. It loomed like a god all its own and basked in a scarlet, celestial glow with lightning sparking all about its feathers like beautiful spiders.

I shifted my footing, stepping into the colosseum—

I was shoved back by an invisible force, and the Phoenix gave a thunderous shriek.

What in Land?

I pushed against the invisible force field with a hand, but couldn't break through. I growled, "Just as with Dream and his Relic…"

Was this Sky's Relic? The true Phoenix of Scarlet?

Glancing at the other Ancients who surrounded me on their own pillars, I noticed no one else could push through. Hecrûshou and Miranda proved unsuccessful as they shoved against the barrier, and Khol peeked over a railing below us while poking at it timidly. The barrier gave glittering ripples where his scaled finger touched. Thörd sat beside me with his leathery wings folded in awe. Even *he* was speechless. That was a rare sight with him.

Hecrûshou slung his glowing trident over a shoulder and rumbled, "What is happening in there?"

Miranda grunted. "I would guess those freak twins have gained their new Hallows."

"Then why do I hear clashing steel?" I asked, my grown cat ears swiveling at each echoing ring that came from below. I could only make out a few figures in those dense clouds.

Hecrûshou hummed broodingly, "Who would be attacking them here?"

My teeth sharpened. "I have a feeling it has to do with the cobra I'll mount on my wall."

Thörd scratched his scaled head and adjusted the goggles over his eyes. "What did Thörd's kitten say husband look like?"

"Black hair," I said, keeping focused on the chaos ensuing below us. "Yellow eyes. Cat shifter… but not the descendant I showed you."

Thörd pointed. "That one not kitten's descendant."

I followed his finger, straining to see past the thick clouds. In a bright flash from the Phoenix, I found a man sidling along the upper row of the colosseum's steps, his black cat ears flattened—and yellow eyes glinting in the flash.

"Kael…!" I pushed against the invisible barrier the Phoenix had manifested, my blood surging frantically. "*Kael!*"

Kael's ears didn't even twitch at my voice, and he kept to his creeping along the row. He stopped outside a closed room, perhaps one of the box-seats.

My screams curdled, trying to scratch my way through this damned barrier…! "*KAEL!*"

KAEL

"*KAEL!*" I heard a voice call my name.

My limbs froze, and I looked about the colosseum… but there was no one in my vicinity. Had I imagined it?

Now is not the time to hear phantom voices, I reminded and shook my head. I crept along the wall of the colosseum's upper row, sure that this room was where the Shadow-half brought his wife. With as much stress as she'd endured, I prayed it wasn't too late to save the child.

Nira Cleanse me, what have I done?

Macar was out of control. I'd agreed to take the Death Princess, that had been necessary, but threatening her unborn child? *I… I can't allow it,* I decided. I'd carried out too many births in my day—so long ago now—all those memories of the mothers, the younglings, my *own* wife's labor for our son…

Pain swelled at the memory, lurching my chest sickly, and I flattened against the wall.

"Cilia…" My Angel's name was heavy on my tongue. "What would you think of me now? After all I've done…?"

"She would think you no better than herself," came a scratched voice.

I whirled. A slouched man was leaning against a pillar nearby. His azure hair dripped from his chin, blue eyes rimmed red and haunted.

"You!" My sorrow was swallowed by pure, blistering rage. "*You!*" I snatched Dream's scrawny neck with both hands, his veins pulsing under my fingers.

"I have waited so long for this, Dream…! I needn't use any poisons for this. I want to watch the life flee from your frosted eyes as slowly as…"

"She's… here…!" Dream choked, desperately prying at my hands around his neck. "Cilia is… here…!"

Cilia? My fingers snapped open.

Dream dropped to the ground, coughing.

"L… lies," I whispered, finding my wits again. "*Lies!* I'll not hear anymore!"

"Then *look,* you blind fool!" shouted Dream, thrusting his hand upward behind me. "She's right in front of you!"

The chilled rain turned freezing. My breaths went ragged, and I nearly turned my gaze away to look—

"*Argh,* I'll not hear any more of your lies, Dream!" I clutched my cat ears and squeezed my eyes shut. "The moment I turn away, you'll trap me in that timeless prison again—!"

"You damned fool!" Dream seized my chin and forced it up toward the weeping sky. "She's right above you!"

I blinked the rain from my eyes.

There were five dark figures perched atop several pillars above us. Four, I didn't recognize in the slightest. Yet in the blinking flashes of the storm, mouthing as if screaming my name and scratching at an unseen wall, was a grey-haired woman with the face of an angel.

My Angel.

The world fell away. "Cilia…?"

Dream released my chin and stepped back, rasping, "She cannot enter with the Phoenix here. Demons are forbidden from nearing the Relics."

"Demons?" I hadn't felt the word leave my lips, lungs like cotton, my heart inflating so, I wasn't sure my feet were still grounded.

As the Landish prince claimed…

My teeth sharpened. I spotted a metal ladder embedded against a nearby lodge's wall, and thrust myself up the rungs like a madman.

With the wind licking my wet hair, I craned to look at where my Angel waited. She bounded off her pillar with incredible speed, landing on a second one, then a third. The other figures joined her path.

Cilia…! I heaved up the ladder, blinking back tears and rainwater. Could this be a trick? Could I be falling for another lie? Or an illusion…?

But if it's real…

I reached for the last rung—but a cutting gale hit so strong, my footing slipped and I tumbled toward the stone floor—

"*KAEL!*"

My Angel appeared on the lodge's roof. She lunged over the edge and snatched my wrist, her teeth grinding as she hauled me onto the roof with her. Now that I was stable, she threw her arms round my ribs. She fit so perfectly there, nestled against my chest. As she always had.

"Kael," she whispered, her voice ghostly. It was the voice of a faerie. "I've searched so long…" Her grip strengthened around me; her touch as real as the skin on my bones. She was no illusion. She was no phantom.

"Cilia—" I choked and sucked in a breath, but it came as a sob. I drew her as close as my grasp could allow for fear she'd slip away; that I would wake any moment from this glorious dream. "You're alive… You're *alive…!*"

"No, Kael." She pulled away, gazing at me with those ethereal, green eyes—the ones that had graced my dreams for so long. But now, her pupils were white and iridescent, and she wiped at tears. "My life ended centuries past. I've… become a demon. A monster."

My chuckle was strained as I cupped her pixie face and stole her lips—lips that tasted sweeter than my memories could imitate, the storm outside pale compared to the bliss now raging my soul.

"In life or in death," I hushed, brushing my thumbs over her cheeks, "you will always be my Angel."

She pushed her face against my hand and wept joyously…

But a vicious shriek cried from the Phoenix of Scarlet, and our attention ripped to the battles in the colosseum.

"Macar…" I growled and turned to my Angel. I trapped her hand in mine. "Cilia, I must know. Have you been dealing with Macar all this time? Since Everland?"

Her celestial features contorted with uncontested ire. "It is far worse than that, Kael."

XAVIER

Crrack-zap!

I let loose the lightning in my soul, strengthening Roji's bolt that he aimed at Macarius.

The cobra caught the bolt, throwing it back at us.

I slid in front of Roji and braced while taking the strike in his stead, the static prickling my blood and drawing my lips into a thrilled grin. *Death* this was amazing! I felt so invigorated—so *alive!*

The sparks tingled down my arms, my lungs quivering a laugh as I rerouted the lightning out of my palms and shot for Macarius again.

Macarius deflected it with a jerk of his hand, sending the bolt to the ground at his feet in a furious hiss, his fangs unfolding from his mouth.

I laughed again; his anger suddenly humorous… But then I blinked, watching as the crowned Sky mark on Macarius's chest faded black. Now, I was staring at a tri-leaf of three black diamonds. *He has the Crest?* I thought with a sinking stomach. Why would *he* have the Crest?

Macarius roared and shot a new bolt at me, and I braced.

But Alex slid between us and caught the bolt, throwing it back at him. Macarius leapt out of the way, his glare vicious.

"Alex!" I panted, flicking a glance at my brother. "He has the…"

"The Crest," Alex finished for me, his jaw clenched. "I know."

"Why?"

"Now that, I don't know," he admitted. His fingers cracked as they balled. "But Dream had better have some Gods damned answers after this."

Shhhhrrrreeeeee!

A piercing shriek rang from the Phoenix above us, the glassy creature curling its wings and rising higher, disappearing into the clouds.

Then, poking through the haze, was an armada of sails and masts. The Airships emerged from the billowing storm and surrounded the arena, canons lowered and crew members shouting over the harsh gale. Powerful drums beat and thundered their songs of war as the ships drifted in a tight perimeter around us, serving as a wall of ships.

Anabelle's fleet had arrived.

Macarius had apparently seen the fleet as well, his head whipping from vessel to vessel. He gave a curse.

In the pause, Roji stepped beside me, wheezing for breath. At his side came Dalminia, gripping her icy trident, and beside her strode Ana.

"Macarius Lysandre," Ana boomed with an imperial timbre. Her golden locks lay heavy over her shoulders as she hefted a glowing, stone sword in each hand, her bare feet set in an offensive stance. "I pray that you yield. My fleet has come for you."

Macarius glared at her with dripping fangs fully displayed. Then realization dawned in his newly scarlet eyes, and he paused. "Is that… little Ana?" His voice was stunned. He began chortling in spurts, clutching his chest as if grasping for air. "Good gracious, you… you were never Dream's daughter, were you!" He wiped at entertained tears. "Oh, he fooled us all—yes, gold suits you far better than blue, Anabelle." His lungs quivered, throwing his head back while clasping a hand over his eyes. "I should have seen it! You look so much like Genevieve—that was your real mother, wasn't it? You were never like Crysa. Dream, you clever fox! Did Adam even know?"

"Yield now, Macar," Ana repeated, her lion ears curled. "I will not ask again."

Macar was trapped in his guffaws. "Do you even remember me, Spirit Daughter? Little Ana? Why, you were such a small thing, you'd hop on my knee and demand that I lift you up!" His laughter worsened. "And here you are! The fabled Lost Relicblood of Land! *Adam's own daughter!*"

A terrible cry burst from the clouds above. Bursts of light exploded in the nimbus. The Phoenix's silhouette could be seen within, its feathers deteriorating and dripping into tiny pieces. In a swirling twister, scarlet sands spiraled into the hourglass-shaped tower, every grain collecting in a glowing mound... until the last bits sprinkled in, and their glow dimmed.

I stared blinking at the mound up there. *Had that been the Phoenix...?*

A furious scream ripped my attention back to Macarius—just as he was tackled to the ground.

By Kael.

"You...!" Kael's voice blazed with unmatched hatred, wrapping his poison-infested fingers around Macar's throat. *"You lying worm!"* His grip strengthened, causing Macarius to gag. Kael roared, "You were my friend...! You were my friend and you *KILLED HER...!*"

Macarius's hands exploded, thunder cracking as Kael was hit chest-first and thrown back several feet by a powerful bolt of lightning.

"Kael!" Cilia cried from five rows above us, and I stepped back when the demon queen threw herself over the rail and cracked the ground under her heels, running to Kael.

She's found him! I watched in disbelief as she helped the groaning Kael to his feet.

The ground shook three more times, and I had to grapple the railing to keep steady. Our other demon royals had joined, surrounding Cilia and Kael like a personal guard. Where had they been? Could they not approach before because of the Phoenix?

Macarius pushed to his feet, spitting venom off to the side and scratching at his blistered throat. "Well, if it isn't our missing demon queen," he hissed bitterly. "So, you joined the Reapers I sent you to kill after all. What a surprise."

Cilia growled. "I remember that night, Macar. Adam was not my killer. It was you."

Macarius threw up his hands in an annoyed sigh. "Yes, so I was! What does it matter now? I hadn't expected you to become a demon when Kael and

I escaped Aspirre. I thought it was quite poetic when I found you on your little island."

Kael snarled, "And you said *nothing* to me. You said nothing for five hundred years, feeding me lies. Was any of it true? *Any* of it?"

Macarius gave an impassive shrug, offering, "I truly needed you, Kael. It was your own fault you hadn't listened to me in the first place. I wouldn't have had to resort to such drastic measures."

Kael's infectious fists tightened at his sides. Then a thought seemed to dawn in his yellow eyes.

"The child," Kael began, glancing at Cilia, "the child she'd housed. You told me it'd belong to your brother… Was that a lie as well?"

Macar flicked his eyes up, his tongue clicking. "Oh, very well, *yes*. It was mine. Not that she knew any more than you did, simpletons. All she saw—" He let slip a chuckle. "—All she *ever* saw was her dearest husband come home from one surgery after another. She never once questioned his silence." His chuckles curdled. "She even said once it was better."

Kael's voice faltered. "Why would you do this…?"

"Curiosity," Macarius considered, amused. "It was an experiment, to test my illusions. I was curious if she would even notice the difference." He slipped another chuckle. "It seemed her time in the brothel desensitized her far too well—"

Kael charged for him in an enraged yell, his poisoned hands raised.

Crr-ACK!

Macarius struck Kael with an incredible, blinding bolt, showering Kael as his screams crackled under the splintered light.

When the bolt dissipated at last, Kael's burnt skin snapped with excess static, and he swayed. Then he fell over the rail and spiraled into the clouds beneath the open-air arena.

"KAEL!" Cilia leapt after him, the two figures vanishing in the dense clouds.

The remaining Ancients yelled for Cilia, and the newer, Skydragon Ancient that had joined them recently spread his wings and soared into the squall after the two.

Now the storm crackled in the new silence, echoing through the colosseum.

Macarius inhaled deeply and slicked back his scarlet hair, gazing at the many Airships surrounding the arena. His eyes flicked to Anabelle, then to the three Ancient Necrofera. His gaze darkened at the demons. "You're one of her kind then, aren't you? Those with Clean souls haven't such radiant eyes."

Hecrûshou gripped his glowing trident and pointed the fork at the cobra. "An observant one. With such insight, one would think you'd have the wit to know what danger you've now brought yourself, bringing such grief to our comrade as you have."

Miranda stepped beside him, and Bloody Death, even Khol stood at his side, shivering though he was.

Screeeeee…!

Shrieks trumpeted from outside the colosseum, distant at first until the screams grew into a crescendo. From the storm emerged skeletal beasts, their boney wings flapping for the arena in incredible numbers.

Macarius cursed, turning toward the open-air center—

He propelled off the railing, using the winds to guide him safely to one of the floating, stone platforms that littered the open center of the arena like a checkered board. They were connected by chains that wavered at his added weight when he landed on one.

"Get back here!" I shouted and leapt onto the platforms after him, fury hot in my blood as I felt the gale wrap around my skin. With my Aerovoking, I *pulled* on the winds, gliding as if part of the air itself.

My feet touched down lightly three platforms away from Macarius, the gusts pushing me back into balance as the platform dipped at my weight, the anchoring chains clattering.

Then it dipped a second time, and I turned to see Alexander had evoked his own Aerovoking, having created winds from his soul, and hopped to this platform beside me.

"If you think you can run now, Macarius," Alexander yelled, and my hands sparked with electricity beside him as I finished, "you're sorely mistaken."

Macarius grinned, his fangs on full display. "Am I?"

Thnk-tnk!

Our platform jerked, the chains shuddering.

Then the sound of propellers fluttered to life beneath the arena, and from the veiling clouds sprouted the sails of an Airship—one that was *not* of Ana's fleet.

The thick masts speared between the floating platforms, snagging the chains and tugging them higher and higher until—

Our chain *snapped* apart.

Alex and I screamed, grabbing the chain that was still attached to our platform as we swung downward, dropping through the open center and dangled amongst the clouds below the arena like a chaotic pendulum. Alex gripped the chain near the broken end beneath my feet while I held on above him, the two of us spinning wildly out of control until I thought I'd be ill.

The gusts bit at my cheeks, the rain cold and harsh, my hair falling loose as it whipped along with the breeze. My knuckles screamed to keep hold of the slippery chains. Alex hollered something up at me, but his voice was drowned by a burst of thunder. I heaved, seizing control of the winds at my feet and trying to calm the gale that threatened to thrash us into oblivion. I managed to keep the two of us in a bubble of calmer winds, but there was little I could do for anything outside of it.

In the new calm, I caught sight of Macarius climbing a rope-ladder onto the intruding Airship in the distance, which sank into the dense clouds and…

It vanished.

"Damn it!" I yelled, kicking the air, but held tight to the chain as it quivered. "He's gone!"

Alex called from under me. "*We'll* be gone if we don't get back on solid ground!"

I looked up, the arena's stone ledges far, far above us. In this weather, I doubted we could climb that far without slipping to our deaths… Or would we even die if we did? With our new Hallows, riding the air seemed fairly simple. Of course, so far, all we'd managed was to *glide* with the wind, so it wasn't exactly flying. I was able to lighten my landing earlier, but would it be so easy from a greater distance…?

Best not to risk it. In any case, if we fell, there was no getting back up. And my wife was still delivering our son up here.

Calling Hugh it is, I decided—

"Xavier!" the voice of my mother's vassal, Aiden, called over the wind. I couldn't find the robin in the nimbus, but his voice pierced through between the thunder. "Alexander…!"

Dalen's voice followed him. "*Da'torr!* You still out here?!"

I hollered, "Aiden, Dalen—*ahh!*" My wet fingers slipped down several links, accidentally kicking Alexander's head. "We're over here!"

"Ushar be merciful!" Aiden cried, his winged visage coming into focus from the left as he and Dalen soared toward us. "You had us worried we'd find your bones in Everland! Oh, but your mother would have Cleansed me, she would… Rossette! Rossette, they're over here!"

Rossette's viridian wings wafted away the clouds as she came next, sighing in relief while flying to us alongside Aiden and Dalen.

Rossette, who Willow had thankfully resurrected days ago as an older, stronger version of her vessel—wings fully developed, to my good fortune— grappled my left shoulder and arm while Dalen seized my right. Aiden caught Alexander by the chest and hefted my brother up alone.

It took several chaotic minutes to reach the stone arena again, but once we were set on solid ground, we puffed for air, assessing the situation as it now stood. Ana's fleet still surrounded the colosseum, but the benches held only those of our company.

"Macarius's followers are gone as well," Alexander observed, spitting rain-water. "They must have left with that ship."

"How did they know?" I panted, coughing. "How did they know where we would be? And when we would call the Phoenix?"

Alexander's nose crinkled in a brooding snarl. "I don't know. But I am damn well going to find out."

I ran a hand through my drenched hair and freed my face of their sticky strands—

Master, Hugh's voice suddenly fuzzed in my thoughts. *Your son is crowning…!*

My limbs jolted. "Death!" I sprinted up the stone steps toward the lodge where I'd left Willow, my feet skipping against the dying wind.

33

A NEW PRINCE ARRIVES

WILLOW

"*AAARHH!*" I shrieked, the ripping pain at my groin unspeakable...! "*AHHH!*" I was in tears, feeling the most uncomfortable mixture of numbness, coldness and wet splashes leaking and spurting between my legs, but Nira, I didn't care! I needed this baby *OUT*...!

The ceiling lamps were now burned into my vision. Every glance I dared to inch at Bianca, who was masked in a yellow cloth that covered her mouth and nose, was blotted by the speckled, bluish afterimages. There was little I could see beyond the covering cloth Bianca had draped over my legs, but I still caught the stains on the towels underneath me. Bianca's gloves dripped red and pink and... oh, Gracious Nira, even brown? Bloods, but I hadn't expected so many damned people to be in here for this...! The smell was already ungodly, now I had to bear the embarrassment of it afterward.

Mikani gripped my hand, another burst of fire escaping my palm as I tried like Death to keep my breathing even... but it only brought me dizziness.

I screamed when something felt like it tore. "*RRRRRAAAAAH—!*"

The door slammed open.

"Willow?!" Xavier came panting inside—but he flinched once spotting me, horror breaking his drenched, bearded face.

"*XAVIER!*" I shrieked, turning my head up to watch his upside-down face blanch. "*WHERE IN DEATH HAVE YOU BEEN—AAAaaaaAAAAAH!!*"

A sucking squelch came from my groin, pushing, groaning, screeching— *THMP!*

When next I looked up, my husband was on the floor.

XAVIER

The world splotched into existence again.

The first thing that came into view was Bianca's guild assistant, Red, who was holding a jar of smelling salts under my nose. When he saw I was finally awake, he pulled down his large goggles and grinned. "Mornin', Daddy."

"*Nngg…*" My tongue was numb, and I swayed when propping my elbows up. "What… what happened…?"

A chuckle came from the center of the room, and Willow's voice hummed. "You fell unconscious, darling. You missed most of the excitement."

My head snapped to her.

There, resting on my wife's bosom, already cleaned and swaddled in soft blankets as his ashen wolf ears flicked against Willow's skin…

Was a newborn baby.

I drifted to Willow and kneeled. Kissed her fingers, a breathless laugh spilling from my lips as I gazed at our son in wonder.

Our son… my son.

Willow held him up, offering him to me.

I stilled my breath, lungs like ice. Then so, so gently, I lifted him, keeping his neck stable in the crook of my elbow. I felt him wriggle in his blankets as his wolf ears folded down and his wrinkled face scrunched as though confused.

"Hello, Lucas," I whispered, kissing his crown where the smallest wisp of ashen hair curled. "Your Daddy's here… lovely to meet you, at last."

The newborn peeked his lids open the smallest bit, and I found myself staring into two deep pools of clear, alabaster eyes. They closed almost as fast as they'd opened, and he squirmed one last time before settling in my arms to return to his sleep.

"Look at you." My voice wavered, tears hitting as something strong and eternal sprouted deep inside me, rooting there until I knew it would stay until the day my soul Descended to Nira.

I brushed a cold finger against my son's cheek, steam rising as his Pyrovoker's heat combated my Glaciavoker's frost. I whispered, "Just like your mother…"

Beside me, Willow cupped my cheek and stole my lips. Then she lay her head on my shoulder, sighing while caressing our son's brow.

"He looks like his father," she said. "It's there in his nose, his chin, his brow… It all looks like you."

Another wave of tears stung, and I laughed. "Save for his hair and eyes, you mean. That is from his mother."

"Well, he *is* a Relicblood of Death," she considered, pulling down the blankets the baby was swaddled in to show the crowned Death mark on our son's left shoulder. "But only Death, it seems. He has no Dream mark, strangely. It seems the Gods decided there were enough Relicbloods of Dream walking about."

"I suspect that is thanks to Eryn," Crysalette said above us. I only now realized she'd been looming there the whole time. Baby Eryn was in her arms, and she knelt to bring Eryn closer toward Lucas. "Well, Eryn, what do you think of your new great-nephew, mm? It looks as though you'll be growing up together."

The fox-eared babe's azure tail swished as he reached for the newborn.

Crysalette pulled him away and chuckled. "No, no, dear! You can play after Lucas has had time to rest. He and his mother have had quite an eventful night."

"So has his father," I grunted, brushing another finger over my son's soft, soft cheek, the touch sparking another burst of delight. Lucas shifted in my arms and grumbled at the disturbance. I sighed, glancing at Willow. "Macarius and his followers fled in an Airship… there's no telling where they've gone."

Willow's expression hardened at the news. "Is the danger over then? At least for now?"

"It seems so."

"All right, all *right!*" Alexander's muffled voice sounded from outside the door. He abruptly entered with a peeved scowl, holding a com with the screen of light displaying my father's frantic face. "They're all here, now settle down! Bloods…"

Alex stalked to us and handed the com to Willow as he stepped aside with crossed arms, annoyed, but a pleased smirk still tugged at his lips.

"Bloods be good, that must be him!" Father guffawed and peered closer through the screen. *"Look at that! He looks just like his father…! Why, he has the same face as when you were born, Xavier."*

I laughed, glancing at Alexander. "I believe I already shared a face with someone."

"Well, yes, yes, but I mean… Oh, you know what I mean." He was panting on the screen, the scenery behind him zipping by as if he were running. *"Alice! Alice, come look! Our grandson has been born…!"*

34

AFTERMATH

OCTAVIUS

"Well?" I asked Matt, ignoring the drizzle slapping my face. "Anything?"

Matt held a hand to the dead Cloak's exposed chest, violet light seeping into the corpse's skin and filling into his ribs like a storm cloud, visible even to Dad, Neal and me as we hovered over him.

Nothing started shining in the corpse's chest.

Matt shook his head, his tone thick. "No soul here, either."

Dad cursed. "I don't get it. They should still have their NecroSeams, our demons didn't eat their souls. Right?"

I looked over my shoulder at Hecrûshou, Khol and Miranda—the only three demons who *hadn't* jumped into the storm. They were peeling off hoods and masks from the bodies two rows above us. Hecrûshou was being assisted so helpfully by his little Bindragon, who suctioned off a mask or two with the suckers under its belly.

"Hey!" I called up, cupping my mouth. "Did any of you eat these guys' souls?"

They grunted a simultaneous *no* and went back to unveiling the masked faces of the dead.

Matt pushed to his feet and wiped his hands, grumbling. "This is concerning. What do you suppose happened?"

I knelt to the corpse under us and peeled off the guy's mask. His skin was rotted and burnt away, cheek bone poking through, and his eyes were rolled back and dripping with tears of blood.

This looks too familiar. Hesitant, I pulled down his jaw to look in his mouth. There were two fractured halves of a Metaglass lozenge wedged between his gums and molar.

"Land," I said, slicking back my drenched hair. "I know what happened. They all had those poisoned lozenges. Like what we saw in Neverland."

"Yeah," Dad rasped, "looks that way all right."

Neal clicked his tongue. "Great. So much for questioning anyone."

"Tavi!" El called down from the same row as us. "Tavi, come quick! This one is alive!"

We scrambled over. I was panting by the time I reached her, looking at the groaning, masked girl under El. Her feathered hair was the same shade of indigo as her wings, and when El took off her mask, I saw a scar running down her face. Land, she didn't look any older than fourteen.

I waved a hand over her heaving chest, feeling a broken rib with my Infeciovoking 'static', along with a punctured lung.

"<P... please...>" the girl wheezed in Culatian, shivering. "<I... I don't... want to die... I'm not ready...>"

El gingerly touched the girl's cheek, speaking in the same tongue. "<We'll find you a Healer.>"

Neal scooped up the injured girl, nodding to me. "I'll take her to Mom. You guys look for any more survivors."

"Right," I said, trotting down the row toward the next body with Dad while Matt went the other way. *Nope, this one's dead.* It was another Culatian bird.

In fact, the more I looked, the more I noticed that most of the bodies were Culatian. Why? The ones who attacked the twins in Neverland were, well, Neverlandish.

"Dad?" I asked, turning to him behind me. "Does Macarius have people in every realm?"

Dad grunted. "I don't know. I only knew about the schools in Neverland and Everland. He never said anything about having people up here."

My brow scrunched at him. "Schools?"

"The Lysandre schools," he explained. "His wife runs them, from what I understand."

"This guy's married?" I rubbed my eyes. "Who in Void would want to marry a psycho like him?"

Dad gave a grim laugh. "Probably another psycho. I've never met her, actually. But Macarius mentioned her every once in a while, when I was with him. But it wouldn't surprise me if they opened up more schools in the other realms—or if they were there all along—to spread their anti-Relicblood propaganda. Makes sense, at least."

I shuddered. "Bloods. Just how many people are we... up against...?" I trailed off, spotting a cluster of people huddled under that looming, hourglass-looking tower. They were *our* people.

Anabelle was there along with Kurrick and Linus, Dalminia and Roji… Roji was sobbing. There was a slumped body in Roji's arms. The body had scarlet wings.

"Oh, Land." My chest froze over. I inched my gaze to El behind me. *Should I tell her? Should I…*

El caught me staring and questioned, "What is it?"

"El…" I pushed my lungs to work, but they clenched up, my throat icing. "I… I think Zyl is…"

El's wings drooped, confused. Then she looked ahead. Confusion drained into fear.

She screamed, "ZYL!" and launched off our row's railing, flying to the cluster of people.

I ran after her with Dad, stopping when we reached the circle of people. El landed in front of Zyl and Roji. She collapsed to her knees, shrieking a hollow cry. She fell over her friend, her blue wings draping and cat ears falling to her neck, every heaving sob pulling my heart.

I watched her quietly beside Dalminia.

El…

JAQ

The last of the rain fell into a calm drizzle, and I wiped the cold droplets from my scaled nose with a sleeve. Not that it did any good since the sleeve was soaked through anyway. Bloody Sky realm and its annoying rain…

"So," Lilli began as she sauntered over and slid an arm around my waist. "I hear I have you to thank for my engagement-vines?"

I grinned. "Heh, yeah, well… it's not like Alex was gonna do anythin'."

"Indeed." She thoughtfully fiddled with the vines in her hair, the pink jewels glinting in the colosseum's glowing lamplight. "I was curious as to when you had the time to find them… and then happened to remember that we'd rescued a certain jeweler in Neverland when the Necrofera invaded."

I laughed, forgoing my peasant dialect and sliding into my more natural speech. "Sharp as ever, you are. Now then." My pulse fluttered, hoping this wasn't too bold. "Well, perhaps this is sudden, but I don't suppose you'd… like to keep them?"

She blinked. "Jaq. Are you proposing?"

I sucked in a breath, my laughter turning anxious. "Well, today was… interesting. And dark. And incredibly chaotic by the end of it, but… this morning, when everyone was getting ready for your wedding, and *you* were there, gown and all, and…" I exhaled. "It Bloody killed me. I don't think I can go through that again and come out standing, so." I took her hand and cleared my throat. "What do you say?"

She chuckled, hiding it behind prim fingers. "Well… I would feel awful for having put the planner through a whole month of work for nothing."

I laughed, pulling her face to mine and kissed her properly.

When we parted, she asked, "No more venom?"

"Nope," I said, going back to my poorer persona, just for the Void of it. "Safe to explore too, if ya want."

She snorted and playfully smacked my chest. "Perhaps in a more private setting…"

A sudden *cr-r-r-shlp!* of dripping water made us flinch. Matthiel was apparently standing there the whole Bloody time, wringing out his drenched sleeve and wearing a smug grin on his face.

"I don't wish to say I told you so," Matt hummed, flinging his hand back in a gesture, the wet sleeve flopping over, "but I did tell you so."

BIANCA

"Look at him!" I squealed, petting the newborn's super soft wolf ears with excited fingers. "He's so cute!" I kept the baby cradled in my arms and nudged Xavier with my hip. "He totally looks like your wife, though."

Willow hid a chuckle from her place on the floor, and Xavier scoffed, "He has *my* eyes… Eye. Well, the right eye, in any case. Twice."

Willow wavered a disagreeing hand. "His eyes are my father's, like all of Death's Bloodline. I was an exception, being mixed."

Xavier shut his mouth. Then tried, "Well, he has my wolf ears, primary or not."

Willow lifted a finger, singing, "Still the Death Bloodline."

"Oh, will you give me something!" Xavier cried. "Does he at least have my face, or is that your Bloody father as well?"

Willow laughed and looked at me, making my rabbit ears perk as she asked, "What do *you* think, Bianca?"

I squinted at the baby's face, studying his tiny nose and the shape of his lips. "Yeah, I'd say he looks like you, Xavier," I concluded, smirking. "Either that, or he looks like Alex."

Xavier snorted. "You both won't let me claim any part of my son, will you?"

"Calm down, he looks like you enough," I said, handing him back to Xavier. "He's obviously yours." In the back, Alex talked with his father on com, explaining everything that happened before the birth. I caught him stealing glances at me over his shoulder, flashing a dopey smile my way before addressing his father again in a weirdly whimsical voice. What was wrong with him?

Jaq and Lilli walked inside, laughing and joking and… Why did Jaq look super hyper? He was smiling so wide, I thought his face would split open. And Lilli was giggling like a giddy schoolgirl next to him. *Weird.*

"Oh!" Lilli clasped her hands when she saw the baby in Xavier's arms. "This *must* be him…! He has Willow's hair and eyes, to be sure!"

Xavier let out a hurt groan. "But he has my face…"

Jaq pushed a fist on Xavier's shoulder, heckling. "Sorry, mate. The hair is way more noticeable. Still, you made one cute kid. Congrats."

Xavier chuckled and handed the baby to Willow, sighing. "Well, now that you're all here, we can hold the Spirit Parent ceremony."

"Yes!" I hopped in a circle. "Yes, yes, yes!"

Xavier cleared his throat behind a fist. "Jaqelle Tyler Mallory."

Jaq straightened and folded his arms behind him. "Right."

"Under the watch of the Mother Nira, and the witness of those here today, will you swear to take on the duties expected of a Spirit Father to my son, Lucas Rouhell Ember, and protect him from harm, folly, and sadness to the best of your ability?"

"I swear," Jaq answered, squaring his shoulders to stand taller.

Xavier nodded to me next. "And will you, Bianca Gertrude Florenne, under the watch of the Mother Nira, and the witness of those here today, swear to take on the duties expected of a Spirit Mother to my son, Lucas Rouhell Ember, and protect him from harm, folly and sadness to the best of your ability?"

"I swear, I swear, I swear!" I said, bouncing and biting my lip to try and stifle my excitement.

Willow turned to Lilli next. "And will you, Lilliana Violette Tessinger, under the watch of the Mother Nira, and the witness of those here today, swear to take on the duties expected of a Spirit Mother to my son, Lucas Rouhell Ember, and protect him from harm, folly and sadness to the best of your ability?"

"I swear," Lilli breathed wistfully, her bat wings folding primly.

Willow and Xavier bowed their heads, speaking in unison, "Thank you for being here for our son."

The room rippled with applause and laughter, and Lilli asked to hold the baby, bending to Willow to scoop him up as Jaq knelt beside her, the viper petting Lucas's wolf ears with a huge, toothy smile.

"…ery well, fine," Alex grumbled from the back corner, still on com, though the face on the screen was now the twins' mother. "But this is the last time I pass them over."

He strode to Xavier and handed him the com again. Then he caught me staring, and he grinned.

I groaned inwardly. *Idiot.*

I hurried to the corner where Rochelle and I had dumped the used towels, pretending to adjust the sheet covering them to make myself look busy.

From my peripherals, I saw Alex walking over. I folded a rabbit ear in annoyance and went to the other side of the room, now pretending to look out the window at the hazy overcast.

Still, he changed course and headed for me. *Will he get the hint already?*

He stalked over, weirdly cheery, and leaned a hand over the window, bringing his face too enticingly close to mine.

"Well," he sang low, not caring that my eye narrowed at him suspiciously, "I believe you and I have some unsettled business to attend."

Bloods, why is he so close? "Alex," I grumbled, "We talked about this. You can't keep acting like we—*Mnf?!*"

He shoved his lips over mine, caution thrown out the damn window.

He pulled back in a chuckle. "Who's acting?"

I stood there, blubbering. "But.. but I… your wedding…" His enthused laugh made it click, and I gasped. "You called it off?"

"Lilli and I came to a mutual understanding," he said, proud of himself as he curled a formal arm behind him and cleared his throat. "Though, it was inexcusably late… and I do apologize. What say you, Mistress Chemist?" He offered a hand to me, smiling. "Take me back?"

I couldn't help my giggle, reaching for his fingers.

Then my eyes flicked behind him, catching Lilli handing the baby back to Willow. Jaq slid his arms around the High Howless from behind, murmuring in her ear and making her chuckle as he kissed her cheek and rested his chin on her shoulder.

WHAT.

I retracted my hand, startling Alex.

Smack!

Alex's neck flung to one side when I slapped him, his pale cheek reddening from my fingers. His shock split into fear when he saw my face.

"You come back after you get *dumped?*" My voice shook, trying so hard not to cry. The others were looking at us now, the room painfully silent.

Alex touched his cheek, blinking. "It… we both decided…"

"Death, and I actually thought you…!" My eyes stung, tears coming up anyway and spilling over as I shoved past him and walked outside. I let the door slam shut behind me.

He didn't follow.

I kicked the stone wall, letting out a muted scream. *IDIOT! IDIOT, IDIOT, IDIOT!*

Why did I let him in again? Even for a damned second—I should know better by now! *Why do I keep falling for this bullshit and getting my hopes up?!*

My vision blurred as I kicked the wall again, wincing at the pain in my toe. I puffed for breath as the anger simmered down, draining into misery. I sniffled and wiped my flooding eyes.

This proved it. He didn't actually care about me. He didn't want me back on his own, he only thought of me as an afterthought—a backup option if things fell through with Lilli… a rebound.

I sat down against the lodge's wet wall, not caring that my back got soaked as I dabbed my eyes, pain squeezing my chest. I shouldn't care, damn it. *He doesn't care,* so neither should I. It'd be better for everyone if I just forgot about him for good…

But why couldn't I…? I rubbed my eyes harder, my vision sparkling with annoying stars.

"H-hey! Bianca!"

My head snapped up. And I was suddenly shocked out of my dumb brooding. Neal was hustling toward me, carrying a bloody, beaten girl in a white cloak.

He hollered, "We found a survivor!"

35

A CLOUDY FUTURE

XAVIER

When Bianca slammed the door behind her, Lucas fussed in Willow's arms, and she bobbed him gently with shushing sounds. I was pulled out of my com call with Mother, wondering what in Bloods was going on.

I found Alex frozen where the rabbit had left him, touching his reddened cheek and staring at nothing.

"What happened?" I asked my brother, glancing after where Bianca had stormed out.

Alex's gaze was haunted. He stared at his fingers. An azure Dream mark was gleaming from his knuckles, only now dimming to their usual, black crest of diamonds. He took a breath and said, "Something I… can't fix."

There was a strained silence in the room, Jaq and Lilli looking particularly guilt ridden.

Jaq rubbed his neck. "Maybe I should talk to her?"

"I… don't think it will matter." Alex cupped his eyes and whispered, "Gods, why does this keep happening…?"

The door was kicked open—and Bianca stormed inside again, shouting. "Sirra! Rochelle! I need tools!"

She stalked across the room—bypassing Alex without so much as a glance—and grabbed her bag of tools, Sirra and Rochelle scrambling for theirs as well.

"Bianca?" I began, beguiled as I left my wife's side to see what had gotten into the rabbit. "What's the matter?"

"We have a new patient in critical condition," she said, hefting her bag to a spot on the floor. "Neal, bring her this way!"

Neal entered, carrying a winged girl covered in gashes and bruises, and laid the patient where Bianca had indicated.

She gathered her stethoscope and began checking the victim's pulse.

The girl was wearing a familiar, white cloak. "Bianca," I said, shocked. "Is this one of Macarius's people?"

The girl wheezed something in Culatian, every breath sounding painful.

Willow translated behind me. "She says she only went because her mother forced her to go. She didn't take the lozenge because she wasn't ready to die."

"Bloods," Alex said, smearing a hand over his mouth. "She may have information. How bad is her condition, Bianca?"

The rabbit's ears didn't even flinch. She ignored him entirely and asked for tools from Sirra-Lynn and Rochelle, focused on her work.

The despair on Alexander's face was not missed by me.

—an explosion burst from the com screen I still held, having nearly forgotten I was still on call with my parents.

"Mother?" I pulled the screen to my face, searching for her, but she'd vanished. As had Father.

Screams and commands poured through the speaker, smoke pluming in the screen—

The call was cut off.

"Bloods!" Panic shot through my fingers, dialing to call her back, but the line was dead. "Something's going on down there! And we're still in Culatia…!"

Alex snapped out of his fog. "Death! I'd nearly forgotten today was the day we'd planned to meet with them. This island is floating right above the capital now. If we descend tonight, we may get there by dawn."

"Will it not be too late?" Willow asked from the floor, bobbing the fussy baby.

Alex shook his head. "It may be… but we've little choice left. We must try. In any case, Anabelle must reclaim her lands."

I knelt to Willow, brushing a cold thumb over Lucas's soft cheek. "Darling," I took a breath, then exhaled. "Stay here with Lucas. Have the Healers look after you both. I have to—"

"Your parents aren't the only ones down there, Xavier." Willow handed the baby to Lilli and slowly pushed to her feet, taking back Lucas. Her brows arched worriedly. "And Nira take me if you don't return. Not now."

"You are *not* coming," I said firmly. *Blast her, she will not shove her way into this one.* "I will not risk you both by thrusting you into the heart of a warzone."

"Then we will wait for you outside of it." She shuffled to the door, moving lethargically.

Rochelle leapt from Bianca's white-cloaked patient and hurried after Willow. "Your Highness!" Rochelle protested. "You shouldn't be up so soon after delivery!"

"I'll be fine," Willow said, "I just need to move slowly."

Sirra-Lynn sighed and, after making sure Bianca had control of the winged patient, rose and looked at me. "We will be with her," Sirra assured. "And I'll ask Claude to guard the ship, should any stray soldiers find us."

Claude? With his Infeciovoking, there were few mortal men who could oppose him...

"And," Willow considered, "We can ask our demons to guard us as well."

"Bloods," I mumbled, deliberating. "Immortal bodyguards would be difficult to kill..."

Willow muttered. "If not impossible."

I groaned. "Oh... Oh fine. You can come *only* if they agree to guard you. And you're not to come *anywhere near* the battlefield until the dust has settled."

She patted my cheek. "Oh, darling. It's precious how you think I wouldn't have come regardless. But I do appreciate the concern."

She walked out, and rueful, I followed after my wife. As we circled the arena, we found a cluster of comrades under the looming tower where the Phoenix of Scarlet's sands lay resting. Everyone surrounded Roji and his sister's body. Anabelle was at Roji's side, silent and in tears.

El held Zyl's limp hand, choking on sobs with Roji.

Willow passed Lucas to me, and I watched her approach Roji, laying a solemn hand on his shoulder.

"Sky," Willow sighed, her tone melancholy. "Nira Cleanse the man who took Zylveia... but he's likely to return. Grieve as long as you need, but we must prepare for what's to come."

Roji held his sister tighter, sobbing.

"My father and his Reapers are now in battle in Everland's capital," Willow said.

Anabelle straightened from Roji's side. "So soon?"

"They were taken by surprise moments ago. This was to be the final battle for Everland's crown."

Anabelle inhaled a slow, reflecting breath. "Then it is time," she said, "I must reclaim my lands."

Roji's breath shuddered, "The snake. Is he the one responsible for the war?"

Anabelle nodded but once. "Yes."

Roji lifted to his feet, carrying Zylveia's body close to his chest. "Then you have my fleet, Land. We leave tonight. Death?" He turned to Willow; his red eyes pained yet resolute as he gazed at his sister. "I have a request."

We stood in the palace chapel. Roji, Ana and I waited by the left pews; Dalminia, El and Octavius stood within the right pews; Jaq, Alexander and Lilli waited behind me. Those who hadn't soul-sight wore white masks, the rest of us bare-faced.

Lucas wriggled in my arms, the boy giving a croaking whine. I hushed him and bobbed him gently, keeping my attention to the front of the chapel.

Willow stood before the altar, looming over Zylveia's neatly laid body.

Zylveia had been dressed in a simple, jade dress, her blood cleansed from her neck, the gash hidden under a green ribbon. She lay on a stone bench, looking as if she were sleeping.

Willow lifted the pure, Spiritcrystal scythe in her hands, and brought its glowing blade over Zylveia's heart, slicing through her NecroSeam.

Zylveia's ghost rose from her pores, the pale specter glimpsing her surroundings in a daze.

"What…" Zylveia's ghost breathed sleepily in broken Landish. "What this…? You take Zyl out again?"

"No," Willow sighed, "Not this time."

Zyl's ghost shivered. "Zyl… dead…?"

Willow bowed her head. "I'm sorry, Zylveia."

El broke into a sob behind her soul-seeing mask and ran out of the pews, throwing her arms around the ghost.

El's touch phased right through, wrenching a louder cry from the hybrid. She jabbered in Culatian with a tight voice, Zyl breathing consoling replies as she motioned to touch the hybrid's head.

Roji leapt over the pews from beside me, greeting his sister in Culatian as well, his eyes long wet behind his mask.

The four spoke in that tongue for some time, their hushed echoes bouncing round the chapel. *What were they saying?* My Culatian was poor at best, and they were so quiet, I doubted I could understand even if I did know the language.

Willow lifted a gesturing hand to her own chest. Zylveia's ghost shook her head vigorously. Willow twisted to look at me, gesturing in my direction. Zylveia's white mouth twisted, thoughtful, then she shook her head again, instead pointing at Lilli behind me.

"Oi!" Zylveia's ghost called. "Grim bat! You speak Culatian?"

Lilli stiffened behind the bench. "Yes?"

"Good!" Zylveia snorted, turning to Willow again. "I be wanting her!"

I flicked a sidelong glance at the bat. "What does she want you for?"

"She, er…" Lilli blushed slightly. "She wishes to form a Bloodpact with me."

"Does she?" I asked, surprised.

"From what I could hear earlier," she explained in a murmur, "she was glad to go to Grim, if El was traveling there regardless. But she denied Willow and you both…"

Zylveia waved impatient, translucent hands at Lilli. "Come on, come on! Being the quick one! We having things to do!"

I hummed. "She's accepted her death rather quickly, hasn't she?"

"Apparently," Lilli said, shyly sliding out of the pews to approach the altar.

They performed the Bloodpact, marking Zylveia as Lilli's vassal, and Zylveia was resurrected. When Zyl awoke once more, physically, sucking in a reviving breath, El clung to her so tight Zylveia chuckled dimly.

Although it seemed odd, I supposed this wasn't the first time I'd seen someone accept their death so hastily. But in those cases, from what I'd seen, the misery came upon them soon afterward. *Will it hit Zyl later, I wonder?* I supposed her acceptance could have another explanation. She'd had her soul taken out of her body for a month before, perhaps she had grown familiar with the state. *Or more likely,* I considered, *she's stifling her grief by telling herself she can still be with El when she leaves.*

The floorboards creaked behind us. I turned, finding a face I hadn't seen in hours under the doorframe.

King Dream was a dripping mess. His azure locks lay heavy at his chin, trails of rainwater leaking down his neck. He leaned his face against the doorframe for but a moment, then quietly turned around and walked down the hall.

Alex growled in the row behind me. "Oh, no you don't."

He slid out of the pews, and I kept Lucas close to my chest as I followed Alex out of the chapel.

"Dream," Alex barked down the hall.

Dream froze, his head flinching at us.

Before he could scuttle away, Alex grabbed his shirt collar. "You're not slithering away this time, Dream," rumbled Alex, his glare deadly. "Why does Macarius have the Crest?" Alex lifted his right hand, turning his knuckles to show Dream his Crest of black diamonds. "Why does *he* have this Crest?!"

"Alex," I snapped, bobbing my son to hush him when he gave a small wail. "Let him answer before you start shouting… Dream? There must be an explanation?"

Dream had braced himself for a strike, looking at the wall instead of us. He swallowed hard, his throat stuck, and whispered, "How was I to know…?"

Alexander's grip loosened slightly on Dream's shirt. "Know what?"

"I was never given a clear answer, was I…?" Dream laughed, a dark, empty chuckle. His eyes were lined with tears. "This one, that one. Either can be our deaths. Either can be our salvation. Either can switch whenever they choose, and their methods could be as unpredictable."

My brow furrowed. "What are you saying…?"

"*One will save,*" he recited, speaking the prophecy he'd once claimed Iri had spoken to him millennia ago. "*One will ruin. One will defend, or cometh the True End…*" He took a separate breath and spoke a new line he hadn't mentioned before. "*All could be he, by choice or by say, and can change if they please, by claiming thy name.*"

Alex released him, and Dream dropped to the floor.

My brother's voice shook. "What is that?" He pointed, accusing. "*What is that second part?!*"

This time, I didn't care that Lucas began wailing. I stared at Dream who lay slumped like a sorry whelp over his knees, and whispered, "That was the full prophecy. Wasn't it?"

Dream's tone was so quiet, I almost couldn't hear. "Yes."

Alex growled, "Then what he was saying… Macarius said *we* were to bring the End. He was right?"

"I don't know," Dream hushed.

Alex grabbed his scrawny arm and heaved him to his feet. "How could you not know?!"

"I'd always thought the Shadowblood would be the one to save us." He stared unblinking at the ceiling, his expression absent. "I thought, of course, the one who doesn't need to spill the blood of the Relicbloods would be the just one. And yet…" His lungs quivered, either with a laugh or a sob. "And yet I let myself hope I was wrong. He had the Crest, after all, as did his brother… I wanted to be wrong. I wanted so badly to be wrong. Yet still, after all that's happened…" His throat released an undignified squeal. "I don't know if it was wrong. I don't know if *this* is wrong. If *you* will bring our deaths or if *he* will—*I JUST DON'T KNOW!*"

Alex dropped him again, letting the pathetic wretch sob at our feet.

Everyone else had shuffled out at the noise, forming a crowd around us. Herrin and Marian watched round the corner behind Dream, their expressions cracked with dismay.

"I'm done." Alex announced, trying with difficulty to calm his breaths. "I'll have no more of this business. No more Blessings. No more Hallows we shouldn't have—I'm finished."

"As am I," I grunted, ripe to vomit.

Dream sniveled on the floor. "You can't walk away. Macar is out there. He'll kill us all—Zylveia, Roji, Dalminia, Fuérr... He'll kill Willow." His bloodshot eyes found mine. "He is after the deaths of all Relicbloods. He'll kill her... and he'll kill your son."

My grip tightened over Lucas. "He'll not go near my son," I snarled, teeth sharpening.

"How are you to stop him, then?" Dream laughed weakly. "He has all of Sky's Blessings now. He'll soon have Ocean's, then perhaps Land's, mine... and then Death's." The hall fell eerily silent. "He will have everything. You will have but three. If you cease your Blessings now..." He reached into his drenched sweater's pocket and produced the velvet sack which held the Orbs of Azure, then lifted one of the globes, where images flitted. "We all die."

I watched the faces of Alexander, myself, Willow... of Lucas... pale and lifeless, staring into empty space—

"But if you continue," Dream said, the images changing to a fainter scene within the Orb, those same faces full of life and breath, "The ones we care for have a chance at surviving."

I echoed. "A chance..."

Dream sniffed, rubbing a crude arm under his nose. "A chance is better than certainty, at this point. I've spent so many years searching for a better way, one that would tell me once and for all what to do... but this is the best I could find. I'm sorry..."

"You've no right to apologize." Alex spat at Dream's feet. "You've no right to tell us what to do. Fuck you. Fuck your prophecy. Fuck your Blessings." He spun, sneering, "We have a war to help my parents with."

I steadied my grip on Lucas and followed my brother angrily, glaring back to find Dream wallowing in his well-deserved misery.

EVERLAND

36

DECEPTION

CAYDEN

"What do you mean the Reaper's are advancing?!" Father snarled at the com screen, his general on the other side ducking in fright. "How close are they to the palace?!"

The general swallowed visibly and meekly answered, *"E-erm… they're perhaps twenty minutes out—"*

"Gardener sow me!" Father slammed his com against the wall. The device clattered noisily as a gear popped out and rolled over the carpet. He ripped his gaze to me, Rilla and Revinna. "Cayden, gather your siblings! We're leaving through the hidden tunnels! We'll escape through the eastern mountainside!"

When he began to storm off, I bent to retrieve the com, examining the damage and assessing it was still usable. *Luckily for me.* I tried to suppress a smile as I called after him. "But Father, what of the war?"

"We'll fight another day!" he sneered, then began yelling for my siblings.

This time, I couldn't help my wicked smile as I dialed the number of Henry's com. When the rabbit-eared Blacksmith answered, I announced, "He's retreating to the eastern mountainside." I was downright chortling now. "Tell the others to meet us there before we arrive."

XAVIER

As dawn split through the circular window of our Airship cabin, I tied back my shoulder-length hair and strapped on my black-painted grieves, pulling the drawstrings tight around my calf. I wasn't accustomed to black armor. I hadn't expected to get different plate than the rest of our team, who all slid on silver armor around me. Before we left, Roji had ordered one of his servants to fetch this for me. I'd discovered that he, Ana and Willow had ordered it some months ago for me, to prepare for the coming battle. A Death Prince, they said, needed to stand apart from his guard. It was simply the way of things. Or so they said.

I picked up the last piece of my ebony set: the sleek, polished helm. It was so watery and reflective, I could see my heterochromic eyes staring back at me on its dark surface. Wrapped around the brow of the helm was a glittering ring of silver with spiked tips and decorative skulls, the Death emblem featured at the front as a centerpiece. It mimicked my crown—the one Willow had given me during our stay in Neverland.

Beside me, Alex slid his shoulder guards on in silence. He didn't glance my way. He didn't glance at anyone while lacing on his plate one set at a time. His wolf ears were long grown along with his claws, which he couldn't retract, making it difficult for him to tie the knots. He was beyond furious still. I wasn't sure what I felt anymore. Numbness, I supposed. My mind was just so… blank.

The others chatted amongst themselves fervently, though. Most of their conversation regarded Jaq and Lilli's impromptu wedding. The two had held a small, brisk ceremony before leaving Culatia. It was a shock to most, but to others, Alexander included, it was hardly any surprise. The two themselves weren't present in this cabin with the rest of us. They'd snuck off somewhere private to, I imagined, make the most of their married life before throwing themselves into battle and risking death.

We'd landed in Everland's mountains some moments ago, and the cabin buzzed with an eclectic mix of emotions among the team. Some were laughing to ease their nerves, others were murmuring skeptically about the coming battle… others commented on the smoke pluming from the city far below us in the mountain city, small *pop, pop, pops* from what could only be explosions echoing up to where we were.

Amongst the chatter, as if encased in our own bubble of bitter asperity, Alexander and I were dead silent. We'd barely spoken a word to each other—or anyone else—since we left. No one approached us either, which suited us fine.

Once everyone had donned their armor and funneled out of the cabin, Alexander and I followed behind sluggishly. I tucked my crowned helm under my arm, but Alexander slid his on and slammed down his visor, as if cutting himself off from everyone and everything.

Creee!

A cabin door squealed open ahead, and a bat-winged woman emerged beside a scaled, blond man. The rest of the team cheered and jeered at the messy state of Jaq and Lilli's armor, which they were unabashedly still adjusting as

Jaq fastened his belt buckle and Lilli primly smoothed back her tangled hair to tie it in a sloppy bun. Lilli wore her pink and silver marriage-vines proudly over her forehead while Jaq's new diamond stud glinted from his left ear, his ring kept on his finger as he slid his gloves and gauntlets over it. They were both bombarded with hearty thumps on the back, congratulations, and overall good cheer as they joined the front of the pack.

Alexander and I made no attempt to approach.

We all stepped out to the deck, the boards and masts awash in the golden light of the rising sun that spilled through the clouded mass of Culatia's capital isles far above us and slit between the peaks of Everland's mountains in warm rays. Anabelle's and Roji's fleet of Airships soared ahead of us toward the smoking city, their cannons already beginning to fire onto the city. Only a handful of ships had landed here in the mountain paths, including ours, to deploy troops on foot. The royals themselves had taken their own separate ships and were likely already on their way down alongside the walking troops. Although, most likely, Roji was with his Stormchasers I saw riding the backs of feral Skydragons down to the city, crossbows at the ready as they whooped and hollered into action.

I watched our team climb down the ramp to begin the trek, Alexander dragging his feet behind them, but I spotted my wife at the bow of the ship and strode to her.

I passed Vendy and Hugh along the way, nodding to our three demons who had agreed to stay behind and watch over those who needed protection.

At the bow, Willow sat on a stack of tied-down crates while nursing our newborn son. Her long hair draped down and flowed over the floorboards like a silver river that was painted gold in the sunlight. When I approached and knelt to match her eyelevel, she flicked her exhausted gaze to me. Heavy bags darkened her lids, white fox-ears grown and lying flat against her neck. Lucas's small wolf ears flicked and swiveled every which way as he suckled his mother's teat and grumbled a soft coo.

I kissed his crown and cupped Willow's face to take her lips, sighing, "You'll be sure to flee to Aspirre with your grandfather should anything happen?"

She leaned into my cold fingers, her warm cheek heating my skin. "We will. Though I doubt anything will get past immortal demons."

"Even so," I said. My messenger raven, Chai, flapped down from the upper mast and landed on my shoulder. He nuzzled my beard with his beak, our Bond straining with worry, but also determination. I offered a weak grin at Chai and scratched his neck feathers. "You ought to stay here as well, Chai," I told him. "Keep them company. Warn me should anything happen."

Chai gave a low croak and hopped onto the crates beside Willow. Her own messenger, Jewel, fluttered from the veil of her ashen hair and chirped fervently with Chai now.

I chuckled hollowly, stealing one last kiss from my wife before rising. With an anxious breath, I slid on my crowned helm and strode to the ramp. But I paused, twisting back for a final glance at her sullen face. My wolf ears grew and my legs screamed to walk back to her, but I dug my heels into the floorboards. This was the first time I would be going into battle without her. The first time she wouldn't be there beside me. It was strange. It was unfamiliar.

And so very, very wrong.

"Please," I said softly, hesitating. "Be safe."

Her eyes welled, and she hurried to dry them. "And you as well. *Myel ma amya.*"

"*Myel ma amya,*" I returned. Then forced my feet to leave.

LUCAS

Explosions burst from every direction as Alice, Serdin, Myra and I hustled toward the mountain castle with our troops of Reapers, Henry and Apson shouting orders at the rebel soldiers we fought beside. It was chaos, but a controlled and orderly chaos. Our formations held strong despite the frequent losses that threatened to break us. Soldier after soldier fell, Reaper and rebel alike, yet we pushed on, crossing blades with the Rockraiders, dodging their Shockglobes and Flameglobes, forming up with shields when a volley of arrows and Shotri fired at us.

Airships had arrived moments ago over the mountain peaks, descending from the floating isles of Culatia that speckled the sky and partially blotted the sun. These must have been the reinforcements from Land's and Sky's fleet. The ships burst with cannon fire, their own Shockglobes and Flameglobes splashing onto clusters of enemy soldiers and rumbling the ground at my feet.

Smoke clung to the air, flames raged from the bones of building after building, blood stained the bricks and rubble at our feet as the body count climbed wherever we stepped. It stank of death and destruction, a horror no man should ever have to face more than once.

But we were prevailing. By Nira, we may see the end of this madness within the hour!

My ear suddenly buzzed when the com hooked there came to life. I tapped the engraved button to answer the call. "Sir Lucas reporting," I barked over the chaos.

"Lucas," the voice of my wife rasped from the speaker. *"Henry has finally gotten word from Cayden. He says to pull out of the city and climb toward the eastern mountainside. Galden and a handful of his remaining soldiers are attempting to retreat there. Cayden wishes to head him off beforehand."*

"Understood," I affirmed and ended the call, then whipped my head to Serdin who soared on his Flamedragon nearby over my head. "Sire!" I shouted up. "Pull the troops back! Head for the eastern mountainside! Our quarry is fleeing!"

Serdin called down a confirmation and pulled his Flamedragon in that direction.

WILLOW

Lucas fussed in my arms and wriggled in his swaddled blankets. The little pup finished his nursing and I gently patted his back over my shoulder, letting him burp over the cloth I'd set there. A bit of spit up spurted from his lips onto the cloth, and his fussing subsided.

Grandmother Crysa, who'd come to sit on the crates beside me with baby Eryn on her knee, wiped a wettened cloth over Lucas's chin to remove the spittle. "You're getting the hang of it, dear," she praised me. "Far better than the first time when you started earlier in the night."

I cradled Lucas against my chest, sharing our Pyrovoker's heat, and sighed dismally. "At least I'm doing something right, I suppose."

Grandmother put a consoling hand on my shoulder and gave me a sidelong look, her rust-orange hair tumbling over her collarbone. "What's the matter, dear? You're doing splendidly for a first-time mother."

"It's not just being a mother that's a first for me, Grandmother," I said.

My gaze drifted over the bow. Our three demons paced the ship as if on a noble patrol mission. Vendy and Hugh walked back and forth from one end of the ship to the other. A sword was strapped to Vendy's belt and a brand-new pair of dual-scythes gripped in Hugh's fingers. Xavier hadn't thought him ready for direct combat, but admitted it would be foolish to leave the boy without some form of protection. Hugh seemed all the more determined for it, at the least, he and Vendy acting as my personal guard.

Far below us, the battle raged on in the city. Smoke plumed and hazed between the buildings that were quickly becoming rubble, fire and lightning flashing every few seconds as explosions burst in the distance. It all sounded so gentle from where we were, but I knew that somewhere down there my husband must be fighting for his life and the lives of others. Alongside my father.

Alongside my mother. Alongside Lilli and Jaq and Octavius and Matthiel and Anabelle and Roji and…

"Everyone's risking so much," I told Grandmother, a wave of shame flooding as my grown fox ears fell to my neck. "They could be dying as we speak—or already dead. I should be out there with them; I should be looking after them—"

"The only ones you should be looking after," the voice of Grandfather Dream interrupted, "are your child and yourself."

Grandfather's azure-haired figure stood under the cabin doorway. His face was dark and morbid, clearly not having gotten a wink of sleep, like myself. A book of some sort was clutched in his hands, the ancient thing raggedy and torn at the edges.

I rose to my feet and hefted Lucas. "Grandfather…"

He raised a pausing hand, then turned to his wife. "Crysa, darling? Could you please give us a moment alone?"

Grandmother nodded and left, disappearing into the cabin.

Grandfather gestured for me to sit on the crates again, and slowly, I did. He lowered to my other side and cupped his hands over his knees.

"I can only imagine what you must think of me now," he began quietly. "What everyone thinks of me. But it doesn't matter. What's done is done. Whether or not my mistake caused all of this won't change what has to be done to correct it."

He set his tattered book between us and grunted, "I'll leave this with you. It may not give you the answers you seek, but perhaps you can draw better conclusions than I have with it."

I balanced Lucas over my shoulder and ran a hand over the book. There was no title left on the cover, the letters had been chipped and rubbed away over time. "What is it?" I asked.

"It documents the various births of the previous Shadowbloods and Lightcasters over the millennia," he said. "All their incarnations that have been recorded. I only ever scribed this one copy, but never released it. I wanted to find the answer to my question before then." He leaned back and lifted his gaze to the sky. "But I never found it. When I finally thought I had, I… discovered I was wrong, in the end. I should have listened to you. I was a fool to doubt my own granddaughter, but damn me, here we are."

I blinked. "To doubt me with what?"

"That the Lightcaster was our enemy." His head rolled back as he looked at me with heavy, azure eyes. "When I was a teen, you came to me often in our shared visions. You warned me of what would happen." He sighed hard. "And when the moment came to meet the Lightcaster—the one you warned me of so many years before… I thought I could change the outcome. I thought I could change his future. I just…" He buried his face in his hands. "I just wanted a friend. A *real* one, that I could die alongside instead of having everyone I ever cared for leave me time and time again, one lifetime after another while I barely aged, and…"

He inhaled deeply and unveiled his face, lifting to his feet and stepped toward the ship's railing. He gazed out at the horizon, sucking in another breath as if trying to remember the scent of the thinning air and peppered smoke.

"I'm ready," he said, and turned to face me with hollow eyes. Vendy walked by him during her patrolling and lifted an eyebrow at him. "I'm tired of running." He gave a defeated shrug and let his arms drop at his sides. "I'm tired of hiding. No matter what I choose to do, this is always where my visions end, for me."

Chai and Jewel began screeching from the crates, and a sickened pit knotted my stomach. I rose to my feet cautiously. "Grandfather…?"

"But know this." Grandfather's throat ripped in warning suddenly, flicking his eyes over his shoulder at Vendy. "It will take more than your cheap tricks to kill my granddaughter."

—Something drove through Grandfather's back and slid out his chest in a spurt of blood.

Shock numbed my pulse.

Grandfather grunted and dropped to his knees, coughing up a slosh of blood. He hovered a shaking hand to the long, Metaglass blade that was skewered through his back and chest, black tendrils of poisonous veins leaking through several cracks in the sword. The veins slithered and crept to Grandfather's skin and sank into his pores. His flesh rotted black. His bones poked through as his cheeks burned away.

"Will… ow…" Grandfather wheezed as a white mist rose from his skin, his soul evaporating as the infection devoured him. Still, he smiled. "I love you."

He collapsed onto the floorboards, the last of his soul hissing away. When the mist cleared, all that was left standing was Vendy, her twisted smile stretched so wide and chuckles so demented, her body shook.

But a *second* Vendy trotted from the rear deck, screeching to a halt when she saw herself standing there.

"Damn you, Dream," the first Vendy snarled. But that hadn't been her voice at all. Then the teen's visage dripped away, her rabbit ears disappearing and brown skin turning into bronze scales. Her eyes bled scarlet, hair shortening into the same shade of red while her feminine face turned masculine. When the illusion vanished, Macarius stood in its place, shivering with laughter. "You couldn't even grant me the satisfaction of catching you off-guard, even now. Clever bastard."

From within the velvet sack tied to Grandfather's belt, something gleamed with bright, azure light. The light leaked like smoke from the sack's opening, wavering into the air as it latched onto Macarius's skin like a leech. Macarius breathed in deeply, absorbing the light, and half of his scarlet hair streaked with azure strands, one of his rose-red eyes changing blue. The black Crest of diamonds over his chest, visible through the tear in his tunic, brightened azure and morphed into a crowned Dream mark.

Macarius exhaled a satisfied breath and plucked the sack from Grandfather's belt, the Orbs of Azure clinking from inside.

"Much thanks, Dream." His smile showed his long fangs. "Ah, the wonders of foresight!" His smile fell slightly as he looked at me with unseeing eyes, as if observing a vision. "Hrm. How disappointing. It seems no matter what I do in the next few moments, you'll escape and I risk dying on this ship thanks to your immortal entourage heading this way. I think I shall take my exit now, thank you." He lifted the sack that held the Orbs of Azure—

A bright flash blinded my vision, and when it dimmed… Macarius had vanished into Aspirre.

And all that remained was my grandfather's disfigured corpse.

37

A REALM UNITED

ANABELLE

My plated footsteps clattered as I stepped calmly through the numerous lines of rebels and Reapers, all soldiers at attention with their chosen weapons. I peered through the slit of my helm and noted that many of the Reaper's black birds speckled the sparse trees around us. The mountainside was far quieter than the chaotic city below us in the distance. It was oddly… serene. It reminded me too much of Neverland—the day I overthrew their teenaged queen. Was this to be a pattern for me now?

To my right strode Linus; to my left, Kurrick; behind me, Genevieve. Their bronze armor clanked and clicked alongside mine and filled the resounding silence that smothered the mountains. I slid off my helm and tucked it under an arm, letting the curls of my golden hair tumble down my shoulders. Now the troops turned their heads as I passed. There were whispers, there were murmurs and disbelieving prayers. Most simply stared.

As the four of us made our way to the frontlines, Roji flew down from atop a saddled Skydragon and landed beside me. He slid off his reptilian mount, which tucked in its leathery wings and shook its head with a snort. The Sky King's jade armor glistened in the sunlight as he removed his helm and set it on the ground at his feet, his scarlet, feathered hair as bright as his wings. He nodded to me, glanced over his shoulder to see that his armada of Stormchasers had landed and joined the ranks of women and men behind us, then leaned against his Skydragon and crossed his arms.

"Well," he said to me, "Feels weird with just two of us Relic Children, huh?"

I hummed, "It does. But nothing for it. Death is still recovering from labor. Ocean is only a child. Dream is not fit for combat of this magnitude in the physical realm."

"Yeah," he grunted. "Just feels weird, you know? Kinda makes a guy feel naked."

"—Then I hope you find us suitable garments," came a voice from above.

A waft of air fanned my hair back as an armored Flamedragon landed between Roji and me. Its three riders, a man wearing black plate, an azure-haired woman, and a little sheep girl wedged between them, dismounted. My gaze locked onto the woman.

"Myra!" I cried joyously and raced to my sister, squeezing her in a strong embrace. "Bloods be good, it's been so long!"

Myra chuckled and returned the embrace. "That it has, Ana! It's so good to see you—and without a disguise for once!"

"It took some time to grow accustomed to it, but yes, it's quite relieving." I frowned at the little girl lingering at her skirts, then asked, "Who is this?"

Myra's lips tugged with a grin. "Someone I'm looking after."

"I see… But what are you doing here? I know this battle is likely to be short, but that does not exempt it of danger. Should you not be in hiding?"

"She intends to," said the Death King, who had stood off to the side while Myra and I had our reunion. He pulled off his crowned, black helm, his ashen hair slick with sweat, then peered from Roji to me with piercing, clear eyes.

"Lovely to finally meet you, Lady Land," he said to me with an acknowledging nod. He did the same for Roji. "Sky. Good to see you back. And with your senile father's crown, no less."

Roji flicked him a lazy, two fingered salute. "He's having an early retirement."

"It was vastly overdue," the Death King muttered. He turned back to me. "Where is my daughter and new grandson?"

I pointed with my chin and murmured. "They are safe with Dream and Crysalette near the peaks. Your son-in-law and his brother are on their way here, though they landed farther away from the battle than *we* had, so it will take them time."

The Death King twisted back toward the lines of troops and called back. "Do you hear that, Lucas? Your sons are on their way."

The frontlines broke apart briefly to make way for Howllord Lucas and Fangs Alice. They were accompanied by the rabbit-eared Henry, Roarlord Apson, and a bat-winged man who, like themselves, rode on the backs of trotting Bonedragons.

When they came to stand beside us, Howllord Lucas uplifted his visor. "It's about Bloody time," he said in a laugh. "And do you know where our new grandson is?"

"Secure in the peaks, away from the danger," the Death King said.

Fangs Alice snorted. "As they should be."

The Death King turned to Myra. "There you have it, darling. Take my dragon and bring the girl up to Willow, if you would?"

"Very well," Myra complied and let her husband help her onto the Flamedragon. He then lifted the girl onto the saddle, and the two took off with a rush of wind, the dragon giving a screech as it veered toward the mountain peaks.

The third Bonedragon rider who'd come with the Devouhs pulled his arms over his dragon's skull and asked eagerly. "What about my Lilli? Where is she?"

Roji answered that, "She and her new husband are on their way with the twins."

The bat, who I supposed was Daniel Tessinger, Lilliana's father, let out a sharp guffaw and slapped Lucas's breast plate. "You hear that, Lucas? Her new husband! You and I are finally in-laws! I was beginning to think your son would drag his feet well after we were dead!"

Howllord Lucas chuckled brightly. "As did I."

Roji scratched his nose awkwardly. "Er, actually, it wasn't with—"

"They've come!" Linus suddenly announced beside me. The goat-shifter's Dream mark was gleaming from his shoulder and his eyes had gone stale, Seeing through his Third Eye instead. He was staring at the trap door embedded into the dirt in front of us. His tone turned gritty. "Galden is here, your grace. And he's brought your crown."

I smiled and stepped up to the trap door until my toes nearly touched the edge. "How considerate of him," I said, drawing my golden sword from the scabbard at my belt and driving the tip into the dirt, laying my hands delicately over the hilt while I waited patiently.

A muffled voice sounded behind the trap door, shouting and cursing and bellowing as the door was thrown open.

The blond man's crowned head popped up before my feet—

He saw my violet-painted boots and froze. His lion ears grew as his gaze inched up and stopped at my face, a look of horror whitening his bronze cheeks.

I sang a jolly note, "Hello."

He let out a yelp and started to rush back down the ladder—

"Ah, ah," I chided and lifted a golden-glowing hand, evoking my rock Hallows to lift the man up by his armor. My word, he was heavy, I actually had to strain a bit to get him hovering in the air before my face. I flicked my eyes at his headpiece. "You've nearly forgotten to deliver my crown, sir."

I lifted my other hand, my gilded sword staying erect where I had it skewered in the dirt, and had my Hallows pluck his crown off his head and slide it over mine. "My thanks, kind sir," I said softly, smiling. Then ripped a strong heave and shoved the man several yards back, the pitiful craven slamming into a tree with a harsh *crack* before collapsing on his back in a winded groan. His arm flailed from the ground but once before flopping over his chest limply. He certainly wasn't dead, only unconscious. The poor tree, however, was now splintered where he'd made contact.

I knelt to the trap door and offered a hand to the young lion girl who carried a large crystal ball. "Why, good day, miss," I said cheerily and helped her to her feet to one side of the door.

The girl dazedly stared at my hair and eyes, clutching the large crystal ball to her chest. "G-good… good day, my lady…" She curtsied, still in awe.

Next to climb out were several blond children of varying ages, and I asked Linus, Kurrick, Genevieve, and Henry to help pull them all out safely. Even Lord Apson broke away from Howllord Lucas's side to help in the effort. There were so many of them—and all riddled with purple and black bruises, countless cuts and scrapes from claw marks…

Linus pulled out a woman wearing glittering marriage-vines, but then paused as he clasped hands with the last man to climb up.

"Cayden." The goat broke into a wide smile and hauled the lion-eared man to his feet, keeping hold of his fingers as he laughed in delight. "I told you I'd come back this time, didn't I?"

Cayden was breathless as his eyes began to well. Then he yanked Linus in for a crushing embrace, causing the goat to wheeze in a chuckle.

"Come now," Linus laughed. "Let's not be rude to our queen, shall we?"

Cayden rubbed his eyes dry and found my face. My lion ears flicked, and I gave a warm smile. He returned the gesture with a winded laugh, then dropped a knee and bowed his head.

"Your Majesty Land," he said reverently. "Forgive me. If I'd known you were among us from the beginning…"

I raised a hand to stop him. "It was my choice to hide who I was. If you'd known then, you may have insisted on joining our voyage overseas. And then Lord Apson may not be standing here now." I tilted my head toward Lucas's resurrected vassal beside me.

The old viper grinned and stood taller as he clasped hands with Cayden cheerily—

A groan rolled from the miserable slump that was Galden farther back in the dirt. He blearily sat up against the splintered tree and rubbed his head, lion ears grown and folded to his neck in bewilderment, as though unsure of where he was.

Then he spotted me. Scrambled on all fours to get away—

"Good morning, sir," I sang, and thrust a golden-glowing hand toward him and pulled him back to us by his armor.

The coward yelped and clawed at the dirt, but it was for naught. I dragged the sniveling man to my feet and spread my fingers, forcing his armor to spread his limbs wide open. Then I jerked him up to stand. He was a prisoner in his own plate, shaking and sweating like a feral hog.

I looked at the many bruised and beaten children standing behind me. "Are these wounds your doing?" I asked calmly.

His answer came in a blubbering sob, "P-p-please…! Please—don't… don't kill me…!"

I clicked my tongue like a patronizing parent. "Oh, Galden. Do you realize how simple it would be for me crush you under your own armor? All it would take would be a simple, gentle curl of my fingers and…" I curled my fingers slightly.

His armor began to squeeze inwardly, pushing a scream from his lungs.

"But." I paused his crushing. Then flicked my gaze to Cayden, raising my voice so the troops behind me could hear. "I believe there is no one here who would covet that prize more than Land's Servant."

Excited murmurs rippled through rebels in the frontlines, the message sent to those in the lines behind them and so on, spreading like an infection.

I kept hold of Galden with one hand while using the other to pull my gilded sword out of the dirt. I tossed it to Cayden. He hurriedly evoked his own Terravoking to have the hilt latch onto his fingers.

"Prince Cayden," I announced loudly. "The one they call Land's Servant. For your years of service to me and the revival of the Old Kingdom, I grant you the gift of your father's death."

The murmurs from the troops broke into shocked cries, the news flooding in waves down the lines.

Cayden stared in awe at me, stammering. "Are… are you certain, my liege? It is your honor to…"

"To bestow upon whomever I deem worthy," I finished with a sharp-toothed smile. "I have been told of the horrors that this insect has brought you and your family. I should think there is no one worthier of this honor."

He looked overwhelmed with emotion, sucking in a resolute breath as he gripped the sword with more determination. "Thank you, my lady."

I pushed Galden to his knees and cracked his spine forward, keeping his neck straight and exposed. "After you, Lord Servant."

Cayden inhaled deeply and raised the sword. "For Gerard," he said, his teeth and claws sharpening as he lifted the blade higher.

"For Apson…!" he cried louder, taking another strong breath as he stretched his arms, and the sword, as high as they could reach. The troops began cheering in their lines, the Reaper's black birds croaking and cawing in a storm from the treetops as they fluttered and screeched wildly.

Cayden widened his stance and took a final breath before screaming, "For *my MOTHER—!*"

Crrack—ksplishh!

Cayden's blade barely moved a hair before he froze stiff, the sword still raised over his head. The previous cheer dwindled into stunned silence.

Skewered through the back of Galden's skull and poking out his left socket was a scaled, webbed hand. Galden's eyeball was held in the hand's bloody fingers, the stringy nerve still attached until the hand pulled back into his skull and *ripped* it loose, blood and brain matter sloshing out the back of his skull.

I quickly released my hold of Galden's armor, and the man's corpse collapsed.

A little girl with webbed ears, emerald hair, and green eyes that shone with white pupils, tossed the detached eye up and down playfully.

"*Oscha*, you Clean Ones take so long to kill someone," the little girl whined. She experimentally squished Galden's eye between her scaled fingers, popping it like a grape. Then her glowing-white pupils focused on the shadowy figures who emerged from the forest. "Was anyone else getting bored?"

Guffaws rippled from the new mass of shifters who stepped forward. All of them gazed upon our soldiers with glinting white pupils.

38

CHAIN OF COMMAND

LUCAS

Cayden and the Land Queen leapt back in line with us as the Sentient Fera stepped behind the little scaled girl. Was the girl leading them? From her emerald hair and eyes, she must have been a Relicblood of Ocean…

Could this be the Ancient my sons warned us of? The one who stole the corpse of Neverland's queen?

I turned to the Death King beside me. "Serdin, I think the girl is—"

"La'Lunaî," the Land Queen snarled. "We'd met her in Neverland months ago."

Alice growled to my other side. "What is she doing here?"

Serdin readied his long-staved scythe. "Walking into her death." The Death King sucked in a breath and shouted, "Stay back, demons! We have thousands of Reapers here to send you to Nira!"

Alice, Daniel and I raised our own Crystal blades around him, the Reapers in line behind us hollering supportive cries.

The little girl turned up her nose, and her horde chortled as if entertained. "And we have thousands to do the same to you all."

—an arrow sailed through the air from one of the Sentient's bows and slammed into Henry's thick hand beside Apson. The glass arrowhead shattered in a puff of sharp debris over his knuckles, digging into the Blacksmith's skin as he grunted in pain.

Black veins sprouted from the arrowhead's shattered pieces. The tendrils sank into Henry's bleeding pores and burned away his flesh, a black mist rising from his fingers in a simmering hiss.

Horrified, I heaved an alerting yell, "IT'S THOSE POISON-ARROWS!"

Henry's face wrenched with alarm, and without another wasted second, he raised his sword over his vein-infested hand—and sliced it off at the wrist.

The infected hand dropped at his feet. He cried in agony, tucking the bloody stump of his wrist under his opposite armpit, but managed to clench his teeth and bear the pain. It was horrific, but… impressively efficient, I had to admit. He'd stopped the poison from spreading just in time. Better his hand than his life.

—The demons hurtled after us in a frenzy, half brandishing swords and daggers imbued with infection Hallows and the other half falling back to let loose a hail of those same arrows.

"Shields!" Alice bellowed to the soldiers behind us. "Don't let those arrows so much as scratch you!"

In a cluster of metal screeches and clangs, the Reapers nearest us rushed to bring their shields forward and shoved them upward, connecting them to form a walled barrier around Alice, Serdin, Daniel and me, shrouding us in darkness.

Tnk! Tnk! Tnk! Tnk!

The thunderous storm vibrated against our barrier, hundreds of Metaglass arrowheads shattering on the other side of the shields.

Serdin barked. "Drop your shields! Before the infection spreads around them!"

The soldiers did so hurriedly, and once the daylight poured over us again, we saw the black tendrils of the poisons slithering over the shields at our feet. We leapt backward to keep away from them—

A demon from their frontlines rushed in and *sliced* a Metadagger over my neck, and I cried out in pain. It was a shallow cut, but the veins that spewed from the blade's new cracks latched onto the wound.

I growled and sliced my scythe into the Fera's chest, cutting his NecroSeam and felling him, but the pain in my neck swelled and pulsed, making me drop to one knee, using my staff as a crutch, panting heavily.

Alice noticed me drop and screamed, "Lucas, above you!"

My head snapped up. A second Sentient demon, one with wings, flew down from the skies wielding an infected longsword, cutting straight down toward my skull—

Screee—cuh-clang!

SMASH!

The clash of metal on glass sounded as two Crystal scythe blades, each held by different men in black and silver armor, caught the enemy sword in their crooks, shattering the Sentient's weapon in a shower of glass shards. The infectious veins inside were set free, clinging to the two aiding soldiers' weapons. The soldiers quickly discarded their scythes and readied their second blades which they held in their other hands—hands which each held a black Crest of diamonds over their knuckles.

I stared breathlessly at the helmed faces that hid behind their contrasting visors, whispering, "Boys…?"

My sons shoved both of their blades into the Sentient's chest and snapped its NecroSeam in unison. They turned their heads to me and lifted their visors, and I found myself gazing at two pairs of heterochromic eyes—a sight I hadn't seen in a very, *very* long time.

"Father," they said together, panting, "Sorry for the delay."

My boys… My eyes began to mist, the sudden flood of pride and bliss catching me by surprise to see my sons—both my sons, here together! —in the flesh. My laugh was nearly a joyous sob. "Boys—*rrgh…!*" I doubled over as the wound on my neck festered and pulsed. The infectious tendrils there crawled up to my jaw, numbing my mouth.

"Death!" Xavier cursed and crouched beside me, fetching one of the several pouches tied to his belt and pulling out a vial filled with violet-glowing liquid. "They have the infection weapons here?"

Alexander growled as he kicked back another Sentient. "I'd hoped we'd seen the last of them in Culatia."

"Apparently not," Xavier growled, his wolf ears growing through the slits in his helm. He popped the cork off the radiant vial he held and poured the strange liquid over the wound on my neck. "I'm only glad we still have some of these cures left over."

The pain in my jaw and neck quickly dissipated, a hissing sound rising from under my wolf ears. The cut at my neck still stung slightly, but the rooting veins seemed to have dissipated entirely. I clutched my neck, stupefied. I'd heard they'd discovered a soul-cure, but Bloods, I wasn't expecting it to work so swiftly.

Xavier clasped my hand and pulled me to my feet, his lips tugging into a bearded smile. "Father, good to see you in person again."

I let out a hollow laugh, tears hitting again as I squeezed his hand heartily. "That it is, son. That it is."

"Boys?!" piped Alice from a yard away in the mass of fighters. "Bloods be good, is that you?!"

They both held up their weapons briefly in greeting. "Hello, Mother. We've brought your vassals back, as requested."

"Aye!" Nathaniel guffawed as he ran to my side and sliced his Crystal cutlass into an approaching Sentient. My bear-eared vassal gave me a toothy grin. "Long time no see, *Da'torr!*"

My wife's vassal, Aiden, flew down from the skies and touched down beside her dutifully, launching Crystal arrow after Crystal arrow at a cluster of demons. "And what a long time it's been!" he said to Alice.

Serdin kicked away his own foe and leapt backward beside Xavier, flicking him an acknowledging glance. "Xavier, awfully good to see you alive. And not attached to your brother, I suppose."

Xavier grimaced. "Yes, it's been quite relieving, Sire."

Serdin snorted. "Don't bother with any 'sire this' or 'sire that' nonsense. I see you've a crown of your own now, I expect my daughter would rather you act like royalty." His eyes narrowed. "How *is* my daughter? And grandson?"

"Far away from here," Xavier emphasized. "I've been instructed to return posthaste, else I'll likely never hear the end of it even as a ghost."

"Likely not, no," Serdin agreed.

I cut down another Sentient and grunted. "That is *if* you still have a soul to listen. These infectious weapons make this battle more dangerous than we're familiar with."

Alexander muttered, "Not to mention, we only have so many cures left after what happened in Culatia. Best we didn't get cocky."

I lifted an eyebrow. "What happened in Culatia—?"

Three Sentients came charging at me with Metaswords, and I prepared my scythe—

Crrrack—ZAP! BRUMMM!

A powerful bolt of lightning suddenly shot out of Xavier's thrusting hand, his Crest of black diamonds shifting into a scarlet Sky mark, and the bolt crashed over the demons coming at me. All three beasts were sent flying several yards back by the blow, lost in the mass.

We all stared at the static still snapping from Xavier's fingers, stunned into silence. Xavier looked at his hand and, seeming to brood over a resentful thought, let out a sigh. "A lot happened in Culatia, Father. We can explain later."

"Yes," Alexander grumbled ruefully. There was something foreboding about his expression, his scowl darker than usual. But he snapped out of it quickly as another cluster of Fera came for us, and he swept his hand in front of him, a powerful gale blowing from the motion and sending the demons spiraling away. His furious gaze returned as he rumbled, *"Later."*

From within the mass, Daniel came to join our protective group. Daniel saw the twins and paused. "Xavier!" he laughed with delight. "Alexander! Seamstress prick me, it's been ages since I've seen the both of you in the same place!"

They both nodded in kind and greeted cordially, "Good to see you, Father Daniel."

Daniel's bat wings folded in question as he frowned at Alexander. "Hang on. You aren't wearing your marriage-stud, Alexander? Did you decide to wait on it?"

Alex grunted a laugh. "Not exactly, Father Daniel." His eyes flicked up as he spotted someone flying over Daniel's head, and he pointed with his chin. "You can ask your daughter about it, though."

Behind Daniel, Lilliana touched down and touched backs with him, her dual-scythes held before her at the ready. "Father," Lilliana greeted, "Good, we arrived in time."

"Lilli!" Daniel cried with glee, craning his neck to see her. "I wish it were under better circumstances, but Bloods am I glad to see you!"

"You as well, Father," she said in a chuckle. "Since you're here, I may as well introduce you to someone."

"Hmm—?" Daniel was cut off when a chained scythe swept through a mass of Sentients and cut them down, clearing a path for the plated Reaper who leapt over their corpses.

I knew that chained weapon anywhere. The Reaper, Jaq, lifted his visor as he trotted up to Daniel and Lilliana—then reeled Lilliana in by the waist and stole a deep kiss.

Daniel and I staggered at the sight.

When they finally parted, Jaq panted. "Bloods, when I lost you in there, I thought you might've been skewered!" He feverishly kissed down her neck. "For the love of Death, don't just fly off next time! Scared me damn near to death!"

"All right, all right," Lilliana chuckled and pushed him at arms' length, turning to Daniel. "Father, I don't think you've formally met. This is my husband, Jaq."

Daniel and I stared blankly.

Jaq grabbed Daniel's hand and gave a vigorous shake. "Hey there, nice to meet ya, pops. Love your daughter. You raised one Void of a woman."

"—Jaqelle?!" the voice of Apson blurted from the mass. The old viper shoved his way to us, spotting his grandson and laughed. "Hah, *hah!* You're here! Thank Land you made it in one piece!"

"Grandad!" Jaq clasped hands with Apson cheerily—then both men pulled the other aside as two separate demons charged for them, and they shoved their Crystal blades into the beasts' chests. Jaq threw his head over at Lilliana. "Glad you're here. You can meet my wife."

Lilli interrupted. "We've already met, Jaq. Good to see you again, Roarlord. Though I wish it were under better circumstances."

"You're Jaqelle's… wife?" Apson said incredulously. Then he belted a laugh and shook her hand. "Hah! Hah, hah, hah! Splendid, *splendid*, my girl! When was the wedding?"

"Last night," Jaq said. "It's a long story."

Daniel and I still stared, stunned. Then we questioned in unison, "What?"

—A piercing screech split through the clamor. All Sentients suddenly dropped their weapons and cowered at the sound, clutching their ears and dropping to the ground as if a great weight were pushing them down.

The only Sentient left standing was that little Seadragon girl. The leader of the horde.

"Cilia!" She shrieked, causing the lesser sentients to writhe and squeal in fright. "CILIA! I know you're here with the Reapers somewhere, little kitten! Come out with your pathetic band of weaklings and meet your Cleansing!"

The girl rushed through the mass as quick as a whip, and as she passed *us*, the Sentients in our area uncurled from their unseen suffering and pushed to their feet, engaging in combat once more. Only this time, there were more of them.

We all braced as the onslaught came again and again. We cut them down, they sliced us with their infection weapons, we administered the soul-cure, and repeated the cycle over and over and over…

It was utter madness.

Serdin hollered mid-combat, "There's too many of them—*ARGH!*"

Serdin was struck in the throat with an infection-arrow. The glass tip shattered on impact and didn't pierce through, but the shower of shards lodged in his neck regardless, the poisonous veins slithering into his pores.

The king hacked and stumbled, but didn't fall as the other soldiers did. His flesh remained as it was, if bleeding and scraped.

I pushed out a breath of relief. *Thank the Seamstress for Serdin's Infeciovoking,* I thought. *His immunity must be keeping him alive—*

The little fish-girl from before, the Sentient demon queen, shoved her hand straight into Serdin's chest while he was still recovering. A trickle of blood flooded up his lips, and he collapsed to his knees, struggling to even wheeze as the fish-girl ripped out his heart—along with his soul--and devoured them whole.

"SERDIN!" I shouted and scrambled for him, cutting through the Sentients in my way—

Another beast drove their Metasword through a seam in the back of my armor, piercing through my chest and breastplate. The poison within it festered through my stomach and burned into my chest, gripping my throbbing heart and choking my pulse.

The battlefield became blurred, swaying and thumping along with my fading heartbeat. The noise dimmed in my ears, hearing my wife shouting my name. Dizzy, and wheezing, I turned and found her running toward me. She didn't see the arrow coming for her. She didn't know to evade as it drove into the base of her neck under her helm, the glass arrowhead shattering, infectious tendrils crawling into her brain and burning the flesh from her face.

I fell to the dirt, my pulse pounding softer as I heard my sons calling desperately, their voices faint.

"No…!" Xavier hurriedly rummaged through the pouches at his belt for a vial of the soul-cure, but each glass was empty. "No, no, no, we've used them all…! Father…! Stay with us!"

My gaze drifted blearily to Alice. Her disfigured face dripped with Alexander's tears as he cradled her head, screaming.

"Father!" Xavier was panicking, still looking for a vial that hadn't been emptied. He found no success. "Please—We'll find Bianca! She can make more, just…! Just hold on…!"

My vision began to spot with black patches, dimming Xavier's heterochromic eyes as I strained to keep focus on them. "Bloods how… long it's been…" I wheezed, touching my shaking fingers—which had rotted in some places and showed my boney knuckles—to his bearded face. Feeling him there, so tangible and real, somehow brought such… ease… "At least I… was granted one last chance…" I hacked painfully. "To s-see you alive again…"

"Father!"

His face was blotted out entirely.

XAVIER

"FATHER!" I screamed, cradling his head—now burned and rotted as his sockets had sunken and his cheekbones poked through his flesh—heaving another cry. *"FATHER…!"*

His eyes glazed over. The hand he'd touched to my face limped to the dirt.

He was gone. Mother was gone. The Death King was gone.

They were all gone.

I laid father down, blinking through tears as the rage burned in my chest, lightning thundering through my blood as I leapt to my feet and *thrust* my hands out wildly, letting the lightning in my soul explode in a vicious scream. With each Sentient who dared to approach me, I alternated between lightning and ice, zapping and freezing, zapping and freezing, each hand assigned its designated Hallows—

That same, grating shriek came from La'Lunaî again, causing the Sentients to cringe and drop to their knees, like they did before. La'Lunaî sped away from the battlefield and began climbing the mountains suddenly. Her horde scuttled after her, funneling up the mountain.

Master! The voice of Hugh split through my thoughts then. *Something's happened at the ship…!*

My rage quelled, tears still hot on my face as fear spiked in its place. "Willow…!" I breathed in horror, watching as the horde of demons climbed the mountains.

Directly where we'd left our ship.

"Hugh," I panted urgently through our mental connection, "Tell everyone to get out of there, now! And for the love of Death, tell our Ancient demons to brace themselves!"

Yes, Master! Hugh confirmed, and the connection line ended in my thoughts.

"Your Highness!" a new voice called from the sky, making me whirl. A wolf-eared man riding a Flamedragon had his beast land in front of me. When he lifted his visor, I recognized him as Fangs Lastings, one of our generals.

From atop the tall, marble-scaled reptile, he surveyed the disaster around us. His face wrenched with shocked grief to see the rotted faces of my father and mother among the dead. When his gaze fell on the Death King's body, his majesty's chest still wide open where the demon girl had plucked out his heart, Lastings absently slid off his Flamedragon, breathless as he cupped a hand to his mouth. Then he looked at me heavily.

And knelt in reverence.

"Your… Majesty," Lastings rasped, his voice gritty and poignant.

The sound of it cut a hole in my chest. *That's right,* I realized as a new fear thrummed in my blood, the gravity of the situation sinking in. *With the king dead, that means Willow and I are now…* I swallowed hard, stifling a tremor.

Those still left alive from the frontlines clustered around me. Countless Brother and Sister Reapers I didn't recognize came forward and knelt to me. Even familiar faces—of Jaq and Lilli and Matthiel—stepped through the mass and mimicked the gesture. Neal and Octavius stood off to the side and awkwardly bowed their heads. Neither man was Grimish, but they seemed to know that following the other Reapers' examples was protocol. Anabelle and Roji came and nodded to me in a dreary acknowledgement. Linus and Cayden stood together and gripped hands as they gave a shallow bow. Kurrick, lingering beside Anabelle, hung his head with curled lion ears. Bloods, having so many eyes on me stiffened my spine, my hands balling nervously.

The only Reaper who had yet to take any action was Alexander. I watched my brother gently lay our mother's corpse on the ground as he rose to his feet, inhaled a pained breath, then turned and strode toward me. He walked past the unfamiliar Reapers. He walked pasted the members of his team. And he walked past Anabelle and Roji, halting before me. With red-rimmed eyes, he held a fist to his chest and, like those before him, sank to one knee, bowing his head.

"Sire," Alex croaked, his throat raw. "What are your orders?"

I shuddered. Hearing it from him, of all people, bit deeper than it ever could with the others. I shut my eyes and sucked in a sharp breath through my nose before turning toward the climbing mass of demons. I bent to pick up my scythes that I'd dropped beside Father's body and pointed up the mountains with one. "The Fera are headed for your queen and infant prince!" I bellowed for all to hear. "We may be out of the soul-cure, but we know they only had a limited supply of those infection-weapons to begin with! If they have any left, they'll be out soon! Hold strong! *For Her Majesty Death*!"

The Reapers ripped determined war cries and moved out. Some climbed on their Bonedragons, Flamedragons and horses while others hustled on foot and launched into the sky if they had wings. Roji whooped and had his Stormchasers take flight to race ahead of them, the Sky King himself mounting his Skydragon and flying after them. Anabelle shouted at her own soldiers, and they trailed close behind the rest.

Alex nodded to me and slammed down his visor, calling for his team to follow him up. Daniel Tessinger, the only one from Father's initial squad still alive, launched into the air beside his bat-winged daughter to soar over them.

Fangs Lastings nearly joined them on his Flamedragon, but I ran in front of the reptile to stop him. "Fangs!" I shouted up at him. "I need to borrow your dragon!"

39

FINAL WAVE

WILLOW

I stared at Grandfather's horrific corpse on the deck, clutching baby Lucas to my chest. Grandfather's azure eyes were splotched with faint black veins along with his spoiled face. Yet his expression, though pained, seemed to welcome the long-awaited relief.

Hugh and Vendy let out a scream, Vendy drawing her sword while Hugh withdrew his scythe blades, the two running over to me protectively.

"What in Bloods just happened?!" Vendy hollered, her rabbit ears swiveling like mad, still looking for Macarius. "Where'd he go?!"

My voice was tight. "He… he took the Orbs. He's gone."

"Gone where?" Hugh demanded.

My two vassals, Rossette and Nikolai, came rushing over from the upper deck to see what the matter was—

"DREAM!" my grandmother shrieked suddenly from the cabin's door-frame. She shielded little Eryn's view with a trembling hand, passing him over to Vendy as she rushed to crouch beside Grandfather's body, sobbing, "Dream…! What's happened?!"

"—What's happened indeed!" Hecrûshou barked as he hopped onto the deck and brandished his Crystal trident in alarm. The demon flicked his glowing-white gaze at Grandfather and growled. "Who is responsible?! Are they still here?!"

The other three demons in our party clambered on deck in a hurry, on full alert as they searched the landscape frantically. With all the noise fluttering about, the rest of those still left on the ship came out to see what was wrong. The Healers and Alchemists were the first to funnel out of the cabin. Then Oliver and Fuérr. Then Dalminia and her two daughters. Ringëd, Mikani and

Claude were last. Their voices stumbled over each other in a noisy tangle as they all fired frightened questions at me, the knot of sound growing so massive, my fox ears draped to my neck and I shouted, "ENOUGH!"

Their jabbering died into a strained, anxious silence.

I took in a slow breath, explaining as evenly as my shaking voice would allow, "Macarius was here. He… killed Grandfather. And has stolen the Orbs of Azure. He fled into Aspirre. We cannot go after him without the Orbs."

There was a resounding silence on the deck. The only sounds came from a passing breeze and Grandmother's wailing over Dream's corpse, her sobs incomprehensible over the constant screeching of our black birds.

"—Aaah!" one of our demons, Khol, suddenly let out an undignified shriek and clutched his chest as if having a heart attack. His webbed ears flicked from under the knitted purple hat that hugged his scaled, bald head. Then his eyes hollowed with fright as he glanced at the other demons timidly. "Did… did you all feel that?"

Miranda also clutched her chest with a hard sneer and tightened her grip on her cane. "You'd have to be dead not to feel that Weight," the old demon growled.

The dragon-winged Ancient, Thörd, folded his lavender wings and scowled. "Thörd be knowing that Weight anywhere."

"It's La'Lunaî." Hecrûshou's voice was dark as he turned to me. "I'm sorry. She pushed her Weight over the land to look for *us*… and even as suppressed as we've kept our Weights, I've no doubts she could feel us here."

Thörd hopped onto the ship's railing and peered down the mountain. "*Skrii!* Whole horde ees being the coming ones," he said and pointed a scaled finger. "Thörd be thinking we want to leave now?"

Miranda grumbled and looked at me. "I think that's best, miss Death. With so many children on board, I doubt you'll want them anywhere near a horde of Sentients that size. Though perhaps if *we* four leave alone, we can direct the horde elsewhere. It's our Weights that are giving away our location."

I glanced at Lucas in my arms, the baby fussing softly. Grandmother still sobbed over Grandfather's corpse, Eryn began crying in Vendy's hold, Oliver and Fuérr clutched Dalminia's skirts alongside her two daughters. Miranda was right—we had far too many children to risk them staying here.

"But," I began, hesitant, "If you leave, we *also* run the risk of being found by stray Fera who wandered from the pack. If you all aren't there to ward them away, we're faced with danger regardless."

Hecrûshou tapped a ponderous finger over his glowing trident. Then, as if having a thought, snapped his head to Khol, whose bald head was occupied by Hecrûshou's snoozing Bindragon. "Khol," Hecrûshou said, "for once, your weaker Weight may be of use to us."

Khol's webbed ears folded as his scaled face blanched. "W-what?"

Miranda laughed and slapped a wrinkled hand over Hecrûshou's shoulder. "Good thinking, Shou! Khol is still an Ancient—he's strong enough to send any newborn Fera away, but is still weak enough that La'Lunaî will ignore him and focus on the three of us."

Thörd guffawed and clapped his hands. "Hah! Thörd see! Ees being a good plan!"

Khol swallowed hard as the Bindragon lifted its head from his crown curiously, Khol's voice fracturing. "W-wh… what plan?"

"Go with the Clean Ones," Hecrûshou said. He shouldered his trident and hopped onto the railing beside Thörd and Miranda, leaping off to dash down the mountain, calling back, "Protect the children!"

Khol paled ghost white, flinching in a yelp as we all stared at him. He looked from me to the others, fidgeting with his knuckles and sweating bullets now. "But… but I…"

Little Fuérr suddenly stepped up to grab Khol's hand. The Bindragon happily slithered down from Khol's head and wrapped around both his and Fuérr's scaled wrists, playfully sticking them together. Oliver fluttered his wings and flapped over next, snagging Khol's other hand.

Khol flushed scarlet. But soon, he stood straighter and declared shakily, "A-all right! Everyone follow me!" His voice still cracked with '*me*' but he managed to keep his stride steady while hurrying off the ship, leading everyone in the opposite direction from the other demons.

My grandmother and I were the only ones left on the deck; the only ones left with Grandfather's corpse. Vendy and Hugh waited for us at the bottom of the ramp, baby Eryn wailing in Vendy's hold.

Lucas whined in my arms, and I held him tighter while walking to Grandmother. I knelt beside her and leaned my head on her shoulder. "He lived a long life," I whispered, my heart squeezing to say it. "Longer than any shifter."

Grandmother threw her arms over my shoulders and wept. "It was still too soon…"

My eyes welled and a tear spilled, but I breathed deep to calm myself and hushed, "Perhaps not to him… Come." I rose and balanced Lucas with one arm while offering her my other. "I'm not the only one with a son to look after."

Grandmother rubbed her eyes and nodded solemnly, her legs trembling as I pulled her to her feet. She composed herself as best she could, her face still wet with tears as she drifted down the ramp beside me like an empty shell. She took Eryn from Vendy with a breathless word of thanks, and followed after

Khol and the others. I stepped heavily behind her with Lucas, and Vendy and Hugh walked at either side of me protectively.

"Willow!" a familiar woman's voice called from the sky.

Then a rush of wind blew my long hair back, and I whirled to see a massive Flamedragon with marbled, black-and-red scales had landed near me. And riding atop that Flamedragon was my azure-haired mother.

"Dear!" Mother slid off the large dragon and helped down a little girl that had ridden with her. Mother's eyes were red and bloodshot, stale tears coating her face. "Thank Bloods you're all right…!"

"Mother," I croaked, "Grandfather is—"

"I know," she said, wiping her eyes. A small squeal leaked from her throat. "As is your father."

I stiffened. "Father is…?"

"I Saw the visions as they happened," she explained, her tone agonized. "I was already on my way to you, I-I couldn't warn them—oh, I'm just glad you're all right…!"

She held me tight, but was sure to make room for Lucas, whose cheek she brushed with a delicate finger. She gestured to him questioningly, asking if she could hold him. I passed Lucas to her gently. She sniffed a soft chuckle, rocking the newborn with a twitching smile as she cooed, "Hello there, little one… I'm your new grandmother."

The little girl who came with my mother peeked her head from around her skirts. I paused at that bronze face. The girl had curling ewe horns and fluffy brown hair, her face so familiar, I couldn't help but stare.

"I know you," I said and knelt to the girl. "You're the girl from Lindel, aren't you? The one whose messenger was…" I trailed off as the memory came back to me. Yes, this was the girl whose mother brutally killed her crow. Bloods, but that was years ago.

The girl shied away, squinting at me. "Who're you?"

I blinked, realizing she'd only seen me in my illusion disguise before. I whistled once, calling for Jewel to come to me, and my little songcrow fluttered over obediently to alight on my extended finger.

The girl gasp at Jewel. "The little birdy!"

"We met in Lindel some years ago," I said and evoked my illusion Hallows over my white hair, changing the strands to a charcoal grey. "I was under an illusion then, so you wouldn't have recognized me. This is how I truly look." I dismissed my Hallows and had my hair bleed ashen again—

The girl flung her arm around my neck and held on tight. "Missy Reaper!" She cried, her grip crushing now. "I-I've been looking for you!"

"Have you?" I chuckled. Then I realized something and asked, "But why? Where are your parents?"

She wiped at her wet eyes and sniffled. "They got crushed when those dragony's smashed a building on them. Then mum got turned'ed into a demon and-and I kilt her with one of the Reaper thingies I found." She presented a radiant scythe-sphere she'd kept in her skirt's pocket. "And I been looking for you after. I didn't know what to do, s-so…"

I held an aghast hand my mouth in shock. For a child of her age to endure events that would break even the most hardened of adults was nothing short of astounding… and *deeply* heartbreaking.

I cupped her face. "I'm sorry… I don't know if I ever caught your name?"

She rubbed an arm under her runny nose. "Milann."

"Milann," I echoed. "Would you like to come with me when this is over? It will be beneath Everland, away from the sun, but we can give you a home there if you wish? Or I suppose we could arrange something with another family if you'd prefer—"

She squeezed my ribs. "I want to go with you!" She bleated and buried her face in my chest. "Please…?"

I stroked her fluffy hair and hugged her back. "Of course. And we'll be sure that everyone knows that you were chosen by a messenger. There will be no question there if I can help it—"

Skririririririririiii!

A grating shriek split the air, and a dark shadow spilled into my peripherals from behind a boulder—

"Get down!" I bellowed, wheeling the girl around protectively and, after plucking the scythe-sphere from her fingers, I pushed her away and pressed the sealing-rune on the sphere.

The glowing metal melted in my palm like liquid, shaping into, thank Death, a long-staved scythe that solidified in my grasp with a hushing clash.

From around the boulder, the shadow I saw before leapt for me, its boney claws dripping black ichor as it ripped a curdling screech. I sidestepped its swipe and sliced my blade into its chest, snapping the beast's NecroSeam, and its corpse dropped at my feet.

—A flash of pain swelled at my back and pelvis, and I doubled over, seeth-ing. *Bloods,* I cursed to myself. *I still haven't recovered from the delivery.*

My step faltered, and Mother hurried to look me over, Lucas now crying in her hold. More guttural screeches sounded in the nearby distance from down the mountain.

Vendy and Hugh slid in front of me with their weapons held at the ready.

"Go on ahead!" Vendy said. "We'll keep them back!"

Hugh swallowed nervously but held his ground beside her, the two of them starting down the mountain where the screeches were sounding.

"Come!" Mother guided Milann and me over to the armored Flamedragon she'd arrived on. "Let's get back to the others quickly!"

"Oh, Death," I grimaced, my neck craning to see the full size of the dragon. I groaned at its leathery wings. "Why is it *always* flying?"

More screeches came from the approaching demons.

Grudgingly, I climbed on the dragon's saddle, helping Milann up next and set the girl in front of me. I reverted Milann's scythe back to its spherical form and tucked it into a pocket sewn to the saddle. Mother handed Lucas to me and climbed up herself before taking Lucas back while I held Milann secure and kicked the dragon into motion.

The reptile blurted a short cry and launched into the air. I had to hold down a gush of vomit that lurched up my stomach, the ground shrinking smaller and smaller as we climbed higher and higher. My grown fox ears stuck tight to my neck in fright, but I set my jaw and latched my claws into the squirming saddle, keeping both Milann and myself on this Bloody thing as best I could. I was relieved my mother had taken Lucas. As much as I wanted to hold my son, I didn't trust that my thighs were strong enough yet to keep straddling the saddle by themselves. I needed my arms to stay on. Mother, on the other hand, *hadn't* just come out of labor and her muscles were far more reliable than mine at the moment—

The Flamedragon jerked downward to avoid a screaming demon with wings. Our reptile spat a slosh of fire at the thing, knocking it back, but three more demons appeared and dove for us. Our dragon lurched and leaned and swatted its tail at the things, but all it could do was distract them. I touched the pocket sewn on the saddle where I'd put Milann's scythe-sphere, and my fingers itched to grab it. If I could just rely on my legs long enough to slice at these things…!

Another beast swiped for us, and Milann screamed.

I shouted, "Oh, to Void with it!" I clenched my legs around the saddle and plucked out the scythe-sphere, having the scythe materialize in a golden glitter and slicing at the swarming Fera in a furious snarl. "Get away from my family—!"

I leaned an inch too far off the saddle. My legs lost grip, and I slipped off, screaming as the wind rushed up and I dropped straight down—

My stomach lurched to a sudden stop. Someone had caught me.

"For the love of *you*," the black-armored man who held me said in an exasperated tone, "will you at least *try* to be more careful?"

I was staring up at the heterochromic eyes of my husband.

"Xavier?" I questioned, incredulous. "Where did you…?"

My gaze whipped around us. He was on a Flamedragon of his own, the reptile breathing streams of fire at the winged demons to keep them back.

Xavier grunted and set me in front of him, lacing his arms through mine and keeping a secure hold of my waist as he gripped the saddle's horn. "The horde we were fighting down there changed course straight for you all suddenly," he explained. "Where is Lucas?"

"With my mother up there," I said and pointed to the Flamedragon above us.

"Thank Bloods." He pulled on the saddle to make the dragon lift upward until we flapped beside my mother and the children. He frowned when he spotted Milann. "Don't I know you?" he asked.

I cleared my throat. "Darling, this is the girl from Lindel some years ago. We've a few things to discuss when we get the chance—"

"Hold that thought." Xavier shoved a hand to the side—and a bolt of lightning blasted from his palm, striking a demon who'd soared by us and sent it flying back at an incredible distance. He re-secured his grip on the saddle and muttered, "Perhaps we ought to talk later?"

"Right," I agreed, craning my neck down to see the rocky walls of the mountain far below us. I felt sick and grimaced. "And of course, I had to drop the Bloody scythe."

"You're in no condition to fight regardless," Xavier chided. He nodded to my mother. "Come, I can keep them back for a time, but we need to find a safer location." He zapped another flying demon and turned back to me. "Where are our Ancients?"

"Most of them went a different way to lead the horde away," I explained. "They left Khol with us, but we were separated."

My mother called from her dragon and pointed with her chin. "I think I see them down there, dear!"

Xavier blasted three more demons with ice this time, then moved our dragon in the direction she indicated. "Let's get to them quickly, then."

HUGH

I hurried down the mountain path while keeping the scythe blades Master gave me ready, running beside Lady Vendy toward the demonic screeches.

When the horde fell into view—

A skeletal monster screamed and thrashed for my face, and I quickly ducked under it and *slammed* my scythe into its chest, ripping it toward the heart as

Master had taught me. A solid snap sounded, and the demon's corpse dropped at my feet, its rotten soul hissing off its bones.

I panted in shock. "I… I did it!"

Lady Vendy thumped my back encouragingly. "Great! First kill. Congrats—"

Another beast came for her and she twirled around it, swept her Crystal sword over its neck, lopped off its head and sliced into its chest in a grunt. When the Fera dropped, her rabbit ears swiveled forward, her brow furrowing. "Wait. The little guys aren't the only ones here."

I trotted to her side and overlooked the terrain. There was a moving sea of shifters—demons and soldiers alike—brawling in a chaotic heap. The few lesser creatures that leapt for Lady Vendy and me were the most disorganized, thrashing at anything that moved without true purpose.

Our Ancients were here fighting as well, trading blows with that same little girl demon from Neverland. Familiar faces sprouted in the mass, and my grown lion ear perked. "Look, it's *Da'torr*!" I said to Lady Vendy.

Da'torr Alexander sliced into demon after demon, Sentients and sticky beasts falling in quick succession, *Da'torr* seeming lost in a furious haze like I'd never seen in him before.

Lady Vendy cocked back her sword and sprinted toward him. "Come on!"

I fumbled after her—

"*Ghk…!*" Someone's boney fingers caught me by the neck from behind, and I was yanked back and lifted off the ground. I squirmed and wriggled, but my assailant's hold was too strong.

They flung me several yards back, my spine *cracking* against the rocky wall of the mountain path, rock and dirt crumbling around me as pain flared from my back. I let out an agonized cry, trying to move, but it hurt to do even the smallest motion. I simply sat there against the rock wall, helpless as my attacker stalked toward me.

"*D… Da'torr…*" I wheezed while tapping into our mental connection to reach Alexander. "If-If you can reach me, I… I'll need a resurrection soon…!"

Da'torr's voice thankfully fuzzed in my thoughts soon after. *On my way, Hugh,* he said. *Hold on.*

My attacker was only yards away now. With it being so close, I could finally make out some of its features. It was a girl's figure, a teen's, maybe. She had cropped, blond hair and wore a simple, violet smock that was torn and ragged from all the fighting. When she was only a few feet away, she peered down at me with glowing white pupils.

My breath fell away from me. Looming over me now with a puzzled expression and perked lion ears was a painfully familiar face.

It was the face of my sister.

"Sy…?" I wheezed.

She stopped cold, her lion ears flicking back as she registered my face. Her brow knotted desperately as my vision started fading.

"Hugh…?" She whispered hauntingly.

Then the world boiled black as I fell into numbness.

ALEXANDER

I cut down another demon and made my way to Hugh.

The boy was just up ahead against a crumbled wall. By the look of his bloodied and crooked state, I wagered he was already dead.

There was a Sentient standing over him, and my legs hustled faster. Vendy had arrived and helped slice down the demons in my way, also seeing that Hugh was in trouble of having his soul eaten, and she let out a curse while speeding up. I only thanked Death the horde seemed to be out of their infection-weapons. It certainly made killing them easier—

That damned little Seadragon Ancient was thrown to the ground in a powerful *crrrack* of lightning, blocking Vendy and my path.

The one who'd zapped her, apparently Thörd, touched down beside the new crater and folded his leathery wings, his arms still snapping with electricity. Hecrûshou and Miranda came to stand over the crater as well, taking offensive stances.

An angry snarl came from the crater. La'Lunaî's scaled arms reached over the hole and she dug her claws in the dirt to keep herself up, glaring at the three Ancients surrounding her.

"Thörd!" She sneered at the lavender-haired Skydragon. "What are you doing here?! And where is Cilia?!"

Hecrûshou lowered his trident threateningly beside her skull and growled, "Cilia is on her way here… with reinforcements of our own."

I scowled. We'd lost Cilia in Culatia when she and Kael fell down the arena. He must have been lying to throw La'Lunaî off.

Miranda huffed and lifted her chest. "Look at your pathetic army now, La'Lunaî. Your numbers are almost squandered entirely. Your advantage shattered with the last of your infection-weapons. Do you truly risk being Cleansed by all these Reapers for the sake of your pride?"

La'Lunaî's face paled, and her webbed ears folded down as she looked about the battlefield. Indeed, her soldiers were dying by the second.

Fear wrenching her features, she let out a hideous shriek, her face flickering with black sludge, and the surrounding demons—Ancients and underlings alike—were forced to their knees by some unseen force. Miranda, Hecrûshou and Thörd were all pushed back, and the moment she had her opening, La'Lunaî sprang out of the crater and grabbed the nearest Sentient of hers with wings.

"Away!" She screeched—and her horde jerked into action to obey.

She launched out of the battlefield wildly, and the rest of her horde, as if compelled to follow her against their will, scattered in a heartbeat.

But the Sentient who stood over Hugh's corpse, I noticed, hesitated. Her limbs twitched and pulsed as if trying to move as she was ordered, but still, she lingered. Only when La'Lunaî gave another shriek from the skies did the Sentient girl snap out of her daze and scurry away with the rest of them.

As the fading mass of beasts retreated over the mountains, I gripped Hecrûshou's shoulder appreciatively.

"Brilliant work," I commended, sliding off my helm. "We can't thank you enough for the support."

The shark dug his trident in the dirt and grunted. "Testify on our behalf when we plea for citizenship," he said, "and I'll consider that enough 'thanks'."

"That's more than fair." I shielded a hand over my eyes to watch the dissipating horde against the sun's glare. "I should think this turn of events will only help your case. There are far too many witnesses here that can testify how the demons we fought against were wielding infection-weapons. That links them directly to Macarius's cult. They must have supplied them to La'Lunaî, which gives us undeniable proof that they colluded with demons." I grinned. "Which means our excuse for colluding with *other* demons will seem like the obvious 'self-defense' choice any sane shifter would make."

Hecrûshou chuckled at that. "Fair."

40

THE ONLY CHOICE

ANABELLE

I sat poised on my new throne in Everland's palace, accepting each individual favor that my new, adoring subjects lined up to offer me.

It had been three days since the war resolved and the fires were dampened. There was much to repair within the city, many families were without homes. I'd ordered for government buildings to house those unfortunate shifters until the repairs were finished, and opened trade with Neverland to import produce and grain that this country was severely lacking. Now that I had reclaimed both continents in my father's lands, after five centuries of separation, the realm of Land was united again under a single domain.

My domain.

The thought of it shuddered my blood in fright, but I kept my proper posture and thanked another shifter for their gift, which Cayden and Linus took from the left side of my throne and set in the ever-growing pile behind them. Genevieve then directed the person around the line toward the exit, allowing the next shifter in line to come forward. *This is what I've prepared for,* I reminded myself. *This is why Dream kept me alive for so long. To bring back the Old Kingdom and aid the Shadowblood.*

The reminder of Dream, my foster father, was a bitter dust in my chest. Dream was dead. Macar had finally killed him.

And now he has the Orbs of Azure.

To the right of my throne, an armored, lion-tailed man cleared his throat, snapping me out of my daze. It was Kurrick. he stood at attention with his sword strapped to his waist and his hands folded behind him in a formal manner. He wore no helm today, his scarred face and honey-blond hair free and exposed for all to see. The coin he used to wear around his neck was gone, as it had been for the past few months. Its absence was irking, but I supposed that was his intention.

He cleared his throat again and flicked his amber eyes at the line in front of me, gesturing to the next person in line that I had accidentally ignored.

I quickly thanked them for their gift, Cayden and Linus took it from them and set it aside in the pile, and Genevieve directed the shifter around toward the exit. It had become a rather monotonous routine for us.

Kurrick leaned to the side and murmured under his breath to me, "Distracted, Your Majesty?"

I thanked the next person before whispering a reply. "How can I not be? There are a few dozen changes shifting the political paradigm in nearly all the realms—and that's just from *this* year. My head is spinning simply attempting to count them all."

I was the new queen of two continents that had been at war for centuries, Macar was surely building a resistance in the background, Roji was the Sky King of Culatia and setting a new standard due to his marriage with the Ocean Princess, I needed new generals, new Hands, new representatives for the courts, new ambassadors for each continent—Bloods, I needed to re-establish the original capital in the Gyle Islands and reveal my father's hidden palace that had been buried in a dense jungle for centuries and claim it as the Land realm's Grand Capital…

I sighed and sank back into my throne. My country wasn't the only one that needed major changes in authority. Grim's monarch has passed to its new successor. The Death King, his Eyes, and his First Fangs of Low Everland needed to be replaced. With Willow as the new queen, she had to establish her cabinet… and introduce new policies that, for the Death realm, would no doubt prove to be controversial for her people. There was no guarantee the Grimish council would allow such drastic changes to be implemented. To start, she wished to amend one of the Laws of Death and add certain allowances for living shifters whose souls were severed too early. Changing a law that has been around since Death's first incarnation was challenging enough—but perhaps not as challenging as her plan to grant citizenship rights to Sentient Necrofera. The Reapers had spent thousands of years killing the Necrofera indiscriminately. For her to propose that we give them rights would surely be met with resistance. But, as Roji, Crysalette, Dalminia and I discussed, we fellow Relicbloods would stand with Willow's proposal and give her our unified approval across the realms.

A chuckle bounced from beside my throne where Cayden and Linus were stacking the last of the gifts. When the last shifter in line bowed and took their leave, leaving us to our privacy in the expansive throne room, Linus slid an arm around Cayden's waist and pulled the lion's face to his, stealing his lips.

I saw Kurrick grow rigid to my other side. He blushed slightly and looked at me questioningly, starting to point at them weakly, but paused midway as a thought seemed to dawn on him, and he mumbled, "Ah…"

I chuckled and patted his plated arm. "So oblivious." My back cricked softly when I rose to my feet, relishing the break from sitting on that chair for the past two hours. "Where is the Death family?" I asked Kurrick. "I wished to speak with them for a moment."

Kurrick strode at my side as we left the throne room. "They're in the gardens, I believe, assessing their travel plans back to Grim. There is much for them to do upon their return to the caves."

I hummed. "When do they plan to leave?"

"They hope to depart tomorrow."

"Then I haven't much time to convince them to make a detour, have I?"

His expression sagged, knowing which 'detour' I meant. "Yes… though I think, given what they've learned, they will need quite a bit of convincing."

I pursed my lips. "Then I will have to be extra persuasive."

XAVIER

I laid Lucas in the hovering basinet we'd brought with us to the gardens, the child finally having dozed off again.

Beside the trickling fountain which had a centerpiece of a lion statue, Willow and Alexander were discussing the lengthy list of items that needed addressing upon our return to Grim. One of which, as Willow and I already discussed in private, involved the little ewe girl who clung to Willow's skirts. She wished to adopt the girl. Given that Milann's parents were dead, her messenger killed, and her home destroyed years ago, it wasn't as if she had any direct plans to find a new family on her own. She was only nine, for Death sake. We offered her a range of alternative options, but she chose to stay with us in Grim. Willow and I hadn't an issue with it, so of course we agreed.

Nearby in the gardens, Myra and Crysalette sat under a pergola wrapped in newly-flourishing vines and blossoms. In Crysalette's hands was a Storagecoffin. Her husband's body waited inside, hidden in a polite cloth.

Dream…

After the final battle, Willow told us how he'd died. How Macarius had tricked his way onboard with an illusion. How he'd killed Dream and destroyed his soul with a sword laced with infection Hallows.

How he'd stolen the Orbs of Azure.

I shivered despite the sun's warmth. Dream had said Macarius planned to make Aspirre a sanctuary for the people of Nirus and bring them into the subconscious realm physically to save them from the End of Existence… an End that *we* may bring, whether we intended to or not.

I glared at my left hand, where my Crest of black diamonds was displayed under my knuckles. I didn't want to bring the End of Existence. And even if there was a chance we wouldn't—if Dream had been right and we were instead supposed to prevent it—why did that impossible responsibility have to be ours? I was already expected to be a father *and* the Death King now. Looking after my family while overseeing an entire kingdom was one thing, but protecting the Gods damned *world* on top of it all? It was too much.

I sighed and lowered into the stone bench beside my son's basinet. His ashen wolf ears flicked every now and then, the boy stirring in his swaddled blankets as if dreaming.

Yulia, whom we'd found after the battles, was watching over the daytime sleepers in Aspirre. Myra and the other Dreamcatchers had built a strong barrier around us and stationed hundreds of sentries in the city to watch for Macarius, should he intervene from within Aspirre. If he chose to do so, I doubted there would be much any of us could do to stop him at this point. It wasn't a very comforting thought. But the fact that we hadn't seen him since Dream's death must have meant we weren't his immediate priority at the moment. Either that, or his newly bestowed foresight showed him we would eliminate him if he tried. I prayed it was the latter.

I reached into my silken vest's pocket and pulled out the Storagecoffin I'd had in there. The wrapped, shrunken remains of my father waited inside. Alexander carried our mother; Willow, her father. We were to bring them to Grim for a proper burial. Since their souls were destroyed, there would be no reaping. No ghosts to greet. Their souls were with Nira now, having skipped their afterlife and, perhaps, gone straight to their next incarnation.

My fingers tightened over father's Storagecoffin, and I sighed before putting it back in my pocket for safekeeping.

"Young sirs?" a familiar voice said from behind.

I twisted on the bench. The three ghosts of Nathaniel, Aiden and Apson floated around me. Their spectral faces were glum and heavy, all lingering hesitantly as they waited for Alexander to notice them as well.

My brother paused his discussion with Willow and strode beside me to address the ghosts, asking, "Is something wrong?"

Nathaniel's pale bear ears folded down morosely as he cleared his throat. "Well… ye see, lads, we been talkin' for a bit an'…"

"Given the circumstances with your parents…" Aiden added with folded wings. "We haven't any *Da'torr* now."

Apson clasped his scaled hands and finished, "We thought perhaps *you* both would, well… have us as vassals in their stead?"

Alex and I exchanged surprised glances. Bloods, I hadn't even thought about what would happen with our parents' vassals. Alex and I nodded our mutual confirmation, and turned back to the three ghosts.

"Of course," I said. "We would be honored… but what of Thateus and the others back at the manor? Will they want the same?"

Nathaniel shrugged his burly, wispy shoulders. "It's somethin' to ask, I says. Might want ta give 'em a call, while yer at it. No tellin' what panic they're dealin' with down there now that their Bloodpact is gone."

Alex hummed low. "We can ask Grandfather Edric to stop by and check on them. Perhaps we'll need to transport them all to Low Rastiria, should they choose to accept our vassalship."

"A right good idea," Nathaniel agreed as he, Apson, and Aiden start back into the palace, the bear calling back. "We'll have Octavius ask 'im for us and get it taken care of."

I nodded in thanks as the specters fuzzed behind the stone wall in a quiet ripple.

Then footfalls echoed from the breezeway, making us turn.

Anabelle and Kurrick approached. Kurrick wore polished armor today, different from what he'd worn in battle. This plate fostered no dents or scrapes, and looked far too formal to have ever tasted blood. His steps clinked and clanked beside Anabelle as his gilded plate flashed like brilliant fire in the sunlight. In contrast to her warrior's metallic wardrobe, the Land Queen was dressed in fine, violet silks and wrapped in a velvet robe, her crown placed delicately over her flowery locks as she and Kurrick strode regally toward us.

"I hear you're leaving for Grim within the hour?" Ana said softly.

I nodded. "There is much to do, now that so much has… changed."

One of her lion ears folded down. "Indeed. Though, I wondered if you would accept an alternate route to Grim?"

Alex folded his arms in a frown. "Alternate route?"

"I would like you all to accompany me on one last excursion in my lands," she said. "As you know, with two continents to rule over, I must assign a Grand Capital. And my choice is neither within Everland nor Neverland."

My brow knitted. "Where else is there?"

"The Gyle Islands between the continents," she explained, "where the *original* Grand Capital resides, abandoned and forgotten. The city that, today, would be called Old Aldamstria. It is the place of my birth… And the home of the Blossom of Gold."

My spine crawled to hear the name of Land's lost Relic. The place where Dream would have taken us to received Land's Blessings. Either taking us one step closer to Nira's salvation—or to its destruction.

Alex must have felt the same wave of fear that itched my own blood, because we answered at once, "No."

Anabelle seemed to expect this and folded her hands over her skirts patiently. "I'm afraid I cannot take 'no' for an answer. I intend to reclaim my father's original throne and reveal it to the world again, along with the Relic. Since you would have had to cross the seas below to reach Grim's Grand Capital, it will be no different to cross here on the surface and descend once reaching Neverland afterward—"

"We aren't gaining anymore Blessings," we growled, both our wolf ears growing as we stood our ground. Alex scoffed separately, "If you can even call them 'Blessings'. We're finished with this Shadowblood business. We will *not* risk being responsible for the End of Existence by obtaining Hallows we shouldn't even have in the first place."

"—But you *are* supposed to have them," a new voice interrupted.

From behind a stone pillar in the breezeway, Herrin meekly peeked his head around to show himself. His assistant, Marian, peered from around the other side of the pillar, the two eavesdroppers abashedly shuffling forward. Herrin clutched some sort of tattered book in his hands while Marian gripped a fist-sized crystal ball.

Herrin repeated, "You *are* supposed to have these Hallows. See…" He opened the fragile book and flipped through the ancient pages. "Dream took a record of all the people ever born with the Crest. All the stories and family histories that he traced all the way back to the same time the Relic Children came into existence. It was *always* a pair of twins. One pair *always* started with Dream Hallows, and the other pair *always* started with Death Hallows. But in the majority of these cases, they all died before reaching the age of ten. Very rarely did they survive past that, and when they did, one twin or the other still dies. This is the first time all four Crest bearers survived past the age of twenty that we have on record—"

"Wait," I interrupted. "Four? Are you saying Macarius has a twin?"

"Had," Anabelle corrected in Herrin's stead. "Accursius and Macarius were from *our* era, five centuries past. But the night Macarius was sealed away in Aspirre, he killed his brother—who was the fourth bearer."

Alex growled, "So, what, the four of *us* were randomly selected to be the next bearers?"

Herrin flipped through the book's pages again. "I don't think so. I mean, this is a theory, but I actually think it's *always* been you four. At least, it's always been your souls. For whatever reason, you all seem to be on a constant loop each time you're reincarnated. For instance, the second to last entry explains that a pair of twins in Grim, born with the crest, were born at the *exact* day and year as Macarius and Accursius. But *those* twins were stillborn and died during delivery while Macarius and Accursius went on without them."

I protested. "But that was five hundred years ago. If your theory about us being reincarnated holds any ground, then it would have only taken us *three* hundred years to be born again, as is the typical cycle."

"You probably would have," Herrin agreed, "but then Dream sealed Macar away in Aspirre, where time doesn't exist. My theory is that Dream *broke* the cycle, creating a sort of glitch in the system. Since Macar didn't exist within 'time' anymore, I think your souls were dormant, like you were waiting for the other pair to come back into the timeline. You only came back when Macar's seal started to deteriorate."

Alex rubbed his eyes. "Then, you think the four of us are trapped in an endless loop?"

"That's how it seems," he said in a shrug. "But I don't know why. Dream didn't know why either. But we *do* know that of all the incarnations, this current one is where the End begins."

"Then we'll break the cycle our own way," I snorted. "If we stop acquiring Hallows, we can't be the ones responsible for the End—*ow!*"

A flying ledger smacked me in the head. I blinked at the one who'd thrown it: Marian. The cardinal girl was red-faced and angry, her scowl filled with furious tears.

"Don't be so Bloody foolish!" she snapped, rifling through her satchel to toss another ledger at Alexander this time, chucking pens and inkwells and books at the both of us. "You've seen the future! You've seen what happens! *I* see what happens every Gods damned night in my dreams…!" She stalked toward us, making us cringe, and she thrust her crystal ball at our faces. "*This* is what happens if you don't receive all of your Blessings!"

Alex and I hesitantly stared at the ball, waiting for the images to swirl into view within.

Yet, nothing appeared.

"It's blank," I said, confused.

"Precisely," Marian huffed. "There *is* no future. Not in the timeline where you decide to stop. It's only a blank, *empty* slate. But if you decide to *continue…*"

Images finally flitted inside the crystal ball. They were so faint, I had to squint to see it at all.

"We have a *chance* at a future," Marian said. "It's by no means guaranteed, but a chance is far better than nothing at all."

Footfalls echoed around the gardens. Several familiar faces now surrounded us meekly: Ringëd stood under the breezeway, Linus lingered under a pagoda with a heavy gaze, little Oliver had flown down from the skies and perched on the fountain's lion-statue to stare down at us, and Cayden's younger sister, Rilla, emerged and shuffled beside Anabelle. It was all of our Seers. Each of them held a crystal ball of their own, of many difference sizes.

Alex and I huddled together as we tensely glanced from ball to ball, the same images Marian showed us flitting inside all of them.

Marian lowered her ball. "I know it's a daunting task," she said softly. "And I know you didn't ask for this responsibility to be thrust upon you without your say. But would you really be so selfish as to risk the lives of your friends and your family?" She jerked a hand toward Lucas in the basinet. "When *you* had the choice to let them live?"

I stared at my slumbering son, nausea bubbling as I clenched my fists. Alex and I exchanged a hard glare.

Then sighed.

GONE

MILANN

Everyone got really quiet in the garden, and the missy Reaper I clung to... she said her name was Willow. My new mum... she looked real serious now. Almost scared.

I was scared, too. I didn't like all this talk of the End of Existence and people dying. People I didn't *want* dead. I gripped the glowy sphere that dangled from my necklace, the one Miss Myra gave me. It was a smaller scythe than the one I had a couple years ago, so it fitted me better than the huge one I got in Lindel after the city was crushed. After my real mum got crushed... and after I reaped her soul when she turned into a demon.

My eyes stung with water, and I rubbed them dry, that empty pain knotting from my chest again. Miss Myra said that pain was from my Bond being torn when my 'messenger' birdy was kilt. I'd never forgive my real mum for killing it, but... that didn't mean I wanted mum *dead*...

I clenched the scythe-sphere on my necklace angrily. I didn't know who was thinking of killing Miss Willow and her new baby, but whoever they were, they'd have to get through *me* first. I lost one mum already, I wasn't gonna lose another. And I 'specially wasn't gonna let them get my new baby brother.

Miss Will... *mum*... went to check on the baby in the basinet as she started talking with the wolves again, real quiet. From what I could hear, they were talking about plans for the trip to these islands the gold-haired queen mentioned.

I sighed and sat on the fountain's stone edge, kicking my feet while I waited for them to finish talking. Then my stomach rumbled hungrily. I rubbed my belly and went to get the sandwich I'd packed away and shrunken in my Storagesphere earlier—

I stopped when I twisted to get the Storagesphere chained to my waist.

There was a feral ferret half-way inside my sphere, his teeth sunk into the wrapped sandwich that was all itty bitty inside. When I caught him, he stiffened. Then hurried to yank out the tiny sandwich—which grew big when it came out of the sphere and fell apart over the furry guy. The ferret huffed in fright and grabbed the deli ham with his teeth, then hobbled over to a crow with a clover on its tail who was hiding behind the fountain. The ferret climbed onto the crow's back and they flew up—with my deli ham they stole—to perch on the fountain's lion-statue, sharing the food between them.

I blinked up at the statue, confused. Wasn't there some winged kid up there just a minute ago?

Then someone made a *psst* sound next to me.

I looked over my shoulder. It was that same owl boy I was just thinking about. The one with the glittery, rubber ball. He was one of the Seers, the littlest one, and he was hiding behind the fountain with his chestnut wings tucked low to his back sneakily. He looked my age, maybe younger, wearing a fancy suit with his feathered hair neatly combed back to one side. The boy slinked up to me, trying not to be noticed by my new mum and da.

He waved a 'come here' hand at me and hissed, "Milann! Come on. We gotta go."

My face scrunched up. "Go? But… wait, how do you know my name—?"

"I know you when we're bigger," he said and snatched my wrist, dragging me out of the gardens and around the palace's side pathways. The crow that helped steal my sandwich earlier flew off the statue, the ferret still riding on its back, and followed us overhead. "It's a long story that hasn't happened yet anyway, so it doesn't matter yet. But we gotta hurry."

No one noticed us leave as he dragged me behind a tall wall of rosebushes. I tried to keep up with his fast steps, but tripped a few times, trying to figure out what he was talking about. Then I looked at his rubber, glittery 'crystal ball', and it hit me.

"Oh!" I blurted. "You mean you know me in the *future!*"

"Yeah," he panted, still in a real hurry. "I'm really glad to finally meet you— like, *actually* meet you. In the *now* times. Oh, uh—and I'm Oliver, by the way."

"Milann," I said, but paused. "Oh, right. You already knew that… So, how *do* you know me, though? Like, what happens in the future?"

The owl, Oliver, took a sharp turn and tugged me along a branching path to the right. "We get married."

My face screwed up so bad, I felt it twisting the muscles. "We *what?*"

"Well, we might not," he said with a shake of his head. "We're probably gonna die in the next year or two, but *everyone's* probably gonna die by then, so that's not new or anything. But if we don't hurry, my friend won't even last *that* long."

I slowed down a step, confused. But when he ran ahead, I hurried after him again. "Wait! Are you talking about this End of Existence thing?"

"Duh," he snorted. "We're on track to get to Fuérr early, but there's still a chance things will go bad. It'll depend on whether he chooses to swim around some more, or stare at an interesting cloud."

Oliver finally slowed down when we reached the outdoor pools, screeching to a stop just at the lip of the biggest pool in the center.

The little green-haired Ocean Prince was here, relaxing against the pool's stone lip on the opposite side of us. He was halfway in the water with his scaled arms propped up while his dragon tail stayed in the water and waved back and forth. His fin-like hair fell over his shoulders all the way down to his stomach, drifting in the water along with the ripples.

When Oliver and me came up to the pool on the opposite side, Oliver grimaced. "Aw, Land," he cursed. "He's looking at the cloud…! Fuérr! FUÉRR!"

The little prince's webbed ears flicked to us, turning his green eyes our way. "Oleev-a?" He asked in a super heavy Marincian accent. "What eez proh-bleem?"

"Fuérr, get outta there!" the Seer shouted, spreading his wings and flapping across the pool in a rush.

The prince's brow scrunched up. "Why eez yuu zo een hurray—"

A pair of bronze, scaled hands suddenly wrapped around his head and clenched over his mouth, the fingers glowing blue.

Fuérr wriggled in surprise, his shouts muffled and tail splashing the water as he was yanked out. But as the blue lights sank into his skin, the prince went limp, falling asleep in the arms of the scarlet-and-azure haired snake shifter whose grin was so wide, his long fangs were showing.

Oliver screamed, "FUÉRR—!"

In the blink of an eye, the prince and the snake disappeared into thin air.

"No…!" screamed Oliver as he landed on the other side of the pool, stamping his feet on the stone lip. "No, no, no, no, *no*…!"

I ran around the pool to meet him, panicked. "Where'd they go?! They just *poofed* into nothing!"

"They went into the Dream realm," the owl growled angrily. "He's taking Fuérr back to Marincia's palace. He's going to be used as bait, to force his papa to lead the snake to the Pearl of Emerald. That's how he's going to get his Ocean Hallows."

My hands shook, scared. "So… so that snake was the bad guy everyone was talking about? The one who wants to kill my new mum?"

He nodded. "Yeah, that was him." The owl spread out his wings and turned his back to me, crouching down. "Hop on. We have a long way to go if we're gonna get Fuérr back."

I gawked at him. "You wanna *fly* us over there?! All the way to a different country?!"

"It's the only decision *we* make that leads to Fuérr staying alive!" He snapped, glaring back at me. "And I need your help to get to that ending. I don't have a scythe yet, and Mama doesn't want me to have one until I've been trained more, and we're gonna need yours. Now get on, Milann." He waved for me to get on his back. "We have to go *now*."

I glanced over my shoulder, biting my lip. I didn't want to leave my new mum and da so quickly after I just found them again… But if we were going to where the bad guy was…

Maybe we can help them our own way?

"O-okay, fine!" I climbed on his back. "Let's go help him."

Oliver nodded and pushed off with his feet, flying us in the air as his crow—and the ferret riding it—followed beside us.

NEWBORN DEMON

CILIA

I overlooked the mountain side to see the ruined city of New Aldamstria. It had been three days since what happened in Culatia, and, it would seem, the Land Kingdom had been overtaken in that time. From my perch on the boulder on the edge of the mountain's forests, I saw the city was being rebuilt.

Soon after I crashed down to these mountains alongside Kael, I'd felt the heavy Weight of what could only be La'Lunaî. She must have fought with Hecrûshou and the others… but was she still here? *And how long would it be before she found me here.*

I shivered at that last thought, turning toward Kael's corpse that lay in a patch of soft pine needles I'd gathered for him. His pale skin was pulsing with blackened veins, slithering up his arms and torso and legs and face…

Until they all poured into his closed eyes, draining away like ink in water.

I hurried to crouch beside him, looming over his face as he slowly, wincingly, opened his yellow eyes. His pupils were now white and shining, staring up at me with a puzzled, distant look.

"Kael…?" I whispered hesitantly, cupping the new Sentient's face. "Do you remember me…?"

He squinted at me in confusion. Then he touched my hand on his cheek, and he drew in a sudden breath, startled.

He jerked up and pulled my lips to his, cradling my head. "My angel…" He hushed. "Am I dreaming…?"

I chuckled and pulled him at arms length. "No, darling. It's really me… but we must leave."

His brow furrowed. "Leave…? But where?"

I smiled. "Home."

DEAR READERS,

Thank you so much for reading Phoenix of Scarlet, the fourth book in the NecroSeam Chronicles pentalogy. If you liked it, I would be extremely grateful if you tell others what you think by writing an honest review. It doesn't have to be long…a few words, or even just a rating would be much appreciated. Reviews are vital to an author's career and helps us not only sell books, but provides valuable feedback. For your convenience, my website has links to various book review sites at www.necroseam.com/reviews.

Want to find out more about the NecroSeam Chronicles universe, including world notes, deleted scenes, character artwork, and even recorded songs from the books? Visit my website at www.necroseam.com!

And while you are there, feel free to sign up for my newsletter to receive announcements on new releases, upcoming conventions I'll be attending, and special promotions!

You can also follow me on my social media accounts below:

http://www.NecroSeam.com
www.Facebook.com/officialEllieRaine

Thank you again!
~Ellie Raine

Sneak Peak for Book V: Blossoms of Gold

PROLOGUE: OMINOUS VISIONS

ASTER

In the hollow depths of the endless Void, wedged between the fragile dreams of help-less shifters, the Seamstress of Souls rattled the abyss with her grueling screams.

The other Gods circled her protectively, their iridescent skin radiating with colors of gold, scarlet, emerald, and azure—and their freshly spilt blood dripped with a luminosity of their own.

Shel, the golden-haired Gardener of Life, dug his gleaming sword into the emptiness as though the blackness were as solid as granite, then leaned against the hilt and puffed for breath.

Ushar, the puckish Archer of Thrill, was hardly his energetic self as he wilted in pain, his scarlet dragon wings scraped bloody and drooping in misery while he limped against his vibrant archer's bow for support.

Rin, the proudest of the Gods known by the mortals as the Artist of Grace, suffered from a cut along his scaled brow, one emerald eye pooling with shimmering blood as his trident nearly slipped from his weak grip.

The child Shepherd of Dreams, Iri, was mounted on his floating shepherd's crook with shaking limbs, looking toward the ashen-haired Seamstress he'd come to call his mother in their small, sundry family.

The Seamstress of Souls, Nira, was crouched over her fallen scythe in the center of them all, curling inwardly in hopes of escaping the searing pain that splintered from the enormous gash split down her middle. The wound shined as bright as a supernova across her torso and thigh.

The Gardener knelt to his injured wife, dragging a golden-glowing finger over her wound to seal it closed. He helped Nira to her wobbling feet and hushed with a voice like grinding stones that rippled through her mind. THAT WAS NEARLY

THE END FOR YOU, MY LOVE... YOU WERE ALMOST SPLIT IN TWO, ALONG WITH YOUR LANDS.

It was true. Nira could feel the lone continent within her caverns split apart and drift away. Her people were screaming in terror, their voices crying in her grown wolf ears and quaking her essence.

Rin stabbed his trident down into their barrier's invisible floor, causing an azure shimmer to radiate from the point of impact.

THIS IS RIDICULOUS! *Rin protested, his voice trickling like a flowing river in all of their minds.* IT MATTERS NOT THAT OUR CHILDREN ARE STIFLING THE CHAOS OUT THERE! IT DOES NOTHING TO AID US IN HERE!

Ushar flapped his leathery wings in agreement, his thunderous voice booming. WE CANNOT ALLOW THIS TO CONTINUE. IF WE ALL SUSTAIN THE SAME INJURIES AS MOTHER, THERE WILL BE NOTHING LEFT OF OUR LANDS.

Iri shivered over his shepherd's crook, the azure-glowing child turning to Nira as his crisp voice trilled like a bell. MOTHER...? THERE IS ONE OPTION LEFT FOR US. BUT IT IS A SLIM CHANCE...

Nira panted heavily, ignoring the radiant blood draining onto her tongue as her teeth sharpened, and she growled. WE MUST TAKE IT!

The vision ripped apart.

My perspective was thrown back to the present time so fast, I jolted upright, my shriveled throat burning with a gasp. The sudden intake of air stung so bad, a surge of black blood rushed up my stomach—and spewed onto the prison cell's dank floor under my hands.

The mongrel Necrofera surrounding me hissed and snarled, letting me know they were annoyed with all the noise. Then they went back to sleep in the shadows of the abandoned cell.

I groaned, the pool of black vomit on the floor starting to bubble. It peeled off the stones, crept over my skeletal fingers and slithered up my arms like an army of maggots. They slurped up to my chin, then marched up my lips and slid down my throat, dropping into my stomach where they belonged.

When it finally ended, I flopped to the floor, curling into myself as my starved belly rumbled in agony.

Another day, I thought miserably, *Another unexplained vision...*

I was convinced I would never remember why I was in here—and what I was supposed to do with all these visions when I got out.

If I *ever* got out.

With nothing else to do, I went back to sleep, clutching my empty stomach with a grueling, hungry whimper.

NIRUSSIAN TRAVEL GUIDE

CHARACTER REFERENCE LIST

Accursius Lysandre	Lightcaster half, killed by Macarius five centuries back, cobra shifter, Seer
Aiden Rogeteller	Vassal of Alice Devouh, robin shifter, former Stormchaser, Aerovoker
Alexander Devouh	Half Shadowblood, wolf shifter, fiancé of Lilliana, possesses seven half-Hallows with an emphasis on Necrovoking for vessel manipulation (Vassals: Vendy, Dalen, and Hugh), Reaper (Messenger: Mal)
Alice Devouh	Twins' mother/ Death King's General, wolf shifter, wife of Lucas, Necrovoker (Vassals: Aiden and more unmentioned), Reaper (Messenger: Ethil)
Anabelle Goldthorn	Relicblood of Land, rightful Queen of EverLand and Neverland, Land's reincarnation, Lion shifter, Terravoker/Healer/Arborvoker
Apsonald Coult	Jaq's grandfather who was executed by Galden, now Lucas Devouh's vassal, viper shifter, Hallowless
Bianca Florenne	Childhood friend of the twins, Doctor and Alchemist, rabbit shifter, Healer
Cilia the Grim	Kael's wife and Everland's Ancient demon queen, ancestor of the Treble family, cat shifter, Pyrovoker
Claude Treble	Father of: Octavius, Cornelius, Connaline and Mikani. Descendant of Kael and Cilia. Cat shifter, Infeciovoker
Connaline Treble	Octavius's youngest sister, cat shifter, Healer
Cornelius (Neal) Treble	Octavius' brother, cat shifter, son of Claude and Sirra-Lynn, descendant of Cilia and Kael, Hallowless, Reaper (Messenger: Ace)
Crysalette Sandist	Queen of Aspirre and Dream's wife, Dreamcatcher, fox shifter, Somniovoker
Dalen Tesler	Vassal of the twins, hawk shifter, brother of Herrin, Hallowless
Dalminia Skrii'etey	Relicblood of Ocean, princess of Marincia, wife of Roji, aunt of Fuérr, sister of Ninumel, Seadragon shifter, Aquavoker/Glaciavoker/Pregravoker
Daniel Tessinger	Lilli's father, Bat shifter, Necrovoker, Reaper (Messenger: Dawn)

Dream Sandist	Relicblood of Dreams, King of Aspirre, original Relic Child of Dreams, Dreamcatcher, fox shifter, Somniovoker/Decepiovoker/Seer
El Lochīst	Zyl's Aide, cat/blue-jay hybrid shifter, Dual-Evocator: Pyrovoker/Imbrivoker, Reaper (Messenger: Salfwy)
Fuérr Aschît'aqua	Relicblood of Ocean, the little prince of Marincia, Ocean's reincarnation, Wavecrasher, Seadragon shifter, son of Ninumel and Veyazelle, nephew of Dalminia and Roji, Aquavoker/Glaciavoker/Pregravoker
Genevieve Lysandre	Macarius's step-daughter, snake shifter, Hallowless
Hecrûshou the Hunter	Ancient Demon King of the Western Seas, shark shifter, Aquavoker
Henry Cauldwell	Vendy's uncle, blacksmith, rabbit shifter, Terravoker
Herrin Tesler	Archchancellor of Enlightener's Guild, Dalen's younger brother, hawk shifter, Hallowless
Hugh Lowery	Vassal of the twins, Xavier's apprentice Reaper, younger brother of Syreen, lion shifter, Arborvoker, Reaper (messenger: Lady Lilac)
James (Jimmy) Grieves	Dreamcatcher, elk shifter, Somniovoker
Jaqelle (Jaq) Mallory	Xavier and Alex's friend, viper shifter, grandson of Apsonald, Hallowless, Reaper (Messenger: Bridge)
Kael Treble	Macarius's partner, Cilia's husband, Surgeon, ancestor of Treble family, cat shifter, Infeciovoker
King Galden Relekin	False King of Land, father of: Cayden and Rilla, Lion shifter, Terravoker
Kohl the Kindhearted	Ancient Demon King of the Northern Seas, fish shifter, Hallowless
Kurn	Ringëd's pet ferret who thinks he's an exiled emperor from the planet *Hcah-Ah-Ah-Hcah*
Kurrick Everstien	Ana's bodyguard and lover, Lion shifter, Hallowless
La'Lunaî the Little	Ancient Demon Queen of the Southern Seas, deceased Ocean Relicblood, Seadragon, Aquavoker/Glaciavoker/Pregravoker
Lannyse Lysandre	Macarius's wife and Headmistress of the Lysander Academy, snake shifter, Hallowless
Lëtta Russeaux	Sirra-Lynn's *Da'torr* & apprentice doctor, bear shifter, Necrovoker
Lillianna (Lilli) Tessinger	Willow's Aide, Bat shifter, fiancée of Alexander, Necrovoker, Reaper (Messenger: Dusk)

Linolius (Linus) Rennegaurd	Cayden's lover, Goat shifter, Seer: emphasis on visions of the present
Lucas Devouh	Twins' father / Death King's Eyes, wolf shifter, husband of Alice, Necrovoker (Vassals: Nathaniel, Thateus, and more unmentioned), Reaper (Messenger: Barrach)
Macarius Lysandre	Lightcaster half, cobra shifter, Dual-Evocator: Decepiovoker/Somniovoker
Matthiel Inion	Willow's former fiancé, wolf shifter, Dual-Evocator: Necrovoker/Pyrovoker, Reaper, (Messenger: Paschal)
Mavis & Prylan Skrii'etey	Relicbloods of Sky and Ocean, the young daughters of Roji and Dalminia, Seadragon/swallow hybrid shifters, possesses 6 Hallows: Sky & Ocean
Mikani Fleetfûrt	Octavius's eldest sister and Ringëd's wife, descendant of Cilia and Kael, cat shifter, Pyrovoker
Milann	Young girl who lost parents in Lindel's Necrofera attack, sheep shifter, Hallowless, Reaper (messenger: killed)
Miranda the Miserly	Neverland's Ancient demon queen, jackal shifter, Arborvoker
Myra Ember	Relicblood of Dream, Queen of Grim, Dreamcatcher, wife of Serdin, mother of Willow, fox shifter, Somniovoker/Seer/Decepiovoker
Nathaniel Jorrechoh	Vassal of Lucas Devouh, bear shifter, former pirate captain, Pyrovoker
Nikolai Voux	Vassal of Willow, tigerfish shifter, Glaciavoker
Ninumel Aschît'aqua	Relicblood of Ocean, King of Marincia, Wavecrasher, husband of Veyazelle, father of Fuérr, Seadragon shifter, Aquavoker/Glaciavoker/Pregnavoker
Octavius Treble	Xavier and Alex's friend, cat shifter, son of Claude and Sirra-Lynn, descendant of Cilia and Kael, Infeciovoker, Reaper (Messenger: Shade)
Oliver Tessinger	Lilliana's adopted son, owl shifter, Seer of the Future, Reaper (Messenger: Clover)
Prince Cayden Relekin	Crowned Prince of EverLand, also known as Land's Servant, Linus's lover, Rilla's eldest brother, son of Galden, Lion shifter, Terravoker
Princess Rilla Relekin	Cayden's younger sister, Lion shifter, Seer
Revinna	Cayden's forced wife, Lion shifter, Hallowless
Ringëd Fleetfûrt	Seeker detective & Mika's husband, feral human, Seer: emphasis on visions of the past

Rojired (Roji) Skrii'etey	Relicblood of Sky, heir to Culatia's throne, Sky's reincarnation, brother of Zylveia, son of King Rojired, Stormchaser, husband of Dalminia, swallow shifter, Astravoker/Aerovoker/Imbrivoker
Rojired Skrii'etey	Relicblood of Sky, King of Culatia, Stormchaser, swallow shifter, Astravoker/Aerovoker/Imbrivoker
Rossette Roroan	Vassal of Willow, macaw shifter, Astravoker
Serdin Ember	Relicblood of Death, King of Grim, Reaper, husband of Myra, father of Willow, wolf shifter, Necrovoker/Pyrovoker/Infeciovoker (Messenger: Locke)
Shefeaux the Gelid	Ancient Demon King of the Eastern Seas, killed by the twins, walrus shifter, Glaciavoker
Sirra-Lynn Treble	Claude's deceased wife, mother of: Octavius, Cornelius, Connaline, and Mikani. Vassal of Lëtta, cat shifter, Healer
Syreen Lowery	Newly awakened Sentient Necrofera, former queen of Neverland, older sister of Hugh, lion shifter, Arborvoker
Taymen Bucannan	Newly awakened Sentient Necrofera, Somniovoker, Fera grunt in demon troupe with Syreen
Thörd the Thunderous	Culatia's demon king, Skydragon, Astravoker
Vendy Cauldwell	Vassal of the twins, rabbit shifter, niece of Henry, Terravoker
Willow Ember	Relicblood of Death and Dream, Heiress to Grim's throne, Death's reincarnation, Reaper, wife of Xavier, daughter of Serdin and Myra (Granddaughter of Dream), fox-wolf hybrid shifter, 6 hallows: Dream and Death (Messenger: Jewel. Vassals: Rossette and Nikolai.)
Xavier Ember	Half Shadowblood, wolf shifter, brother to Alexander, husband of Willow, possesses seven half-Hallows with an emphasis on Necrovoking for soul manipulation (Vassals: Vendy, Dalen, and Hugh), Reaper (Messenger: Chai)
Yulia Vivelle	Devouh's hired Dreamcatcher, fox shifter, Somniovoker
Zylveia Skrii'etey	Relicblood of Sky, Princess of Culatia, sister of Prince Roji, daughter of King Rojired, Stormchaser, swallow shifter, Astravoker/Aerovoker/Imbrivoker

NIRUSSIAN WORLD NOTES

Dragons of Nirus: For every element of magic Hallows (with the exception of Dream Hallows), there is a dragon that embodies that element. Land realm: Stonedragon/Barkdragon/Landragon, Sky realm: Skydragon/Shockdragon/Nimdragon, Ocean realm: Seadragon/Bindragon/ Frostdragon, Death realm: Bonedragon/Flamedragon/Poisondragon.

Evocators: A shifter born with magic Hallows is called an Evocator. Most Evocators only possess one element. In rare cases, some are born with two Hallows and are known as Dual-Evocators. Only the Relicbloods have ever possessed all three of their realm's Hallows.

Land:	Terravoker	Healer	Arborvoker
Sky:	Astravoker	Aerovoker	Imbrivoker
Ocean:	Aquavoker	Glaciavoker	Pregravoker
Dream:	Somniovoker	Decepiovoker	Seer
Death	Necrovoker	Pyrovoker	Infeciovoker

Hallows: These are the "Gods' Blessings", which are elemental magics to which certain shifters are born. A shifter's Hallows element is defined based on the realm they are from. There are fifteen Hallow elements in total. For each of the five realms in Nirus, there are three elements, as shown in the charts below.

LAND		SKY		OCEAN	
Rock	Terra	*Wind*	Aero	*Water*	Aqua
Plant	Arbor	*Rain*	Imbri	*Ice*	Glacia
Remedy	Healer	*Storm*	Astra	*Pressure*	Pregra
DREAM		DEATH			
Dream	Somnio	*Fire*	Pyro		
Illusion	Decepio	*Death*	Necro		
Prophecy	Seer	*Poison*	Infecio		

NecroSeam: A ghostly thread which sews a soul to its vessel. When a shifter of Nirus dies, the soul is still bound to its body by their NecroSeam. If three days pass without a Reaper coming to cut the NecroSeam and free the soul from its deceased vessel, the trapped soul rots inside its corpse and merges into an undead creature called Necrofera that can only be killed by a weapon made of Spiritcrystal.

Nirussian Calendar: A month in Nirus is 60 days, or six weeks. One week is 10 days. There are 5 months in a year (300 days).

Realms of Nirus: There are 5 realms in this world. Land (surface realm split into two continents: Everland & Neverland), Sky (floating islands of Culatia in the sky inhabited primarily by flying shifters). Ocean (seaside isles of Marincia inhabited primarily by fish shifters), Dream (subconscious realm of Aspirre where shifters' souls visit in their dreams), Death (underground caverns of Grim where souls of the dead are protected in their afterlife).

Relicbloods: Shifters who are descendants of the Relic Children (those chosen by the Gods to be the ruler of a specific realm). The only Relic Child still alive today is Dream, who doesn't age at a regular pace due to his timeless residency in the subconscious plane of Aspirre.

The Relics: Magical artifacts of the Gods which are the sources of each realm's Hallows. (Land: Blossom of Gold, Sky: Phoenix of Scarlet, Ocean: Pearl of Emerald, Dream: Orbs of Azure, Death: Willow of Ashes)

Sentients: Necrofera who possess Hallows (Class 1), or a mongrel demon who has eaten ten thousand souls (Class 2). Sentients look like normal shifters, except their pupils are white.

Shifters: The world of Nirus is inhabited entirely by shifters, but they aren't quite the traditional shapeshifters who can transform from one human form to a full-on beast form. The shifters of Nirus are seen possessing traits of some kind (Ringëd Fleetfûrt is the only exception) but these traits usually only consist of wings, horns, claws, teeth, ears, tails, scales, fins, etc. Most shifters are born with a majority of their traits already showing (referred to as Primary Shifts), but some only appear when they are threatened or upset (teeth/talons/claws and even extra feathers/scales/fur). Mammals seem to be the main beings whose traits actually shift, with their ears, claws and teeth. Antlers and horns are always out and don't retract, nor do wings and scales. The fish shifters are the most unique due to their inherent ability to switch their Primary Shift to tails or legs when they are in or out of water, and this is the largest range of shifting that happens among the shifters.

The Void and Great unknown: A place that is considered purgatory for rotten and sinful souls in the Harmonist religion. It is believed that once the Goddess Nira has Cleansed these souls of their rot and sin, she takes them to the Great Unknown, which is thought to be the "waiting room" for souls to be reborn again.

NIRUSSIAN MINERALS/TECHNOLOGY

Olium: a lightweight, extremely durable mineral that is found in the deeper caves of Grim, where the veins are closest to the planet's magma-filled mantle and are in a constant liquefied state until extracted and left to cool. Once cooled, the metal can be crafted, but forging the material is incredibly difficult and only skilled smiths are able to handle the task.

Spiritcrystal: a mineral found in the caverns of Grim. It is a unique crystal which physical skin cannot touch. Adversely, it is one of the few things ghosts can make contact with. The Reapers use this crystal to forge their specialized scythes which allows them to cut a shifter's NecroSeam without damaging the body.

Vision-gems: minerals found in the Land realm's mines which, when broken apart, can show what the other piece is reflecting. Modern technologies led by Culatia's top inventors in 2102 A.B. have learned to harness Vision-gems to bring devices such as Vision-screens, communicators, and other numerous devices.

Levi-stones: magnetized rocks that are repelled only by the planet's core, causing them to be pushed into the air and kept suspended so long as the oppositely-charged side is facing the core. Culatia's islands are made of these stones, which is speculated by many geologists as to the reason Culatia's islands float.

Storage-gems: a gummy, gel-like mineral found in Everland's mines. When an object is pushed inside it, that object's size and weight shrinks to a small percentage of its original mass until that object is removed.

Yinklît Gel: a sap from a long-leafed plant that is native to Culatia. It is similar to the Aloe vera plant, but instead of possessing soothing properties when applied to burns, Yinklît Gel dampens all Hallows effects when an Evocator's hands are coated in the substance. If the gel is ingested, it can cause serious damage to an Evocator's Hallows for several days, and in some cases, it can wipe their magic connection permanently.

Shotri: The latest ranged weapons created by Culatia's top weapon-smiths. They require ammunition made of meta-glass pellets with entrapped elemental magics which, when fired, cause damage or temporary paralysis on a target, depending on the element the pellet housed.

Meta-glass: an alloyed material which combines Flexi-glass as the outer layer and Yinklît Gel as the inner layer. With this, Culatia's top weapon-smiths have used these to make Shockspheres, Flamespheres, Splashspheres and the like, which are then used as ammunition for Shotri.

Flexi-glass: A gummy, gel-like glass found in Culatia's mountain peaks that can be stretched and manipulated with ease while still wet. Once it has been through a kiln, it solidifies and become as fragile as normal glass.

ABOUT THE AUTHOR

Ellie Raine is a voracious BookWyrm when it comes to epic adventures, detailed world-building, and thrilling battles. Growing up in a family of book lovers, comic readers, and video gamers, she always dreamed of making the next explosive game that would catch fire with her darker themes that put the spotlight on her favorite fable: the Grim Reaper. Her ongoing Hard Epic Fantasy pentalogy, *NecroSeam Chronicles*, was originally intended to be that video game series, but she's found that the book adaptation is far more fulfilling and exciting. Her other works include a paranormal-noir novella entitled *Nightingale*, published with Pro Se Productions.

Fueled by coffee-bean concoctions brewed by the finest caffeine alchemists in Georgia, Ellie only emerges from the depths of her daring tales when she is summoned by her loving king and their darling daughter: the Dragon Princess Felicity. She is a lover of ravens and a dreamer of dragons, but above all else, she is a scribe to the stories that guide her.

You can find out more about Ellie Raine and her
books at: https://www.EllieRaine.com